"Mr. de Lint's handling of bits of ancient folklore to weave into an entirely new pattern has never, to my knowledge, been equalled. This is one of those books which one reads first in a gulp and then rereads with closer attention to savor the fine flavor. I know that of all the fantasy I have read lately few, if any, books have moved me to the extent that this one has."

—ANDRE NORTON

"Charles de Lint is a folksinger as well as a writer and it is that voice we hear in The Riddle of the Wren, both new and old, lyric, longing, touched by magic."

—JANE YOLEN

"De Lint knows what he's doing. His world-set is luminescent, his narrative touch deft and clean in a genre choked (!!) with tin-eared dialogue and warmed-over Dunsany and Tolkein."

—PARKE GODWIN

Other fantasy titles available from
Ace Science Fiction and Fantasy

and many more!

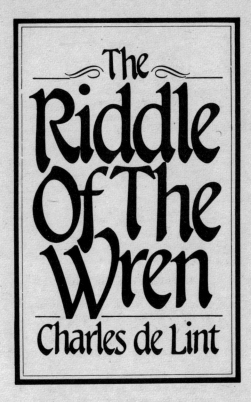

The Riddle Of The Wren

Charles de Lint

ACE FANTASY BOOKS
NEW YORK

for
my mother
Geradina

THE RIDDLE OF THE WREN

An Ace Fantasy Book / published by arrangement with
the author and his agent, Valerie Smith

PRINTING HISTORY
Ace Original / June 1984

ISBN: 0-441-72229-6

Ace Fantasy Books are published by The Berkley Publishing Group,
200 Madison Avenue, New York, New York 10016.
PRINTED IN THE UNITED STATES OF AMERICA

Contents

The Riddle
of the Wren

*"as we perceive our dreams at centrifugal spin
so green leaves grow
the rowan bears the crown. . . ."*
                              —*Robin Williamson*

The Heart of the Moors

chapter one

The town of Fernwillow was the picturesque conse-
quence of centuries of unplanned and disordered growth. Situated in the lower northwest corner of the Penwolds, it straddled
the Keeping River in a pleasing sprawl of stone and timber-
framed buildings all clustered around Fernwillow House, the
original manor from which the town took its name. Its streets
were narrow, twisting haphazardly from the outlying farms to
empty into the town squares on either side of the Keeping. A
stone bridge connected the two—Marketsquare south of the
river, Craftsquare on the north.

Weekdays and Saturdays, both squares bustled with activity.
In Craftsquare, every manner of craft was represented. Tinker
stalls stood elbow to elbow with pottery and weaving booths;
there were portrait painters, dressmakers, candlemakers, leather
workers, metal workers, ink and paper sellers, furriers, time-
keepers and instrument makers. Every sort of manufactured

goods was on display, from bolts of cloth to carved wooden "catch-the-mouse" games.

In Marketsquare, the butchers cut lamb, beef and pork to the direction of their customers. Geese, ducks and chickens raised a cacophony from their wicker cages. Farmwives and their daughters boasted the quality of their vegetables, each raising her voice to be heard above the cries of her competitors. There were baked goods, tobacco, herbs for stewing and salads and sauces, cob nuts and almonds, apples, quinces and grapes, hops, scouring materials, tallow and flax.

Fernwillow was the trade center of the Penwolds, situated as it was south of the hills that grew progressively more rugged as they marched into the Hinterlands, yet lying just north of the patchwork farmland and forest that swept in ever more cultivated leagues south to the Lakelands. Low barges travelled from the north and south along the Keeping so that their drovers and badgers might sell goods in Fernwillow and buy others to dispatch elsewhere. From the east and west, traders came in wagons from as far way as Bentyn on the coast and Cranstock in the Midlands, travelling the King's Road.

Sitting on a low stone wall on the Craftsquare side of the river, Minda Sealy watched one such wagon creak its way up Elding Street, the horseshoes of the big Kimblyn draught horse clopping on the cobblestones, the wagoner crying, "Make way! Make way!" to a crowd which was slow to take heed of his cries, and slower still to obey. Minda was a small, slender girl of seventeen, with shoulder-length brown hair framing an oval face, and dark otter-brown eyes. There was a wicker basket by her foot, topped full of cabbages, carrots and leeks. She wore an oak-green dress with flounced sleeves, a cream-colored smock overtop, and leather shoes that were more like slippers than the sturdy footgear a countrywoman might wear. She tapped the heels of her shoes against the wall, letting her gaze drift and her attention wander. Though the sun was warm, she shivered. Her eyes had a hollow look about them, with dark circles underneath.

"Silly Sealy!"

Minda turned with a frown. The nickname had followed her all through school. But the girl who joined her on the wall wore a gentle, teasing smile and meant no harm by it.

"Hello, Janey," Minda said.

"My, don't you look glum. What some licorice?" Janey dug in her pocket and gave Minda a piece. Her father owned Darby's Bakery farther down Elding Street, and she always had a bit of sweet tucked away in one pocket or another. She was a month older than Minda, twig-thin for all the sweets and pastries she put away, with skin dark as a tinker's, black hair all a tumble of ringlets, and eyes darker still.

"What's the matter, Minda?" she asked. "I haven't seen you for a half week or better. Have you been sick? You don't look at all well."

"I can't sleep," Minda said. Because when she slept, she dreamed, and when she dreamed. . . .

"Well, you should see Mother Tams, then. She'll have something hid away in the back of her shop that can set you right. A pinch of her herbal tea, or some bitter root of one sort or another."

Minda sighed. "It's not that I can't get to sleep; it's that I don't *want* to."

Janey cupped Minda's chin with a small hand and regarded her with mock seriousness. "You're not in love, are you?" she asked.

That woke the first smile to touch Minda's lips in many days. "Not likely."

"Well, what is it? I'm all ears."

"I . . . no. It's nothing that makes sense."

"Now I *must* know."

"It's not something I want gabbed up and down Elding Street."

"Come *on,* Minda. Tell."

She leaned closer, elbows on her knees, chin propped on the palms of her hands. Minda sighed again.

"It's . . . I've been having these dreams," she began.

"Of Tim Tantupper, I'll wager!"

"No. This is serious, Janey. These are dreams so strange they make my skin crawl just to think of them. I . . . they're the same, every night. I've been having them for two weeks now. I think . . . I'm afraid I'm going mad."

"Oh, Minda," Janey said. She clasped her friend's hand and squeezed the fingers tightly. "How horrible. But it's not true. They're just nightmares . . . terrible nightmares. They're not real."

Minda bit at her lower lip, determined not to cry, not here in the middle of Craftsquare with everyone to see. "They seem so real, Janey."

Her friend nodded. For a moment she shared Minda's chill, felt the afternoon sunshine go cold. She blinked quickly and stood up, drawing Minda to her feet. "Let's go see if we can beg an ice from my dad," she said with determined cheerfulness.

"I can't..."

"It'll cheer you up."

Minda shook her head and tapped her basket with the toe of her shoe. "I've been two hours getting these as it is."

"I shouldn't wonder if your dad's not to blame for these nightmares you're having," Janey said. "The way he treats you would shame a tinker. I don't know how you can stand it."

"I've nowhere else to go. My uncle's asked me to live with him, but Hadon won't allow it, and if I ever tried to run away he'd be after me so quick I'd be lucky to get a half mile before he took me by the ear and dragged me off back home."

Janey regarded her friend, hands on her hips, uncertain of what to do.

"Let me come home with you, then," she said. "I can help you with your chores and maybe your dad'll give you the rest of the afternoon off."

"I don't think you should," Minda said. "He's been in a foul mood all day long and I don't want him yelling at you."

"He doesn't scare me."

Minda looked steadily at her until she shrugged.

"Well, not a whole lot," Janey said. "Besides, if he ever tried to lay a hand on me, my dad'd whack him for a loop!"

Minda smiled. "Thanks for listening, Janey. Are you working tomorrow?"

"Only in the morning."

"I'll try to get away after the noon meal."

"Where shall we meet?"

"At Biddy's corner," Minda decided.

Janey lifted her eyebrows. "Are you going to have your fortune read?"

Minda shook her head. "We could go visit Rabbert."

"Or Wooly Lengershin. He's promised to teach me how to juggle."

"Does he want his payment in kisses or sweets?"

"Both!" Janey said with a laugh.

Minda picked up her basket. "I have to go."

"All right. Try not to dream, Minda. And if you do—try to remember that a dream's all it is. Don't be a Silly Sealy."

"Janey Jump-up!"

"Minda Miggins loves Tom Higgins!"

Giggling like the schoolgirls they'd been only a few years before, they went their separate ways.

Minda was still smiling when she returned to the courtyard of her father's inn. It was a two-story timber frame building with a stone foundation that stood at the corner of Cob's Turn and the King's Walk, which was the name the King's Road bore as it wound through Fernwillow. Hadon Sealy, recently widowed and with his two-year-old daughter in tow, had bought it fifteen years ago when the previous owner retired. It was called The Wandering Piper—a name Hadon kept both because of the goodwill that was already associated with it and the fact that he didn't have enough imagination to give it a better. There'd been no great increase in trade since the change in ownership, but there'd been no noticeable drop in business either, a fact that had kept the local gossips' tongues wagging all through the first winter, considering what a dour face Hadon turned to the world in general, and to his young daughter and help in particular.

Minda winked at Pin the stableboy as she hurried through the yard to the kitchen. Slipping through the door, she prayed her absence had gone unnoticed, but no sooner had she set her basket on the long counter that ran the full length of the kitchen's west wall than her father entered from the common room, his bulk filling doorway. Hadon was black-haired where she was brown, heavy-set where she was slim. His eyes were a pale blue—the sort that flickered dangerously for no discernable reason and were quick to anger.

"Where the hell have you been?" he demanded.

Minda swallowed dryly and pointed to the basket.

"Two hours it took you to buy a couple of cabbages?"

"I met a . . . a friend . . . and we talked a bit."

For all his bulk, Hadon could move quickly. He crossed the room in three strides and struck Minda open-handedly across the side of her head. The blow made her teeth jar together and brought tears to her eyes, but no sound escaped from between her lips.

"You've no time for friends," Hadon said. "Not with the work there's to be done about here."

"It wasn't busy," she said, "and Kate was here—"

She broke off as he lifted his hand again and quickly dropped her gaze to the floor. "I . . . I'm sorry," she mumbled.

Hadon let his hand fall to his side.

"See that you are." He looked about the kitchen. "Place needs sweeping—and there's soup to make for dinner."

"I'll start right away."

"I won't have you slutting about the marketplace like the rest of those girls you know."

"They're not—"

He glared at her.

"I wasn't doing anything like that," she protested.

"Not much, you weren't. Think I don't know what goes on there? Think I haven't seen you gawking at the farmlads flexing their muscles as they're unloading their carts, or those damn tinkers with their greasy hair?" He shook his head and stomped to the door. "Don't know why I bother with the likes of you," he muttered as he left the room.

Minda leaned weakly against the counter, lifted a hand to her burning cheek. Tears shone in her eyes and she blinked them furiously away. He had no right to treat her this way, to talk about her friends as though they were nothing but trollops! He had no . . . She sighed bitterly. No right? So long as he was her father and he kept her here, he had every right.

Kate came in as she was starting to chop cabbage for the soup. A buxom woman in her late twenties, Kate Dillgan had been at the inn for five years now. She had dark red hair, a broad, cheerful face, and Minda had yet to see her lose her temper. Stacking dishes in the sink, she glanced at Minda, then went about her business, filling the sink with a pailful of water drawn from the big storage barrel by the door.

"He's in a rare mood today, that one is," Kate remarked.

Minda nodded, chopping the cabbage with quick angry motions.

"Never you mind him," Kate continued. "You won't always be here. A pretty thing like you—you'll be off and married in no time."

"I hate him," Minda said, "but I don't want to get married just for a change of masters."

"Well, there's that," Kate agreed. "Never married myself for much the same reason—though my dad never once lost his temper with me. I just couldn't see myself spending day after day looking after some oaf with never a good word given in return." She laughed. "And look at me now: working for your dad. La, but the world's a funny place."

"Why do you stay on?" Minda asked.

"Well, it's a job—and they're scarce enough at the best of times. The only worry I have—when your dad gives me the time to even think of such things—is where I'll be in another twenty years. There's a certain security in marriage, I'm thinking. Where else can you find somebody to keep you company when you've gone all old and wrinkled and flabby? So one day I might marry—a widower, perhaps, with a nice big farm, or a craftsman. But never an innkeeper. Working here, I've had my fill of innkeepers."

She glanced at Minda again as she worked, washing down a plate and setting it aside, reaching for another, all with the mechanical movements of a task known too well.

"You're looking somewhat pale of late, Minda," she said.

"I've not been sleeping well."

"At your age you need your sleep. Try a tot of hot milk and rum—I'll pinch you a splash when his lordship's not looking. You'll be sleeping like a babe in its swaddling in no time, mark my words."

"I don't think I'll need it," Minda said, "but thanks all the same."

"Suit yourself. But I'll tell you, I have the odd nip myself, from time to time, whether I'm sleeping well or not. Does no harm, my dad used to say."

Minda paused in midstroke. "Not from Hadon's . . . ?"

Kate grinned. "The very same. That lovely cask of Welan brandywine he keeps hid under his bed. I have a little flask that I fill with a drop or three whenever I'm in there sweeping up."

Minda laughed. "Well, good for you."

That night she sat up in her bed and lit a candle to help keep sleep at bay. Her room was just above the kitchen. Its door opened onto the landing at the top of the back stairs and

its window overlooked the courtyard and stables. Her bed was
against the west wall, with the window to her right. On the
left her clothes hung from hooks on the wall, or were stored
in the oakwood chest set underneath. There was a narrow table
in front of the window on which she kept various knick-knacks—
from a small carved stag that her uncle Tomalin had given her,
to her pebble collection and a foot-high painted vase that Janey
had made for her. Beside the table was a small shelf where
she kept what few books, pennysheets and chapbooks she'd
managed to collect over the years. Her friend Rabbert owned
a bookstore on Elding Street, and it was there that she'd bought
most of them.

Except for the sound of her own breathing, her room was
still. The whole inn was quiet. There were no guests staying
tonight—only the locals had been in, the last of whom had
staggered out just before closing. Pin would be asleep in the
loft above the stable, Kate in her room, two doors down. Hadon
had long since tramped up from the kitchen to slam the door
of his own room behind him. By now he was deep in slumber.

Huddled in her bed, with the blankets pulled up to her chin,
she stared at her reflection in the mirror at the far end of the
room. The reflection was little more than a shadow. She was
shivering again, though the night was not cold. Her whole body
cried for the sleep it was being denied and she knew she couldn't
stay awake much longer. Already her eyelids were drooping.

She forced herself to stay awake. The candle banished the
darkness from around her bed, but it awoke shadows that danced
around the room, shadows that reminded her of the dark thing
that stalked her dreams. Frowning, she leaned over and blew
out the candle with a force that surprised her. Clutching her
knees, she rocked back and forth, striving to stay awake, trying
not to remember the dreams. It was a bitter lesson in futility,
for awake or asleep, they would not let her be.

At length she found herself losing the battle. Her eyes closed
and a certain measure of calmness came to her. She was so
tired, and it felt good to just lean her head back, to close her
eyes. Drifting in a state somewhere between drowsy wakeful-
ness and full sleep, the fear began to slip away and suddenly
she was indeed asleep.

Then she felt that touch again, the touch that heralded the
nightmares. The dawn took forever to arrive.

chapter two

"I didn't think you'd make it," Janey said as she saw Minda approaching.

It was an hour past noon and Janey was sitting on her heels, back against a wall, watching Biddy go through her routine with a farmwife who, by her accent, had to be from the farms bordering the Hinterlands up north. The farmwife was a stout middle-aged woman in a plain brown dress, with her corn-yellow hair tied back in a green scarf and a basket over her arm. She sat on the small stool that Biddy provided for her customers and listened intently to what the fortune teller was saying.

Biddy herself was a frail-seeming but tough old woman in her sixties. Her hair was a collection of grey wisps that moved whichever way the wind was blowing, her eyes dark with gypsy secrets. She wore heavy black clothing with red seams, and yellow cuffs and collar. Faces and palms were her specialty, though she also sold charms and herb packets. She lived in the back of Camston's Woodworks, in a one-room lodging filled with all manner of wonderful and mysterious odds and ends. Janey and Minda had been there once before—Janey for a charm, Minda just tagging along—and the two of them had come away with both giggles and a certain awe. There were so many strange things to be seen—beaded charms, rams' horns filled with weird powders, a stuffed monkey with gills and wings that hung from a thread in front of the single window.

"Someone's just sewn on those wings," Minda had whispered to Janey.

"No, they're real—look for yourself," her friend had replied, but neither of them had wanted to get too close for a proper look. Biddy just sat in her chair by the small hearth, smiling enigmatically.

"How did you get away from the inn?" Janey asked now.

"I had a bit of luck," Minda replied softly. Biddy gave the pair of them a hard stare for the noise they were making. Minda plonked herself down beside her friend and whispered in her ear: "Hadon's gone for the afternoon—maybe even the evening meal. I saw Master Dryner in the front hall with a handful of unpaid bills clutched in his hand and Hadon ducked out the kitchen door and was off."

Janey nodded sagely. "And when the cat's away, the mice—"

"If you girls can't be still," Biddy cried, "then be off with you! You're disturbing the spirits. And they're not fond of being disturbed, if you get my meaning."

The two girls quickly stood, curtsied, and were off, hiding laughter behind their hands. They followed Tucker's Way, ducked through an alley and came out into the crowds on Elding Street near the Craftsquare. Janey found a mint in her pocket, offered it to Minda, popped another into her own mouth.

"How did you sleep last night?" she asked around the mint.

Minda's smile left her. "The same . . . Janey, I don't know what to do. One day Hadon's going to notice these rings under my eyes and think I've been sneaking out at night and then I'll really be in for it. Do you know what he said about us last night?"

"I don't think I want to know."

"That we're nothing but a couple of trollops, slutting about the marketplace."

Anger flashed in Janey's eyes. "He's a beast!" she cried, loud enough to receive stares from several passersby. They pushed their way through the crowd and found a perch on the back of a tinker wagon from which they could watch the bustle but remain insulated from it.

"I hope you gave him a good kick in the shins," Janey said.

"He gave me a good whack on the head," Minda replied, touching the side of her face.

Janey sighed. "Oh, let's find something pleasanter to talk about than Horrible Hadon and your dreams. You need to forget them for a while—thinking about them all the time'll just make them worse."

For a few minutes they sat in silence, savoring their mints and watching the crowd go by. The tinker whose tailgate they were borrowing for a perch was a dark, handsome man with a ring in each ear and a bright red scarf tied to the wrist of his left hand. He winked at them as he worked, doing a brisk trade with his knives. He sold three of them while they were finishing their mints—each for a few coppers more than the previous one.

"Don't you go running off, ladies," he called to them. "You're bringing me the best luck I've had all day."

"What sort of commission are you offering us?" Janey asked.

Dark eyes glittered. The tinker reached under the front seat of his wagon and withdrew a pair of small objects from a leather sack. He tossed them over, grinning as Janey caught them easily.

"Oh, look," she said to Minda. "Aren't they lovely?" They were figurines, crudely carved from bone—one a bearish shape, the other a goose with a long neck and pointed tailfeathers. "Did you make them?" she asked the tinker.

"Na, na. It's my grandad does them—a few quick strokes and he's got a wee bone beastie all carved out, neat as you please. Do you like them?"

"Very much. Thank you!"

"But now you must earn your keep," the tinker said. "Sit there and bring me some more luck for a while."

"What's your name?" Minda asked.

"Periden Feal—from over Bentyn way of late." He winked at them again, then turned as another potential customer paused to look at his display. He launched into his sales patter, hands moving quickly as he spoke, red scarf flashing at his wrist.

"Which do you want?" Janey asked.

"The goose."

"Done! Because I like the thought of a bear better. Geese are too silly."

"And bears have a sweet tooth, so we're well matched."

Janey licked her finger and made a mark in the air. "One for you," she said.

"I wonder that he can just afford to give them away like that," Minda said, turning her gift over in her hand.

"Oh, they're all like that, the tinkers," Janey replied. "Loose and easy. You heard him—takes his grandad but a few minutes to make each one."

"But it takes time to become skilled enough to do them so quickly."

"And once you have the skill, Minda, why then you can make a zillion a day and afford to give them away. He probably sells them, two for a penny."

Minda smiled. "I'd like to think he keeps them just for special people—and that he'll only give them away then, not sell them."

"Too romantic a notion—even if he is a tinker," Janey said. "He's just happy he's sold a few knives—probably paid his stall-fee for the rest of the week. Oh, did you hear about Ellen? Just last night I heard that she's run off with Han Dowey."

"Han? Wasn't he the one—"

"That pushed you in the Mill Pond last year? The very one! He was 'prenticed to a tinsmith in Belding—least that's what Tim Tantupper says. I met him on the way home last night, you see, and . . ."

The afternoon passed all too quickly. From the hour they spent gossiping on the back of Periden's wagon, to wandering up the King's Walk as far as Yold's Corner and back, with a stop in the bakery where Janey begged a pair of apple tarts from her dad, it was an hour to supper before they knew it. They said their goodbyes in the Marketsquare, Janey running off home while, after a quick look to see that Janey wasn't watching where she went, Minda hurried back to Biddy's corner.

"Thought you'd be back," Biddy remarked as Minda ran up, breathless. "Had that look about you, you did."

Minda sat down on the stool, fingers working nervously at the hem of her smock as she caught her breath.

"So what can I do for you?" Biddy asked.

"I've only two coppers," Minda began.

Biddy waved her hand nonchalantly. "One'll do for you, my dear. Now what's the trouble? Got a young lad you want to charm?"

"Well, no. I have these dreams, you see. . . ."

She wasn't quite sure where to go from there, but Biddy was already nodding her head. A grey wisp of hair fell across her eyes and she brushed it aside with a skinny hand.

"Disturb your sleep, do they? Nasty things, dreams—when they're unpleasant, at any rate."

"It's always the same one," Minda explained.

They came at the first touch of sleep, with a power that undermined her will and bore her helplessly away before it. Alien realms roiled and spun before her eyes—gaseous vistas of black and ochre. She choked as foul air filled her lungs; gagged on the stench. Voices whispered in the dank mists. They told her she was mad, that this torment came from inside herself and could never be driven away. And always, chasing her through the nightmares was a vast and nameless evil. Relentlessly it pursued her, night after night, dream after dream. No matter how far or fast she fled, the presence was always upon her, whispering: *No escape, no escape. . . .*

"They scare me something fierce, Biddy."

The old fortune teller leaned forward and placed the tips of her fingers to either side of Minda's head, nodding to herself and muttering. "A sending, perhaps . . . witchy dark . . . strong, too. Who'd be doing that to a sweet young thing like you? None around these parts even has that skill, not since Cidjin died—what? Three years ago now?"

Minda sat wide-eyed, unable to speak. She didn't believe in witches and magic and such, but the queer look on Biddy's face awoke a weak trembling inside her that started at the base of her spine and travelled to the ends of all her nerves.

"Has . . . has someone put a curse on me?" she asked.

"Could be, could be," Biddy replied.

She dropped her hands from Minda's head and tugged a bulging tattered sack from behind her own stool and started to rummage about in it. "Valerian for the nerves," she said, taking out a small pinch of the herb and placing it on a square of paper. She folded the paper with quick deft movements and handed it to Minda. "Put this in your bedtime tea tonight— with a bit of mint, for the taste, you know, and the head as well. Clears the cobwebs from your wee mind, as it were, my dear."

"That's all?" Minda asked as Biddy pushed the sack back behind her stool with her foot.

"No more's needed. One penny now—that's all I ask. If it doesn't work, you come back and tell Biddy and she'll give you the penny back."

Minda studied the herb packet in her hand. She opened her mouth to ask something else, thought better of it and stuffed the packet into her pocket, digging out a penny as she did. Biddy accepted the coin solemnly.

"Off with you now," she said. "There's others'll be needing my services before this old soul gets herself home. Off with you! Tell me tomorrow how you slept."

"But who . . . who's sending the dreams?" Minda had to ask.

"Can't know that, dear. Can't know if it's dreams being sent, or your own nerves being a wee bit highstrung. You try that in your tea and I'll see you tomorrow."

"Well . . . thank you," Minda said, standing up.

"Yes, yes. Off with you now."

The fortune teller pretended a great interest in the ball joint of her right thumb, moved it around and studied the motion with pursed lips. She didn't look up again until Minda was half a block down the street, and then she sighed and shook her head. A strange sensation she'd felt, touching fingertips to that young girl's head. Was as though she wasn't quite what she seemed to be. Was a feeling of . . . oldness, Biddy supposed. Not the oldness of years stacked one upon the other, but an oldness like a hilltop cairn or the feeling in the air when the May fires burned. A strange feeling indeed.

Minda wasn't sure what to think as she hastened home. All this talk about witches' curses and sendings was nonsense, of course, except that there was always something a little spooky about Biddy—like the winged monkey hanging in her window. More than likely it was all talk—to set the mood and give it a magicky feel—but . . . Well, she'd try the herb in her tea tonight and see what came of it. But she'd never tell Janey or anyone else—not unless it worked.

Pin was lugging water to the horsetrough when Minda entered the inn's courtyard. He was about Minda's height, a thin boy in trousers that were too short for him and a ragged old shirt. Freckles dotted his nose and cheeks, and his hair was like a thatch of straw.

"How do, Minda?" he said.

She smiled at him, then asked, "Has Hadon come home yet?"

"Not likely. Master Dryner's still sitting in the common room, waiting to serve his bills."

"Oh, good. See you, Pin."

She rushed into the kitchen and immediately started in getting supper ready, making enough of a mess in a few minutes to give the place the look of her having been working away in it all afternoon, just in case Hadon did show up. As she was cutting carrots for the stew, she remembered that she hadn't dropped by to see Rabbert today as she'd planned. Tomorrow then—if she could gather up the nerve to sneak out a third afternoon in a row.

"And don't you look busy," Kate remarked as she came in. "Did you have a nice afternoon?"

"Perfect," Minda replied. (Barring witchy talks with Biddy, she added to herself.)

"Well, it's not been busy till about a half minute ago, and Hadon's still off making himself scarce. Don't know why he doesn't just pay the man and be done with it."

"If he's not about, then he doesn't have to pay," Minda said, knowing her father's ways all too well. "And Master Dryner will still send round the week's wine. It's the same every month."

"True enough," Kate said. "And then, because it's a month's worth of bills, he barters the poor sod down a silver or two. He's not a stupid man, your dad."

"He's not a very nice one either."

"I didn't say that," Kate said, "but if you pressed me, I wouldn't deny I was thinking it."

chapter three

That night in her bedroom, Minda added the tinker's gift to her tabletop collection in front of the window. She set the goose down in among three clay mushrooms that she'd made herself. They were unfired and crumbling at the edges from the odd knock they got when she rearranged them. She spent a minute or two puttering about the table, then slipped on her nightgown and climbed into bed. She read a bit from a new chapbook that someone had left behind in the common room—*A Journeyman's Travels* by Jon Geady.

Well, he didn't travel very far, Minda thought as she flipped through the slim booklet's pages. Not if this was all he had to show for it.

She sipped her valerian-and-mint tea and was nodding off before she'd finished the third page. Sleep came quickly and, despite Biddy's charmed tea, the nightmare came fast on its heels.

In some dim recess of her mind she knew it was only a

dream, that she would wake from it and be safe, but that didn't help her now. Her soul was swallowed by a darkness that mocked her with a bitter cold glee and left her body writhing on the bed, screams stillborn in her throat, while she fled, deep and deeper into the hidden places inside her, only to find that there was still no escape.

She fled and the darkness pursued with hollow laughter that boomed around her. She knew her flight was futile, but panic would not let her be still. She tried to hide, but the thing was suddenly behind her . . . around her . . . inside her . . . its laughter clawing trails of fear up her spine. She wept and her tears stung her cheeks like acid. She tried to curl herself into a ball like a hedgehog, but the shadow had already pierced her. Her pulse drummed in her ears. She broke free only to hear its laughter echoing all around her. It toyed with her, letting her go only to catch her again. She felt its touch slide over her. Then she seemed to be falling from a great height, the mocking laughter trailing behind her like ragged spiderwebbing when—

The feather-light touch of another presence brushed against her. She read its surprise as it enveloped her gently, drawing her away from the terror. The darkness clotted inside her, deepening, intensifying its grip; the new presence worked each tendril free of its hold on her mind, its touch quick, but gentle. The darkness fought to regain its control, thinking she had found some last reservoir of strength, unaware of the new presence.

For a long moment she was held fast between the two opposing forces, stretched thin as a thread near its breaking point. The darkness roiled inside her, the new presence undoing each hold the former gained. Then, when surely she could be stretched no further, the dark was gone and she was spinning through soft amber and grey mists. Their touch soothed her. A calmness eddied and filled the hurt places where the darkness had been and all about her rang the sweet notes of a faraway harp and the breathy skirling of reed-pipes.

She spun like a slow top, drifted like a leaf on a gentle wind. Something formed underfoot and her legs folded under her. She tumbled to . . . ground? Her hands grasped thick grass and soft soil. Her heart knew a quiet sense of peace. The music had stilled. Slowly she pushed herself up from the ground to crouch on hands and knees. She opened her eyes.

No sooner had she looked than she shut her eyes firmly.

Surely this wasn't real? She should be home abed, not here ... wherever here was. But the grass under hand and knee was real. Again she opened her eyes.

She was on the crest of a high craggy hill, in the middle of a circle of huge longstones. Rough heath swept from the horizon to the hill, broken only by occasional granite outcrops and thickets of rowan and thorn. Overhead the moon was full and richly gold. A chill wind whipped up from the heath, blowing her hair against her cheeks. She shivered with the cold for she was still dressed only in her thin white nightgown.

Immediately in front of her was the henge's kingstone. Where the grey-blue menhir were old stones heavy with age, the kingstone was older still; the epochs it had endured rested on it as lightly as a spray of vine upon an old fencepost. Etched upon it was a swirling symbol of interlocking knotwork that stood out from the great stone with a sudden clarity. As though it were the right thing to do, though she couldn't say why, she reached out to touch it.

When her finger came into contact with the rough stone surface, a small shock thrilled warmly through her. Absently she watched her finger trace out the swirl of the symbol's lines; it followed the pattern without faltering. As she completed the final curve, a word drifted into her mind. Again without thinking or stopping to wonder where it came from or what she was doing, she spoke that word aloud.

"Caeldh."

A brilliant flare of light burst before her. Dazed, she stumbled back from the stone and sprawled in the grass. The outline of a figure appeared within the glow. As the glare faded, she found herself staring at a strange man, no taller than herself, with eyes of the deepest gold. He stood motionless in front of the stone. The moonlight threw his sharp features into relief, showed her the small pointed ears nestled in his curly hair, the two small horns that protruded from his brow.

She edged away from him. Please, oh, please, she thought, let me wake!

"A-meir, kwessen," the horned man said.

His voice was musical and haunting, like an old memory only half recalled, and held a faint echo of the harp music that the mists had carried.

"I don't understand you," she said slowly. "Who are you? What do you want of me?"

"Forgive me," he said, and this time she could understand him. "I spoke in the speech of my kin, thinking—hoping— you were of them." He shook his head. "I have been stone-bound too long, I fear. Already my thoughts take on a craggy slowness. You . . . you are the first I have reached from my prison—though not from want of trying. I looked for aid, you see. My spirit went questing for a power that might free me and then I sensed such a strength. . . ."

He broke off to stare at her. She shrank under his frank scrutiny. The gold gaze seemed to bore straight through her body to weigh the worth of her soul.

"There is a mystery about you," he murmured almost to himself. "You are some fey creature, surely—yet cloaked so I do not know your kin. You keyed the stone—sure as the Moon's my mistress—but. . . . Carn ha Corn! *Ildran*. After all this time, Ildran alive and loose once more! His touch is on you, lass, and . . . now I see. . . ."

His brow furrowed with anger and Minda edged still further away from him.

"Ildran!" He repeated the name as though it was a curse. "'Twas he who bound me; I was a fool not to recognize his foul touch. Yet he has been gone so long, and he never had such power."

"Please," Minda said. "I want to go home."

"He will pay," the horned man said, not hearing her. "For what he has done to me, for . . ." His gaze focused on her once more. "For what he has done to you. What have you done to gain his ill will?"

She shook her head—partly in answer to his question, but more because she couldn't believe what was happening. "You . . . you're not real, are you? None of this is."

He laughed hollowly. "Not real? Perhaps you've the right of it. I scarce feel real. Stone-bound for how many Moons' turning? Aie! But I *am* real. As real as you. Can the dead— could an illusion walk the silhonell?"

"The . . . ?"

He gestured broadly about them. "All of this is the silhonell. In the common tongue you would say 'the inner realm where living spirits walk.'"

"Who are you?"

"I? I am Jan Penalurick—the heart of the moors, the arluth of the longstones. And your name?"

"Minda. Minda Sealy."

Jan shook his head solemnly. "Nay, lass. Do not claim such a poor lineage. The name you claim is a mernan's, and once-born you never were."

"But—"

"I would name you Talenyn—Little Wren—for you will prevail like the wren that the Winter Lads chase . . . chase but never catch. Minda Talenyn. It has a ring to it, does it not?"

She nodded numbly, rubbing at her temples.

"You. All this," she said. "The stones. The moors. It's all in my head, isn't it?"

I'm going mad, she thought.

"Not mad," Jan said, catching the stray thought. "This is real enough. But how do I explain? See: as your body houses your spirit, so do the worlds house the silhonell."

"Worlds?"

"Oh, aye. How could there be but one? Even Grameryn— the Wysling who first discovered the gates—knows not how many worlds there are. And my own kin—the muryan—we have wended the worlds since time out of mind, before ever Wysling or Loremaster keyed a gate.

"Longstones—such as this henge—are the gates. We call them porthow in the high tongue and they are on all the worlds for they are all that remains of Avenveres, the First Land. When Avenveres was destroyed in the Chaos Time, her rocky bones were scattered through all the worlds; but they are still bound, one to the other, and by keying them one can bridge the void between the worlds, as easily as stepping from one stone to another across a stream."

He drew a small pouch from his belt and shook a handful of smooth blue-grey stones into his palm. He held them up so that Minda could see.

"My kin," he said, "have gone the Wyslings one better. These are porthmeyn—gate-stones. With these we can move between the worlds without need of henge or longstone."

"I don't understand the half of what you're saying," Minda told him. "In fact, I don't believe that any of this is real."

Jan frowned. "Believe it or not, still it is real. Just as Ildran is real—Ildran the Dream-master. Tell me this, Talenyn: was this the first time he touched your dreams?"

The dreams. Minda stared at the ground as the memory of them flooded her. Her brow broke out in a cold sweat. She shook her head. "No," she said in a small voice. "They come . . . night after night."

"We could help each other."

"How?"

"I can help you to free yourself from Ildran's grip—while you can set me free from my prison."

"But . . . where are you? Where is your . . . body?"

She stumbled over the word, just as her mind stumbled over the entire concept.

"I . . ."

A shimmering rippled through the muryan's body. For an instant he became so transparent that Minda could see right through him. On the outer edges of her consciousness she could feel the presence of her nightmares—the thing Jan had called Ildran—groping for her, trying to entangle her in its snare once more.

" 'Twill not be as easy as I'd hoped," Jan continued as he became more substantial again. "Ildran builds his prison stronger still and my own strengths are rapidly dwindling."

He returned the porthmeyn to their pouch and tossed it to her.

"Take these. They will do me little good, fettered as I am. There is a pendant inside the pouch as well. Wear it and you will dream true—safe and true. Ildran will need to bind your body now if he still wants you for his own. Your spirit will be safeguarded."

His body shimmered again. In another moment he would be gone.

"But where are you?" Minda cried. "What of freeing you?"

"The porthmeyn," the fading form replied. "Use them to seek my kin on Weir. Tell them I am in the Grey Hills on Highwolding. They will understand. Remember . . . the pendant and the stones. . . ."

A golden fire shone in his eyes, warning her with a strength that she could feel, but not call upon. Her fear still clung to her, and again she felt the Dream-master's grip tighten.

"Dream strong, Talenyn. Little Wren. Strong and fair. Dursona. . . ."

A vague outline of him remained. Minda lunged for it, but he was gone and she was brought up sharp against the kingstone. Then Ildran's grip grew stronger, the noose of his thoughts taut and choking. She found she couldn't breathe. The muscles in her chest constricted. Ildran's laughter mocked her, and an uncontrollable shudder racked her body. She knew she was succumbing to the darkness once more. It grew thick in her mind and she had only one defense against it. With trembling fingers she worked the pendant free of the pouch. It was nothing more than a common old acorn attached to a leather thong. She gazed at it, horrified, disappointment welling inside.

Fairy gold, turning to dust and leaves when the spell was done.

Darkness fingered her, tore and pulled, drawing her back into horror. The whispers grew more insistent, fierce with their success.

With the last shreds of her will, she made her hands move, tugged the thong over her head. As the pendant lay against her skin, a long wailing shriek rang and faded inside her. The Dream-master's presence vanished. Freed, she slipped from the kingstone to lie face down on the grass.

For long moments she lay there, smelling the dark earth, breathing deeply. Then, slowly, she sat up. The moorman's pendant had worked, but she was still alone amongst the long-stones, still lost in some strange place that she could not quite believe was real.

"What do I do now?" she asked the silent henge. "How can I get home?"

She stared at the symbol etched on the kingstone. Softly, as though from a great distance, she heard Jan's voice murmuring a word in her mind. She let her finger trace the pattern of the symbol and repeated the word, keyed the gates.

"Tervyn."

Again the fey music came to her ears—harpstring chords and breathy reed-pipes, their notes intermingled. The amber-grey mists swept in and once more she was slowly spinning.

She awoke in the dark in her own room, and remembered the dream. It had been more pleasant than the others to be sure, but only a dream all the same.

But in her hand she still held the small pouch filled with rounded hard objects, and around her neck hung the acorn pendant. She touched the pendant, tightened her grip on the pouch, trying hard to understand.

If that place with the henge and the moorman had been a place of spirits, how had she brought pendant and stones back

with her? Surely they should be like so much mist here? But
she felt them, held their weight in her hand. They had sub-
stance. The pendant was curiously warm where it hung between
her breasts, the stones tingled against her palm, but they were
all undeniably *here*.

Was it their magic? The magic the moorman said they held?
That could explain how they had come back with her... back
from.... But if they were real... then... then it was all real.
Something, someone called Ildran really was tormenting her.
The dreams were meant to trap her, as surely as the moorman
was imprisoned.

Ildran will need to bind your body now.

The horned man's words rang in her mind. The thought of
confronting this Dream-master who was responsible for so many
nights of terror sent new chills of fear coursing up her spine.
She hefted the stones. He... Jan Penalurick... had said:

We could help each other.

Did he really think she could be of any help to him? She
wasn't even sure what she believed. The stones were proof
enough, and the pendant... and Ildran's presence, gone at last.

Then just as her natural good humor bounced back from
every ill treatment that Hadon had laid upon her over the years,
she took the final step to acceptance. She wasn't really sure
how much she understood, but as Jan had helped her, she would
help him in return. She would go to this Weir place and.... Only
where was it and how was she supposed to find her way there?

She regarded the stones thoughtfully. He'd said the stones
would take her. She lined them up on her blanket and wondered
how they were supposed to be used. Remembering the symbol
on the kingstone in the silhonell, she turned each of them over
in her hand, looking for a twin to it. The stones were worn
and smooth, devoid of any design. With a sigh, she returned
the last one to the line and stared at them once more.

Leaning back against the headboard, she closed her eyes.
There had to be a way to make them work, or why had Jan
told her to use them? She pictured the kingstone's symbol in
her mind. Tracing its knotwork lines with her thoughts, she
murmured the keying word.

A great weariness washed over her. How long had it been
since she'd slept... truly slept? She tried to concentrate on the
symbol, to call on some power that might unlock the riddle of
the stones. In the end, without even realizing it, her thoughts

drifted. She thought she heard the moorman's voice again.

Dream strong, Talenyn. Strong and fair.

She smiled at the name. Little Wren. It had a comfortable, familiar feel to it. Snuggling against her pillow, she fell asleep, her first true sleep in weeks, and dreamed common dreams.

chapter four

Minda awoke the next morning to the sound of her father pounding at her door. She sat up, her mind filled with muddy thoughts, her gaze fixed glassily on a shower of dust motes that danced in the sunlight pouring through her window.

There was a cart passing by outside. The protesting clack and creak of its wheels and the clop of iron-shod hooves on the cobblestones rose clearly to her ears. In the mirror, her reflection returned her bleary stare, tousled hair and all. She grinned ruefully, then her gaze froze on the stones that lay scattered across the blanket.

Porthmeyn.

Her gaze returned to her image in the mirror. She touched the acorn pendant with trembling fingers.

"Minda! Are you getting up, or do I have to come in there and pull you out of your slug's bed by the ear?"

Hadon was still at the door, growing angrier by the minute.

How late *was* it? She rubbed the sleep from her eyes, thrusting stones and pendant from her mind.

"I'm up!" she called back and slid her feet to the floor.

"Well, you'd better be coming quick," Hadon growled. "Jicker's by this morn and there'll be traders for the noon meal."

She listened to him stomp off down the hall before she stood up. Sighing, she struggled into the first dress that came to hand. This wasn't promising to be a good day. A roomful of noisy traders for lunch was the last thing she needed. Slipping an old smock overtop her dress, she combed her hair with her fingers and hurried off to the kitchen.

She thought of the horned man a lot that morning as she went about her chores. Either he was another dream or—she would think, fingering her pendant—dreams could be real. Whichever, she felt as though a great weight had been lifted from her. That sense of doom she'd worn for the past few weeks was gone and the moorman could take full credit for its going if he wanted to. And those moors . . . the hill and its henge. . . . She could not forget them either. Compared to them, the inn, its courtyard, and the town beyond seemed so mundane.

She hummed to herself as she bustled about the kitchen, preparing the noon meal and hugging her secret to herself. Hadon came in once and stared at her strangely, but she ignored him. Her thoughts were off and far away and she didn't come back from them until just before noon, when Janey popped her head in through the kitchen's back door.

"Is Hadon about?" Janey asked.

Minda nodded. "But he's closeted with Master Jicker upstairs. What are you doing here?"

"Now isn't that a fine welcome? I'm worried about you, Silly Sealy. How did you sleep?"

"Better." Minda touched the pendant where it hung under her dress.

"Well, that's something," Janey said. "Now if we can only get you out of this place for the afternoon, things'll be better still."

"I was thinking of visiting Rabbert today."

Janey wrinkled her nose. "With all those dusty books for company?"

"I *like* Rabbert, Janey."

"And so do I—but it's a lovely day. Too fine to spend

indoors. We should go down to the Wens for a swim."

Minda shook her head. "Thanks all the same, but I'm sure he thinks I'm mad at him because I haven't been by for ages."

"Well, do you want a hand? We'll get the noon meal done away with and I'll walk as far as Rabbert's with you."

"You don't have to—"

"Nonsense. I like mucking about in a kitchen—just so long as it's not my mum's." She looked about with a smile. "This place is like an adventure all on its own."

"You wouldn't say that if you had to be here every day."

"But that's just it. I don't, do I?"

Minda laughed. With Janey's help she had a stack of ham sandwiches and a platter of beef pies ready as the first noon meal customers began to straggle in.

"What do you think of the name Talenyn?" Minda asked when they were both back in the kitchen, buttering a new array of bread slices. Kate was out in the common room taking orders.

Janey glanced at her. "Well, it's a bit foreign sounding," she said. "Is it a man or a woman's name?"

Minda thought about that. "I suppose it could be either."

"Where did you hear it?"

"It just came to me."

Janey regarded her friend fondly. "You really are a Silly Sealy sometimes," she said.

Minda brandished a half-buttered slice of bread at her and the two of them laughed.

When the noon meal was over and they had finished with the washing up, Minda ran upstairs to put on a clean dress and smock and tucked the pouch of porthmeyn into a pocket before hurrying back down.

"If Hadon asks," she said to Kate, "tell him I've gone grocery shopping in the market."

Kate rolled her eyes, but nodded.

Rabbert's shop stood at the northern end of Elding Street, a half block down from Darby's Bakery where Minda bought a half-dozen muffins from Janey's father while Janey scooped up a handful of jawcrackers from a jar by the window.

"Are you sure you won't come in?" Minda asked as they neared Rabbert's.

Janey shook her head. "I'll see you later. If you get tired

of breathing musty air and poring over old books, I'll be at Dailla's."

"Thanks for the help."

"That's all right. Don't get lost in there."

She went off with a jaunty wave of her hand and Minda turned to the shop. It was built of stone, with oaken door and windowframes, and crouched between a silversmith's and a dressmaker's shop like some poor country cousin of an otherwise wealthy family. The bay window was jammed full of books, their dusty spines facing the street. Just above the door there was a shabby awning that half hid a small sign that read:

MacENCRACKER'S BOOK EMPORIUM

A small bell tinkled as Minda opened the door. She saw Rabbert start at the sound and trip over a pile of books in the middle of the floor. He teetered a moment, trying to balance an armload of a dozen other volumes, before gravity took its toll.

"Damn that bell!" he muttered, untangling his gangly frame from the mess. One bony hand scrabbled about for his missing spectacles. Finding them, he examined them critically before perching them on the end of his nose.

"Well, at least they're not broken," he continued. "But what a way to come in on a body—bursting through the door like some unmannered dolt, frightening me out of my wits, and me with all this work to do. Why, look at this mess! I was just in the middle of cleaning up when . . ."

Looking up as he spoke, he seemed to notice her for the first time. "Minda! Well, what a surprise. I hadn't expected to see you today. But you've picked a bad time to visit, I must say. The work I have waiting for me! There's inventory still to do, at least half a dozen special orders to ship out with the morning post—or have I missed it already?—not to mention all this cleaning up."

"Hello, Rabbert," Minda said, smiling.

Rabbert sat on the floor, picking up three or four books, then setting them down to make room for three or four others until he finally put them all down and stared disconsolately about himself. He wore a tweed jacket and trousers, patched at the elbows and knees, and a shirt with two buttons missing.

His hair was short and raggedly cut with wild locks sticking up every which way and a matted tangle just above his left ear where a bit of twine was caught and apparently woven in.

And he was forever talking of cleaning up, or had been for as long as Minda knew him. "A tidy room shows a tidy mind," he would say in all seriousness, but the books and papers were scattered everywhere. There were tottering stacks on the floor and on the desk, on the chairs and leaning in precarious piles against the bookshelves—in fact wherever there was room, for the shelves were always overflowing and he seemed to buy twice as many books as he sold.

"I've brought some muffins," Minda said, "so I hope you've got a pot of tea on."

"A pot of tea, a pot of tea. . . . Now where did I put the teapot? I'm sure I had it just yesterday. Or was it last week?" He began to fumble about with the books again as he spoke.

"Oh, here! Let me give you a hand."

Minda set aside her bag of muffins and helped him gather up the books. Twenty minutes later the kettle was rescued from a corner where it lay hidden under last week's pennysheet. Filled to the brim, it was soon rocking merrily on the pot-bellied stove that stood just inside the door that led from the shop to the kitchen in back. Minda found a saucepan to steep the tea in (the teapot remaining steadfastly hidden) and two mugs (one without a handle, the other chipped along its rim) that had been filed on a shelf labeled "History."

As she was cleaning them in the kitchen, Rabbert joined her. Industriously he threw books from the big sofa that stood against the wall near the stove, raising clouds of dust, and cleared a space on the low table in front of it. With the tea poured and muffins passed around, Minda found herself talking about her dreams—last night's especially—and ended up asking Rabbert what she should do, which, she realized once she'd gotten to the shop, was mostly why she'd come.

"Can I see these things?" Rabbert asked with his mouth full, trying manfully not to spill too much of the muffin as he spoke.

"Of course." She handed over the pouch of gate-stones and pulled the pendant from under her dress. "I'd rather not take this off," she added.

Rabbert nodded. He took the pouch and leaned forward, adjusting his spectacles to get a better look at the pendant.

"It's an acorn," he said. "A common acorn." He put out a finger to touch it and drew back with a startled look on his face. "It gave me a shock."

Minda looked down at her acorn with bewilderment.

Rabbert stared at the pendant with a growing curiosity, then turned his interest to the stones in the pouch. "Porthmeyn?" he asked, looking up. "Is that what they're called? And this Penalurick man—he said they worked like gates? Gates between the worlds?"

Minda nodded. "He said henges were gates and that these could be used in the same way. He disappeared before he could tell me how."

Rabbert replaced the stones in their pouch and set them on the table in front of them. "Of course," he said, "they always disappear—at least in anything I've ever read. I suppose it makes for a better story. But I've always preferred to know more at the beginning. I mean, if it were to happen to me, I'd like to be absolutely certain of all the rules before ever I'd go off traipsing into some fairy land." He paused and gave her a questioning look. "You *are* going, aren't you? What I mean is, you've already decided, haven't you?"

"I'm not really sure what I've decided."

"Because it could be dangerous, to say nothing of—"

"Rabbert! It already *is* dangerous. This . . . this Ildran has been doing things to my mind. I'm not talking about a story in some old book."

He shrugged. "Who's to say how true or untrue the old tales are? For any legend or tale to be handed down through the years, no matter how wild or fanciful, there must be some truth upon which it's based. I mean, how else could the tale survive? Truth rings true, no matter if it's only a tiny germ of truth; and it's truth we've got to look for."

"But what's that got to do with—"

"Don't interrupt. It's got everything to do with you and your dreams and your wild talk of moormen and worlds and the gates between them. Everything you've told me . . . I've read similar stories in my books." He waved an arm loosely about the kitchen. "It's in many of them. Mortals falling into the realm of fairy, lost for seven years or seven centuries. The Middle Kingdom, the Isle of the Undying, the Hidden Lands, the Hollow Lands . . . countless tales. They lend credence to what you've told me. But the thing I want to know is, why do you have to go yourself? What would it do for you? You've never struck me as the lusty adventuring sort, you know."

"You've forgotten my promise to Jan. And the fact that this Dream-master is looking for me."

"You're right, of course," Rabbert said, frowning. "But what's to stop him from finding you in these other worlds—just saying you could find a way to get into them? You might be delivering yourself right into his hands. And how would you find this Weir place, or any of Penalurick's kin?"

"You're making it sound impossible."

"Impossible? Perhaps it sounds impossible because it is. Minda, you're a dear friend and if trouble comes to you, I want to help. But this . . . I know you've already made up your mind to go. You're just waiting for me to nod and say, 'Yes, that's a good idea.' But I don't know that it's a good idea at all. I'm not sure I even understand the half of what you've told me. But if you like, you can stay here with me a while. If your Dream-master shows his face, we'll just give him a good thrashing and send him on his way."

"But—"

"Minda! We're not in the Dark Ages. Someone can't just come along and kidnap you. People wouldn't stand for it. Why Hadon—"

"—Wouldn't give a damn, and you know it! Fiddle! If I told him what I've told you, he'd have me locked up as a crackerbrain quicker than you could shake a fist at him. No, Rabbert. I know what you're saying and why—honestly, I do—but I've got to go. I suppose I did come down here to have you give me a pat on the head and tell me I'm doing the brave and right thing or something. I don't know. It confuses me as well. But I made a promise. Jan kept his side of the bargain, so I've got to at least try to keep mine. If you could only imagine what it's like . . . that touch in your mind . . . how helpless I felt. If I were to meet him face to face. . . ."

She shuddered.

"I wish you'd come to me sooner," Rabbert said quietly.

Minda met his gaze. "I should have. I don't know why I didn't. I only just told Janey a couple of days ago." She rubbed her temples. "I've still got my own doubts," she said. "Even now. But the pendant and the stones—they're real enough. And that makes it all real. Don't you see that I have to do something? If I could just key these porthmeyn Jan gave me. . . ."

Her voice trailed off. For a while they sat in silence, each caught up in their own thoughts. Minda stood up and crossed the room to look out the window. The sun was just dropping behind the buildings on Hart's Row.

"It's getting late," she said, returning to the couch. "Hadon'll have my hide if I'm not back soon." She scooped up the stones, deposited the pouch back in her pocket. Looking down at Rabbert, she smiled. "Thank you for listening," she said. "I couldn't have told anybody else about it *all*—not even Janey."

Rabbert returned her smile, but there was a far-off look in his eyes. "I've had a thought," he said. "If you really mean to go through with this quest of yours, and the porthmeyn won't work, have you thought of Caldwer Henge?"

Caldwer Henge. She could almost hear Jan's voice in her ear, as clear as though he stood beside her.

Longstones. . . . They are the gates . . . and they are on all the worlds.

On all the worlds. She remembered the henge in the silhonell and the swirling symbol cut into its kingstone. The keying word whispered through her thoughts.

Caldwer Henge. It was almost a full day's journey north, on the way to her Uncle Tomalin's farm set in the hills between Fernwillow and Woldley. If it was a gate, why, surely she could make it work for her?

"No," she said dreamily. "I'd not thought of it. But just maybe. . . ." Her smile widened, eyes sparkling. "It's worth a try in any case."

"When will you go?" Rabbert asked. "I'll go with you."

Minda shook her head slowly. "No, Rabbert," she said. "This is something I have to do on my own. Besides, the countryside's all wild up there and when was the last time you went roughing it, Rabbert?"

He grinned ruefully. "There's so much to do just in the shop that there never seems time for anything else. But what about you?"

"Oh, I hike around all the time. This'll be different, but I'm sure I can manage. I've read all about journeying in the wilds and know just what to take."

"I can remember that picnic we went on—was it last summer?" Rabbert said. "I enjoyed that."

The memory blossomed happily in his eyes, then faded and

he frowned. He stood abruptly, spilling his tea in the process. He looked down at the mess and shrugged. His eyes were glistening when his gaze lifted to meet Minda's.

"Luck be with you, then," he said softly. "I . . . I'll miss you."

Minda stepped over to him and threw her arms around him. "I'll miss you, too," she said, hugging him tightly.

They clung to each other for a long moment, then Minda stood back, biting at her lip. Sighing, she straightened her shoulders, her resolve hardening once more. But her eyes, too, were shiny with unshed tears.

"I'm off," she said, keeping her voice light. "Not a word to anyone, all right?"

"Not a word," Rabbert said. "Goodbye, Minda."

"Goodbye, Rabbert."

He followed her to the front of the shop and out into the street. She hugged him again, then raced off to The Wandering Piper, waving over her shoulder. Rabbert stood in the doorway, watching till she had turned the corner. He brushed a sleeve across his eyes. A sense of loss welled up inside him. More tears built up in his eyes and he brushed them away as well.

Why did he feel like he would never see her again?

Because, he answered himself, he never would.

"Goodbye," he repeated.

For all the crowds, the street seemed empty. With drooping shoulders, he walked back into the shop. The door closed with a lonely click behind him.

chapter five

That night, when Hadon and the rest were long abed and the inn was quiet, Minda crept from her bedroom onto the landing outside its door. She had a journeypack slung over one shoulder and her shoes in her hand as she made her way down to the kitchen. Each creak of the stairs made her freeze, ears cocked, breath held in. By the time she reached the kitchen without mishap she was trembling from tension.

She was a little proud of herself. She was actually seeing this thing through. There had been a moment, while she lay in bed waiting for the inn to quiet down, when the full enormity of what lay before her had pressed against her like a lead weight and she felt unable even to lift a finger. Thoughts of security forsaken—even if it was a security that included Horrible Hadon—and of friends like Janey and Rabbert left behind skittered through her. It had taken every ounce of bravery she could summon to convince herself that she had to begin this journey. Once she did, a feeling of rightness settled in place, calming her.

In the kitchen, she added bread and cheese to the few belongings in her pack and filled a waterskin at the barrel by the door. She wore a pair of thick brown cotton trousers and an old dusty blue shirt, with a jacket overtop. A small knife hung in a sheath at her belt.

Easing the back door open, she slipped out into the courtyard and closed the door as quietly as she could. The only sound she heard was the latch clicking shut. Putting on her shoes, she left the inn behind and made her way through the sleeping town.

Her shoes tapped softly against the cobblestones of Fernwillow's streets. Small teasing gusts of wind lifted the hem of her jacket and tugged at her hair. She was alone in the still streets, walking through a ghost town with only the moon high above for company.

When she had put a couple of miles between herself and the outskirts of town, she left the roadway. Squeezing through the hedgerow, she made herself a bed in the grass, using her pack as a lumpy pillow. Somehow she didn't quite dare go too far on her first night—but she hadn't wanted to chance oversleeping at the inn, either. She lay there, waiting for sleep to come, but the excitement of what she had just done kept her awake. It was only the first step of—how long a journey? Did it even matter? It was enough now to be free of Hadon and of the inn, to be responsible only to herself . . . and the promise she'd made to the moorman.

Looking up at the stars, she wondered how soon Hadon would come looking for her. The stars seemed so far away, the dark between them so very dark. It would probably take Hadon until tomorrow night to realize that she'd really run away. The first place he'd check would be her Uncle Tomalin's farm, but by then she'd have reached the henge and . . . be gone? Into other worlds?

It didn't seem quite so possible, lying out here in a field all by herself. The moon had set. The field rustled with small scurrying sounds that her imagination turned into Hadon crashing through the hedge, looking for her. Or, what if the dreams came back? *Ildran.* She fingered her pendant, shuddering. It was only an acorn. How could it keep the Dream-master at bay?

With one thought leading into another, she tired herself out and was soon asleep without even knowing it.

When she woke, it was from a dreamless sleep.

Well-rested, for all that the field was an uncomfortable bed, she sat up, stretched and looked around. The sun was just rising over the eastern woods and the whole field sparkled with dew. She grinned ruefully. Her first night of freedom had only brought her a rough bed, and a damp one at that. But she didn't really mind. The sun and brisk walking would soon dry her out. She munched on some cheese as she set out.

It was spring and she'd almost forgotten. In town you didn't notice it so much, but here the roadside was choked with purple orchids, yellow buttercups and cowslips, hawthorns and stark white jack-by-the-hedges. The road was overhung with the drooping branches of oaks and drowsy elms, light green buds flaring the lengths of their boughs. Wild apple trees, heavy with blossoms, dotted the fields.

Minda walked along at an easy pace, staring with wide eyes at the rich, bursting colors, the sweep of the hills as they rose and fell in a rolling march to the horizon. The distance sobered her somewhat, reminding her that she was but one little speck in a vast world.

Worlds, she corrected herself. And how was this little speck supposed to find her way?

One worry often leads to another and soon she was wondering if Hadon had guessed right away that she'd run off and was now on the road behind her in swift pursuit. Or what if . . .

Ildran will need to bind your body now.

Suddenly, she was sure she was being spied upon. She looked to either side and over her shoulder, but there was no one in sight. The northern road to Woldley seldom had much traffic and this morning she had it all to herself. Still the feeling persisted.

Minda pushed through the hedgerow and followed the road by way of the accompanying fields, hopping over ditches and scrabbling over brush-choked fences, nettles stinging her hands and forearms. The feeling grew stronger. She panicked a little, stepping up her pace until she was running. At last she collapsed under a stand of young beech and lay gasping.

There was nothing following her, no one spying. She looked back the way she'd come. A light wind stirred the grass and weeds. The sun was near noon, straight above her, and everywhere she looked there was no sign of threat. Two magpies chattered on a dead maple stump nearby and in the hawthorns along the road a young hare peered shyly out at her. A kestrel was winging lazily in the sky above.

"Silly Sealy," she mocked herself.

As she stood, the hare vanished and the magpies turned to regard her. When she pushed back through the hedge to the road, they lifted into the air and scolded her with sharp cries. Once on the road, keeping to a brisk pace, she began to relax, embarrassed by the way she'd let her fears run away with her. She concentrated instead on the way ahead.

The road would take her into Woldley if she followed it that far but she meant to turn off at the track that led to the henge, a good six miles or so before the village. She'd come this way with Uncle Tomalin a few years ago, the time Hadon had closed the inn for two weeks while he went south.

She liked her uncle. He was everything his brother wasn't. They were both big men, but Tomalin's bulk gave him a cheery look, while Hadon was nothing but a bully. It was in the eyes, Minda supposed. Tomalin's were a pale blue as well, but there was a kind look in them that made you warm right up to him. The day they'd travelled this same road, he'd taken her to the henge.

"What matters an extra day or two?" he'd said in his countryman's brogue. "We've a whole two weeks, lass, an' that's the truth o't. We'll make Woldley in plenty of time, an' if not—why we'll sleep in t' ditch!"

They'd been the best two weeks of her life, Minda thought, remembering them with a smile. She often wished that her mother had married Tomalin. When she'd said as much to her uncle, he'd only shrugged, saying:

"That's the way o't, in't, lass?"

She wondered what her mother had been like and what she could ever have seen in Hadon. There was no one in Fernwillow she could ask because by the time they'd moved there, Minda was two and her mother had already died. Nobody in Fernwillow had ever known her and Hadon would only glower when she asked him. Sometimes Minda thought that she remembered, but the memories were never very clear. Tomalin wasn't much help either.

"She was a grand lady, she was," he'd say in answer to her questioning.

"But what did she look like? What was she *like?*"

"Well, you look like her when you're smiling, an' she'd a quiet way 'bout her—not at all like you! But I never kenned her all that well. She came from a far way away, she did, an' never talked much. She came back with Hadon from one o' his travels—ah, he was always t' one for travelling in those days. She'd you in tow an' you were no more 'n a year old. She died here, a year later, an' then Hadon bought t' inn."

Tomalin took her to her mother's grave, the first day they arrived at his farm. She'd stood before it, reading the inscription. "Here lies Morwenna, wife to Hadon Sealy."

She hadn't felt any closer to the stranger buried there. "Do you think she would have liked me?" she asked.

She could still remember the sad look in her uncle's eyes as he replied, "She would o' loved you, lass, an' make no mistake o't."

Minda kicked a pebble into the bushes as she shook the memories from her. Tomalin hadn't been by the inn since those two weeks. There'd been a terrible row over her, her uncle insisting that she come and live at the farm with him, Hadon shouting vehemently back that he'd never let her go.

The farm was the first place Hadon would go in search of her but she wasn't worried about it. Tomalin was the only one she knew who could stand up to Hadon's temper. He'd be delighted to learn that she'd left the inn and would send Hadon packing the moment he arrived.

She wished there was time to stop by the farm, but knew she couldn't chance it. Tomalin would ask where she was going and, when he found out, he'd never let her go—*if* he even believed her story in the first place. It wasn't that he'd be trying to rule her life the way that Hadon did, but because he cared about what happened to her and it was a mad thing to be doing. But it had to be done—for herself as much as for the promise she'd made to Jan Penalurick. After just a half day of freedom, she felt she could never give it up again.

She forced herself to keep a steady pace. As she continued

along her way, she tried hard not to think of anything except
the road that unwound under her feet, mile by dusty mile.

The henge lay silent and dark-cloaked by the twilight. As
Minda left the road and walked the last half mile along the
rough track that led to it, she watched it grow into colossal
proportions. Her heart beat fast when she stood in the shadow
of the great longstones. The looming megaliths and triad dolmen appeared otherworldly and the air around them was charged
with energy. She could easily believe that the henge was a
magical gate. The pendant grew warmer against her skin.

She felt very small when she stepped in between the stones.
When she reached the kingstone, there was still a flicker of
light in the western sky. She laid her hand on the stone's rough
surface. A tingle ran up her arm. A curious assurance filled
her. Trembling with excitement, she backed away from the
stone.

A wind rose up, pushing her hair into her face. She tied it
back with a strip of leather, then gathered the makings for a
small fire. She struck flint against steel until the spark jumped
to her kindling, then kneeling on the ground, she cupped her
hands around the tiny glow and blew gently on it. The glow
awoke into a feeble flame. Slowly she added bits of wood until
a small fire was crackling merrily, throwing its light onto the
kingstone. She peered closely across the stone's surface,
searching for the keying symbol that was supposed to be there.

Nothing. It simply wasn't there.

Minda edged closer and ran her fingers along the stone. At
the touch, a tingle arose in her again and the darkness shrouding
the henge seemed to draw back, the old longstones huddling
closer to the kingstone and to her. She heard a murmuring
about her like the wind travelling through the henge, but in her
mind she fancied that the stones were speaking to her. As from
a great distance, she heard a faint trilling of music, soft amidst
the murmur of the wind. A comforting warmth spread out from
the pendant. She brought it out from under her shirt to find it
glowing with a muted amber light. When she laid her hand on
the kingstone once more, the rock's surface shimmered.

She stifled a small cry of delight when the symbol's swirling
lines appeared in the midst of the shimmering. Solemnly she
traced the lines with a steady finger, holding firm in her mind

an image of what she thought Weir was like—of a place where moormen like Jan Penalurick would be at home. She pictured low hills and sweeping moors, standing stones topping craggy heights.

"Caeldh."

She murmured the keying word as she completed the last turn of the symbol. The word rustled up from her memory, soft as a feather's falling, but seemed to thunder in the still air when she spoke it. She waited for the mists and fey music with a breathless expectation.

I've done it, she thought. Oh, Rabbert, if you could be here. . . .

The murmuring of the wind—of the stones?—stilled until all she heard was the spluttering of her small fire. Then that too was gone. With a rush the darkness beyond the henge swept her up. Her pendant flared, and the henge disappeared. She was spinning again, falling in silence. Instinctively she knew that she was in the dark between the worlds—that it was here that she must control her destination.

She closed her eyes and held to her images of Weir with a desperate hope. Almost she thought she saw it in her mind. The wild heaths were there, cloaking low hills. Stones were scattered in straight lines as if to mark some boundary and high winds rode the sky, tumbling grey clouds before them. She reached for the image, willing herself closer.

Then something grew closer to her and the image dissolved. She knew that what drew near was alien to the land she had seen. Alien to that land, but hatefully familiar to her.

Ildran had come.

She tried to escape him, but there was nowhere to flee in the darkness. Her hands opened and closed, searching for something to hold on to, but found nothing. She tried to hold to her image of Weir, but fear clouded her mind. Like a fat snake, the first tendril of the Dream-master's thoughts wrapped itself around her. Her flesh cringed from its touch.

I have the pendant! You can't touch me when I have—

Jan's charm burned against her skin, pouring strength into her that she didn't know how to use. Ildran balked at the pendant's power, but only momentarily. Then his grip tightened.

"The power is not enough," the darkness hissed, "without the skill to use it."

With a disdainful flick, Ildran sent her whipping through the void.

On all sides of her, golden flares of light flashed. She knew they were gateways to the other worlds, and that one was the gateway to the world she sought; but she was plunging into some deeper darkness with a speed that defied reason. Her terror was such that she couldn't concentrate enough to reach even one of them—any one. And once in that deeper darkness, she would be lost forever.

"You were the last of them." The whisper followed her like a curse, sibilant and fierce. "With you the line dies."

Blind panic exploded in her as gate after gate sped by. She was very near the darkness now and the gates grew fewer in number, further apart. Soon that darkness would be all she knew.

She grasped the pendant.

Please . . . help me. . . .

Its warmth cut through some of her fear with an echo of the power that had come from the stones in Caldwer Henge. She was speeding towards the last gateway. Numbly she watched the approaching golden flare. What strength remained in her drew her in an arc towards it—an arc that would fall just short.

Ildran's mirth rang in the void. She knew why he mocked her. For all that she had the pendant, for all that she struggled with every last ounce of her strength, she was still going to lose to him. The realization stung. But curiously, on the heels of it, her mind filled with incongruous thoughts of that one day's taste of freedom she'd had. Again she knew the pride of making a decision of her own and following through. Again it seemed she walked the road from Fernwillow, revelling in spring's dance across the hills.

"That was life," Ildran told her. "That was life—yours no more."

No! With the pendant, Ildran couldn't enter her mind—Jan had told her so. He could feed her fears, make any illusion seem real, but with the pendant, she was in control. She had to be.

The last gateway came rushing up. Her fingers tightened around the acorn charm until the knuckles went white. As she tore through the void, as the gateway was directly opposite her, she screamed the closing word.

"Tervyn!"

The flare sucked her into its heart. Winds howled about her. The dark between the worlds vanished as the gateway burned bright, then brighter still. Its glare blinded her. She could feel her strength rush from her. Utterly spent, she drifted on the borders of unconsciousness.

"Ildran," she mumbled to the void. "This time I...I've beaten you. And no matter...what lies before me...I'll always know that I...beat you once and...can do it a... again...."

She knew no more.

2

Towers of Stone

chapter one

Slowly the darkness drew back its veil.

Minda finally opened her eyes to stare into a clear sunlit sky. She lay still, blinking in the brightness and savoring the deepness of its blues, only peripherally aware that she lay in a canyon of some sort. A minute or so passed, then a dull throb in the back of her head brought a rush of memory. Ildran. The void. The gates.

She sat up and the sudden motion caused a short spell of dizziness. Where was she?

This was a canyon—but the like of it she'd never even heard of before. On all sides tall stone buildings rose to tower about her like the ribcage of some fossil behemoth. Up and up they reared into the sky, hundreds of stone fingers pointing out some remarkable sight overhead.

Time had taken a grim toll on some of the structures. Their once flat surfaces were crumbled and pock-marked, worn by

wind and weather. Here and there some of them had toppled
to form small mountains of rusted metal beams and wagon-
sized slabs of stone. Those still standing formed long neat rows
that stretched away as far as the eye could see. Their surfaces
were black or a dull grey. Their huge windows seemed to watch
her with brooding menace, the sunlight not so much reflected
from their dark panes as swallowed by them.

Scattered like tiny knolls in between the monolithic structures were the remains of what, upon closer inspection, must
have been vehicles of some sort—metal wagons, rusted and
broken, heaps of scrap that lacked shafts for horses and had
once had glass windows. Minda touched the door of one gingerly and the metal flaked away in her hand.

The ruined metropolis was so immense that if Fernwillow
were dropped into it—the bridge, and all—it would be swallowed in an instant to disappear without a trace. But why was
the city deserted? What had driven its inhabitants forth, allowing the wilderness to reclaim its lost heritage?

Where once the roadway had been smooth, now tall oaks
and elms forced their way up through the cracked surface. Their
leaves were mottled, gold and red and brown. Had she lost the
whole of the summer to get here?

She saw apple trees as well, heavy with fruit, and berry
bushes. Vine tendrils clung to the stone walls and creeping
bushes engulfed the lower doorways and windows of the buildings. Clumps of dark cedars huddled in corners, whispering in
the light breeze. Scraggly juniper bushes clambered over heaps
of rubbled stone and the strange wrecks of the metal vehicles.

Minda stared about herself, utterly at a loss. This wasn't
Weir, of that she was sure. But what was it? And where was
the henge—the gate through which she had come?

The thought of being trapped in a weird world of cliff-high
buildings in ruins, trapped perhaps forever, sent a new shiver
of fear through her. And Ildran. . . . She cast a nervous glance
over her shoulder. The sense of being watched beset her once
more. If he wasn't here yet, he would be. He would follow
her and there was no use pretending otherwise.

She turned in a slow circle, staring at the gaping maws of
doors and windows, at the shadows where cedar stands pressed
against walls, at the eerie metal wagons. Her gaze settled on
her journeypack lying forlorn in the roadway where she'd woken.
Biting her lip, she made her way to it, skittish as a hare. For

a long while she crouched beside it, touching its familiar woven side as though proximity to this one remnant of her homeworld would somehow protect her from whatever dangers might lurk about her now.

At length, she shouldered her pack and stood. Gathering her courage, she studied her surroundings once again, searching for some hint of the blue-grey stonework that made up a henge. Were the longstones part of the buildings—hidden in the rubble that was mounded in the street? In this world did a henge look different, made of some other sort of stone than the kind she was familiar with?

She closed her eyes, trying to remember what the moorman had told her about the gates. She drew the acorn pendant from under her shirt, held it tightly, and some of her tension began to ease. Almost she could hear Jan's voice, explaining to her:

Longstones . . . are the gates. . . . They are all that remains of Avenveres . . . rocky bones . . . scattered through all the worlds . . . bound, one to the other.

She opened her eyes, sighing softly. The gates were the same on every world. Henges shaped from slabs of blue-grey rock. She looked around once more, her panic stilled as though just the remembering of the moorman's voice was enough to give her strength to go on. For go on she must. There was no henge here—however it came to be that she'd arrived here—so she must go on until she found one.

She chose a direction at random, tramping down one long street after another, skirting piles of rubble where she could, pushing her way through the undergrowth where it blocked her passage. She kept to a cautious pace, conscious that a twisted ankle or any sort of accident would harm her far more, alone in this desolation of stone towers, than even Ildran might.

Once she made her way up to an age-widened doorway. Pushing aside vines, she peered in to see a great hall as big as her father's entire inn. She was tempted to explore further, when a rat scampered across the smooth marble floor and she fled back into the streets where at least the sun shone.

Were there any people still living in this city of ruins? she wondered. Or did it just go on and on forever, forgotten and empty? The chill of fear returned and not even the pendant could entirely banish it this time.

•   •   •

She spent the night huddled in a small stand of cedar, hidden in a hollow made by bare boughs that never saw the sun. With nightfall came a stronger wind. The wind sped through the streets, in and out of the buildings, waking a strange sound like piping as though the city were alive and singing. Sometimes the sound was strident and high-pitched, sometimes it echoed in fitful moans.

The discordant music cried all night long. Minda slept only in snatches, waking from dreams that—though they were not some sending of Ildran's—nevertheless left her shivering with fear. She clutched at her pendant with damp palms, praying over and over for the night to end.

When the sun finally tipped the shadowed towers, the wind and the music died away with a sound like ragged breathing. Minda crouched in her shelter longer than necessary. Not until the sun was bright on the streets once more did she shake her fears from her and step into its welcome light.

She was angry with herself for having allowed the darkness and wind to frighten her so much. To compensate, she walked with reckless courage, daring the city to send forth its goblins. Yet street after street passed by underfoot, and nothing changed. Loneliness settled upon her like a heavy shroud.

By midafternoon Minda realized that instead of making her way out of the ruined city, she'd been faring deeper into it. Since she'd stopped for her noon meal—munching bread that was going stale and cheese—the buildings had grown progressively taller. They were clustered closer together, often with no room between them at all. She had half decided to turn around and retrace her steps, when she turned another corner and came to a wide plaza.

She stood at the edge of the huge square, gazing across. It was about a mile wide, sparsely dotted with trees and almost bare of brush. In the center, on a raised platform, were the remains of a long neglected monument. Once it had held a host of statues. Now only one figure stood proudly amidst the surrounding rubble, sunlight glinting on the oxidized bronze of its limbs. Its companions lay about the platform, broken, limbs scattered, torsos cracked.

The plaza was hemmed in by the same towering ruins that she'd found everywhere in the city, except to the north where a low building squatted. It was built like a castle, complete with battlements, and was only three stories high. Minda's gaze lingered on it. After looking upon the alien heights of the city's architecture for so long, the smaller building drew her as with a sense of the familiar. It reminded her of a picture-book castle— not a fairy palace with slender spires, but the fortresses that could be found in the Hinterlands, north of Fernwillow. It seemed very old.

She crossed the square, pausing at the monument to look up at the one standing statue. There was a sad look on the figure's face. He was dressed in clothing unfamiliar to Minda— a uniform she supposed, but nothing like what the militia wore in her homeland. He held a staff of sorts that was broken off near his shoulder. On the ground by her feet, Minda spied a bronze flag with an unfamiliar design upon it. That must have belonged to him, she thought as she skirted the rubble about the monument. He must have been a standard bearer, leading a charge. Now he bore nothing, led nothing. She looked back a last time, then made her way across the square to where the castlelike structure stood.

The building had seemed almost small from a distance. Now it loomed over her. The size of its massive brass doors staggered her. When she pushed against the right one, it opened sound- lessly to reveal a large darkened antechamber, dimly lit by small vine-choked windows set high in the walls. Stepping through, she saw an open doorway to her left and made for it. A cloud of thick dust arose from her scuffing feet.

She found herself in an enormous room filled with the re- mains of long rows of glass display cases. As her eyes became accustomed to the gloom, she could make out knives and swords, crossbows and even more exotic weaponry lying in what was left of the cases, or scattered upon the floor. She reached out and touched a strange implement made all of metal, curious as to what it was. Something about its shape sent a shiver running up her spine.

She walked along the aisles, crunching glass underfoot, touching the frames of the cases, blowing dust away from some objects as she tried to make out what they were. One was a king's sword—its hilt all encrusted with jewels and inlaid with gold. It lay askew on a case, its scabbard on the floor. There were other swords more plainly fashioned, still more in bizarre shapes. One like a winding forest track, another like a crescent moon. There were iron clubs, maces and then the things she could put no name to—gleaming weapons that had neither edge nor bowstring, which yet filled her with awe. Some appeared so fragile she couldn't imagine how they were used.

Far down the first aisle her pendant began to grow warmer. She stopped and stared about her. A warning? If so, a warning of what? She could hear nothing, see nothing threatening. What if it was Ildran, come at last?

Nerves all on edge, she started to retrace her steps to the door, then froze again. The sense of imminent danger cut through her like a dagger. She looked about her, gaze falling on a short sword that lay at her feet, half sheathed in a plain leather scabbard. She grasped the weapon's hilt and drew it forth, held it in a trembling hand. She knew as much about how to use a sword as she knew about sailing a ship, but with the leather hilt hard in her hand she—

A high-pitched skreeing cut through the chamber and Minda spun about, the blade held out before her with all the finesse of a floormop. From the gloom of the chamber's lofty ceiling, a dark, winged shape descended in a rush, fangs and claws flashing. Yellow eyes bore into her soul, paralyzing her. An obscene stench clogged her nostrils. Her throat constricted with her fear and the scream rising inside her never passed her lips.

Numbly she watched the winged thing dive. There was nothing she could do. She would die here, in the claws of a nightmare.

Then the sword she held flared with a blue glow and lifted with a will of its own, dragging her arm up with it. The diving creature veered to one side. A wingtip brushed Minda, bowling her over. She fell in a sprawl, cutting her knee on a shard of glass. The sword hilt was hot in her hand, but she was unable to let it go. The creature swooped upward, skreeing its frustration, then dove once more.

Responding to the renewed attack, the sword exploded with a brilliant blue-white glare. A strange power filled Minda with an alien strength and knowledge. Her pendant screamed a warning in her mind, but the power lifted her to her feet to meet the creature's attack.

Her eyesight cleared in the glare of the sword. The shadows in the chamber were banished and she saw her enemy for what it was: a bat the size of a small hound. As it bore down on her, she dodged claw and fang with a stranger's skill and thrust upward with her blade, deep into the monster's abdomen. The shrieks of rage twisted into pain and the beast careened along the aisle, spraying pale blood from the ghastly wound in its underbelly.

It thrashed about savagely, shattering showcases. Shards of wood and glass ricocheted through the vast room. Minda dropped to her knees, rubble whining about her. The knee she'd cut gave out from under her and she fell again, narrowly dodging a jagged piece of glass. She crouched on the floor while, slowly, the flailing wings of the bat-creature grew weaker. It tore at the air in one last fruitless attempt to fly, then lay still.

Sick with horror, Minda pulled herself to her feet. Some trace of the alien presence that had filled her remained as she looked at the dead thing. The sword in her fist lost its glow and hung loosely in her hand. Hardly aware of what she was doing, she cleaned the blade on the dusty velvet lining of a case, retrieved the scabbard and thrust the weapon into it. She hobbled slowly towards the exit, still carrying the sheathed sword.

At the doorway she looked back to see the silhouette of a wing lifting from the shattered display cases. Her gaze dropped to the weapon she held. Something in it had taken over her body, killed the monster with skills and strength she couldn't hope to copy. Magic. The thought of being possessed by what-ever it was that inhabited the sword revolted her. She wanted to fling it as far as she could from her. But it was magic. . . . If Ildran came and she had this to fight him with . . .

A shadow moved across the doorway. Something had entered the antechamber.

A wolf padded into sight, head cocked to one side as it paused to study her. Minda felt weak. The dead bat behind, the wolf blocking her way . . . the ruins were coming to life. Dully, she closed her hand about the sword's hilt and tugged it free of its sheath once more.

chapter two

The wolf bared its fangs, growling low in its chest as the sword cleared its scabbard. Its guard-hairs bristled and it took a step towards her.

Minda moved back, gaze locked on the reddish-grey shape that blocked the doorway. The scabbard fell from her hand to clatter on the floor. She waited for blue light to flare from her weapon again, but no more than a pale blue sheen touched the blade.

Do something! she told the sword.

She clasped it firmly in a sweaty hand, waiting for the wolf to attack. Her legs were trembling. If the sword didn't possess her quickly she was going to fall to the floor. She tried to hold the blade pointed at the wolf, but it kept dipping as her hand shook. Her pendant retained its normal warmth. She was puzzled at its lack of warning.

She edged a little to her right.

"Ruhn?"

A voice spoke from beyond the doorway and the wolf turned to look over its shoulder. A woman appeared and moved to its side. She laid her hand on the wolf's head, smoothing the raised guard-hairs absently, and regarded Minda with curiosity.

She was a small, delicately boned woman, no taller than Minda herself, though something about her gave her the appearance of greater stature. Her mouth was wide, nose thin, eyes a deep sea-green. She wore a red and grey cloak over a kirtle that was dark blue. Though she didn't seem old, her long hair was a strange mingling of grey and white.

"I give you greeting, stranger."

Minda took another step back, keeping the sword in front of her. "Put down your weapon," the woman said. "You've nothing to fear from us."

Minda thought of the bat-creature and her gaze flicked to one side where a huge wing still poked above the display cases. The woman's gaze followed hers and her eyes widened. "A skeller! You've slain a skeller. Is that it? Do you think we're in league with the likes of that?"

Minda didn't know what to say. The more the woman talked, the less inclined she was to think that either she or the wolf meant her any harm. But she couldn't be sure, not in this strange place.

The woman bowed slightly from the waist. "My name is Taneh Leafmoon. I am a Loremistress from Wistlore—on Langlin. The wolf answers to Ruhn. What is your name? From what world have you come?"

The woman's voice held a strange accent, but she spoke the same language as Minda did—just as Jan had, Minda realized. Surely they didn't all speak the same language on all the worlds?

The arm that held the sword felt leaden. She lowered it slowly until the sword tip rested on the dusty floor, taking the weight off her arm. So long as the blue flare didn't spark along its length, it was about as much use to her as a stick. Could whatever invested the sword with its power tell friend from foe?

The silence lengthened until Minda grew uncomfortable.

"My name's Minda," she said at last. "Minda Talenyn," she added, feeling braver using Jan's naming. "I don't know what world I'm from. We just call it the world—when we speak of it at all."

Taneh smiled. "As did my own folk, before we knew of the gates. Now we name worlds with the abandon of children at play. This world we call Dewethtyr, the Last World; the city, Darkruin. But surely your own people use the gates, else how came you here?"

"I. . . . It's sort of a complicated story. I didn't mean to come here at all. I was looking for another place when . . . in the void . . ." She was feeling more awkward by the minute. "It was all I could do to reach this place," she finished abruptly.

"Yes, but . . ."

"I really should be going," Minda said.

Taneh looked disappointed. "I was going to ask you to sup with me," she said. "So few come to Dewethtyr, and those that do are mostly wrapped up in their own studies."

"That's very kind of you," Minda said, "but . . ."

She shifted her weight from one foot to the other, wincing at the pressure it put on her cut knee. Taneh's gaze travelled down to the torn trouser, the blood that stained it.

"You're hurt!" she said. "At least let me help you with your cut. I've bandaging in my pack—I left it just outside the door as I was coming in."

"I'm sure I'll be all right," Minda said.

The Loremistress studied her a moment, taking in the white knuckles where Minda gripped the sword hilt, the strain that showed in her face. "Don't be afraid," Taneh said softly. She opened her cloak to show that there were no weapons concealed under its folds. "I won't hurt you."

"It's not that; it's just that . . . I don't really, well . . ."

"Know me," Taneh smiled. "You are new to the world-wending, aren't you?"

"A little, I suppose."

"And you're lost?"

Minda nodded, not trusting herself to speak.

"Let me help you, Minda Talenyn. That means 'Little Wren' in the old tongue, did you know?"

Minda nodded again. She concentrated on the pendant hanging under her shirt, trying to read some sort of message in its warmth. It had warned her of the giant bat's attack. Now it told her nothing. The blue sheen had left the sword. She tried to make herself relax. The wolf chose that moment to move towards her.

Panic flitted through her and she started to raise the sword.

"Easy," Taneh said. "Ruhn means you no harm. He sees well enough, but trusts more to his nose. He only wishes to greet you. Such is the way of his kind."

Minda swallowed dryly and stood quiet, hardly daring to breathe. The wolf approached her and sniffed at her free hand, tickling the skin, then nuzzled at her leg.

"You can pet him if you like. He won't bite."

Gingerly, Minda ran a hand along the wolf's back. She stroked the grizzled fur shyly, half expecting that she might still be bitten. The wolf fixed her with a reproving eye, as if reading her thoughts, and returned to Taneh's side.

"Let's see to that knee of yours," the Loremistress said.

"If you're sure it's no trouble," Minda protested as she started slowly for the door.

"No trouble at all. Here. You forgot your scabbard." Taneh retrieved the leather sheath and handed it to Minda.

"But it's not my—" Minda looked down at the sword and thought better of what she'd been about to say. She might still need its magic, if it even worked more than once. "Thank you," she said, accepting the scabbard.

She sheathed the blade, and followed the Loremistress out into the dying afternoon.

"Honey?"

"A little, please."

Minda watched the Loremistress spoon a small dollop into each tea mug, then stir them with a cinnamon stick. They were in a tower about a half mile from the building where Minda had fought the skeller. Taneh's quarters were in a large room just off the vast entrance hall of one of the tall structures. There were windows in two of the walls—one of which had been converted into a smoke vent for a small hearth. It was built from the rubble that lay everywhere in the city, the rocks held together with what looked like a white fired clay.

The room itself was comfortable—cozy, Minda decided when she first stepped inside. There was a table and chair under a window that still retained its glass pane, a pallet by another wall, mattressed with pungent cedar boughs that filled the room with their scent. Minda sat on pillows that were strewn beside the bed. Her bandaged knee still throbbed a little, though the cut had proved to be more messy than severe.

Idly she picked up a sheaf of papers that lay on the floor

beside her. She couldn't understand the writing. It was in a small fine script, illuminated with detailed drawings that she recognized as scenes of the ruins outside.

As Taneh brought the tea over, Ruhn arose and scratched at the door that shut them off from the main lobby. The Loremistress let him out, then settled down beside Minda on the cushions. "He goes to hunt," she explained as she arranged herself into a comfortable position. "He prefers his meat uncooked—which reminds me, I can only offer you some hare stew. I wasn't expecting company."

"That would be lovely," Minda said. She held up a sheaf of papers. "Did you draw these? Are you writing a book?"

"Yes to the first, no to the second," Taneh replied with a smile. "Though I've enough notes to write two or three."

"But this is what you do here?"

"I'm a Loremistress, so my life's work is the collecting and studying of lore. I've been here in Darkruin for three years now, trying to understand what made this place what it is; why its streets are deserted, where its people went, why the buildings remain. Three years, and I'm still not much closer to any answer than when I first arrived. Like most riddles, the more I question, the more questions I find to ask."

"I know that feeling," Minda said. "How long do you plan to stay here?"

"I fear I'll be leaving sooner than I'd thought. When I first came, the skellers only hunted at night when I was safe in my rooms. But the game's grown scarce in the city of late and more than once I've seen them abroad during the day. Ruhn's killed two that attacked me in the past month. And . . ." She shrugged. "I'm here to study—not battle with overgrown bats."

Minda shivered, remembering the creature that had attacked her. Without the sword, she'd be dead.

"They're dangerous in more ways than one, you know," Taneh added. "They're quick—deadly with claws and fangs— but worse, they carry diseases in their fur. Ruhn has some natural immunity to their poisons, but the one you slew. . . . You didn't touch it, did you?"

"Only with the sword. And I cleaned the blade right after."

And how, Minda thought, had she known enough to do that—she who'd never swung a sword in her life?

"Luck was with you, then," Taneh said. "Were you long in the museum? Today was my first time inside and all I saw was a glimpse of the showcases. I've tried to go in before, but whenever I've approached it Ruhn stands in the doorway baring his teeth at me till I leave. Did you come across any written records? The few I've found this far are so weatherbeaten there's little left to decipher from them."

Minda shook her head. "I didn't see any books. I wasn't really in there long, and too much happened too quickly. This museum, if that's what it was, seemed to be no more than a storehouse for weapons."

"Is that what it held? Curious. Most such places keep artifacts, records and the like. Weapons would be but a small part of its inventory. Do they not have them on your world?"

"Weapons?" Minda asked with a smile.

Taneh returned the smile. "No. Museums."

"Not in my home town," Minda replied. "It's called Fernwillow and it's about as far from the big cities in the south as Fernwillow is from the moon. I feel like such a bumpkin, really. I've never been farther than a day's walk from Fernwillow, where the tallest building is the Tamtren on Elding Street—and it's only three stories high. Nothing like the towers here."

"Most people feel as you do when they first see Darkruin. There's a tinker come recently—in the company of a Wysling, how's that for a curious pairing? He just stood and stared at the towers as though his eyes might pop out."

"What's a Wysling?" Minda asked, remembering her moorman mentioning them in the same breath as Loremasters. "Some sort of wiseman?"

"You might say so. Wyslings are wizards and some of them are wise enough."

"Wizards?" Minda's eyes grew wide.

Taneh smiled and nodded. "Spellworkers," she said. "It was a Wysling who first discovered the gates."

Minda remembered something else Jan had told her. "That was Grameryn, wasn't it?" she asked.

"Just so." Taneh looked puzzled. "Now how could you have known that if they have no knowledge of the gates on your world? And to take the riddle a step further: how did you learn of the gates yourself and so come to use them?"

Minda couldn't meet the Loremistress's eyes. She looked about the room a moment, uncomfortably aware of Taneh studying her. "I was only in the one room of the museum," she said abruptly, "and saw no written records there. There might be something in the other rooms. I did find this sword, though."

She nudged its scabbard with her foot as she spoke. Taneh looked at the sword, lifted her gaze to regard Minda with gentle humor.

"Ah, Minda. You may profess to be a bumpkin, but you surely don't act the part. You changed the topic bluntly enough and I can take a hint. But remember this: if you need help or guidance, and I can provide either, feel free to ask. You've piqued my curiosity with your riddles. I can sense an uncertainty about you—for all your closely guarded secrets. You're seeking something, but you seek it in darkness."

Taneh's words hit too close to home for Minda's liking. She was enjoying the company after two days on her own, but what had brought her to this place, the dreams and her promise to Jan; Ildran; she could not share these with a stranger. The Loremistress was kind, but she wasn't Rabbert or Janey.

Taneh rose to her feet. "The stew should be ready now," she said briskly, the tone of her voice closing the subject until Minda chose to reopen it. "Will you have some?"

Minda nodded, happy to think of something else. "Can I help?" she asked.

Taneh shook her head and spooned the steaming stew into a pair of wooden bowls.

The evening passed pleasantly with Taneh telling stories of her homeworld of Langlin, and the curious things and beings she'd found on Dewethtyr and the other worlds she'd studied. She spoke of her home in Wistlore—of its halls of learning for which the people of Langlin were renowned; of the mysterious Drarkun Wood that lay south of Wistlore where the kemys-folk were said to live, beings that were half human and half beast; of how history and myth were often retellings of the same past and to understand that past better one should be prepared to study both. That made Minda think of Rabbert. She smiled and felt sad at the same time.

Ruhn appeared halfway through the evening and settled down in front of the hearth with a self-satisfied grin. Minda was still somewhat in awe of the great red-grey wolf, but she did her best not to let her nervousness show.

The question as to whether or not she'd stay the night didn't arise again. It was tacitly accepted that she would and—with the wind's eerie piping faint but audible, even in Taneh's rooms—Minda was content to sleep indoors, with the Loremistress for company and Ruhn as their guardian.

She lay awake for a while once the candles were blown out, comfortably snuggled on the pillows, thinking of how far she'd come in just a few days. It wasn't the distance alone. Inside, a sense of independence was growing, a self-assurance that come what may, she would prevail.

One hand clasping her acorn pendant, she fell into a dreamless sleep.

chapter three

At Taneh's urging, Minda agreed to stay another day
with the Loremistress, if for no other reason than to give her
knee a chance to recuperate more fully. The cut was clean,
Taneh told her, not deep, and healing well.

"You were lucky," the Loremistress said. "The glass missed
cutting any major tendon. But you must not allow the wound
to become infected. Dewethtyr suffers from a lack of healers—
a lack of most civilized comforts, to be honest. A long day's
trek will do you a good deal of harm, alone in the ruins with
an infected leg."

It was an unsettling prospect, Minda had to agree.

Taneh had a tendency towards lecturing—reminding Minda
of a schoolteacher, though in a pleasant way. If the teachers
in the school back in Fernwillow had had the Loremistress's
patient manner, Minda was sure she wouldn't have had to find
her learning in the books that Rabbert lent her.

After a good night's sleep, and with a breakfast of porridge and tea still comfortably warm in her stomach, Minda had no real objections to staying another day. She could use the time to sort things out a bit. Since meeting Jan, everything had become something of a blur.

They spent the morning packing up Taneh's notes and the odd curious artifact (carefully labelled and wrapped in cloth) that the Loremistress was bringing back to Wistlore with her.

"What's this?" Minda asked.

She held up a hand-sized wooden object, square with a crank in its side. Taneh smiled as she took it from her and pried open the lid with the tip of her thumbnail. Inside was a small ribbed cylinder set against a number of irregular slivers of metal.

"It's a music box," the Loremistress said. She turned the crank. As the cylinder moved slowly, its ribs struck the tiny metal rods, and a clear bell-like tune arose from the small object.

"I've seen something like that before," Minda said. "In the Craftsquare in Fernwillow. Only it was much bigger. This is so tiny."

"Oh?" Taneh looked up with interest. "Have you seen anything else in Darkruin that you're familiar with from your own world? There are so many things that I can't even begin to guess the use of."

Tugging a bundle at random from the floor, she unwrapped a flat rectangular object and handed it to Minda. It had a small narrow bit of glass set over the top of one end and a number of indentations that might be buttons of some sort below. Minda turned it over curiously, then shook her head.

"Ah, well," Taneh said. "They're mostly toys, I'm sure," she added, indicating the artifacts they were packing. "Like the music box. But it's very frustrating all the same. If I could only find some more complete records—a library of some sort, a storehouse for records, *anything* more than these tantalizing snippets I've managed to scrounge so far."

"How do you plan to get this all back to Wistlore?" Minda asked. "Is there a gate nearby?"

"No. The closest is Jasell Henge—outside the city to the west. It's more than a few days' journeying."

Minda swallowed her disappointment. "Then how will you get all this to the gates?"

Taneh smiled. "Not easily! No. I mean to store it here, all except for my notes. I'll come back with others of my people to transport the rest."

Minda was quiet for a moment, digesting this new information.

"I'd like to travel with you," she said. "At least as far as the henge. Would you mind?"

"I'd welcome the company."

There was a question in the Loremistress's eyes, but when she saw that Minda still wasn't ready to speak, she returned to her task, talking lightly of other matters. Minda rewrapped the rectangular object and added it to the almost full box that stood on the floor beside them, listening with only half an ear. Excitement hummed in her and she was hard put not to ask that they should go now . . . today . . . this minute.

The gates would take her to Weir, to Jan's kin. She was sure of it. Then she remembered Ildran. Did he still wait for her in the void? Perhaps when they reached the henge, she could then ask Taneh if she knew the way to Weir. Safeguarded by the Loremistress's presence and with Ruhn. . . . And if Ildran should attack them all?

"Are you all right?" Taneh asked.

"What?" Minda looked up, startled.

"You went pale. Perhaps you should rest and let me finish this."

"Oh, no. I'm all right. I was just . . . thinking."

Taneh regarded her with worry. What is it, child, that you fear so? she thought. But Minda returned to the packing with an exaggerated enthusiasm and the Loremistress could only shake her head.

In the late afternoon, when the last case was packed, they spent an hour or two exploring the city near Taneh's quarters. They took an easy pace for Taneh was worried about the strain it might put on Minda's knee, but Minda brushed off her worries.

"Look," she said, flexing her leg. "It doesn't hurt a bit."

"You heal quickly," Taneh said.

"I always have," Minda replied. "Ever since I can remember."

Darkruin didn't seem half so grim in the Loremistress's

company, Minda decided. Rabbert would have loved the place.
Janey would have been bored to tears after an hour or so, but
Rabbert. . . .

Minda felt very safe with Ruhn scouting ahead and the sun,
while lowering, still bright on the buildings. She could almost
forget the skeller; hardly worried about Ildran. Her newly acquired sword she'd left behind, propped against a wall in Taneh's
quarters.

The rubble and buildings that she'd simply passed by before
acquired a new sheen of interest as Taneh pointed out highlights
and explained what she knew of the vanished civilization that
had once inhabited the ruins.

"It would have looked very different then," Taneh said.
"Many of the towers were not even used as living quarters;
they were workplaces. Perhaps the city was once a great place
of learning, larger than Wistlore could ever dream of being;
but all the records were removed when the people vanished."

"Where did they live, then?"

"There are living quarters in some of the towers," Taneh
said, "but most of the people lived further from the central
core—in smaller structures not even a fraction of the size of
these buildings, though still as big as a lord's keep for all that.
What evidence we have shows that they were a wealthy people.
Do you see this?"

They were walking near one of the rusted metal wrecks that
littered the streets.

"These were vehicles of some sort—self-powered somehow, rather than drawn by beasts." Taneh tugged on the thin
metal sheet at the front of the wagon, managing to lift it a half
foot or so. It rose with a squeal of protesting metal. "Odlum—
a colleague of mine—has made a study of these wagons. His
research has shown that it was this complicated jungle of metal,
here in the fore of the wagon, that actually powered it."

"It's like magic," Minda said.

"No. More like the music box or . . . a waterwheel. Yet the
actual source of the power has eluded our study. Hand or water
would be impractical at best. Clockwork has been ruled out as
well."

"I can't imagine riding about in a wagon without a horse
to pull it."

"And yet the original inhabitants of Darkruin did just that.

Minda, there are so many puzzles. The building of these towers alone defies the imagination. The height of them, the smoothness of the stone, the size of the windows, the sheer weight of all the tons of building material. . . ."

"You don't really want to go, do you?"

Taneh shook her head. "I've not scratched the surface of what's to be found here. But it has grown dangerous, for all that today's peace apparently belies my statement. I've grown to trust my intuition, and my intuition tells me to leave. The skellers may not be the only evil to haunt these strange towers.

"But I will return."

"Did Ruhn come with you from Langlin?"

Taneh returned from the hearth with a pair of bowls filled with leftover hare stew and shook her head as she handed Minda one.

"No. I met him here," she replied. "Or rather, he met me. There's a pack of wolves that ranges through the city. At first I took Ruhn to be one of the mys-hudol—the talking beasts— mute from birth, perhaps, or due to an accident. He seemed so intelligent, you see. But no. He's a wolf, plain and simple— though wise enough in his wolf ways. For some reason he's taken a liking to me and appointed himself my protector."

"There really are talking animals?" Minda asked between spoonfuls of stew. "Like in the old tales?"

"What a world you must come from! No mys-hudol? You might as well say that there's no such thing as erlkin, or wizards."

"But there aren't, at least not on my world. Not any that I've ever seen, anyway. I *did* meet an erl, though . . . sort of. It was in a dream; a very real dream. He was as tall as I am with pointed ears and two small horns on his brow. He told me he was the airloos of the longstones."

Taneh's green gaze fixed seriously on Minda. *"Arluth,"* she corrected. "It means 'lord' in Sennayeth—the old tongue. Arluth gan Menhir would be his proper title: Lord of the Longstones. Or even Arluth gan Hal: Lord of the Moors. He was the lord of the muryan, the moor folk."

"That's what he said."

"And you met him in a dream?"

Minda nodded, not trusting herself to speak. Taneh saw

something of the conflict on her face and, wisely, turned to her stew, saying nothing.

"It was in the . . . silhonell," Minda said suddenly.

"I have heard of it," Taneh replied, "though I have never walked it."

Minda's hand found the shape of her acorn pendant through the material of her shirt and she fingered it nervously. "I was having these dreams, you see," she said.

"You needn't speak of them if it brings you pain."

"No. I want to tell you about them. You've been so kind to me last night and today, just accepting me and not prying."

"But that does not give me an automatic right to your secrets."

"I was afraid," Minda said. "To trust you, I suppose. Or that you'd . . . I don't know . . . laugh or something. But you've told me about things that I always thought were just stories as though they were real and—"

"They *are* real."

"Yes. I mean, I believe you. But you see I also need your help and it could be dangerous."

Taneh smiled. "Why don't you let me be the judge of that?"

"It gets sort of complicated."

"My teacher's name was Aniya Marrow," Taneh said, "may she sleep with the Mother, for she's been dead these ten years now. She always said: 'Begin at the beginning, and let everything else follow.'"

"I'll try," Minda said.

". . . And so when you told me about the gates outside the city, I thought perhaps when we reached them you'd show me how to get to Weir. The pendant's helped me; it's kept Ildran from my dreams. But I know he's going to follow me. He tried to kill me in the dark between the worlds and I *know* he'll try again."

While Minda spoke, the wind had risen outside once more. Its piping as it made its way through the ruins echoed her words with a discordant music. Strangely, it fit the tempo of what she was saying. Or perhaps she ended up fitting her words to its curious rhythms.

"The city sings," Taneh said absently. "I've grown used to the sound by now. I wonder if I'll miss it?" Her eyes held a faraway look that slowly faded as she focused on Minda. "I don't know if I can help you. I'd like to, but I've never heard of Highwolding, and as for Weir, only the muryan know its location. What I *can* do is take you to Grimbold—the Wysling I told you about last night. Wyslings discovered the use of the gates, as you know, but the muryan always knew of them. Some call them the keepers of the gates, the Piper's children. They are hill-wenders and stone shepherds. When Grameryn keyed the gates for the first time, it's said the muryan came to him and exacted a promise—" Taneh shook her head. "I'm letting lore get in the way of a simple explanation. We could look for Grimbold. He and the tinker were headed north, the last time I spoke to them. The tinker was seeking star-silver in the ruins; Grimbold was looking for who knows what? Perhaps the journey for its own sake. Who can say what drives a Wysling?"

Minda fiddled with the edge of one of the pillows, pulling at a loose thread. "This Wysling," she said, "he's not like his name, is he?"

Taneh shook her head. "He's not near as grim as his name." She gathered up their bowls and left them in a basin of water on the table to soak.

"You were lucky to reach Dewethtyr," she said as she returned to sit on the pillows. "The arluth should have explained to you how keying the gates works, for it can be dangerous if not done properly. First, as in all magical doings, you must know exactly what it is you wish to accomplish. Or, in this case, where it is you wish to go. With the gates, the pattern-tracing on the stone and keying words are not enough. You must hold an image of your destination clear in your mind or when you speak the closing word you could well end up anywhere...or nowhere.

"When the Wyslings first began to use the gates many of them were lost in the void. Then the muryan gave them the images to hold in their minds and showed them how it was to be done. The Wyslings, in turn, showed Loremasters of Wistlore. That was many long years ago, but still very few people travel between the worlds. Most folk know nothing of them. Those that do are careful to fare to deserted worlds, such as Dewethtyr, or to tread cautiously in the others. There is a Balance involved, though no one seems to be sure exactly what it entails, except perhaps for the muryan. And they . . . well, they seldom use the gates. It's said they have some other means of faring between the worlds."

Minda remembered the porthmeyn and dug them out of her journeypack.

"I forgot to tell you that Jan gave me these as well as the pendant," she said as she handed the pouch to Taneh. "He said that they could take me to Weir—though he never said how."

Taneh studied them, rolling them in the palm of her hand. "Ah, this is a dangerous thing you've done," she said, "showing such a riddle to a Loremistress." She laughed lightly at the sudden wariness in Minda's eyes. "No, no," she added. "Don't be afraid. I was jesting with you, that's all. But I *am* a Loremistress and any riddle or puzzle—be it magical, historical or whatever—draws me to it. My mother was a Loremistress— it was she who 'prenticed me to Mistress Aniya—and my grandmother before her was a Loremistress as well. Knowledge—and the seeking—is a delight in itself. To add one stray idea there to a bit taken from a book here and mix the two with some of the scrolls in Wistlore's Library. . . ."

"You remind me of a friend I left in Fernwillow."

"This Rabbert fellow who has the bookshop?"

Minda nodded.

"Yes. When you spoke of him, I thought I'd like him."

"You'd get along famously."

Taneh smiled. "Who knows where the road takes us? But these stones, now. I wonder how *do* they work?" She returned the porthmeyn to their pouch and watched Minda put them away. "Grimbold might know. Tomorrow, if you're willing, we can see what we can do about finding him. But for now your eyes are closing of their own accord and I've watched you stifle a half dozen yawns this past hour or so. It's time we were both abed. Depending on how far they've gone, we could have a long trek ahead of us on the morrow."

At the word yawn, Minda felt another build up in her and couldn't hold it back. "I think you're right," she mumbled.

Taneh arose. "If the pillows were comfortable enough last night, you're welcome to them again. And if you should wake before me tomorrow morning, the kettle's along the side of the hearth already filled with water and there's kindling in that box by the table. The tea's in the second tin to the right on that shelf."

Minda curled up on the pillows and murmured a sleepy goodnight. She felt as though a great weight had been lifted from her. What will a real wizard look like? she wondered. Will he have a tall peaked hat . . . ?

The piping of the wind rolled through her thoughts as it travelled through the city. Warm and comfortable as she was, she never gave it a second thought. It merely lulled her to sleep.

Taneh stood over her and gazed thoughtfully at her face, the features peaceful now that sleep had eased her tension. "And here's an even greater riddle," Taneh said softly to Ruhn.

The wolf lifted his head to regard her steadily.

"So young and with such grave trials placed before her," Taneh said. "Who is she?"

Ruhn let out a long breath and lowered his head on his crossed forepaws, closing his eyes. Taneh smiled at him and, pulling her kirtle off over her head, laid it on the foot of her bed. She braided her silver-grey hair, then lay down. She glanced at Minda.

"I hope your moorman named you well," she said as she blew out the candle, "and that you will prevail. Sleep well, Talenyn."

There was no answer, but the Loremistress hadn't expected one. She turned over, searching for sleep, but it lay entangled in a myriad riddles and was long in coming.

chapter four

She stood in a stretch of wild moorlands, wearing only the shirt she'd gone to sleep in. Low-backed hills, blanketed with bell heather, sedge and deer grass, stretched out before her, disappearing into a horizon of mountains overhung with clouds. It was night, but she'd acquired night vision that allowed her to see as plainly as though it were day. The ground was cool against her bare feet. A lean wind rustled heath rushes against her legs. There was a rich smell in the air and, from a distance, she could hear a soft piping.

Minda knew she was dreaming. She knew the sound she heard was no more than the piping of the wind as it travelled through Darkruin's towers. But in this place the sound was that of a low skirling music made by an instrument—of reeds lipped, of a tune stirred by living breath. In this place . . .

The music haunted her. It seemed to come from the mountains, yet simultaneously from all around her. And as surely as the moon draws the tide, it drew her.

She moved through the reeds to walk towards the distant heights. The wind followed her, teasing her hair, setting up a motion in the heather that ran like waves from hill to hill. An image came to mind of the musician whose music lured her on. Rabbert had once lent her a large, leather-bound volume crammed full of odd tales and legends, illustrated with water-colors and ink drawings. One picture in particular arose in response to the reedy music. It was of a curious being crouched by a stream, reed-pipes in hand, his haunches and legs like those of a goat, and on his brow were two small horns—like Jan's.

But most of all she remembered the eyes of that being—wild eyes, filled with a mystery for which there were no words, only the breathy sound of the music.

She tried to recall what the book had called that being, but the name eluded her. Was it he she heard piping now? He'd been a god of some sort. Did they have the same gods on all the worlds? In the country of Elheron, of which the Penwolds and Fernwillow were but the smallest corner, there was only one god, Koevah. All others were pretenders, pagan devils. Koevah alone was worthy of worship. He was a vengeful god, given to sudden and great angers.

Minda much preferred the little gods in Rabbert's book. She'd delighted in the fanciful tales told of them. Were they memories of an older time? Or had they filtered into her world from the others? If a language could be the same on many worlds, might there not be more that was familiar?

The questions lazed through her thoughts without real need of answer. Not here in this place. Looking up, she realized that she was almost in the mountains. The horizon now lifted above her in high jagged peaks. She stepped lightly from stone to stone, her tread sure on the loose shale underfoot, and climbed steadily higher.

If this was the silhonell, would she be meeting Jan again? Or Ildran . . . ?

The music swelled momentarily, washing the fear of the Dream-master from her. A cleft opened before her, a pass that cut a crooked way through the mountains. She made her way through it, marvelling at the heights that reared to either side. Then she was through and saw the wide slopes of a valley leading downward and away.

Cedar and spruce cloaked the higher banks, dipped to become grasslands with the mountains climbing high behind them once more. She stared at their heights and then searched the lower ground. The source of the piping was very near now, though its breathy tones reached her ears no more loudly than before. The moon broke through the cloud overhang and then she saw him, perched on a ledge far to the right. The piper.

He was the same as the being in Rabbert's book. Though he was some distance away, she could see him as clearly as if he was within arm's reach. His cheeks were slightly puffed from his playing. The moonlight was bright on his horns. The wind tossed his curly hair. His gaze mets hers over the top of his reed-pipes.

She felt herself drawn into the amber depths of his wild eyes, and a strange deep warmth issued from her pendant and spread to her every nerve end, loosening tight muscles. Wild eyes . . .

In a strange double awareness she felt her body where it lay sleeping in Taneh's quarters, so that she was half dreaming, half awake—her body aroused, but in a languid, nonphysical way. Her spirit on the mountainside moved in the steps of a dance that her sleeping body could never perform. Wave upon wave of wonder moved through her. She swayed in time to the music—that strange sweet music—until the tune died away. The wild eyes locked on hers misted. The piper faded, the last echo of his presence melting away on a long breathy note.

She stood alone once more, the valley spread out before her, her spirit revelling in a new clarity that seemed to spread to every one of her senses. She hummed the last strains of the piper's tune, swaying still, caught in a timelessness to which she wished no end.

When Minda awoke, the sun coming in through the window told her that she'd slept late. Sitting up, she remembered her dream. The sensations it had kindled stayed with her. Taneh's room took on a sudden brilliance as she looked about it. Taneh had a golden glow about her where she sat at her table, sipping tea and making marks on her map. The same glow hung about the sleeping wolf at her feet; each hair of Ruhn's grizzled red-grey fur stood out in sharp relief.

Minda thought of Rabbert and his spectacles. This must be what it was like when he put them on first thing in the morning. Everything acquired a sudden edge.

Taneh looked up as Minda stirred. "So you're up," she said. "I thought you might sleep away the whole of the day. Did you sleep well . . . and without dreams?"

"I slept well," Minda replied, "though I did dream."

Jan's words returned to her. *Dream strong, Talenyn, strong and fair. . . .*

Minda sighed. "And strong and fair my dreams *were.*"

Taneh's eyebrows lifted quizzically.

Minda smiled. "I couldn't explain. What are you doing?"

"Daryn-seeking. There's still some tea left and cornbread for toasting if you're hungry."

Minda poured herself some tea and crossed the room to stand by the table. She looked at the maps and saw they were of Darkruin. There was the plaza and the museum.

"Daryn-seeking?" she asked.

"Dowsing." Taneh lifted a small stone tied to a thread that lay by her hand. "The pendulum can show us where Grimbold and the tinker are. Though I'm no dralan, I can use a tool like this and copy some of their seeking skills."

"How does it work?"

"Like anything concerning the will," Taneh explained, "it merely needs a goal and focus. So I keep thoughts of them strong in my mind and pass the pendulum over the map like so. . . ."

Brow furrowed with concentration, the Loremistress held the pendulum above the map and moved it slowly back and forth. Minda stared, fascinated, then gave a little cry of delight when the stone seemed to stop of its own accord and spin in place. Taneh removed the pendulum from that spot and approached it from another direction. Again the stone paused and spun. Dipping a quill into her inkpot, Taneh drew a small circle on the map to mark the site.

"You've brought me some luck, it seems," she said. "That should be them. I've been at this for over an hour and was beginning to despair. Some days . . ."

"Could I do something like that?"

"Why not? Would you like to try?"

Minda nodded. Setting down her tea, she took Taneh's place at the table.

"What should I look for?" she asked.

"Well, not for them. For one thing, you don't know them, and for another, now that we've marked the spot, you'd subconsciously start the pendulum spinning in the same spot. Why don't you try looking for water? It's really the traditional use of daryn-seeking and I can check your results. I know where most of the major waterways are and have them marked on another map."

"All right," Minda said. "So what do I do? Just think about water and pass the stone over the map?"

"Basically. Only remember—keep clear in your mind what it is you're looking for. It takes concentration, but you have to remain relaxed at the same time. I know it sounds contradictory, but that's the way it works. Be focused but open."

Minda tried to think of water. She held the thread between two fingers and stared at the stone.

"No, no," Taneh said. "Don't pay attention to the pendulum."

Minda nodded and stared at the map instead. She called up an image of water again . . . a small stream, water flowing over its pebbled bottom . . . a crayfish scuttling over the stones. . . .

Something clicked in her mind and suddenly the image was alive inside her. She could hear the water's bubbling, see the flash of sunlight on its surface, feel a wet spray on her cheek. The pendulum jerked in her hand and traced out a line on the map. One, another. A third. Taneh stared, transfixed by the motion of the threaded stone. Her gaze lifted to Minda's face, comical with astonishment. Minda caught the look and pulled the pendulum away from the map.

"Heart of the Moon!" Taneh said. "Are you sure you haven't done this before?" The tone of her voice implied that she didn't believe it for a moment.

"Never," Minda said. "Honestly."

Taneh shook her head. "I've never seen anything like it. Some people are simply born with the talent, and you must be one of them." She pulled another map from a folder that lay on the floor and spread it across the table, covering the first. "See this? You traced this stream perfectly, moved to this one without so much as a moment's hesitation. I certainly could have used your help when I first came to Darkruin."

Minda nodded, still bemused by the weird feeling of having the pendulum come alive in her hands. After a moment she set it down on the table.

"Could we use daryn-seeking to find Weir?" she asked.

Taneh shrugged. "If we had a chart showing all the

worlds . . . why not? But we haven't, so we must go afoot and—"

"Ask a Wysling," Minda finished.

"Just so."

While Minda toasted cornbread for her breakfast, spreading each slice generously with honey, the Loremistress finished setting her quarters to rights. By the time Minda was done, Taneh had their packs ready by the door. Ruhn was already outside.

"Don't forget your sword," Taneh said as Minda joined her.

"The sword," Minda repeated.

She looked at it, leaning against the wall by the hearth, remembered the blue flame that had run its length in the museum, the strange knowledge filling her mind, the possession of her motor-reflexes by whatever it was that inhabited the weapon.

She was slow in crossing the room, slower still in picking the sword up. Taneh regarded her curiously. Minda had never told the Loremistress exactly what had happened in the museum, only that she'd picked the weapon up and somehow *known* how to use it. And when the danger was gone, so too had her knowledge of swordplay left her.

Gingerly, she drew the sword partway from the sheath, studying the blade. She was afraid to see the blue sheen touch it, disappointed when the grey metal remained dull. And yet it had a presence that was more than the weight of it in her hand, more than the memory of what had happened in the museum. Sighing, she resheathed it and buckled it to her belt.

"What is it?" Taneh asked.

It's alive, Minda thought. "I don't know," she said aloud; "I'm just not terribly comfortable with weapons, I suppose. But it won't hurt to bring it along."

"It's already served you well once."

"That's right." Minda smiled to cover her misgivings. "We should get going."

Taneh nodded. "With any luck, we should reach their campsite by tomorrow night."

She stepped aside, letting Minda precede her out the door, allowing herself a last glance at her quarters—the hearth, its coals almost cold now; the stack of boxed artifacts by the wall. But when she turned to join Minda, her thoughts were not so much on what she was leaving behind as to the curious riddle

her young companion presented her. There was an undercurrent
about Minda as though the air about her was stirred by a wind
that originated with her, a disturbance in the ether as if from
invisible presences hovering near, just out of sight.

What will you make of her, Grimbold? she thought.

They walked through the ruined streets all day, heading
steadily north under the watchful eyes of the towers. Ruhn
loped ahead to wait impatiently for them, then bounded away
again once they'd caught up—"Playing dog," Taneh said with
a smile. Minda and the Loremistress walked side by side,
speaking sometimes, but mostly sharing a companionable silence. The sword bounced against Minda's thigh, giving rise
to a curious mix of feelings that she never did sort out.

The clarity that had come to her from last night's dream,
the feeling of all her senses being heightened, never quite left
her either. She heard more, felt more, saw things with a greater
depth and sharpness; could see the sap flowing in an oak tree,
the promise of the seeds in the fruit of the apple trees, the slow
deliberate pace of growth—from the yellow-topped weeds that
clustered at the base of the towers, to the highest grey-barked
elm they walked under.

The sun was beginning to set, heralding dusk's approach,
and the long shadows of the towers were already cutting across
their way, when Minda turned to her companion.

"Where will we spend the night?" she asked.

The Loremistress shrugged. "Ruhn will find us a shelter of
one sort or another—some place free of skellers and rats. He
won't hunt far once the night falls—not if we camp out of
doors." She glanced at the setting sun. "But you're right to
think of it. We should start looking now. Ruhn!"

The wolf returned from his scouting at her call. Minda
watched him as Taneh spoke and wondered how much, if any,
he actually understood. But when the Loremistress was done,
he seemed to know exactly what she wanted for a half hour
later he led them into a stand of old pines. He lay down on
the thick carpet of needles as if to tell them that this was where
they would stay tonight, and not in a building.

Minda dropped her journeypack gratefully and unbuckled
the sword from her belt. During the past few miles her legs
had been cramping and she ached all over. The worst was that
she knew she was going to feel twice as stiff in the morning.

Sighing, she helped Taneh build a fire and longed for the meal to be done with so she could go to sleep.

That night she tried to recapture her dream of the piper and his haunting music. She lay on her back, her head pillowed on her journeysack, hands clasping the acorn pendant at her bosom. When the wind arose and began to pipe through the towers, a small chill ran through her. Then she absorbed the sound, let it fill her, while she set her spirits in search of the moors of her dreams.

Heather hills flashed into her half-awake mind, clear and sharp under her scrutiny, touching all her senses. But they were not *the* moors, not the dream. More asleep now than awake, in that borderland that separates the one from the other, she tried to relax, to move from the self-induced images into true dreaming. But when sleep finally came, it swept across her consciousness in a dark wave, cloaking her without dreams.

chapter five

Just before the dawn, Minda awoke with a start. She sat up, alert and expectant, looking for what had disturbed her. The wind continued its piping through the towers, its melody unbroken. In the dim light she could make out Taneh, still sleeping peacefully by the ashes of last night's fire.

"Ruhn?"

The wolf stood, hackles raised, staring to the north, and gave no sign that he'd heard her soft call. Minda followed his gaze with her own, but could make out nothing in amongst the dark pines. A prickling of some sixth sense touched her. Then, across the sound of the wind, she heard the distant winding of a hunting horn. Minda frowned, pushed aside her blanket. The city was supposed to be deserted—so who went hunting?

Ruhn padded out of sight, a low growl rumbling deep in his chest. When the darkness swallowed him, Minda stood hesitantly, then buckled on her sword and followed. As she slipped away from the camp and the shadowed boughs of the pines closed in above her, fear iced through her. Ildran . . .

She shivered as the horn sounded again—closer now. She could barely make out Ruhn's form in the shadows ahead. The wolf ignored her presence, all his attention focused on what approached. Minda paused just under the last pines. The towers rose to their smooth heights, lifting from the edges of a clearing that was actually a crossroad of two broad avenues, fairly clear of underbrush. With the towers in view, the sense of being in a forest left her. Under the trees it was easy to forget that Darkruin lay all about, league upon league of deserted buildings.

By now the dawn was pinking the sky to the east and the wind was dying down. The eerie sound of its piping faded. In the middle of the clearing, Ruhn stood stiff-legged, still no more than a grey shadow. Minda could feel his tension from where she was hidden. The horn sounded for a third time.

Ruhn melted into the shadows of the nearest building at the sound. Minda drew farther back into the trees, felt for the hilt of her sword as the pendant grew warm against her skin. She wasn't sure she was capable of drawing the blade, of letting it possess her once more. Then the first hounds came into sight and her hand tightened against the leather-wrapped hilt.

They were tall gaunt shadow-shapes that loped with a fluid stride. As they entered the clearing, the foremost lifted its muzzle and bayed. One by one the others took up the sound until their howling filled the air. It *was* a hunt. Minda shrank behind the bole of a tall pine, her heart quaking at the din.

As the dawn broke in the east, she saw the hounds' master. He appeared suddenly, a tall muscular man in a fur tunic, horn in hand, bow and quiver over his shoulder. He had a helm with stag's antlers on his head and carried himself proudly, with a bold spring to his step. The light grew in the clearing. As the huntsman drew nearer, Minda saw to her horror that the antlers were not part of a helm. They sprang from his brow.

He cast his gaze about the clearing, turning in a full circle until he faced the pines where Minda was hidden. She clutched her sword hilt with a sweaty palm, not even daring to breathe.

She was the quarry.

The hounds left off their howling to stalk about their master.

He took a step towards her, then paused to look skyward. The sun topped the eastern buildings, casting a long shadow across the clearing. When his gaze returned to her, his eyes were like molten gold, piercing the boughs that hid her as though they were just so much gauze. With a savage snarl, he charged her hiding place.

Minda froze. Her mind screamed "Run!" but her body refused to obey, paralyzed by fear. She couldn't even draw the sword. It wasn't until the stag-browed man was almost upon her that she bolted, panic flooding her with adrenaline. She dodged his grasp and raced deeper into the pines—away from the clearing, but away from the camp as well.

The huntsman whirled in midstride and tackled her before she had gone a dozen yards. Strong hands clamped on her shoulders, but the adrenaline lent her strength as well as speed. She twisted in his grip, clawing at his face. He whipped his head back so that her nails met only the rough fur of his tunic, caught in the thongstrap of his horn. Her fingers closed about the thong. Before either she or her attacker knew what she was doing, she had the horn in her hand and yanked it free, breaking the thong.

He dropped his hands from her as though she'd become a live coal. Backing away, Minda held the horn in a white-knuckled hand and faced him. His features twisted with rage, but he wouldn't come any closer to her than he already was. Was it because she held the horn?

She was trembling all over in the aftermath of their struggle, her breath ragged. The nervous way he was watching her hold the horn made her want to smash it on the ground, grind it underfoot. It was a delicate thing. One good stamp should do it.

"Na!" he cried and shook his head emphatically. His voice was gruff and throaty. "Coldas het yn ne."

The outstretched hand made his meaning obvious. Minda switched the horn to her left hand and drew her sword with the other. She waited for the blue fire, but it didn't come.

Magic, where are you? she thought.

With the point of the useless blade holding the huntsman at bay, she tried to think of what she should do next. She couldn't quite see herself killing him out of hand, but neither could she just return the horn to him. He shifted his weight as she debated silently, the gold gaze darting from her sword to the horn. She backed up a step.

"Who are you?" she demanded. "What do you want with me?"

Where was Ruhn? Where was Taneh? Surely the noise should have woken her.

As though replying to her silent call, Ruhn appeared at her side. He sat beside her, dark gaze fixed on the antlered man. He nudged her leg and she stole a glance behind. In the growing light she could see through the pines to the clearing. The huntsman's hounds were surrounded by a pack of wolves.

The huntsman shifted his weight again. She returned her attention to him, lifting the sword meaningfully. "You . . . you haven't answered my questions," she said. To Ruhn, she murmured: "Bring Taneh."

Please, she thought, let him understand me. . . .

"Taneh," she repeated. "Can you bring her?"

"No need to."

The Loremistress approached from the direction of their camp. She eyed the huntsman, her features puzzled.

"Tyrr, preserve us! Minda, what's going on?"

"Ask him," Minda said, nodding to the horned man. "He was hunting me."

Taneh frowned. "Hunting?"

"Bren ser a Langlin?" the huntsman asked, his voice still harsh.

"I am of Langlin," Taneh replied. "But that is neither here nor there. What do you want with us? And have the courtesy to speak in the common tongue so that we can all understand you."

"What courtesy do I owe to the Shadowed? And I do not hunt you. Only her—the tainted one. What does one of Langlin do in the company of her kind?"

Taneh's eyes went hard as he spoke. She made a ward sign in the air between them. Without taking her gaze from him, she said: "Destroy the horn, Minda."

"No!" the huntsman cried.

He lunged forward only to be brought up short by the double threat of raised sword, a flicker of blue running its length at his movement, and Ruhn's bared fangs.

"Then answer," Taneh said coldly.

The stag-browed huntsman's shoulders drooped. "I am named

Huorn," he said wearily. "As you've guessed, yon horn holds more than my power over the pack. Destroy it and you destroy me."

"Why do you seek my companion?"

The gold eyes went bitter with grief. "Why? She is Ildran, the Dream-master, and three days past she slew my sister Gwerynn. No. Save your lies for another. I can read scent—and she reeks of Shadow. It's a sad day when those of Langlin league themselves with her kind."

Minda went chalk-white. "Ildran?" she blurted. "Are you mad?"

Taneh stepped beside Minda and touched her shoulder gently. "Peace, Minda," she said. "Madness is on him true enough, but surely it's the madness of grief." She chose her next words carefully. "Listen to me, Huorn. Open your eyes and look upon her. Read her with the wisdom of your spirit—not with the blood of your sister fresh in your nostrils. The scent of evil is upon her, yes. But only because she recently escaped the very fate that slew your sister. Read her, Huorn. Then beg her forgiveness and give thanks to your gods that you did not slay an innocent."

Huorn shook his head. "No. You seek to confuse me, to trip me with lies. Gwerynn lies dead—dream-slain. Ildran can take on any guise—"

"But Ildran has not taken on this one," Taneh said softly. "Read her and know the truth. I am of Langlin and we would never league with any evil, even if it meant that our world would fail unless we did. Better that it fail than we be blighted by such an alliance."

Huorn nodded slowly. Raising his eyes, he held out a hand towards Minda. She backed away and Ruhn growled, low and throaty.

"Let him touch you, Minda."

Minda looked at the Loremistress as if her companion had taken leave of her senses. "Taneh, he wants to kill me!"

The Loremistress nodded. "He did. Now he would read your spirit. Do you want to stand here all day, holding him at bay?"

"No. But . . . I could destroy the horn. . . ."

"And so kill him. Are you no better than he is? Worse, I'd say, for he at least acted in ignorance. What is it that you're afraid of?"

Minda took another step back. "Him," she said. "I'm afraid
of him. It was only by blind luck that I ever got the better of
him. He . . . he would have killed me then and I won't give
him the chance to finish what he began."

She looked from Taneh to the huntsman, trying to understand why Taneh was pressuring her so. Couldn't she see that
the huntsman would kill her, given half a chance?

"Think of his sister," Taneh said. "Think of the fate she
suffered that you escaped only because of the muryan Penalurick."

Ildran . . . For a moment she could feel him in her mind
again and she shivered.

"It was only his grief that blinded him so," Taneh said.
"You should be allies, not enemies."

"You . . . you're confusing me," Minda said. "I thought you
were on my side."

"I am. Trust me, Minda."

"It's him I don't trust."

Huorn followed their interchange, the dark look never leaving his face. A pang of uncertainty grew in Minda. She looked
at the stern huntsman, at Taneh. The sword wavered in her
hand.

"Please, Minda," the Loremistress said. "Let us end this
charade."

Slowly Minda lowered her sword. Holding the horn behind
her back, she moved forward, still hesitant. "Let him read me,
then," she said. "Whatever that means."

Huorn lifted a big calloused hand, touched the tips of his
fingers against her forehead. The pendant flared at his touch.
For a moment she was the huntsman, watching her, who was
watching him, who was. . . . A terrible, dizzying sense of dis-
location raced through Minda.

Huorn's hand fell from her brow. He dropped to his knees
with a moan, the proud antlered head bowed in sorrow. "Oh,
child," he whispered hoarsely. "Forgive me."

Minda stared at him.

"The horn," Taneh said.

Only half aware of what she was doing, Minda handed it
to the Loremistress. Taneh knelt by the huntsman and placed
it in his hand. Rising, she regarded the two—the weeping
Huorn, and Minda, her face still pale, legs trembling. She took
a deep breath and said matter-of-factly:

"Now, who'd like some breakfast?"

Minda roused at that.

"I won't eat with *him*," she said.

"Minda..."

"I won't, I tell you. Don't try and tell me what to do. If he stays with you, then I'll go on alone. I...I don't know what just happened...." Her hand lifted to massage a temple and frowned. "One minute he's trying to kill me and the next he...he's like this—but that doesn't change anything. I don't—I *can't* trust him."

She sheathed her sword, the hilt ringing against the top of the scabbard with a clank of finality.

"She has the right of it," Huorn said in a subdued voice. "I will not break bread with you until I have proved myself worthy. I will go."

Taneh shook her head. "No. We've all seen the mistake and there was no harm done. Can't we just forget—"

"I can never forget," Huorn broke in. He inclined his head to the Loremistress, then glanced at Minda. "When I read you, I gleaned some understanding of what you mean to do. I would help you, but..." He sighed, then finished softly: "Cern serr lamm bren."

Without another word he stalked towards the clearing. Ruhn followed. Blowing a long clear blast on his horn, Huorn sprinted back the way he'd come. The hounds lifted their voices and fell in behind him. The wolves cleared a way so that huntsman and hounds could pass through their ring, fading into the undergrowth once the last dog had rounded the far tower and vanished from sight. Only Ruhn remained in the clearing, the sun bright on his red-grey fur.

"Cern serr lamm bren," Taneh murmured. "The Horned One be with you as well."

She glanced at Minda, then turned and began to make her way back to their campsite. Minda watched her go. Her anger ran from her, leaving only a confused mixture of dispossession and guilt. The last look in the antlered man's eyes stayed with her. He's all alone, Minda thought, just like me.

Slowly she trudged back to the campsite. When she reached it, Taneh was sitting by the fire, stirring the embers into life.

"Tea'll be ready soon," she said.

Minda nodded, found a trace of a smile in reply. Ruhn lay down near her and she ran her fingers through his thick fur.

"Where did the wolves come from?" she asked Taneh.

"They were Ruhn's pack, I should think. It was strange the way they came to help us."

The Loremistress regarded Ruhn thoughtfully as she spoke. She'd never seen or heard of such a thing before. What was it about her companion that the very beasts of the wild came to her aid? And this Ildran—twice now mention of him had arisen, from two different sources. She wished she had access to the Library in Wistlore to see what the records had to say about him. If she only knew more. She was sure that she'd run across references to him before in her studies, but nothing clear came to mind. Perhaps Grimwold would know.

The water was boiling. She took it from the fire, dropped a handful of dried rosehips into the agitated water and set the tea aside to steep.

"He's really very nice," Minda said.

Taneh looked up. "Who is . . . ?" she began, then smiled. Ruhn lay with his head on Minda's lap, fast asleep.

"You have two friends now," Taneh said.

A whisper of sadness touched Minda's eyes, then she nodded and smiled brightly. Taneh pretended not to notice what remained in her young companion's features.

chapter six

The tinker's name was Markj'n Tufty. He was tall and lean with a teasing sparkle in his eyes—eyes that were a startling green against his dark complexion and shock of blue-black hair. His clothing was a flood of color: yellow shirt and boots, green trousers, bright red cap and coat, with a rusty orange scarf tied about his neck. From each earlobe hung a golden hoop. Thrust into sheaths buckled to his broad leather belt were a pair of long knives—tinker blades, the sort the travelling people made and rarely sold, for they kept their finest work for themselves.

He was alone when they came upon him at day's end. The sky was just darkening, the wind rising to begin its nightly piping through the ruined towers. The camp was in a clearing in the middle of a broad avenue, hidden from prying eyes by a thick stand of poplars.

"Ho, Markj'n!" Taneh cried.

The tinker was stirring a rich-smelling stew in a battered cookpot, occasionally leaning forward to add a sprig of chopped greenery from a flat stone by his knee. His pack leaned against a tree, its contents strewn about the grass in a fine disarray. A small flute wrapped in a dusty rose shirt lay upon two leather-bound books and a much-folded map. A half-dozen blades were heaped beside their unfinished handles, a ball of twine and a pair of battered tin cups.

He looked up, grinning at the Loremistress's call and languidly beckoned them closer.

"No need to shout," he said as they approached. "I heard you coming a mile or so back. You'd do well to relearn your woodslore, Taneh. Aye, aye. I know what you'll say. 'Tis naught but a dead city with little to bother you in it save for the odd skeller, but you can ne'er be too certain." He laughed suddenly. "Ah, where's my manners? A-meir, Taneh. Well met. I see you've not lost that wolf yet. Here, boy. An' you too, lass. Well met. Pull up a stone an' rest yourselves. I've stew on, as you can plainly see, an' though I've no idea how it'll turn out tonight—it's Grimbold's recipe, broom and heather!—still you're welcome to give it a try."

Taneh smiled. "A-meir, Markj'n. I see you're still as shy as ever. Where's Grimbold?"

"Where's he ever? Prying about, I dare say. What's your name, lass?"

"Minda."

"Ah! An' it's as fine a name as any, no doubt about it. I suppose you'd both like some tea? It'd be just as well, as I've only the two wineskins left an' one's a third empty, so there'll be more for me 'less—Minda was it?—'less you'd care for some wine, Minda. I know Taneh's drinking habits well enough, thank you, an' they never cease to amaze me. What do you say?"

"I think I'd like a little wine," Minda said, wondering if he ever ran out of breath. "If that'd be all right."

"Ah, well spoken, lass. You've a heart after my own. An' what would you be doing in the Loremistress's company then? Ballan, but she's a dreary way about her sometimes, always poking about looking for some new bit of lore. As if there weren't already halls overbrimmed with the stuff in Wistlore, eh?"

He winked at Minda as he spoke and reached behind him to hold up a beautifully worked brooch made of a sparkling silvery metal.

"What do you think of this? Star-silver. Now there's something to suffer dust and tedium for. Should've seen Grimbold's eyes when I found this, near popped out of his head, they did! Said I was wasting my time, he did—just like you, Taneh. I'll not forget those who mocked me. Wasting my time, eh? Well, when Grimbold saw—ah! Here he is now. Tell them, Grimbold. Tell them what you said."

Wasn't it something to the effect of: even a chattering magpie can find the odd treasure?

Minda had begun to turn to have a look at the approaching Wysling when the voice sounded in her head. She started with surprise, completed her turn, and could only stare, slack-jawed with amazement.

Grimbold was a badger.

He was one of the mys-hudol, the talking beasts. He was at least twice the size of normal badger—more like a bear with his five-foot length from nose to tail tip. His body fur was streaked with age and there were many grey hairs in amongst the black and white markings on his face. But for all the telltale signs of encroaching age, he still had the strength and hardiness of a boar in his prime.

"You—you spoke," Minda stuttered. "In my head."

And how else could I converse when my throat cannot shape manspeech? The badger's deep brown eyes gleamed with good humor. *A-meir to you, stranger, and you as well, Taneh. How go your studies?*

"As well as might be expected. And your own, llan?"

She used the honorific in respect to his status as a Wysling. It had various meanings—holy one, wise one, elder—depending upon the context. With a Wysling, each of its meanings had relevance.

Slowly, he replied.

"Like a chattering magpie?" Markj'n broke in. "Ah, an' perhaps you meant well by it, for the magpie's a wise enough bird—cunning really—unlike the thieving crow or the oh-so-noble eagle. Wise, yet humble."

Markj'n, my friend. Do we not have company?

The tinker grinned. "An' so we do, indeed. Well..." He

set a pot half-filled with water on the fire. "The water's on for your tea, Taneh. An' Minda. Would you like a mug, or will you drink from the skin?"

Minda took the proffered wineskin without really looking at it. Her gaze was fixed on the badger. There was an expression on her face that made her look as though she expected the Wysling to sprout wings at any moment and fly away.

"How can an animal . . . ?" she murmured.

Animal? Nay, say rather mys-hudol. We are kin to the beasts, true enough, but distant kin. And you might as well ask how can I not speak. What world are you from that such a simple thing amazes you?

Minda was suddenly self-conscious. "I didn't mean any harm," she said. "It's just that . . . I never . . . that is . . ."

"It's my fault," Taneh said. "I should have warned you what to expect."

Minda looked at the wineskin in her hand and took a long pull from it. Wiping her mouth on her sleeve, she gave it back to the tinker and sat down by the fire, trying to get a grip on herself.

No harm taken—Minda. Was that your name?

She nodded, not trusting herself to speak in case she should put her other foot in her mouth. Grimbold padded over to her, pausing to rumble a gruff greeting to Ruhn. The wolf seemed to nod a greeting in reply.

But what world are you from? Grimbold asked. *There is that about you that I feel I should know you—though I cannot say what it is precisely.*

"My world doesn't have a name. No one on it even knows that there are others."

Then how came you here?

"This is a long tale," Taneh said, coming to Minda's rescue, "and one that will be full told after we've supped. In it lies the reason why we came looking for you."

I wondered at that as well. It would take almost a Great Mystery to pry you from your studies.

"I'm returning to Langlin," Taneh said.

Another riddle, Grimbold said. *Fair enough. We will speak once we have eaten. Markj'n, is the stew ready? And did you add the tosher root?*

"Oh, aye. It was added—Ballan help us! An' if the whole stew's bitter, let the blame lie with you, not me. My dad had

a way of cooking hare stew that would fair make you tremble.
I remember . . ."

He dished out the stew, talking all the while.

The stew was delicious—with a slight, unfamiliar, but very
pleasant taste to it that Minda decided must be the tosher root
that Grimbold and Markj'n had been bickering about. The
tinker was the last to finish for he kept up a running commentary
throughout the meal—discussing anything from the market
value of star-silver on his homeworld of Yenhanwittle to the
number of companions Guirey the Owen had with him on his
fabled quest to Dunswallow, rarely allowing anyone else to get
a word in edgewise.

Taneh waited for the right moment. When Markj'n paused
to take a particularly large mouthful, she set aside her tea and
spoke.

"Perhaps Minda should tell her story by now." She glanced
at Grimbold who nodded, then added: "Only this campsite
seems a touch too unguarded. With the skellers growing more
bold and . . ."

We are not so uncautious, Taneh, the Wysling said, *though
I wonder about Markj'n from time to time. I set my wards when
we first came here at spring's ending. It would take more than
a skeller to win through them.*

The badger turned to Minda. She shifted uncomfortably,
feeling the weight of too many eyes on her. She cleared her
throat, trying to find the right way to begin. At first her words
came haltingly. Markj'n was quiet as she spoke, his dark eyes
serious for once. Grimbold nodded encouragingly, interrupting
her only once and that was to question her on the dream she'd
had of the piper two nights past. When she ended with the
morning's confrontation with Huorn, the Wysling nodded
thoughtfully.

*So. It was he I sensed this morn. A strange secret that—to
keep his power in the object of his naming. There is sorrow in
his tale, aye, and more brewing in your own, Minda. I fear
for you. Ildran! Who would have thought?*

"You know him," Taneh asked.

*I know of him—which, while not quite the same, is still too
much. There have been rumors among the elder folk—whispers
of a dark power rising, a Master of Dreams—but they were
never connected to his name. It was so long ago. He was high*

*in the councils of the muryan, later cast down for some for-
bidden meddling that no moorling would ever discuss. Aye,
and always he is spoken of as being slain. We know so little
of the muryan.*

The gruff murmur of the badger's voice faded in their minds
as he lost himself to his thoughts. The Wysling's quiet acceptance of her tale put Minda more at her ease, as telling Taneh
had before.

Weir, Grimbold said abruptly. He looked into their faces
and there was a power in his gaze that they could almost feel
crackling in the air about them. *The hidden land of the muryan
is one of the Great Mysteries. It has been said that one can
search for it all one's life and never see even a glimmer, while
another can turn some well known corner to find its wild hills
unrolling into the distance. And this place you would seek?*

His gaze settled on Minda and she nodded.

"I have to," she said. "I made a promise to Jan. He helped
me and now I have to honor my side of the bargain."

*Just so. Oaths are not made to be broken. Especially to
such a one as the Penalurick. He is their arluth, their high
lord. For one such as he to be stone-bound—do you ken what
that means?*

"No. At least, not really."

*The once-born will lock their foes away in some jail deep
in the rocks or under a hill—even a barrow I have heard. But
the elder folk have other imprisonments. They entrap beings
in trees and stones and the earth of the rounded hills themselves—body and soul merged with their prison. To be stone-
bound is to be trapped in stone, to lose oneself to the slow flow
of heavy thoughts. In time they gather and thicken so that the
one imprisoned* becomes *a stone.*

Minda swallowed dryly, remembering almost one of the first
things Jan had said to her: *I have been stone-bound too long,
I fear. Already my thoughts take on a craggy slowness.* What
if she were already too late?

I remember a time, the Wysling was saying. *I was travelling
on Kildree—through that lonely stretch of moor that lies between Sheehy's Keep and Eakin Wood.*

"I know the place," Markj'n said. "My dad used to trade
with the wooderls in Eakin."

*I sensed a presence near me when all I could see for un-
numbered leagues were barren hills and an occasional standing*

stone. I called upon my deepsight so that I might read the land—to see beyond any glamorings, if such there were—and, lo! To my astonishment the nearest menhir held the shape of a muryan—still like unto the stone wherein she was imprisoned.

A simple enough spell freed her, but she had been stone-bound for so long that it took me weeks to draw her spirit back into her. It had fled far and deep into the earth, seeking the heart of the old bones of the hills to which it felt kinship because of the spell. To this day she cannot remember how it was she came to be trapped so—or who did the deed.

It was chance alone that saved her, for there are few enough Wyslings and, since the gates were discovered, we tend to wander far and wide. Had I passed there a year later, I am sure all I would have sensed would have been the stone that bound her.

Grimbold sighed and fell silent.

"Am I too late, do you think?" Minda asked.

That I cannot know.

"But will you help me?"

To find Weir? Aye—I suppose it must be Weir. This High-wolding and its Grey Hills you spoke of . . . I have never heard tell of them. At least we know there is a Weir, even if we do not know where it might lie. But I cannot help you directly. As Taneh brought you to me, so I will bring you to another, one that should know both your Jan Penalurick and the way to Weir. Her name is Taryn Weldwen and she is the very muryan that I freed from that stone on Kildree those many years ago. She is the only muryan I know, if the truth be told. They are a secret people, not given to mingling with those not of their own kin. But she will help. She of all folk should know what it is like to be stone-bound.

"Where can we find her?" Minda asked. "Is she in Dark-ruin?"

I fear not, Minda. We must fare to Elenwood on Gythelen, to the hall of the Lady Sian. Since her trial, Taryn has forsaken the hills of her people and dwells now with the Lady's wooderls.

Disappointment lay plain on Minda's features. Through how many worlds would her search take her?

Do not look so dismayed, Grimbold said. *I will take you to Elenwood myself.*

"You will? But . . ."

*But why? Your tale intrigues me and Wyslings are no dif-
ferent than Loremistresses when it comes to riddles. And there
is this as well: Ildran sought you—perhaps meaning to slay
you. Huorn's sister he did slay. I ask myself: why? And how
many others has he slain?*

Minda nodded. She'd not thought of it like that. Now that
the Wysling mentioned it, it made more sense that she was just
one of many that the Dream-master meant to kill.

"Many riddles," Taneh said quietly, "and no clear answer
to any one of them."

"Save on Gythelen," Markj'n added, his own voice somewhat subdued. "I will come as well. It's been a year an' a day
since I walked those fair lands, aye, an' there was a lass in the
Lady's hall. . . ." He sighed, with a far-off look on his face
that reminded Minda of Janey mooning over Wooly Lengershin, then added: "But even if there weren't, still I'd come.
Such an adventure comes but once in a man's lifetime."

"I will come as well," Taneh said. She looked up from the
fire to give the tinker a thoughtful glance. "Though my heart
misgives me. This is no Fair Day jaunt that we're about to
embark on."

Minda looked from one to the other slowly. She was touched
at their quick acceptance of her and their willingness to help.
It helped ease the way she missed the good things about Fernwillow—Rabbert and Janey, quiet afternoons in the kitchen
with Kate, walks along Elding Street with the quick babble of
stallmen and goodwives all around her.

"Thank you," she said to the three of them. "I don't know
how to tell you how much this means to me."

Grimbold's eyes sparkled merrily, hiding his deeper concern. *No need to say more, Talenyn.*

Minda glowed with pleasure at Jan's naming from the Wysling. It made her feel both brave and safe.

But the hour grows late, Grimbold added. *We should take
what rest we can. Tomorrow we must start for Jasell Henge
and each day has grown precious. I can feel it in my bones.*

"You *could* show your thanks," Markj'n said, ever practical,
"by giving me a hand at cleaning up these bowls an' all."

Minda laughed and stood up, stretching the stiffness from
her joints. With their arms full, she and the tinker made their
way to the stream that lay just within the bordering line of
Grimbold's wards, a dozen or so yards beyond the campsite.

As they scrubbed the dishes with wet sand, Markj'n filled her ears with rambling talk that never seemed to have a point. Still it brought a smile to her lips that wouldn't leave.

Grimbold lay with his broad backside to the fire, his paws crossed before him, one long digging claw tapping on the ground as he stared into the darkness, lost in thought. Taneh poured herself a last cup of tea and sat drinking it, studying the badger.

"You know more of this Ildran than you let on to Minda," she said finally.

Grimbold stirred and turned to face her.

I do, he said.

He glanced to where Taneh's young companion was laughing with Markj'n.

How well do you know her? he asked.

Taneh shrugged. "We met only a few days ago, as she told you."

Aye, aye. But . . .

"Llan, what is it? Do you mistrust her?"

She frightens me.

"But she's just a young girl."

The Wysling sighed. *And yet there is that about her that speaks of old wisdoms—lost and forgotten even by folk such as you and I. An old power moves in her. That dream she spoke of about the Piper is most disturbing.*

"Tonight was the first I'd heard of it," Taneh admitted. "Do you think it was a true spirit-faring?"

I am not sure, Taneh. Ildran, you see, is misnamed. He is no Dream-master—not in the way that we reckon dreams. But he is a master of illusion. When the soul sleeps, when it dreams, it is open, susceptible to the power of a creature such as he. At such a time he bridges distance with his mind—but what he sends is no dream. Only the gods send dreams. Ildran sends illusions. Deadly illusions. And with them he can slay a wakeful soul as easily as a dreaming one, once the initial line of contact has been made.

"You said nothing to Minda of that."

I thought it better not to frighten her. She has her charm, her moorman's pendant. It will keep her safe from dream or sending alike—that much power it has. But also it wakes something in her.

Taneh leaned closer to him. "What does it wake?"

The oldness, I think. I can phrase it no better.

"But she is safe at least from Ildran?"

She need only fear his physical presence now. But, Taneh, what does he want with her? 'You were the last of them,' he said to her in the void. 'With you the line dies.' What line? Who is this maid with the old wisdom in her—wisdom she is not even aware that she bears? It is this that frightens me so, Taneh. You know as well as I what the misuse of power can bring. If what I sense about her is true . . . if she realizes that potential . . . aye, I fear indeed.

"And the dream she had of the Piper?"

Grimbold's dark gaze met Taneh's. In the firelight, his striped head took on an otherworldly cast. *If it was a true dream,* he said. *When the Horned Lord comes to one, in any of his aspects, when the Middle Kingdom stirs, then there are forces at work far beyond my ken, Taneh. What if what lies in her should wake, or if Ildran should come to control her potential?*

"How can she have such power?" Taneh asked. "She comes from an unnamed world that has no magic."

All worlds have magic. And I did not mean to say that she has such powers in her—only that the potential for them seems present. She might never tap it. Or Ildran might. Or . . . He paused, then added: *The muryan charm keeps her safe for now, but if Ildran wants her badly enough, he will send his creatures to fetch her to him. Perhaps he will even come himself.*

Taneh looked again to where Minda and Markj'n were, then her gaze searched the darkness that ringed the camp. She had no fear of the dark, but she shivered. Ruhn moved closer to her and she laid a hand on his thick fur, glad of the contact.

"Now you have frightened me, llan," she said.

Grimbold sighed, but said nothing.

Later, when Minda lay wrapped in a warm blanket with the fire's dying coals toasting her feet, she found it hard to get to sleep. Tomorrow they were going to the gates. Away from Darkruin and its singing winds. She listened to the wind's song. It spoke of loneliness, of forsaken towers and a lost people, long gone, and woke in her once more a feeling of homesickness—not for Hadon and his quick temper, but for the good things she'd left behind her.

Did Hadon wonder where she was? Did her friends miss her? What would they say if she never came back? Surely she'd return—once Weir was found and Jan was freed and Ildran. . . . But what if she never returned?

Goosebumps rose on her arms, but she fell asleep soon enough. The wind that wound through the city's towers lulled her with its eerie plaintive sound. She started once before sleep fully took her, thinking she'd heard from far away the winding of a hunting horn. Then there was only the wind moving among the ruined towers once more and the sound of the horn, a sad and lonely sound, was gone.

chapter seven

"Not bad at all," Markj'n said. "It's not tinker's work, to be sure—whose work it is, I couldn't say—but it's a well made blade all the same."

He and Minda were finishing their breakfast when Markj'n had asked to see her sword. Between helping himself to mouthfuls of batter-pan toast, he studied the weapon with a blademaker's eye, testing its metal, the join of the hilt to blade, the fuller and edge, its slight curving line, the tiny rune marks set high near the hilt.

"Can you use it?" he asked.

"Not really."

The tinker smiled. "But it's nice to have hanging from your belt all the same—hey?"

Minda laughed. "Something like that. It doesn't seem right to go off on a quest without one."

"An' this is just your size. Any longer an' you'd be dragging it about. Any shorter an' you might as well trade it in for a knife."

"What do you know about enchanted swords?" Minda asked.

"Well, now." Markj'n pulled at his left earring. "Not much. Don't like 'em. Don't see much use for 'em, to tell you the truth. Broom and heather! There's too many rules tied up with enchanted blades—at least in all the tales I've heard. Like when the dwarf smith made Tinder Gehr his sword—do you know that tale? The bloody thing would only work if he remained chaste. Well, what's the point in that? It's not that I'm in favor of lechery, understand. But the odd dalliance, when both parties are willing, as it were. . . ."

He broke off to fix her with a questioning look.

"You think this one's enchanted?" he asked, hefting her sword.

"I think so . . . yes."

The tinker's eyes narrowed as he studied the blade with new interest. "These runes," he said, "you should ask Grimbold to have a look at them. It's really more his sort of thing—hocus-pocusing an' the like."

Minda glanced to where the Wysling and Taneh were planning their route, heads bent over the maps the Loremistress had spread upon the ground. Minda shook her head. She still wasn't sure about Grimbold. A talking badger, who was a wizard. . . . He seemed nice enough, but he kept watching her with a measuring look in his eyes that made her uncomfortable.

But if there was a price to pay for using the sword?

"I don't think it's that important," she said.

"You're probably right," Markj'n agreed. "It's not likely that some wonderfully enchanted sword would be lying about these ruins just waiting for you or me to pick it up. Acquiring one of those is usually a whole quest in itself. My dad used to tell me about the bard Eonair—do they tell that tale on your world? He was just a twig of a man who played the harp or lute or some such thing. He went into the Middle Kingdom— the land of faery, you know?—looking for a magic blade. Seems he was in love with this woman who . . ."

Looking up from the map of Darkruin, Grimbold had caught Minda's glance before she turned back to listen to Markj'n's story. He sighed.

I do not think your young companion cares much for me, he said.

Taneh smiled. "I don't think she knows quite what to make of you. Not only are you a wizard, something that on her world belongs only in a tale, but you're a mys-hudol as well."

No, Grimbold said. *She senses my mistrust. I wish I could trust her; it is not so much the maid herself as my fear that what lies in her might bring ruin upon us all.*

Taneh poked him in the side with a finger. "There comes a point," she said, "when worry can be taken too far."

The Wysling shrugged off her comment. *I know what I know—more than any of us, perhaps—and so the fear is more real for me.*

"Perhaps," Taneh said.

There was a moment of quiet, then Grimbold asked: *Last night you said you were leaving Darkruin. It was not just to help the maid, was it?*

"No. The ruins seem to be coming to life; we've been attacked by skellers more times in the past month than we were in the whole previous year. I have a feeling that other evils are waking."

I know. I have that same feeling. And with the coming of your young companion . . .

Taneh shook her head. "You can't blame her!"

I will say no more, the badger told her. *At any rate, it is time we were on our way.*

"I'll gather up my gear and tell the others," Taneh said.

When the Loremistress walked over to Minda and the tinker, Grimbold sighed once more. He tried to study the map laid out before his paws, but found it difficult to concentrate. There was a heaviness inside him that worried and gnawed at his mind. If only he could be certain, one way or the other.

"You'll never get all of this into one pack," Minda said.

She handed the tinker another pot, shaking her head when he managed to squeeze it in. A rolled-up shirt went into the pot, along with a pouch of tea leaves, a handful of knife handles, three mugs that fit one into the other, and a twist of straw tied with a ribbon that he told her was a love charm slipped into his pack by another innkeeper's daughter. He grinned at her.

"It all came in the one pack," he said.

He took his flute from her, tootled a quick scatter of notes and worked it in along the side of the pack, his features a study of exaggerated concentration that made Minda laugh.

"And these?" she asked, holding up a pair of soft leather slippers.

"Into this side pocket."

"The axe?"

"I'll tie it here."

The pack was bulging with all sort of odds and ends hanging from it—a bedroll tied along its bottom, a frying pan secured beside the axe, a smaller bag holding a few slim ballad books hanging underneath them.

"And this?" Minda asked.

Markj'n took the object from her and studied it critically. It was a long length of weathered metal that the tinker had been working free of rust. When he returned to Yenhanwittle, he'd planned to melt it down to make new knives.

"Ah, this," he said with mock sadness. He tossed it into the bushes where it clanked against a stone. "I think I'll just store it over there till I can come back for it."

"Grimbold doesn't have much to pack," Minda remarked.

"Well, now, he doesn't have much use for gear," Markj'n said, flexing his fingers in front of her. "Hasn't got the right sort of equipment to use tools an' the like."

"I wonder what it'd be like, being a mys-hudol," Minda said. "I mean, it sort of seems like you'd feel trapped. You can't pick things up—can't do much more than an animal can, but you're still human inside."

"Well, they're a canny folk, mostly. Many of them are Loremasters or Wyslings an' the like. They've a grand oral tradition—their bards remember all the way back to the beginnings of the worlds—as far back as Avenveres, the First Land, some say. And you mustn't think of them as people trapped in the bodies of beasts. They're far more than that. An' as far as Grimbold's concerned; well, a wizard's a wizard, doesn't matter what skin he wears. I felt a little queer when he first took up with me—or rather, when he let me tag along with him, if the truth be known. Not because he's a mys-hudol, you understand, for we've plenty of them back home, but because he's a Wysling."

"Like they warn in the old stories?" Minda asked. "Do not meddle in the affairs of wizards. . . ."

Markj'n laughed. "Hardly. Grimbold has as much of a temper as anyone, but he's not nearly as dour as his name. What
it is is he sees portents and signs—which can be disquieting
to say the least—an' queer things tend to be drawn to a wizard.
Magic, and magicky beings that wouldn't bother with ordinary
folk like you an' me.

"The first week we were travelling together—up around
the Whelans, a mountain range on Turst—we made camp in
a hollow high up in the peaks an' round about midnight I heard
this eerie sound come drifting down the mountainside—sort
of a cross between a wind's whisper an' the cry of a bird. An'
you know what it was?"

Minda shook her head, eyes wide as she listened.

"A little rock man, about two feet high with greyish skin
and chalky white hair. The sound came from his staff; it was
a hollowed length of wood with holes cut in it an' the whistling
came when he spun it above his head as he leapt from rock to
rock. He was the queerest little man, eyes big as saucers an'
tiny, tiny feet.

"The way we were travelling was a tinker's way, you understand? My dad, an' his dad before him, had travelled that
way a hundred times an' it wasn't the first time I'd been there
either, but I'd never seen or heard tell of a little man like that.
Anyway, he hopped down an' sat by our fire an' he an' Grimbold talked the night away in some language I'd never heard
before. Every once in a while the little man would leap up an'
whirl his staff above his head an' that sound'd start up again.

"Well, in the morning, when the little man was gone, I
asked Grimbold what he'd wanted an'—"

"Are you ready?" Taneh called.

She had shouldered her pack and was standing with Grimbold waiting for the pair of them.

"Just let me close this up," Markj'n called back. His brown
fingers made quick work of the pack's tie-strings. When it was
ready to lift, he hefted it, grimacing at the weight. "Want to
trade packs?" he asked Minda with a teasing smile.

"Not likely."

"Ah, well. No harm in asking. Ballan, but it's getting heavy.
Or I'm getting weaker. I should leave a thing or three behind,
but it's so hard to make a choice." He swung the pack onto
his shoulder and the two of them made their way to where
Taneh and the Wysling were waiting.

"So what did the little man want?" Minda asked.

"What? Oh, yes. He wanted me for his dinner an' all that gabbing was Grimbold talking him out of the idea."

"No..." Minda began, not really sure if the tinker was pulling her leg or not. She glanced at Grimbold and the badger winked at her.

There is a saying among those who know tinkers, he said. *Listen to only half of what they tell you—and believe no more than a quarter of that.*

"The real reason Grimbold has me around," Markj'n informed Minda, "is to have someone he can abuse that's goodnatured enough to stick around. That an' to make sure he gets a few hot meals so that he doesn't have to grub about like some wild boar for his dinner."

Grimbold laughed. *You forgot to mention grooming this time.*

"Ah, yes. But I always drew the line at that."

With the two of them bantering back and forth, the small party set out. Discovering this new side to the Wysling, Minda found some of her nervousness concerning him run from her. And Grimbold, for his part, was glad to forget his worries in a moment or two of the badinage.

We are being followed.

Minda glanced ahead to where the Wysling was padding beside Taneh. It was the third day since they'd met at the badger's camp, making for Jasell Henge on the western outskirts of Darkruin. She and Markj'n were trailing along about a dozen yards behind the pair, while Ruhn was far ahead, scouting. The afternoon was drawing on, the long shadows of the ruined towers growing longer across their way.

"What is it?" Minda asked.

The Loremistress and Grimbold had stopped to wait for them.

Grimbold shrugged. *I cannot tell. Something—perhaps two hours behind us—but nearing rapidly.*

"Huorn?" Taneh asked, echoing Minda's own thought.

I think not. This is something more than the horned huntsman. Something...alien.

Markj'n fingered the pair of long tinker blades at his belt. "Perhaps I should scout back aways," he said.

No. I will set a glamor at the next crossroads. With any

luck, it will throw off what follows. Time is what we need. The gates are not so far now and, once past them, we can easily lose this pursuit. But still I must wonder: what is it that follows?

"Ildran?" Minda asked in a small voice.

Until Grimbold had mentioned it, she'd not noticed the vague tugging in her own mind, a sensation akin to the Dreammaster's touch. The comfort and growing camaraderie she'd known over the past few days—even with the Wysling badger—dissolved as old fears took hold.

It is difficult to—

Ruhn's sudden appearance cut Grimbold off. The wolf padded up to Taneh. Nudging her knee, he made it plain that they should be moving . . . and quickly.

No more talk, Grimbold said. *Fare for the crossroads, and hoard your thoughts lest they be used to track us.*

Without waiting for an answer, the Wysling set off at a surprising speed—long foreclaws clicking on the rocks, the wolf loping at his side. Exchanging worried glances, the others hurried to follow.

Minda was breathless from the short run by the time she reached the crossroads, trailing well behind the rest. In the middle of the crossing, the Wysling stood upright on his hind legs, forepaws cutting the air. Golden glimmers shivered in the air, a flickering pattern that held briefly before it faded. The minutes slipped by as he repeated it across the way they were going, moving from one tower to the other. Once done, he padded to the road that led off to their right. There he repeated his actions, returning to where Minda and the others were standing when he was done.

What had he done? Minda wondered.

She turned to ask Markj'n but the tinker gripped her arm and held a finger to his lips, forestalling her question. With a nod of his head, he led them straight through the badger's first spelling. An uncomfortable tingling brushed Minda as she passed through the invisible glamor—touched her and was gone almost before it registered. She looked back over her shoulder, but could see nothing there. Further back, she caught a glimpse of movement in the undergrowth. Wolves.

Let them be from Ruhn's pack.

She touched Markj'n's shoulder and he glanced back, nodding grimly. The change in him shocked Minda. Gone was the merriment she'd come to know. He moved with a smooth easy stride, suddenly unaware of the large pack on his shoulders that he'd laughingly complained about for most of their journey.

The wolves stole in from the underbrush to lope amongst them. Minda ran beside Taneh, with Grimbold bringing up the rear. Her pendant grew warm, warning her, and she tried to hold back the familiar panic that was welling inside, attempting to draw strength from the others' calm to fight it down.

The danger was her fault. If they were attacked, she couldn't cower in a corner while the others faced the danger for her; but she couldn't imagine what she might do. She knew about as much about fighting as—

A skreeing broke through her thoughts and she looked up to see the sky dark with skellers. The pendant was like fire against her skin. Growls rumbled in the wolves' chests as they bared fangs against their hated foes. The companions raced for the shelter of the nearest tower. With any luck, they might be able to fend off the attack there. Markj'n filled each hand with a tinker blade as he ran.

"In the daylight?" he muttered, glancing skyward.

Evil calls to evil, came Grimbold's reply, *as like to like. Whatever pursues us has sent them to stay our flight.*

The tower reared up in front of them. Just as they reached its door, the first flight of skellers struck. Markj'n's blades flashed in the sunlight, came away stained with pale blood. Two of the creatures fell to die at his feet while he fought another that had landed on his back. Only his pack saved him from the ripping claws. The skeller lost its grip; Markj'n turned, impaling it on a blade, his gear scattering from his pack on the flagstones behind him.

Minda dragged her sword from its sheath, gratified to see a pale glow along its length. She swung it upward with a clumsy two-handed grip to strike a skreeing monster with a jolt that almost knocked the sword from her hand. The skeller fell, nearly cut in two, showering her with its stinging blood.

A wingtip hit her shoulder as another attacked and she was thrown to the ground. The sword flared then, bright and blinding, and its power entered her. She came to her feet with a quick fluid motion, cutting one creature, then another. The power crackled in her, singing through her veins. Skill not hers kept her on her feet as a third and fourth skeller attacked her.

She cut them down, saw Grimbold fall under the onslaught

of a half-dozen of the skreeing creatures. She raced to help him, but an explosion of gold light burst around him, scattering dead skellers in all directions. Then she was at Taneh's side. A skeller's claws were clamped onto the Loremistress's arm, the wide wings flapping as it tried to lift its burden from the ground. Minda stabbed the skeller, supported Taneh as the Loremistress stumbled.

Inside! Inside!

Grimbold's voice was a roar in Minda's mind. She pushed Taneh towards the door, then turned to face another onslaught. Side by side with the tinker, she cut at the maddened creatures. The space before them was a maelstrom of skreeing skellers and wolves. Though dead skellers lay thick on the ground, the sky was still clouded with them.

Inside! Grimbold roared again. *They are too many for us to fight*.

The wolves broke off their struggle and streamed into the building, hard on Taneh's heels. Grimbold followed. But still the skellers attacked. It was all Minda and the tinker could do to hold the door free for the others.

A wild trilling sounded in Minda's head, drowning out the high-pitched cries of their foes. Her blood drummed through her veins and her heart filled with the strange joy of battle. Her sword rose and fell, while she hovered somewhere between herself and something else. Further and further the sword's power pushed her away.

"Yal!" she heard herself cry with a voice that wasn't her own. "Yaln ser brena! Yal!"

The sword sheared through another skeller, then the creatures withdrew to wing high in the air above the tower, skreeing and whistling. Wild-eyed, Minda raised her arm to shake her sword at them.

"Come on," Markj'n said at her side. "Quick before they return."

She turned to face him, the blood-lust still burning in her. Something in his eyes brought her back, gave her the strength to push the sword's power from her mind. She stared at the skellers piled about the doorway and was sickened. Suddenly she felt weak; her eyes unfocused. The sword drooped in her hand and she started to shake.

The tinker dragged her through the doorway. Scurrying down

a long shadowed corridor, they came to where the others waited for them in a defensible room just off the hall. Grimbold stared strangely at Minda, but made no comment.

Minda trembled still, clutching the sword with frozen fingers. The past few minutes drained from her until she could hardly remember the details. The pendant was warm against her skin, soothing her. She tried to recall who it was that had fought at the tinker's side. Then she lifted her gaze and saw Taneh. Her own panic faded as concern for her friend overrode it. She dropped the sword on the floor and hurried to where the Loremistress was sitting against a wall. The whole side of her tunic was red with blood.

"I'll live," Taneh said, trying to smile. "It . . . it looks worse than it is. Remember your knee in the museum? They drew blood and it spilled—but I'll live. If we get out of here."

Minda quickly searched through Taneh's pack for bandages and salves.

"They're not following us in," Markj'n said from the doorway. He was carrying Minda's pack, along with the remains of his own. "They're still out in front of the building feasting on their own dead. We need to find another door out."

It will be guarded as well, Grimbold said. *We won free of them too easily. For all the savageness of their attack, if they had truly meant to see us slain, we would be dead now. I believe they only seek to hold us here until the other—the one that follows—arrives. My glamor will not stay that one now, not with these bedamned skellers outside to guide him. No. It was neatly done and we are trapped.*

"We must try—"

Aye, Markj'n. And so we shall. But first let us clean and bind our wounds. Look at yourself, man! You have been hurt in a dozen places. Skellers carry Tyrr only knows what diseases.

Minda tore Taneh's sleeve open and washed the wound with water from her waterskin. The wound proved, as the Loremistress said, to be shallow, but she felt weak from a loss of blood. Minda dried her friend's arm with a piece of clean bandaging, then gently patted on a healing salve. "Ah," Taneh said. "That feels better already."

"This isn't too tight?" Minda asked, wrapping the bandage around her arm.

"It's fine. What about yourself, Minda? Were you hurt?"

"No. It's just their blood on me . . . it stings."

She met the Loremistress's gaze. For an instant the strangeness that had possessed her when she'd held the blade returned. Then it was gone and she shivered.

"I should be . . . more scared or something," she said slowly. "But I'm not. Taneh"—her hand went to touch her pendant, came in contact with her shirt, wet with the skellers' blood— "what's happening to me?"

Taneh, too aware of Grimbold's fears, only shook her head. "Don't think about it for now. Let's see to the wounds of the others and wash that blood from you. There'll be time enough to think later."

"But—"

"Do as I say," Taneh said soothingly. "Don't worry, Minda."

It was easier to act than to think, but as she helped the Loremistress with Markj'n's cuts and with the wolves, she couldn't stop thinking about what had happened, fearing the sword, but yearning to feel its hilt firm in her hand once more. It felt so good to be strong and fearless.

From whence came that blade?

Minda looked up from the cut she was cleaning on a wolf's shoulder to meet Grimbold's gaze. Taneh had tended to him and was now resting again, her head leaning against a wall. She sat up at the Wysling's question. Markj'n, too, turned from the door, remembering the battle at the door and trying to fit the young girl he saw tending a wolf's cut with the hellion that had fought at his side. He remembered as well how she'd asked him about enchanted swords a few days ago.

"It's the one I found in the museum," Minda said.

It is bespelled.

She nodded.

Have you even an inkling as to the danger of meddling with such a thing? It possessed you when you fought the skellers.

"And once before, in the museum where I found it. But once the danger's past, it leaves me again."

And what if it does not—the next time?

Again the sensation flooded her—the sureness of hand and eye, the strength in her arm, the wild drumming in her blood. Borrowed skills, borrowed courage. But without them she was helpless. She returned the Wysling's stare, and wondered: Does he even know what it's like to be helpless?

"You don't understand," Minda said. "It's not going to hurt us. It's helped us. The sword saved us all. Markj'n and the wolves, your own spells, would they have been enough out there?"

"She's right, you know," Markj'n remarked.

Grimbold nodded wearily. *Aye, it saved us. But at what cost?*

"This isn't really the time to talk about that," Taneh began, but the Wysling cut her off.

Not the time? he demanded. *What better time than with danger upon us and the likelihood of its being used again so close? A blade like that needs payment.* His gaze shifted from Taneh to Minda. *All magic requires a payment, Minda. You spoke in the old tongue when you fought, crying: 'Die! Death be yours!' It was not even your own voice, for all that your mouth shaped the words. Until we know more about this sword of yours, my advice is to—*

"It helped us!" Minda cried. "Would you rather be lying dead out there with the skellers feeding on you?"

Grimbold bit back an angry retort. Instead he asked: *May I see the blade?*

Frowning, Minda finished cleaning the wolf's shoulder. When she was done, she set aside the cloth and brought the sword over to the Wysling. Grimbold regarded the short length of steel lying before him, trying to reach out with his wizard senses and understand it for what it was.

"You use magic," Minda said bitterly. "Why begrudge another?"

The anger Grimbold had held in check edged into his reply. *I use magic, true enough. But I have studied it. For twenty-one years I studied as a 'prentice and I am still learning to this day. I do not begrudge another's use of it, but it must be tempered with a fuller knowledge than you have. Magic is not like some child's skipping game where you have but to see it done once before you can hazard a try, where the worst you might receive for your effort is a scraped knee.*

"I'm not a child!" Minda told him, her own temper kindled.

What if by using the blade it cost you your very soul?

"I—"

What if by using this blade, it caused you to slay your friends in payment?

"But—"

Be silent! I do not speak solely to hear my own voice. Think a moment, Talenyn.

Suddenly she resented it that he called her by Jan's name.

What do you know of this sword? What are you prepared to offer should it demand payment? Will you give it Taneh's life? Markj'n's? Mine? Talenyn, I beseech you—

"Don't call me that!" Tears brimmed Minda's eyes. She grasped the hilt of the sword and sheathed it savagely.

Minda, the Wysling began.

"Just leave me alone!" she cried. "I don't want to listen to you. I don't want to ever see you again."

A gold glimmer awoke in the badger's angry eyes, and he seemed to grow in stature. Minda backed away from him, her hand on the hilt of her sword.

"Don't," she said. "Just don't try and use your magic on me." She backed into Markj'n and spun out of the tinker's arms before he could grab hold of her.

"Grimbold!" Taneh cried.

The Wysling turned to her and Minda ran from the room. She started down the halls towards the front door, but the skellers were still there, tearing at the bodies of their dead with bloodied fangs. Their high-pitched cries rang sharply in her ears. Gagging at the sight, she turned quickly down a corridor to run the other way—away from the battlesite, away from the Wysling and his words that hurt so much because they just might be true.

He had no right! He was acting like Hadon.

But the logic of his argument followed her—the words repeating themselves in her mind, over and over, until she stumbled and fell. Huddling down, she clutched at her temples, cheek pressed against a wall's smooth surface, tears streaming; she rubbed at her eyes, smudging the streaks of dirt and skeller blood until she looked like she was wearing a mask.

In the room she had left an uncomfortable silence reigned. Markj'n had started after Minda, but a wolf with the same coloring as Ruhn and a third again as big blocked his way. They were the only two with the reddish tint to their fur. The tinker glanced at Taneh, eyebrows raised, but she shook her head.

"I don't know what makes them behave as they do," she said. "Why Ruhn befriended me, why they've helped us against the skellers, why that one's stopping you now from going after Minda."

Markj'n shrugged and backed away from the wolf, worry plain in his eyes; but the worry was for Minda, not for himself. He regarded Grimbold, torn between the loyalty he had for the old friend and the new, wanting to say something but not sure where to begin. Where a moment earlier the Wysling had seemed to fill the room, now he seemed diminished, smaller than his normal size. Taneh sighed and spoke before the tinker came to a decision.

"You were too harsh with her, llan," she said. "She's not some fledgling wizard studying under you."

I know. Grimbold's voice was just a murmur in their minds.

"How can you even be sure the sword is cursed?"

I cannot, he replied. *But the potential for power that lies in her coupled with an enchanted blade is too much. I ask again: who is she, this young companion you have befriended, Taneh? She walked the silhonell with an aspect of the Horned Lord himself, and that is no small thing. He is of the Middle Kingdom and now we see that these grey ones*—he indicated the wolves with a nod of his head—*have an interest in her as well. She bears an enchanted blade that says 'god-wrought' to me. What place have we in a struggle between the gods?*

"The old books say that *every* struggle is a struggle between the gods."

Aye, Taneh. But that is a philosopher's voice speaking—as you know as well as I. But this . . . whether it be the Tuathan, the Grey Gods of the Middle Kingdom, or even the Daketh . . . there is the touch of a god's hand in this.

The Loremistress nodded sympathetically, but did not stray from her argument. "Still, I say you were too harsh—whether it be a matter for the Bright Gods of the Tuathan, the Dark Gods of the Daketh, or the Grey in between."

You do not know as well as I the dangers of magic, the dangers of the uninitiated toying with forces beyond their ken. I have seen the horror of such a weapon as Minda's sword turned upon its wielder, and that sight I have yet to burn from my soul.

"And yet," Taneh asked, "what of those of your own order? How came your knowledge into being? I will tell you. It came from those who dared the unknown, who explored and experimented."

Aye. But what need for such daring now? The laws are there for any to take the time to learn them.

"Time is the one thing Minda doesn't have. And remember—there are those who have a natural affinity to magic."

She is not an erlkin, Grimbold protested.

"But neither is she once-born. Or do you disagree?"

Grimbold shook his head. *No. Her moorman was truthful when he told her that. She is no mernan.*

"I told you what happened when she tried daryn-seeking," Taneh continued. "Didn't I? I've never seen anyone with such a natural empathy for the art. I say she knows—to a degree—the chance she takes with that blade, yet faces it bravely for she has no other recourse. She told us of her upbringing—of her father beating her, of needing to creep from her home to spend a few hours with her friends; do you think she will trade that one life of servitude for another? When she now has a choice? Do not belittle her striving, Ilan. Warn her if you must, but do so gently."

You have the right of it, Grimbold replied wearily. He sighed. *She is gentle within and strangely gifted in a way I cannot understand. If the gods have a part for her to play, who am I to sway her from that role?*

"You show your strength now, Ilan," Taneh said.

And you your wisdom. But I will tell you, I would feel much easier if I could unravel the riddle of who and what she is and what part she has to play, for then we could—

"Grimbold!"

The badger looked up at Markj'n's call. The tinker stood by the door, staring down the hall to where he could see the front of the building. The Wysling opened his mind, seeking the source of the sudden strangeness he sensed in the air. He found Minda where she was huddled in the rear of the building, then a wave of evil washed over him.

The one that had pursued them had arrived.

"It's here!" Markj'n said. "By the door."

Grimbold pushed by him to look down the hallway. At the far end by the front door he could make out a figure silhouetted against the outside light. Though the distance was great, the Wysling no longer needed his eyes to call up an image of what had been pursuing them.

A Walker, he said in a wondering tone.

The fur on his shoulders and back stood on end. Once before he'd seen such a creature—tall and scraggy-thin, with a bald scalp pulled tight over a bony skull. A white robe covered him from his throat to the ground, accentuating the pallor of his lean hands and face. His eyes were deeply sunken under thin eyebrows and blazed with a feral intentness.

Grimbold had never faced such a creature before. It was his own master, the Wysling Morcowan, the high llan of the badger's homeworld of Hafelys, who had faced a Walker and died destroying it. They were creations of the Daketh and could only be slain by a caryaln weapon, a shadow-death. Grimbold had no such weapon.

Markj'n, he said. *Go find Minda. You will find her in the rear of the building. When you have her, go with Taneh and flee for the henge. I will try to hold this one, but I fear he is beyond my power.*

"But, Grimbold—"

Go! There is no time for argument. I will try to follow when I can.

Knowing the tinker would do what was asked, Grimbold padded down the hall towards the door. The tall wolf that had blocked Markj'n's way earlier moved to one side as the Wysling passed. Grimbold's claws clicked hollowly on the tiled floor. His heart was filled with a fearful dread for them all.

chapter eight

As the Walker drew near, Minda felt its approach as a growing depression of spirit. It fit in so well with her mood that she wasn't aware of the reality of its presence until it stood directly in front of the tower. Then the same evil that Grimbold had felt lashed at her heightened senses.

She stood on shaky legs to peer down the hall. Though a corner hid the main entrance from her sight, she could still *see* the Walker with her deepsight as plainly as though he was right in front of her. She wiped the tears from her cheek, smudging her face more, and fingered the hilt of her sword.

"Minda! Minda!"

It was Markj'n. Minda turned and bolted. This creature that had come wanted her, not them. She'd made her decision to leave her companions. If she was no longer with them they'd be safe. She didn't think it was the Dream-master, but the sense of evil that came from it was as foul as any touch of Ildran's.

"Minda!"

The sound of Markj'n's voice was fainter now. She sped down a hallway raising clouds of dust. Markj'n could track her in the dust, she supposed, but there was nothing she could do about that. It lay everywhere, thick as a carpet.

An opening appeared to her right, a dark shadow amidst the hall's greyness. She turned into it to find a stairway going up. As she took the stairs two at a time, she heard Markj'n run by the stairwell's opening, still calling her name. So he wasn't tracking her by the dust. Still, she knew he'd discover his error soon enough so she pushed herself harder, trying to put as much distance as she could between them.

She came to a doorway and opened it cautiously. It led into a long hallway with an endless array of doors set into each wall. She took the first one and stepped inside, hand on sword hilt. A new corridor unwound before her, high-ceilinged and broader than the one she'd just quit. She closed the door behind her and bolted it. She was just in time for she could hear Markj'n pounding up the stairs.

Still fingering her sword hilt, she started down this new hall. It, too, had doors along either wall, with a larger pair at its farthest end. She thought for a minute, then headed towards them. Unless she had her directions mixed up, those doors should open up into a room that was at the front of the building. She wanted to see what had been following them with her own eyes—not with the strange deepsight that seemed to bring images into her head from far away. It was still too strange an experience and she wasn't sure that she trusted it.

Perhaps she could face and defeat whatever it was that had followed them, with the sword to help her. She knew she would have to keep using it, in spite of Grimbold's warnings. What other choice did she have? If it demanded a payment, she'd have to face that moment when it came. Right now, it was more important to concentrate on living long enough to reach that moment.

The double doors led into an enormous cavern of a room with tall glassed windows taking up the whole of the outer wall. Again she bolted the doors behind her and walked to the windows. The main part of the wall was taken up with six huge panes of glass. Under each pane there were three smaller windows. Some of these were broken with vines pushing their way in through the jagged edges. The room was furnished with one long table that ran almost its entire length with chairs set at intervals spaced like the doors in the halls outside.

The acorn pendant pulsed with a warning heat as she approached the glass wall, skirting the table. It grew insistently hotter with each step she took. Her courage faltered.

Then she focused her thoughts on Ildran, turning fear into a fuel to fire her anger at what he'd done to her—what he was doing to others. The pendant felt molten against her skin, but she knew that the heat was inside her, that it buoyed her strength, kept her senses alert and taut as a drawn bowstring.

Reaching the window, she looked down at Ildran's newest sending. One hand gripped the hilt of her still-sheathed sword, the other supporting her weight on the windowsill. The Walker looked up as she gazed down, his eyes blazing as he met her gaze.

A flash of gold light burst from the doorway below where Grimbold stood, bathing the Walker's figure. He dropped his gaze to meet the new threat, hands cutting the air with a sudden fluid motion, dissipating the Wysling's attack and sending a flare of red lightning in return. The Walker's gaze rose once more. A hideous grin split his face.

Minda dropped back out of sight, her hands shaking. She began to pull her sword free when a shimmering flooded her sight.

Come to me, a dry raspy voice whispered in her mind.

The room disappeared. She found herself standing on a rocky crag, looking down at the white-robed figure. Desert surrounded them—a vast sweep of wasteland, wind-blown sand and bare red rock. The Walker lifted a gaunt hand and beckoned her down.

Come to me, come to me.

Minda tightened her hand around the hilt of her sword, but grasped only empty air. She was wearing nothing but a thin white shift with nothing to draw on for strength except for Jan's pendant dangling from her neck. At that moment she felt that everything—from meeting the moorman to her escape from the inn, to Darkruin and her companions—had all been a dream. One more mocking move in the game Ildran played with her.

Panic awoke in her again. She looked around, trying to focus on something familiar to orient herself. The sword was gone. Darkruin was gone.

(All a dream.)

She felt stupid and weak, with nowhere to hide, nothing to rescue her from Ildran's control. She shrank inside herself, defenseless, without hope.

Come to me.

The air about her was foul—as fetid as the gaseous reaches that Ildran had dragged her through before. She found she was clambering down the rocks, answering the Walker's call without even knowing she was doing so. The rough stone cut at her palms and feet. She was already almost halfway down the crag. Her gaze swam.

(All a dream.)

But the pendant—she still had that. It was burning like a fire against her skin. It was supposed to save her from this, to stop Ildran from getting inside her head.

Jan . . . everything . . . all a dream. . . .

She couldn't believe it. She must fight the insidious whisper or lie down and die. Admit to Ildran that he'd won. She *couldn't* let him win. Hanging from a precarious handhold, fingers tight with tension, she fought a silent battle inside herself. Below her, the Walker let his grin widen and beckoned once more, the skeletal hand rising and falling, his voice rasping in her mind.

Come to me.

She wished she was Markj'n who didn't have to depend on a magic sword that disappeared when you needed it the most to save himself. Or Grimbold who'd just blast the Walker, or lay a glamor on him like he'd tried to do when they first sensed the Walker was following them. The memory brought with it a sudden inspiration.

Glamor. Illusion. She had the pendant.

(No dream. It *had* to be real.)

The pendant was her magic—Jan had said so. Or at least said that it would keep her safe. It turned warm to warn her of danger. It calmed her when the panic got to be too much.

(Only a fool would believe that.)

Well, she was Silly Sealy, wasn't she? Magic depended on focusing and will—that was what Taneh had told her. She could make a glamor. She *had* to. And so . . .

She let her fears run free. The Walker laughed as he felt them. She didn't care. Because while she let her body continue its descent, while she gave her fears free rein, under them she narrowed her focus to a pinprick of will, sharp and hard. And in that focusing she hoarded her inner strength, like in daryn-seeking, except she kept it close to her, letting it build inside her, waiting, instead of it letting it flow from her, seeking.

Ah, come to me, Ildran's plaything. Too long you have made us wait. Come to me.

Her jaw tightened at the naming he gave her. Carefully she hid the sudden surge of anger under her cloak of fear, let the waxing power inside her wash away the bitter taste while it added strength to strength.

Come to me. We will walk, spirit with spirit, to Ildran's keep, the keep of our master. Come with me.

Spirit with spirit? This was another aspect of the silhonell, Minda realized. Here spirits held sway; here one's inner strength made the reality.

With that awareness, a great wave of power flooded her, loosed from the hidden recesses deep inside her, a vast ocean of strength that she would never have guessed was there. It was like when she'd tried daryn-seeking, when the power came up in a rush from under the surface of her consciousness to set the pendulum spinning. When Ildran had cast her into the void, that power had reached out and drawn her to Dewthtyr. Now that same power would strike back.

Come to me.

She came. She stood before the grinning Walker, small and forlorn, like a penitent child before its elder. The Walker spread his arms and the white robe billowed like wings in the wind. The sand that rode that same wind stung Minda's cheek. Her eyes smarted. But she held the cloak of her illusion—*her* glamor—tautly about her.

The Walker's arms dropped to grasp her. When the talonlike fingers closed on her shoulders, she let her cloak fall. The surge of her hoarded power roared about them with the fury of a deep winter storm.

Too much, she realized.

Desperately she tried to control the flood before she lost herself in it. The Walker's grin twisted into a wild shriek of pain. He fought to loose his grip, but it was as though his hands were sewn to her shoulders. Her power shrouded them. All her anger and frustrated despair beat at his twisted soul, smashing his defenses one by one, until his spirit moaned in defeat.

Minda stepped back. The Walker's arms fell from her shoulders to hang limply at his sides. The blazing eyes were glazed, hatred burning helplessly in him. She had drained him of his power.

Once more she was atop the crag and he was below. A sound like a clap of thunder pounded once, then the tower formed about her. Her breath was labored and her body started shaking in the aftermath of shock. But something had changed in her. She could look at the Walker, at the strewn corpses of the skellers, and not shrink back from the sight. It didn't please her; she had not become one of the Shadowed who revelled in death and pain. But neither would she shirk the battle against such creatures.

The window in front of her had exploded outward, its glass showering the still form of the Walker during their battle in the silhonell. He crouched on his knees now, his arms back, the flesh charred to the elbows. When finally he moved, it was to rock with pain. His gaze met hers, hatred in his eyes. He yearned to strike, but couldn't even stand.

You . . . surprised me. The Walker's dry voice faltered in Minda's mind. *It will not . . . be so again. . . . I am forewarned now . . . and we will have you yet.*

Minda drew her sword and pointed it at him. A whisper of blue light flickered along its length.

"Leave me alone," she said softly. "You know you can't hurt me anymore."

We . . . we shall see. . . .

A swarm of skellers rushed her, skreeing, maws gaping. She let the sword rise to fight them off. Dispassionately, she watched the creatures die. Again she stood to the side—a spectator, nothing more—but this time the wildness didn't speed through her veins and she cried no words in the old tongue.

One moment the air was filled with the creatures, claws flashing. In the next, they were off in a wailing cloud of black against the sky. The Walker was gone as well. And not a skeller had touched her. The sword had seen to that. She stood, the blade's bloodstained edge resting on the windowsill, and stared off into nothingness.

(Who was she now?)

Was she someone Rabbert or Janey might still recognize? Or even Hadon? Would Tomalin still ruffle her hair and give her forehead a kiss?

(What was she now?)

Had Jan reshaped her with his pendant? Or the sword—
was this objectivity its doing? Would it stay, or would it fade?
She remembered the power rising in her. Did every man, woman
and child have that same potential? Except... *once-born you
never were...*. Jan had said that. What did he mean by that?

She had cleaned the sword on the vines' leaves and sheathed
it without even being aware of doing it. She touched its hilt,
then her hand moved to feel the shape of the pendant under
her shirt.

Once-born. Did that mean there were those who were born
more than once? She'd been taught that when you died your
soul went before Koevah for judgment and depending on the
measure of good against bad in your life, you dwelled with
him in the White Halls Beyond or were doomed to drown
forever in the Endless Seas.

Shaking her head, she walked the long length of the room
to the double doors where she could hear Markj'n pounding.
In fact, he'd been banging against them for some time, she
realized, only she'd been too—what? Lost?—to notice. She
unlocked the door and stepped aside as it was flung open.
Markj'n burst through, stumbled and fell, skidding on his knees
on the dusty floor.

He turned, fear for her and anger mixed in his eyes. Minda
offered him a silent hand up.

You are changed.

Minda's gaze went to the Wysling as she and Markj'n returned to the room where the others were. Grimbold had taken
a terrible blow from the Walker and only his wizardry had kept
him from death. His fur was singed and he was weary to the
point of exhaustion.

She nodded in reply to his plain statement, not trusting
herself to speak.

And you bested him, the badger said. *How?*

"I'm not really sure," Minda said then. She was suddenly
very tired, aching in every muscle and joint. She sat down near
the tall red-grey wolf and leaned her head back against the
wall. "It's all mixed up. I remembered your laying a glamor
and tried something like it myself. I pretended to be afraid—
I *was* afraid. What I did was let that fear seem so strong that
the creature would never realize I was building up... strength

to strike back. I knew I had to wait until I was close, until it touched me. I'm not sure how I did it—or if I could even do it again. It came to me as though I'd always known how to do it but only remembered that I knew at that particular moment. Does that make any sense at *all?*"

Taneh shot Grimbold a look as if to say, Was I not right? The badger inclined his head to her.

"I used the sword again as well," Minda said flatly, waiting for Grimbold's reaction.

I know. I felt you using it. We spoke of it—Taneh and I— after you had left. Taneh reminded me of things I had forgotten, or perhaps chose not to remember at that moment. I spoke harshly, Minda, more harshly than I had any right to. Worry drove me to it. You are caught up in a chain of events that wakes fears in me that I cannot understand fully. That I have difficulty in putting into words.

Why does Ildran seek you—so much so that he would send a creature like the Walker after you? Why did the Horned Lord come to you? For what purpose did that Tuathan blade come into your hands—for that is what I pray the blade is. If it belongs to the Dark Gods, then your soul is already lost.

But I do not mean to belittle you, or begrudge your doing your part. Tyrr preserve us! Had you not stepped in when you did, the Walker would have slain us all.

"I don't think so," Minda said thoughtfully.

Taneh glanced at her, trying to understand the change. All that had been queer and wonderful to her so recently, she treated matter-of-factly now. She glanced at Markj'n, but the tinker could only shrug.

"He came for me," Minda was saying. "I was all he wanted. He attacked you because you stood in the way. If you had stepped aside, I don't think he would have tried to hurt you. And it's because of that . . ."

She sighed, rubbed a hand against her temple. For a moment Taneh saw, through the grime and blood that streaked her face, the young woman she'd known these past few days. Then the moment passed.

"I should go alone," Minda said. "If you could show me the way—point it out to me, I'll go on to find the muryan you told me of. I don't even like doing that because of what I might involve *her* in, but I don't know where else to start." She paused and her voice softened. "I *was* angry before, but I'm not any-

more. I know you weren't trying to do anything but help me.
You were taking me to Gythelen, weren't you? You stood
beside me when the skellers attacked. It's just . . . I suppose it
was the way you were telling me. It rubbed me the wrong
way."

And for that I apologize, Grimbold said. *Truly. Before the
Walker made his appearance I was about to go and look for
you to tell you the same. But do not begrudge* our *help now—
as it seemed I was doing to you before. The Walker—aye, and
others—will return, twice as strong as before. You will need
someone to stand by you then. With your powers and my focusing them, we could stand a better chance than either one
of us on our own.*

"Powers," Minda repeated softly. The past few hours were
already growing muddy in her memory. She unbuckled the
sword from her belt and laid it on the floor. "It doesn't even
seem real anymore," she said. "Up there, I was so sure of
everything, but now . . ."

"It's no longer just your struggle," Taneh said. "If it ever
was. There is Penalurick who is stone-bound—so the muryan
are involved. Ildran has sent his creatures against us—so we
are involved. Huorn's sister was slain—so he is involved. And
how many more has Ildran touched—warping them to his own
ends or simply destroying them? No. You can no longer claim
this struggle for your own."

Markj'n nodded. "Just so. No more locked doors, Minda.
We are here to help."

Aye, Talenyn, Grimbold said. He paused to judge her reaction to his using the moorman's name, but she only nodded
wearily. *We must share our knowledge as well as our powers.
Only so can we hope to prevail.*

"I just don't want to be responsible for anything happening . . . to any of you."

*Allow us the responsibility of our own decisions—as we,
and especially I, will allow you yours.*

"All right," she said. "I didn't really want to go on by
myself." She tried a smile. "Thank you."

Taneh returned the smile. "Let me help you clean up. You'll
feel better—I know."

The Loremistress was wearing a clean dress, though her
cloak was still stained. She gave Minda a hand up and together
they left, bringing along Minda's pack and a shirt that Markj'n

was lending her. It was too big, but she managed to stuff the long tails down into her trousers. Her jacket didn't fare any better than Taneh's cloak, but she felt much better when they returned. A proper soak would have to wait until they found a river outside of the city. For now it was enough just to have a clean face and a shirt that wasn't stiff with blood.

Markj'n was mending his pack and winked at Minda as she sat down again. "You look almost human again."

She was feeling much better—enough so that she pulled a face at him. The tinker smiled as he returned to his work. He didn't like the grim face she'd turned to the world when he'd found her upstairs. Everyone had to harden themselves from time to time, but he much preferred the merry friend he'd made at the old campsite to the other.

"What was that . . . Walker?" Minda asked hesitantly.

"A child of the Daketh," Taneh replied.

Minda settled back as the Loremistress's voice took on its lecturing tone.

"They are the Dark Gods' parody of the high erlkin. Dalkwer they are named in the old tongue and the Walker is but one of many. They include demons, wizards and others such—all debased mockeries of the Kindreds, as the children of the Tuathan name themselves. The Walkers are the seekers, the searchers. They follow the scents of the soul to steal spirits from their bodies. And this one . . . he will be back."

"But Jan said the pendant would keep me safe from that kind of attack."

Only if you allow it to, Grimbold said. *Illusion can play any spell false. If you think it no longer works for you, chances are it will not.*

Minda nodded, remembering how she'd felt when the Walker attacked her. She'd almost convinced herself—or been convinced—that everything but the Dream-master had been a dream. "How long will it be before the Walker comes for us again?" she asked.

Too soon. So we must be away to the henge before he does return. Grimbold rose wearily as he spoke.

"Can you travel?" Minda asked. She'd found a genuine affection for the gruff Wysling—a feeling she wanted to nurture and would have recognized far sooner if the misunderstandings between them hadn't come up almost from the start.

I have little choice, the badger replied, *but aye, I can travel. Is the sky still clear, Markj'n?*

"So far as I can tell there's not a skeller to be seen. But the wolves are still restless."

His pack mended, the tinker was dividing his time between the room and patrolling the hall. Night had long since fallen. Wizard lights, spelled by Grimbold, illuminated the room.

"The moon'll be rising soon," Markj'n added. "If we travel by its light, an' are willing to chance the rest of the way by dark, we could reach the henge by midmorn."

If need be, we will walk in the dark, Grimbold decided. *We dealt both Walker and skellers a harsh blow. I think they will wait until the Walker is recovered before they try us again. I give him one day at the earliest—and by then we will be through the gates and away. He will not find us so easy to follow once we reach the henge.*

"An' no welcome at all in the Lady's halls," the tinker added.

Just so. Are we all ready?

Minda and Taneh shouldered their packs in reply. As they left the room behind, the wizard lights guttered. One gleaming orb followed them into the hall, hovering above the Wysling's head. When they reached the outer doors, it too winked out.

Ruhn and Markj'n took the lead, the others following, with a dozen or so of Ruhn's pack flanking them. The other wolves had slipped away, whether to lick their wounds or scout ahead, Minda couldn't tell. Before the tower was out of sight, she paused to look back.

The moonlight gleamed on the ruined tower's windows— all except for the ones that had broken in her battle with the Walker. She stared at it, then slowly turned. The others were some way ahead, though a tall wolf waited for her, loping at her side as she ran to catch up. When she reached the rest, she saw that except for her companion and Ruhn, the rest of the wolves had gone.

"My thanks, grey brothers," she said softly into the darkness, not sure why she'd phrased it in that way.

The wolf walking beside her cocked his head as though in approval and when she reached out a tentative hand, rubbed his head against her palm, before running off into the darkness.

chapter nine

They reached the outskirts of Darkruin just as the dawn was fingering the sky. The monolithic towers lay behind them now—tall silent sentinels, still brooding and dark against the sky. The district they travelled through had narrower streets and the buildings were squat, bringing the sky closer to them. They kept a close watch for skellers while the two remaining wolves—Ruhn and the other of his pack with the same red-grey coloring—scouted ahead. Minda called the second wolf Cabber.

This part of the city felt older to them—which was strange, Taneh remarked once, considering that most cities started with a central core and then spread out as the population growth warranted it.

Perhaps they weren't men who built this city, Grimbold offered.

After consulting their maps, they realized that the gates were still a day's journey away. The flight from the Walker and subsequent battle with the skellers had thrown off their estimations.

"We took a wrong turn," Taneh said as they studied the lay of the streets on the outspread maps. "I thought this was the place we took refuge in." She pointed to a place and Markj'n shook his head.

"No. I remember we turned twice after Grimbold laid his glamor," he said. "We were following Ruhn an' I, for one, wasn't paying as much attention to where we were going as to how quickly we could get there."

He traced their route and the Loremistress nodded in agreement. They decided to rest where they were before going on. A few grey shapes drifted in from the undergrowth. The wolves prowled restlessly about until Ruhn gave a sharp bark and they vanished as quickly as they'd come.

Minda sat down and leaned her back against the wall of a low building, stretching her legs out in front of her. This part of the city didn't hold the same sense of awe for her. The buildings—the tallest of which was four stories—were more like the constructions of her own world, each constructed in its own fashion so that they ran the lengths of the street in a haphazard style.

Her own world. . . . It seemed further away than ever with these reminders of it all around her. Something touched her—not homesickness exactly but a sort of loneliness. So much had been happening so quickly that she didn't have much time to think about Rabbert or Janey or any of what she'd left behind in Fernwillow.

Markj'n and Taneh had settled down on either side of her. The Loremistress was sleeping—or at least her eyes were shut and the worried frown she wore so much of late was smoothed away—while the tinker was scratching patterns in the dirt at his feet with a small twig, watching the sky out of the corner of his eye. Grimbold was still studying Taneh's maps, while Ruhn and Cabber were asleep in the middle of the street.

Minda kneaded the stiff muscles in her calves. She hoped they'd seen the last of the skellers. They didn't have them on Gythelen, Taneh had told her. But there *were* erlkin there . . . and a muryan. A moorling like Jan. She wondered what they'd be

like and why muryan were referred to as low erls and the others
as high. Taneh said that the high erls were even taller than
Markj'n, who was a good six feet tall, but it didn't seem right
that height alone should be the reason.

You look thoughtful.

Minda looked away from the city's skyline that she'd been
staring at without seeing to find Grimbold regarding her quizzically. "I was thinking," she said, "of my home; or rather the
friends I left behind there. And of this muryan that we're going
to meet, Talwen . . . ?"

*Taryn. Taryn Weldwen. You had best keep the name straight.
Erls are great sticklers for names, as are most folks when you
stop to think of it. But for erls there is magic in a name. It
shapes the person and misspoken, they believe it changes the
bearer.*

The badger spoke with a mock sternness that made Minda
smile. Ever since they'd talked in the tower she'd found herself
almost more comfortable with him than with any of the others.
It was something she couldn't have explained if she'd wanted
to.

She may not be so easy to convince, he continued more
seriously. *I have thought on it for a while now. The muryan,
like all the erlkin, can hold a secret, and Weir is a secret. She
may not be so ready to take us there.*

"But certainly she will when we tell her about Jan?"

Grimbold shrugged. *We can only hope. He is their arluth,
but surely even in the tales on your homeworld you have heard
how the erlkin can affect curious humors. Taryn could take it
into her head that neither Weir nor the affairs of her arluth
are any of our concern.*

Minda nodded, but she hoped there wouldn't be any more
trouble. She'd seen enough of it these past few weeks to last
her a lifetime. And who knew what lay ahead?

"What were you doing in Darkruin?" she asked suddenly,
not wanting to think too far into the future for the moment.
"Looking for star-silver as well?"

I? Seeking ster-arghans? Grimbold's gruff chuckle rumbled
in her mind.

Markj'n looked up and tapped his stick against Minda's leg.
"What I found, I found on my own," he said. "That lug wouldn't
lift a hand to help me."

It is not for me, the badger said, *fair though it be. What use would I have for it?*

"Well," Markj'n drawled, "any you found an' didn't like, I'd've been happy to take off your paws."

Pretty baubles—Grimbold began.

"That are worth a prince's ransom in any civilized land," the tinker said.

There is more to Darkruin than such, even if they were worth a king's ransom.

Markj'n tapped the side of his head with a finger and fell back to drawing meaningless patterns in the dirt with his stick. Minda grinned, but gave the Wysling her attention.

"Like the artifacts and records that Taneh collected?" she asked.

In a way of speaking. I seek with my taw—the strength from which my magic grows. There are memories here, more than what can be seen with the eye. They are hid in the stones of the city's buildings, hid in the slow thoughts of the trees that choke the streets. I read them with my deepsight, the wizard sight, and garner these as Taneh does.

"But to what purpose?"

The first thing we are taught as 'prentice Wyslings, as we begin to delve into the hidden lore, is that one can never know enough.

"Except about where to find star-silver," Markj'n complained. "That doesn't rate even five minutes' work. But do carry on, Grimbold. We're all ears." He turned to Minda and added in a stage whisper: "I like to let him think I haven't heard this all a thousand times before. Keeps him smiling, you understand?"

Grimbold laughed. *Given the right topic, I tend to lecture as much as any Loremistress.*

"That's all right," Minda said, giving the tinker a warning look. "*I'm* interested. What did you find here in Darkruin?"

It is not so much what I found, as the questions I learned to ask. There is nothing that one learns that cannot prove useful one day—though that day may be long in coming. I have not been in Darkruin long enough to do more than question; but those questions, in themselves, are fascinating.

We have here a vast city that is deserted, time-worn and maimed by weathering. But what caused its folk to flee, if flee they did? There are no bones, true enough, but there is also little in the way of personal effects. What does remain are the towers, acre upon acre of them. Were they filled with folk? Did they huddle together in them—and if so why, when the lands are broad and wide about them?

"Taneh said she thought they were originally libraries of some sort where the people of Darkruin stored their knowledge."

Perhaps. But imagine then what knowledge they had accumulated. All of Wistlore's learning would fit into one of those towers—and Wistlore's libraries are the most extensive amongst those of all the Kindreds.

"That's still pretty big," Minda said, thinking of the size of the towers. "But still . . ."

Grimbold nodded. *There are hundreds of these towers. What were they? Where did the people go? Could what befell here come to my own world?*

The answer to it all is here, locked in the stones. And one question leads to another. Jasell Henge, the gate for which we are bound, is the nearest gate to Darkruin. It was first used by a Wysling named Feoin, given its name later by the Loremistress Marna but a score of year-turnings ago. Yet you gated into the midst of the city. How?

"I've thought about that," Minda said. "I think there are gate-stones built into some of the towers. Jan told me that all standing stones are parts of Avenveres and wherever they stand, as a henge or a solitary stone, they can be keyed like a gate."

You could well be right, though I have never heard of a lone menhir being used as a gate. That must be another hint of hidden muryan lore. We have been taught that it is the positioning of the stones that is the secret of the gates. And so without a henge—

"How did I gate here?" Minda finished.

Exactly.

She shrugged, having no answer but the one she'd offered already.

The Wysling's eyes twinkled. *And so it goes. We learn one thing, only to find that it does little save open the way to more questions than it answers. I can recall—*

"Grimbold?"

Minda and the badger turned to look at Markj'n.

"This is all fascinating," he said, "but it's time we were away. At least if we're still intent on reaching the henge this side of moonrise."

Minda laughed at him. "I thought you liked to keep him smiling," she teased.

"I do, I do. But—"

He has the right of it.

Minda stood wearily, shouldering her pack. She wondered if she should lighten it of an item or two. Not that she was overburdened by any means, at least in comparison to Markj'n's fat pack. But anything was a weight just now.

"Oh, for the soft beds of Elenwood," Taneh said when they roused her.

She loosened stiff muscles and swung her own pack to her shoulder. Minda grinned at her.

"Just about any bed'd do right now," she said.

As they finally quit the city and were faring across the brushlands that separated Darkruin from the forests to the west, a pale moon rose to cast a shimmer across the hills that lay spread out before them. A nervous tingle touched Minda's shoulders, as though they were being spied upon—from the forest ahead . . . or the city behind. . . .

Ruhn and Cabber appeared restless as well. There was an urgency about the wolves that she would have put down to her own imagination if not for the warm warning pulse of her pendant. When they reached the forest, they paused to give the dark bulk of the city a final look before following the two wolves into the trees.

The thickets were dense and made hard going, especially for Minda who had none of her companions' woodlore to help her. The woods increased her nervousness as well. A hundred foes could be hidden all around them. And what a racket she was making all on her own, while the others moved quickly and nearly in silence. "The trick is to feel with your foot before you put it down," Markj'n told her. "When you feel a branch, you can slide your foot away before you snap it." She tried to follow the tinker's example, but still she made as much noise as Hadon pounding up the stairs of the inn back home. The feeling of being watched continued to grow.

We draw near, Grimbold rumbled in her mind.

Caution!

Minda shot the badger a glance. *Why?* she sent. *What is it?*

As the Wysling turned to her, Minda realized two things simultaneously: the second voice had not been Grimbold's, and she had mind-spoken.

You—Grimbold began.

A lean shadowy shape streaked at them from up ahead, bowling Minda over. The pendant flared against her skin.

Danger!

Not from Cabber who'd knocked her down, but from ahead. She peered in that direction, trying to make some sense of the shadows. By her deepsight she could see Taneh and Markj'n crouched by the trunk of a tall shadowed tree. Crawling on her hands and knees, she followed Grimbold's lead to where the others waited for them. Her journeysack got in her way. Stopping, she dug the porthmeyn pouch from it and put it in the pocket of her jacket, leaving the pack behind.

"Yargs," Taneh whispered, her voice strained, the fear in it plain.

Minda stole a glance around the trunk of the oak and drew back hastily. She'd seen a small clearing. In the middle of it was a small henge not nearly the size of the one near Woldley on her own world. The ground sloped up to it from their side of the clearing. In amongst the standing stones, she'd caught a glimpse of three shadowed figures too tall and broad to be men.

The sky is awake as well, Grimbold said.

"Broom and heather!" Markj'n muttered. "We were so close."

Above the trees Minda could hear a sound, a whisper of leathery wings. A long skree chilled her blood.

"It'll be now or never," Markj'n said, edging forward. "Grimbold, do you an' Taneh key the gates while the wolves an' I an'—"

He gave Minda a sharp glance. She bit at her lip, but nodded.

"—an' Minda try an' deal with the yargs." He leapt to his feet, shouting: "Now!"

Minda drew her sword. The blue flame that awoke along its length filled her with a sense of mingled fear and relief. She drew a deep breath to steady the sudden rush of adrenaline that had her pulse hammering, then charged after the others as they raced from the shelter of the forest. Before they'd gone a dozen paces, a raucous scream cut the air above them. The yargs turned and Minda saw them for what they were. They were like men, but the musculature was exaggerated and the heads triangular in shape, with large wide noses and even larger ears. They had a total lack of body hair and their clothing was only twists of hide wrapped around their loins, held in place by wide scabbard belts; and ill made knee-high boots. Three gnarled hands dropped to the hilts of swords as they spotted the company's approach.

"Take the one on the right!" Markj'n called to Minda as he angled in the opposite direction.

Ruhn and Cabber bounded ahead. From the woods behind them a chorus of howls lifted as Ruhn's pack rejoined them. Minda ran with her heart in her throat, then the sword's spirit rose to possess her limbs again.

Her heightened senses warned her of a diving skeller. She stopped as she ran and the creature overshot. Its claws snagged at her hair but managed no firm grip, as its wings billowed to stop it. She plunged her blade into its chest as she ran by and then was in amongst the longstones.

All around her was a sudden confusion, a welter of sound and movement. Markj'n dropped his yarg with two swift strokes of his long tinker blades; the two wolves brought down a second. The third raised a huge sword above its head and charged Minda.

Her own blade flared in her fist, rising of its own accord to meet the yarg's descending blow. The resulting jar of contact broke the yarg's weapon near the hilt, tearing her own blade from her hand. The sword's will—the skill and strength—vanished. On her own, she turned to meet the yarg's charge.

His heavy reek stung her nostrils. A backward swipe of his fist threw her to the ground, her head ringing. Dazedly, she watched the yarg stoop to pick up her sword. If this creature was possessed by the blade how could any of them stop him?

She tried to rise and a skeller dove at her. Ducking, she wasn't quick enough; the skeller's talons ripped into the material of her jacket and shirt, cutting the skin underneath. The impact spun her around. She lunged for the yarg but his fingers were already closing around the sword's hilt.

The yarg screamed as blue flames leapt up his arm. The hilt burnt his palm. Minda took a half step towards him, hand outstretched, then Grimbold was beside her. He reared back on his hind legs, forepaws cutting the air. A golden fire burst from his claws, leapt for the yarg. The creature crumpled, his chest exploding with flame.

Taneh! Grimbold cried. *Key the gates!*

He turned to meet a new onslaught of skellers with his magefire while the Loremistress raced for the keystone.

"Gather near!" she called to them.

Minda crouched where she'd fallen, staring at the dead yarg with a horrified fascination. Her stomach churned, but she couldn't look away. Markj'n came to her side, lifted her to her feet. The henge was a mass of battling wolves and skellers, the grey shapes leaping with snapping jaws to meet the black-winged monsters that dropped from the sky. The tinker motioned her to pick up her blade and join Taneh while he turned to help the wolves. Golden magefire flared across the dark henge from where Grimbold held his ground, slowly edging his way to the kingstone.

Minda hesitated, her hand inches from the hilt of her sword. She stared at the dead yarg. His yellow eyes were wide and stared sightlessly back at her, lips drawn back to reveal two rows of teeth filed to sharp points.

"Minda!"

Markj'n's cry dragged her from her trancelike state. Stomach roiling, she closed her fist around the sword's hilt. The power lunged through her, lifted her body to cut down an attacking skeller. A shower of its blood washed her, stinging her eyes and the open wound on her shoulder. But with the sword in control once more, it cut down skeller after skeller and brought her to the kingstone.

Taneh's brow was furrowed with concentration. A dead wolf lay at her feet while Ruhn and another kept the skellers from her. Cabber leapt onto one of the batlike monsters just before it struck Minda, breaking its back with a quick snap of his jaws. Markj'n arrived, followed by Grimbold. The wolves ringed them, leaping at the skellers that tried to break the circle.

Taneh took a quick count, then shut her eyes. Her arms were raised high above her head.

"Caeldh!" she cried in a loud voice.

A deep coldness swept through Minda and a pale amber glow pervaded the henge. Thoughts came scurrying into her mind, intruding with a suddenness that startled her. She remembered Ildran and the void and tried to raise a barrier between herself and what was touching her mind.

Be open, Grimbold told her. *Let Taneh's thought guide you.*

Minda relaxed, understanding what he meant. Taneh had

keyed the gates; it was her will that would take them to Gy-thelen. If she didn't allow the Loremistress to enfold her and guide her, she could end up anywhere. She drew in a breath and let Taneh's control wash over her.

3

The Way to Weir

chapter one

Minda had forgotten the horror of the void. It was vast, black and frozen, an endless sea of shadow. She could sense more than see the gateways into the other worlds. They were like tiny specks of gold that teased the back of her mind. Which one led to Gythelen?

But it was Taneh's will guiding them, not her own. Taneh knew the way. They drifted past gate after gate, the cold settling chill in their bones, the unrelieved emptiness of the void deepening.

Each gate looked the same, Minda thought. She'd never be able to tell which was which. She couldn't even focus on the specks—they were so tiny, here and then gone before she could study them. She thought of Ildran and the chill in her tightened its grip.

Taneh led them deftly towards a particular speck that blossomed into a glowing radiance veined with greens and rusts as
they approached. Its light spun around them, pushing back the
cold of the void. Minda tightened her grip on the hilt of her
sword. She hadn't had time to sheath it; what kept it from
possessing her now? Did it need danger to gain a foothold in
her mind?

Tervyn! Though Taneh's cry was silent, the closing word
echoed in Minda's mind. The spinning quickened, intensified.
Pain shot through Minda suddenly, stunning her. She didn't
need the pendant's answering warning to tell her that something
was wrong.

Sealed! Taneh's voice was tinged with a sudden fear. *Cosrandra is sealed!* the Loremistress repeated.

Ildran's working. That was Grimbold.

Minda's chest went tight with fear. Her knuckles went white
as she squeezed her sword hilt.

But how? Taneh was saying. *The timespan between our
leaving Jasell and gating here was too short for a sealing-spell
to be set. How could he even know we were bound for Gythelen?*

No time for wondering, Grimbold replied. *Time grows short
for us. 'A spell woven, may be broken.' Can you hold us here,
Taneh, while I shape a counter-spell?*

Be quick, she said.

Minda! The Wysling addressed her urgently. *I am still drained
from the battle. You must lend me strength.*

How? Her mind shaped the word and sent it to him before
she was aware that she was using mind-speech.

*Remain open to me and I will take what is needed—no
more.*

Remain open? The answer confused her. She could feel him
tensing and something touched her mind. Strange words ran
through her, swift phrases spoken in the old tongue that she
could almost understand. The cold of the void was cutting
deeper. How long could they survive it?

She could taste the Dream-master's touch in this now, a
lingering trace of his presence, a foulness that curdled her spirit.
She was shivering from both the cold and the memory of Ildran's dreams when Grimbold drew the strength he needed
from her.

It lifted from her with the suddenness of a torrent rushing

through a breach in a dam. Its sheer power left her gasping as it burst from her.

Stay . . . stay the flow . . . . Too much . . . .

The Walker flashed in Minda's mind—his flesh charred, his soul blasted—and she tried to pull away from the Wysling. The gate was opening about them, coupled with the increasing pull of the void. It sucked at them, drawing them away from the gate's glow. Taneh was losing her grip. Blackness lapped about the gate until its dappled flare died to a glimmer.

How many were in their company? Minda tried to remember.

Grimbold, Taneh and Markj'n . . . that was three and she clasped them to her, overlaying her thoughts upon theirs, building a net to keep them by her. The wolves? She sensed Ruhn, drew him close, then Cabber. There was something else present as well—another wolf? She drew it into the net as well.

The gate splintered into shards of light. The void swallowed their flares. Minda's hold on the company began to falter. Shadows welled up in her mind.

Guide us, she cried to Taneh. *Guide us!*

An image drifted into Minda's mind. She drew it into focus. A circle of stones . . . the swirling symbol on its kingstone . . . the thick grass between the stones . . . the constellations wheeling above . . . different from those of her own world. . . .

Her blood pounded in her ears, a wild thrumming that threatened to break her concentration. Her teeth chattered from the bone-numbing cold. The net she held so tightly, her friends, all bound to her, threatened to fray.

She forced herself to ignore everything except for the image Taneh had given her. She focused on its wavering shape, held it, lost it. Again she saw the stones . . . for a moment . . . clearer . . . the stars over the henge. . . .

Tervyn! she cried the moment it focused.

The rushing and spinning of the gate's keying crowded her senses. Vertigo flooded her.

Hold them, she told herself as the gate swallowed them. Hold them all . . . badger and tinker, Loremistress and wolves . . . and the other . . . hold them. . . .

The distortion lasted for long seconds, then she felt something underfoot, stumbled on the solid ground to fall flat on her back. Someone jostled her—Markj'n by the curse. She reached out with her thoughts. Taneh was here. Grimbold. Both Ruhn and Cabber. And . . .

The blade in her hand came alive as she realized she'd brought not a third wolf with her, but a skeller. The great wings flapped, but before the creature could escape, the sword had her on her feet and had cut the skeller in two. The sword's blue fire died immediately and Minda stumbled back to the ground.

Pushing her hair from her face, she stared around the henge. It was the same as the image Taneh had given her—Cosrandra Henge.

Before she had time to complete her self-congratulation, she became aware of a crowd of figures standing in amongst the outer circle of the henge's longstones. The night was dark on this world, darker than it had been on Dewthtyr, and it was hard to make out just what sort of beings these were.

With an effort she made it to her feet, biting back a cry as the movement pulled at her hurt shoulder. She'd almost forgotten the wound. Her stomach was still churning from the wild passage through the void. The cold was fading, but she still shivered. Peering into the darkness, she grasped her sword more firmly as she tried to make out who awaited them.

Her deepsight came to her, allowing her to see them more clearly. An indefinable emotion quivered through her. They were not men, but not yargs either. They were tall, lean with thin faces and pale hair, handsome, but grim. Erlkin? But there was one who stood half again as tall as a longstone, broad-shouldered and heavily bearded.

She shot a glance at Grimbold, looking for guidance—but the Wysling lay very still on the grass. His eyes were glassy and froth flecked his muzzle. Taneh lay a few feet beyond him with Ruhn standing guard over her motionless body.

She heard Markj'n rousing. He stood up, toed the dead skeller to assure himself that it was indeed dead, then stepped close to flank Minda. Cabber moved to her other side. The tension in the air lifted the tiny hairs at the nape of Minda's neck. She cleared her throat, trying to decide what they should do. She glanced at Markj'n. The tinker shrugged and dropped his knives on the grass.

"Sanctuary," he said in a clear voice that carried across the henge. "Sanctuary for my companions an' myself."

A figure detached itself from the longstones, a long narrow

sword held at the ready. They *were* erlkin, Minda thought. Pointed ears lifted from his silvery hair that seemed to float light as gossamer about his face. The eyes were deep and golden, almost luminous in the darkness. The features were handsome, though pinched, some might say. They must all be erlkin, Minda decided looking past him to where they stirred between the longstones. All except the big one.

"How are you named—you who have keyed a sealed gate?" the erl demanded. His voice was grim, but underlying it was a clear tonality, like soft flutes or chimes.

"Markj'n Tufty's my name—from Yenhanwittle." The tinker peered at the tall erl, trying to make out his features but his night sight couldn't match Minda's. "My companions are the Loremistress Taneh Leafmoon of Langlin an' the Wysling Grimbold, of Langlin as well, though originally from Hafelys. The maid is Minda Talenyn—of an unnamed world—an' the wolves're from Dewethtyr. Why have you sealed Cosrandra?"

"We?" The fluty voice grew harsher still. "Never we, tinker. We are as trapped here as others are barred."

As he spoke, more of the erlkin stepped forward, swords in hand, some with bows drawn, the points of their arrows leveled at the small company.

"Sanctuary of a sort I can offer," the first erl continued. "You may consider yourselves prisoners. You with the sword—drop it."

"No," Minda said.

She glanced at her sword, willing the blue flames to come, but the blade stayed dark. Her pendant grew no warmer. No danger. But she didn't trust these erlkin with their shiny gold eyes and abundance of weapons.

Markj'n nudged her. "Best do as he says for now, Minda."

"But we haven't done anything wrong."

She stared at the erl. He regarded her dispassionately. Her glance shifted to Grimbold. If he was dying . . .

Markj'n caught the look she gave the Wysling. "The sooner we let them play out their game," he said, "the sooner Grimbold an' Taneh'll get some help." His gaze touched the ripped shoulder of her jacket. "Broom and heather, lass. You've been hurt yourself."

Reluctantly, Minda stooped and laid her sword on the grass.

"Move away now," their captor said. "Away from the weapons."

"The Lady Sian," Markj'n said as he pulled Minda back with him.

Cabber remained where he stood a moment longer, guard-hairs bristling, then he too retreated.

"We've come to speak with the Lady Sian," Markj'n said.

The erl stared at him curiously, then shrugged. He made an abrupt motion with his arm and a half dozen erlkin moved soundlessly forward—two to retrieve the company's weapons, the rest to make sure that none of the prisoners began something they might all regret. The one reaching for Minda's sword jumped back when he touched it, blowing on his hand with a curse.

That was twice now, Minda thought, enjoying the erl's discomfort. But it had never hurt Markj'n when he'd picked it up.

The first erl glanced at his hurt companion. Cabber chose that moment to lunge between the foremost erls. A dozen shafts were loosed but the wolf escaped without one of them reaching its mark.

"Light!" the first erl cried. To Markj'n he added: "Call the beast back."

"Call him back yourself," Minda said. "We've no claim on him. I'll say this much, though: there's more soul in him than you could hope to have. I hope you never catch him."

The erl's pinched features twisted with anger and he took a step towards her, gold eyes glinting dangerously.

Have a care... Camlin Gatewarden. I am not so sore hurt that... I could not blast you. Strike her... at your peril.

The Gatewarden paused in midstride to glare at Grimbold. "Call it back, Wysling," he demanded.

Grimbold raised himself painfully from the ground. *Talenyn spoke the truth. We have no... claim on him.* He shook his head ruefully. *Ah, poor questing this is... for Elenwood.*

Minda ran to the badger's side, ignoring the sudden drawing back of bowstrings. She knelt to support him. Lights flared in the henge. Their source were a number of misty globes raised high on wooden staves.

Are you all right? Minda asked. She hoped she was directing the thoughts so that only he could hear her. *The sword wouldn't flame. One of them tried to pick it up and it burnt his hand—as it did the yarg back in Jasell Henge. How are we going to get away? Should I try the sword again?*

There will be no need, Grimbold replied in kind. *Not once we see Sian.* He broadened his mind-speech so that the others in the henge could hear as well. *Take us to the Lady Sian, Camlin Gatewarden.*

The erl stared at the Wysling for a long moment. "Bind them," he said at length, "and leash the remaining beast."

He turned his back on them. Minda clenched her fists and stood up from Grimbold's side with a determined look on her face. As though he had understood as well, Ruhn backed nearer Taneh, baring his teeth and growling low in his chest.

"No binding," a deep voice boomed.

The Gatewarden paused and looked up as a tall shadow that was lounging against a longstone stepped forward into the light. Minda had to tilt her head back to look the giant in the face. Her earlier glimpse had given him nothing but a bearded face. Now she saw the craggy lines in his huge features, the deep blue eyes under bushy brows, the vast spread of his shoulders. He was more than twice her own height—almost eleven feet tall from the bottoms of his low-heeled boots to the thick mass of hair that topped his hair.

"You go too far, Garowd," Camlin said softly.

"No," the giant replied, his voice still booming, "it is *you* who goes too far, Camlin. Bind a Wysling and a Loremistress?"

"What about a tinker?" Markj'n muttered, but Grimbold hushed him.

"Greymin's beard!" Garowd finished. "Have you gone mad?"

"Someone sealed the gates," the Gatewarden said, accentuating each word as though he spoke to a child, "so that none could pass through—but these came nonetheless. From Wistlore or not, I would be shirking in my duty to allow them their freedom."

"Take them to the Lady by all means. Gods, man, they *asked* to be taken before her. But you will not bind them while I stand here." The giant touched the hilt of a great axe that leaned against the grey stone beside him. "By the shaft of my father's blade, you'll *not* bind them before me. Tyrr! The Wysling even knows you by name!"

"I have seen him in the Lady's hall before," Camlin admitted.

"Aye," Markj'n added. "An' drunk my wine there, too, now that I think of it."

"That means nothing when a gate has been sealed and only

your company can use it. Has Wysling magic become so great,
a Loremistress's wisdom so vast, that they can win through
where our Lady failed? Or is it some hidden tinker lore that
let you through?"

Talenyn brought us through.

The Gatewarden shook his head. "Her?" he mocked. He
took in Minda's slight form. Looking beyond the anger in her
eyes that echoed his own, he saw that there was more to her
than a first glance allowed. There was power hidden behind
those wide brown eyes. "This I must see," he said.

He took a step towards her, one hand outstretched. Minda
backed away, regretting that she'd ever taken Markj'n's advice.
Things were just going from bad to worse. Her sword lay only
a dozen steps away—but it might as well still be on Dewethtyr
for all the good it could do her now.

He only means to read you, Grimbold explained. *As Huorn
did.*

"He can go read himself," Minda retorted. "I don't want
every thrill-starved lout who can't see beyond his own nose
pawing at me."

Her hand lifted between herself and the erl as she spoke—
almost of its own accord. The forefinger and little finger pointed
straight out from her hand, while the two middle fingers folded
in to touch her palm. Camlin blanched and took a quick step
back, shifting the shape of his own fingers to make a ward
sign between them.

Minda stared down at her hand, looking at it as though it
belonged to someone else. A word came into her mind. Pansign. That was what it was. Only how did she know that? For
a moment, she thought she heard a faint sound of reed-pipes
as she wiped her brow, trying to collect her thoughts.

She felt stretched too thin, as though everything that touched
her was pulling at her, trying to spread her out over some vast
distance that she couldn't hope to cover. Or like trying to fit
the giant into her jacket—everything was tight and thin at the
same time. Stillness spread across the henge. She looked into
the erl's eyes and found something unreadable there. Fear almost, mixed with sorrow. What *was* the Pansign?

Talenyn. Grimbold's voice was soft in her mind.

She sighed. Keeping her hands loose at her sides, she walked
slowly up to the Gatewarden, her mind full of confused thoughts

and emotions. When she stood directly before him, she took a deep breath. "Read me, then," she said.

Camlin hesitated. Cautiously, he lifted his hand to touch fingertips to her brow. A shiver touched her slim frame at the moment of contact and suddenly Minda understood what reading was. Something had woken in her since her meeting with Huorn. Then, she remembered, she had watched herself through Huorn's eyes; but now, she realized, as their souls mingled for the briefest of instants, that she could read the Gatewarden too. She knew the fears he held for the safety of his world, and of his Lady. The confusion and helplessness of the sealed gate spilled through her. It was an expansion of the dreams Ildran had sent to her. All that was familiar had become strange. Shadows reared on all sides with no enemy in plain view.

"Ildran?" the erl asked. He was plainly puzzled, but the name was uttered more as a statement than a question.

"Who was Oseon?" Minda asked in a low voice.

She had picked the name from his thoughts in the instant his fingers fell away from her brow. A great sadness shrouded the name, so deep a sorrow that Minda truly regretted the anger that had come between them.

"He is . . . was the Lady's brother," Camlin said. "He died the night the gates were sealed—dream-slain like the horned man's sister." His lashes were damp, his eyes glistening. "Will you pardon me my hard words? I see now that I . . . was wrong."

Minda touched his arm.

"Neither of us knew," she said.

Camlin nodded. "You must see the Lady and tell her— show her what you showed me. Come. I will take you. And you will walk unbound."

There was a sudden motion everywhere at his words—as though a great weight had lifted from the hearts of all that were present. Stretchers appeared to carry Taneh and Grimbold. Two of the erlkin lifted the Loremistress onto one, but Garowd waved the others away from Grimbold.

"I will carry the Wysling," he said.

He lifted Grimbold gently in his arms. Markj'n retrieved and sheathed his blades, motioning Minda to do the same. She glanced at the Gatewarden and he nodded. Bemused, she picked up her sword and cleaned it on the grass.

What a thing this reading, this spirit-sharing was. She wished she had understood it better when Huorn had read her; she had lost a friend there. And the antlered man could have been a great help on their trek through Darkruin for, after all, Ildran was his enemy too.

Sighing, she slid the length of her sword into its scabbard. Falling into step beside Markj'n she worried at her thoughts, seeing little of the way they took to Elenwood Hall.

chapter two

Like many henges, Cosrandra topped a rise in the middle of a clearing. The erlkin, Garowd's tall frame towering over them, headed for a break in the tall forests that surrounded the field. Markj'n kept pace with Minda, matching his stride to her smaller step so that they lagged somewhat behind the others. She wondered if she should give Cabber a call, then thought better of it. Ruhn, she noticed now, had slipped away as well.

The stars seemed closer to the earth on this world than they had on Dewethtyr. The bobbing faery lights of the erlkin pulled further and further ahead. Markj'n quickened the pace a little and Minda tried to keep up with him.

The forest itself was mostly oak—tall spreading giants, thicker about the trunk than three men—fingertips touching— might girdle. Weariness crept into Minda's limbs and fogged her thoughts. She stumbled once or twice along the way until

Markj'n took her arm. But her bleary eyes opened wide when Elenwood Hall came into view before them.

Enchanted was the only word to describe the place. It was a huge towered and peak-roofed structure that seemed to have been carved out of one vast tree and stood as tall as the giant oaks, like a castle of wood growing in amongst its brothers rather than crafted by hands. The Inn of the Wandering Piper could have fit into it three times over, stables, yard and all, with room to spare. The courtyard was lit with the same misty globes that the erls had used to light the henge. They swung from the boughs of the trees that overhung the walls and from the gables of the hall itself. Long strands of ivy hung from the rooftops to disappear into the woad and fennel that leaned against the building's walls. A rich smell hung in the air of wildflowers, apples, and the earthy scent of dark forest soil.

There were erlkin everywhere she looked. All were tall and slender, pale-haired and golden-eyed, with the narrow aquiline features she'd come to expect after the ones she'd met in the henge. The ladies were beautiful, with an eeriness to their beauty that took the breath away; even the serving maids that clustered about the keep's door were radiant. There were solemn lords with shining faces and soldiers in gleaming mail who seemed more fit for a high court ceremony than war. All moved with spare, graceful motions.

Minda moved closer to Markj'n, thankful for the comforting arm to hold on to. She felt suddenly dowdy. The tinker squeezed her hand reassuringly.

"Boggles the mind," he whispered to her, "seeing so many all together for the first time, eh?"

Minda nodded mutely. What a sight their small company presented to this shining folk. Grimbold with his fur all singed, the rest of them with their clothing in tatters and dried blood splattered over everything. No wonder Camlin had balked at giving them their freedom, even if they did have a Wysling and Loremistress in their company.

"Don't worry, though," Markj'n added. "For all that the first part of our welcome was a wee unsettling, we'll be well treated now. The Lady an' Grimbold are old friends, though you'd never know it to listen to that Camlin. An' the wine here! Ballan! If there's one thing that an erl can do better than look like a storybook, it's brew a wine so heady it takes the top off a—"

Camlin was motioning them into the hall; Minda gave Markj'n a tug in that direction. When she stepped inside, she saw that the erls were not all of one type as she'd thought. Camlin introduced them to the woman who stood waiting for them.

"Guests," the Gatewarden said, "this is Tangle Hallwife."

The Hallwife was startlingly different from the other erls. The mass of black curly hair that cascaded down the slim lady's shoulders and back told plainly how she'd come to be named. She was only a half head taller than Minda and wore a light blue dress intricately embroidered with red and gold threads. While she had Camlin's slender features and the ears that came to a pointed tip through the thicket of her hair, she reminded Minda more of her moorman Jan.

"A-meir," the Hallwife said softly, a warm welcome in her eyes.

Behind her, the smooth expanse of polished wooden floor seemed to go on forever. Minda saw more erls of various sizes and hair color, everything from Tangle's dark locks to a rich red as bright as Wooly Lengershin's back home in Fernwillow. There were none taller than the giant, but a few smaller than Minda. She thought they were children until they turned their tiny wise faces to her.

"I will show you to the rooms we have set aside for you," Tangle said. "The Healers will tend to your wounds and you may wash up there before you meet with the Lady."

Minda let the Hallwife lead her away to the room that she would be sharing with Taneh. The Loremistress was already stretched out on a bed with two erls bent over her. These were the taller, silvery-haired sort, dressed in rich scarlet robes; one was male, the other female. The man held a bowl of some clear sparkling liquid in one hand. While the woman laid her palms to either side of Taneh's forehead, her lips moving silently, he would dip a slender finger into the liquid and trace lines above the Loremistress's chest.

"What are they doing?" Minda asked Tangle in a low voice.

"Your companion was sorely hurt, trying the gates," the Hallwife replied. "Arenna seeks to restore the lifeforce that the Loremistress expended in her struggle."

"And the water? What's *it* for?"

Tangle smiled. "Not water. It is colonfrey, the heart-water of Elenwood, that speeds Arenna's work. Halinor is her 'prentice. The symbols he traces are sacred to the forest and they quicken growth, whether it be in a new sapling or a friend's recovery from her hurts."

Minda nodded, understanding not so much the methods of the healing as that Taneh was being cared for. She looked about the room curiously. She could see no seam or join between floor, walls and ceiling. There was a window set in one wall, overlooking the darkened forest beyond, and another bed under it; hers, she hoped, as her weariness came welling up once more. But there was still the Lady to see. She sighed.

Chests stood at the foot of each bed—Taneh's pack was leaning against hers—and between the beds, set out from the wall, was a tall folding screen. Its three panels depicted a band of erls riding golden horses through a meadow and into a forest where a still pool reflected the full moon.

"It's beautiful," she said.

Tangle glanced at the screen. "We all did that once, when we were younger—went out wild and chased down the moon."

"Was this whole place carved out of one giant tree?"

"Not carved," Tangle replied, shaking her head. "This is Colonog, the heart-tree of Elenwood, and she grows in this fashion to house the Lady and the Lady's people."

"You mean it's still alive?" Minda studied the room dubiously, not sure she liked the idea of sleeping inside a living tree.

"Very much so," Tangle said.

"But doesn't it need . . . well, branches and leaves and roots?"

"It has roots," Tangle replied. "They go deeper than any tree in the wood. And as for sustenance"—she touched a hand to her breast—"we provide her nourishment with what lies in our hearts."

It was everything Minda had imagined a magic place to be. Beautiful and unearthly, with just a suspicion of disquiet. Marvelous trees that grew in the shape of small castles, beautiful fey folk to live in its halls, a giant. . . .

"There's a tub behind the screen where you can wash," Tangle said. "The water's freshly drawn and should still be hot. Would you like someone to help you bathe?"

"No . . . I can do that on my own."

"And I have laid out fresh garments for you."

Minda hadn't noticed the clothing on the bed. A long dusty rose dress with green vinework in the collar and cuffs lay beside a more practical set of brown trousers and a shirt the same

color and material as the dress. Undergarments, a loose tunic
of a deeper rose and a dark blue jacket completed the selection.
By the bed stood an impossibly fragile pair of slippers and a
pair of sturdier shoes.

"Were you expecting us?" Minda wondered aloud. Everything looked to be about her size. But if they'd been expected,
why had there been trouble at the gates?

Tangle shook her head. "No. We didn't know until Camlin
sent word ahead."

Well, she supposed that made sense. As Tangle turned to
leave, Minda touched the erl's arm, curious about one more
thing. "All the erls here . . ." she began.

"We are not of the same Kindreds," Tangle finished for her,
"though we are kin. The silver-haired folk are the high erls—
First Born of the Tuathan's children. They are the Lady's own
people. My folk are of the forest; we are the wooderls. There
are many of the Second Born in Elenwood, folk of the forests
and hills, the waters, the meadows and the mountain heights.
And there are always guests as well."

A shadow crossed her face and Minda remembered the sorrow she'd pulled from the Gatewarden's mind. Oseon. The
Lady's brother. Dream-slain.

"Since the closing of the gates," Tangle said, "we have not
been so merry as we might be. Still, we will have a greeting
feast for your company when you have had a chance to make
yourself more comfortable and you will see that, shadows not-
withstanding, Elenwood can still give a merry guesting. I will
leave you to your bath now. If I come for you in an hour or
so, will that be too soon?"

"Oh, no." Minda looked once more about the room, ap-
preciating its simple beauty. "Thank you again," she added.
"For everything."

"It was my pleasure," the Hallwife told her.

She smiled and left the room. Minda turned to where the
healers were still busy with Taneh. Worry creased her face,
but she knew that there was nothing she could do to help them.
They would heal her friend. They *had* to.

She made her way behind the folding screen and smiled at
the sight of the big wooden tub with the steam still rising from
its water. Stripping her soiled clothes from her, she sank gratefully into the bath, dunking her head, then lying back to lean
against the tub's rim. A sensation of dreaminess stole over her

as the heat of the water soaked into her. It was like finally crawling into her bed at the inn after a day of mad work in the kitchen and common room that seemed as though it would never end.

Taneh was sleeping peacefully by the time Minda finished her bath. Arenna had bathed her by hand and the Loremistress lay in a clean white nightshift, her features relaxed. Halinor was gone—taking his bowl of colonfrey with him, Minda supposed. Arenna smiled when she peeped around the corner of the screen looking for a towel. The healer helped dry her, which made Minda feel like a child, though Arenna's ministrations were not nearly so rough as Hadon's had been when she was a toddler. After rubbing a salve in the wound on Minda's shoulder, with hands so gentle they were like feathers on her skin, the healer bound the wound in clean white linen and left Minda to dress.

"Will Taneh be all right?" Minda asked before Arenna could reach the door.

The erl paused to look back. "She sleeps. What she needs most now is rest. Tomorrow she will be up and about and you can speak with her."

Gold eyes warm and smiling, Arenna stepped from the room. So quiet, Minda thought. They all move so gracefully and silently.

She chose the more practical garb, luxuriating in the feel of the clean cloth against her scrubbed skin. The trousers and shirt were softer than any material they had in Fernwillow, but seemed very strong and sturdy as well. She was just putting on the blue jacket when Tangle arrived to fetch her.

Leaving her sword behind, for there was no need for it here, she trailed along beside the Hallwife, staring wide-eyed at everything around her. Erls moved about their business, nodding or calling soft greetings to them as they passed. Fabulous tapestries and paintings hung from the walls. Carved faces peered at her from the doorframes—not carved, she corrected herself. They *grew*.

She shook her head, glad she'd chosen the plainer clothing. She still felt dowdy, but the dress would just have accentuated her feelings of being a coarse lump in these delicate surroundings. When they reached the entrance hall, Grimbold, again cradled in the giant's arms, and Markj'n were waiting for them. Grimbold's eyes sparkled with amusement at his predicament.

His singed fur had been carefully trimmed and his pelt gleamed from a thorough grooming. Markj'n was decked out in replacement clothing as wildly colorful as his usual tinker garb. A bright yellow shirt, brilliant red trousers and a dark green jacket assaulted Minda's eyes. A long red scarf trailed from his neck and a jaunty blue cap was perched on top of his head. Neither of his tinker blades was at his belt, just a small knife, the blade of which was about as long as Minda's hand.

"Don't you look a fine sight," she said.

The tinker shrugged and grinned. "I hardly recognized you with your face clean."

"The Lady waits for us," Tangle said before Minda could frame a suitable reply.

The Hallwife led them out of the hall into an enormous room that, once they were inside, seemed even larger than it had from the outside. Three inns could fit in here alone, Minda thought, correcting her first impression of the Lady's hall. The ceiling was as lofty as a tall oak. Misty globes hung from the walls and the high ceiling to illuminate the whole length of the chamber.

"They're called dalin," Markj'n told Minda, following her glance. "They're made by dwarves an' there's not one, save a dwarf, can tell how they're made. There's some say that they're lit by the souls of the dwarven dead." He shrugged. "So much pigsh—shoes, I think, but who's to say?"

Minda tried unsuccessfully to hide a smile. She'd never expected the tinker to care who heard him say what.

"I didn't know pigs had shoes," she began innocently, "though I do know they—"

"Never you mind what they do or don't. This is neither the time nor the place for such talk." He took her hand and gave it a squeeze. "When we're done hoity-toitying with all the lords an' ladies, I'll show you 'round proper. Till then, we'll play the part of courtly pilgrims an' cause no more rows. Bargain?"

"Bargain."

They turned their attention to the far end of the hall where a number of erls sat about an intricately wrought table on a raised dais. The table's legs were shaped like hoofed limbs, with paws curling about the tabletop to hold the lacquered wood in place. The backrests of the chairs lifted above the heads of the erls in the semblances of various birds and beasts. The wall behind them was a three-dimensional representation of a forest;

tall wide trunks rising up until they split into branches that spread across the vaulted ceiling. Several shapes stepped out from between the trees—a tall bear, a wolf, a stag with twelve-tined antlers, an otter. Higher up, a raven sat perched on a branch, its wooden eyes fixed on the company below.

Tables ran the length of the hall between the door and the dais. Folk of all kinds were there, mostly erlkin, but Minda spotted the odd short broad-shouldered and bearded individual that she thought must be a dwarf. There were hearths set at varying lengths along the walls, tall fieldstone affairs with fires burning in them.

Now surely, Minda thought, the tree hadn't grown those stones as well? And wouldn't the heat of the fires bother it? She'd ask someone about that later.

As they approached the dais, those seated there fixed them with steady stares as though weighing their worth. The weight of those many gold eyes made Minda nervous and she tightened her grip on Markj'n's hand. A lady stood up to beckon them closer—a lady so fair she took Minda's breath away and made all the other erls she'd seen so far seem plain in comparison. She wore a long white simply fashioned robe belted about the waist with a green cord. Her hair was a sunburst gold and hung to her waist; her face was heart-shaped, high cheekbones accentuating its fine lines. Deep gold erl eyes, flecked with rust and green, appraised the newcomers with a gentle scrutiny. When at last they all stood before the dais, she motioned them to take seats at the table.

"Welcome," she said. Her voice was as sweet and soothing as milk and honey. "Welcome to Elenwood Hall. And though you come to us in a dark time, blessed be your stay with us."

At the words "dark time" Minda caught a hint of the deep sadness that weighed on the Lady Sian—for surely this must be the Lady of Elenwood Hall herself—and her heart went out to her. Oseon had been her brother, the brother Ildran had slain.

Blessed be, Grimbold replied from Garowd's arms. He stirred and the giant set the badger gently down. *Our thanks for your welcome, Lady,* Grimbold continued, feeling decidedly more comfortable standing on his own wobbly legs. *We share your sorrow.*

Sian inclined her head sadly to the Wysling.

"Aye," Markj'n said. "It's good to hear your voice raised

in welcome, Lady; an' finer still to see you. Though the times may be bad, just standing here before you makes my heart feel a little lighter. But Oseon—he was a good lad. I'm sorry."

The tinker bowed low, nudging Minda with his elbow. So caught up in the wonder of her surroundings, the jab startled her and she almost let out a yelp, catching herself just in time. She bowed too and mumbled a greeting, gaze cast down at the floor. She was beginning to regret that she hadn't chosen the dress and slippers. She felt very scruffy and unpresentable in amongst all this finery. When she dared to lift her eyes once more, she met the Lady's gaze and blinked at the sudden depths she found in those golden eyes. It was like it had been with the piper . . . not the wildness . . . but she was drawn into them . . . far and far . . .

Though your heart is open and merry and wise, the Lady's musical voice sounded in Minda's mind, *there is yet a shadow upon your spirit—as though a door were shut against any who might pry, be that but yourself. Who are you? What lies behind that door?*

I—I'm not sure I understand.

The Lady nodded. *I see that now. I will trouble you no more tonight, but later we will speak of it. I am Sian Gwynhart.*

My name is Minda Talenyn.

Then, welcome to you, Little Wren. Blessed be.

As the last words sounded in her mind, Minda blinked. Her vision broadened so that she saw the whole of the hall again. Markj'n took her by the elbow and aimed her into a chair. She sat down and gratefully accepted the wine goblet he passed her, but all the while her gaze stayed on the Lady of Elenwood Hall. She understood now why Camlin took his duties so seriously. Here was a wonder worth protecting. If she'd had her sword with her, she would have laid it at the Lady's feet and offered up her service to her.

She took a sip of her wine, hardly tasting its curious flavor, and paid attention as the Lady introduced the others at the high table.

"Camlin Gatewarden you have already met," Sian said, gesturing to the erl at the far end of the table. "At his side is Dayan Harper, from Goldinghall south of the Stonecrop."

The Harper stood and bowed. He was a dark man—not an erl—black-haired, with a tanned complexion and bright blue eyes under bushy eyebrows. He wore light brown trousers and a simple tunic of rust-colored cloth. A gold chain sparkled at his throat.

"Merriwell Harper, our own tunesmith."

Merriwell wasn't tall for an erl; like Tangle he stood only half a head taller than Minda. He bounced to his feet, golden locks tumbling about his face. He brushed them back, straightened his leaf-green tunic and winked at Markj'n before he sat down again.

"Tangle Hallwife and Arenna Healer you have already met as well."

The two ladies nodded greeting. As Sian passed over an empty chair between Arenna and herself, a shadow crossed her face. Oseon's chair, Minda thought.

"Cothwas Holdmaster," Sian continued quickly.

The Holdmaster was a solemn erl, tall and silvery, and he seemed older than the others, though Minda wasn't sure how one could tell an erl's age. He stood to bow gravely. His eyes held a wisdom matched only by the Lady's. His robes were a deep blue.

"Dorren Fieldmistress."

The Fieldmistress was a high erl as well. Unlike the other ladies, she wore trousers and tunic. Her slender hands were rough and callused, her wrists thick from swordwork. She nodded to the newcomers.

"And lastly," Sian said, "Garowd Shenkwin—a cawran, as you can plainly see, from Cleth-hall in the north."

The giant grinned hugely. "Welcome, from one guest to another," he said, his voice still loud though he spoke softly— for a giant.

The Lady smiled but only a trace of humor remained on her features when she turned to Grimbold. The badger's chair was curious, as though made especially for him. It was longer than it was wide and the seat tilted back so that his head, resting on his forepaws, was raised well above the tabletop. Garowd's seat, too, was especially crafted for his size.

"I realize you bear grave tidings," Sian said to the Wysling, "and yet would you pardon me if they were left unsaid until the morrow? So much has befallen, so much that is strange and sorrowful, that I would we had the one night free from them. Tomorrow comes soon enough, I fear, Grimbold. Perhaps all too soon."

Grimbold nodded, much to Minda's relief. *A respite would be welcome, Lady.*

"Aye!" Garowd boomed. "Time enough for troubles when the sun's high. Let's forget our worries for this one eve, that we may face them with all the more strength tomorrow!"

There were other empty chairs about the table—guest chairs, Minda decided, for they held none of the sorrow of emptiness that Oseon's did. She sighed, looking at the chair, feeling guilty that she should be enjoying herself when the Lady's brother was dead, when Jan was still stone-bound and Huorn's vengeance unfulfilled, when who knew how many others were falling under Ildran's power.

There is a time for sorrow and a time to set sorrow aside. The Lady's thoughts came to Minda, rustling like wind across reeds. *Oseon is gone, aye, and we sorrow for his going; but as his spirit has departed, so does a new life quicken in the womb of a young woman of Elenwood. So it goes. Death brings life. The circle turns. Though we sorrow that Oseon has left us, how could we not rejoice at the coming of a child? There has not been a child born in Elenwood for fourscore years.*

Minda caught Sian's gaze. The concept stunned her.

You mean for a child to be born one of your people has to die first?

Just so, Sian replied.

She broke the silent conversation to rise to her feet. Lifting her arms, she called out to the folk gathered in the hall.

"Tonight we have promised ourselves to set aside the troubles that pound at our door." She raised her goblet high and the others at the high table followed suit. "Merry meet, merry part!"

"Merry meet, merry part!" a great swell of musical voices repeated, answering the Lady's toast.

Minda turned in her chair to look at the sea of erl faces, a forest of arms lifting goblets high. As if on cue, young erls of both sexes streamed in from doorways bearing platters laden with food. A touch on her arm brought Minda's attention back to her own table. A grinning erl stood at her side, offering her a platter of dainties with a wide variety of choice. Others came with honey-cakes and sweetmeats, bowls of steaming grains garnished with vegetables, stuffed mushrooms and rich-smelling cheeses, sauces and spreads, baked rolls—more food than she'd ever seen before in one place. A grumble in her stomach reminded her of how long it had been since she'd last eaten.

"A hastily thrown together feast indeed!" Markj'n said beside her. "Ballan! They've been weeks preparing this meal or I'm not a tinker. Still, you won't find me complaining—hey?"

Minda bit into a stuffed mushroom and couldn't have agreed more.

Much later, Minda lay in her bed, staring at the ceiling above her and listening to Taneh's quiet breathing. She tried not to think that she was sleeping inside a tree. Clean, for what seemed like the first time in weeks, and wearing the soft sweet-smelling nightshift she'd found on her bed when she returned to the room, she did her best to let sleep claim her. But tired as she was, the wonders and marvels of Elenwood Hall were still too fresh in her mind.

A strange folk these erlkin, she thought. For all that she'd enjoyed the feast and the songs and harping that followed, she hadn't been able to throw herself into the gaiety with the erls' wholeheartedness. It was a little disquieting how *thoroughly* merry they could be. But for all that she'd smiled and laughed and tried to sing along with the strange erlish songs, the troubles that had brought her here had never quite been dispelled. The wine—and oh, she still felt dizzy from it—had helped somewhat, but lying here in the quiet, her worries all came back to her, lunging through her mind like hounds on the fresh scent of a hart, unwilling to give up the chase though their master's horn called them back.

Foremost on her mind was the muryan Taryn Weldwen. She repeated the name carefully to herself, mindful of Grimbold's warning about names. She hadn't seen anyone that looked like her moorman in all that crowd—though considering how many erls there'd been in the hall, perhaps that wasn't really so unusual. But what if Taryn *wasn't* here anymore?

She frowned to herself in the darkness. It was pointless lying here awake running through an endless list of what-ifs. A council had been called for tomorrow. The best she could do was get some rest before tomorrow came. To distract herself, she tried to remember the words to the ridiculous song that Dayan and Merriwell had sung at the end of the night, ably assisted by a very drunk Markj'n and Garowd.

She was still smiling when sleep slipped over her.

chapter three

Minda awoke at dawn and couldn't get back to sleep. She felt far better rested and had a much clearer head than she deserved with only five hours of sleep on top of all the wine she'd drunk the night before. She sat up cautiously in case the usual effects of overdrinking were just waiting for some movement to make themselves known, but she stayed clear-headed. Markj'n had certainly been right about the erls' wine-making abilities. What Hadon wouldn't give for a keg or three of it in his cellars.

Swinging her feet to the floor, she found the pair of slippers that had been laid out with her nightshift and put them on. Taneh was still sleeping, with Ruhn curled up on the foot of her bed. Now how had he gotten into the hall? She looked around for Cabber, but the other wolf had not reappeared. She wished that Cabber would attach himself to her as Ruhn had to Taneh, but knew in her heart that whatever these wolves were, they weren't pets.

Ruhn cocked an eye at her as she changed into day-clothes and slipped from the room, but made no move to follow. Biting at her lower lip in concentration, she managed to steer herself through the confusing turns of the empty hallways until she reached the huge chamber where last night's feast had taken place. Dozens of erls wandered about the room or sat at the tables. Sunlight streamed through the windows set high in the walls.

Merriwell was sitting at a table to one side of the door and called her over. He offered her some breakfast, but she settled for a mug of tea and wandered out into the courtyard with it to have a look around.

There was supposed to be a river near the hall and she decided to go look for it. The tub in her room was empty and she hadn't wanted to disturb Taneh by getting someone to fill it, but another bath, or at least a swim, would be just the thing for starting off the day. After days of feeling gritty and unkempt, it was a treat to be able to wash frequently. She sipped at her tea, enjoying the early morning quiet. Halfway to the river, she came upon Markj'n and Garowd reclining under one of the tall oaks and conducting a rather bleary conversation with each other. Seeing her, the giant broke off in midsentence and waved her over.

"Ho! Minda! So you're an early riser as well. Come sit with us a bit."

Minda looked ahead to where the blue of the river showed through the trees, then shrugged. There'd be time enough later for her swim. Still sipping her tea, she settled down between the two.

"I should be exhausted," she said, "for everything that's been going on these past few days, but I'm not. I feel like I could tackle a jaunt through a dozen worlds today."

Garowd grinned. "Aye, an erl hall's like that. The erlkin crowd much living into each moment, for all that they live such long lives. When they feast, they're merrier than birds in the spring; when they fight, they're fiercer than dragons. Ah, and when they love . . ."

The giant broke off, embarrassed. Minda laughed good-naturedly at his discomfort.

"What do they love like?" she asked. "Or are my ears too delicate, do you think?"

They both had a rather self-satisfied air about them this morning, she decided, and the erl-maids *were* fair. Then the thought of Markj'n in the arms of one of those radiant ladies awoke a twinge of jealousy in her—though what she'd've done if he'd showed up at *her* bed last night, she didn't know.

Garowd had blushed crimson, but then he laughed. "You're not shy, Minda," he said. "Not shy at all—I'll give you that. Bold as a robin!"

"Or a wren," Markj'n added languidly.

Garowd ruffled Minda's hair and she caught at his hand with a look of mock irritation. Then she stared at that hand, a good three times the size of her own.

"Who'd've thought," she said dreamily, leaning her head back against the tree trunk. "Ah, who'd've thought a year ago that I'd be wandering around worlds—worlds!—meeting talking badgers, erls, tinkers and giants? And accepting it like it happened every day."

"There are no cawran on your world?" Garowd asked, using the old tongue word for his race.

"Oh, there are tall men. But not one of them could top the middle button on your shirt. We've stories about giants, though—thirty feet tall they're said to be and they could level whole villages with just one stomp." She grinned. "And they usually only had one eye, in the middle of their forehead!"

Garowd looked shocked.

"And no magic at all," Minda continued, "or at least none that I ever knew of, none that was indisputably *real*. I lived in a smallish town called Fernwillow in the northern corner of that part of Elheron called the Penwolds. My father owns an inn there and all that makes him content is squeezing every last copper that he can from its patrons. He's very small-minded and the people of Fernwillow are mostly the same—sparing friends like Janey and Ellen, and of course, my best friend of all, Rabbert. *He*'d love to be here right now.

"He always believed in magic and erls and all—or at least kept an open mind about them. Mind, when I told him that I'd actually met one and was going off world-hopping his belief ran a little thin. Still he used to lend me books that told all the old tales of magic and whatnot. I never knew what to believe, but he maintained that if the stories existed, then there had to be some foundation of truth for them to be based upon, no matter how small. I wonder if he'll ever know how right he was."

"Sounds like a most wise man," Markj'n remarked. "Do you think he likes wine?" He took a swig from the wineskin that lay by his knee and offered it to Minda. When she shook her head, he passed it across her to the giant. "Minds me of my old grandad," the tinker continued. "He always held that the old tales were true, that there was more to the world than what we could see just past the tips of our noses. I can remember—"

"Listen to him!" Garowd said, roaring with laughter. "As though the tinkers of Yenhanwittle were some backward people with nary a thought to the rest of Wayderness. As though your folk aren't directly descended from the travelling folk in the Tinkerdales of Lillowen, smack dab in the middle of Langlin! Tyrr's beard! Langlin—home of the Wyslings and the great halls of Wistlore, where there's more magic in one dale than in all the other worlds combined. Ah, Markj'n. How you do go on."

The tinker grinned and shrugged. "But there's none like the Lady in Langlin."

"Aye. You've the right of it there. There's none like the Lady on any world." Garowd took another swig of wine and returned the skin to the tinker. His eyes took on a faraway look. "Have you ever been north of Elenwood, either of you? Far north, into the mountains that rise higher into the sky than ever stone and earth had any right to? Ah, it's a sight to shake your soul. Nothing between you and the stars but one short step. There's many the night I've sat high on those peaks with a skin of good Elenwood wine and talked to those stars. There's nothing like *that*, either—on any world."

"Except for a swim," Minda said, standing up. "I'm off." Swinging her empty mug around a finger, she set off for the river once more.

"But, Minda!" Markj'n cried.

"Too much wine and wine talk for me this hour of the morn," she called back over her shoulder. "I'll see you in a bit."

Ignoring their entreaties to return and at least *try* the wine, she soon left them behind and arrived at the riverbank. She lolled in the cool water, the sun warming her face so that she stretched languidly in the shallows from sheer contentment.

She touched her pendant while she half dozed, at peace with the world. Only when she thought that the danger of becoming thoroughly waterlogged was directly at hand did she step back to the shore. Wringing out her hair, she waited for the sun to dry her skin before she got dressed again, but she still wasn't quite ready to return to Elenwood Hall. So it was that Grimbold found her sitting on a rock, chin cupped in her hands as she stared out across the river.

"Hello, Grimbold," she said as the badger settled down in the grass beside her stone.

Hello, yourself. He glanced at her wet hair, adding: *It was the river that brought you, it seems, but something else that keeps you here, I think. What is it, Talenyn?*

"I don't know. I was thinking—mostly. About my friend Rabbert and Fernwillow and Janey...."

It must be hard. Do you miss them a great deal?

Minda sighed. "When I even get a half moment free to think about them—yes, I do. This place and all these worlds... it's easy for you and Markj'n and Taneh and all to fit right into place. It's always been this way for you, worlds beside worlds, and wonders and marvels. But me, I don't have the same roots you do. Everything's new and different for me and I'm never all that sure of what I'm doing. I keep getting into arguments with people like Huorn and Camlin. And there's all these things happening to *me*. Not just Ildran and the dangers—but changes in *me*."

She turned to look at him and there was a sympathetic warmth in his deep eyes.

"I keep saying it, I know," she added, "but I don't even know who 'me' is anymore."

Such as the wenyeth? Grimbold asked.

"The ...?"

Wenyeth. Mind-speaking.

She nodded. "That and the ... Pansign. What *is* a Pansign, Grimbold? Why did it frighten Camlin so? How did I know how to make it?"

You have heard Taneh and I speak of the gods—the Bright Tuathan and the Daketh, the Dark Gods?

"Yes, but gods ..." She spread her hands in an exasperated

fashion. "What do gods have to do with anything? They're not going to pay attention to anything *I* do. They're not even *my* gods."

Perhaps not, Grimbold agreed. *And yet who did you meet in the silhonell, but an aspect of the Horned Lord himself?*

"And which is he, Bright or Dark?"

Neither. You see, Talenyn, there is a third group of gods, if such is even the correct term for them. The Many Worlds, which we call Wayderness, existed long before Tuathan and Daketh came. There are conflicting tales as to how they actually came to be. Some say that when Avenveres was destroyed the Many Worlds grew from her scattered bones. Others have it that Wayderness already was and that the destruction of the First Land merely cast those same bones upon those lands. Whichever theory you hold, most agree that before ever Tuathan or Daketh came to Wayderness, the Many Worlds were tended by other beings—a Lady and a Lord.

Anann is the Lady's name. She is the mother of the earth and the moon, called Arn by some, and she wears three aspects, that of maiden, mother and crone. Her mate is Cernunnos, the Horned Lord. He comes like a man with a stag's legs and antlers cresting his brow. He is the WerenArl—the lord of the weren, the Wild Folk. When Anann wears her mother aspect and the Cernunnos his stag's antlers and they come together, they are fertility and fruitfulness and the worlds know spring and soon swell with summer's bounty.

When Anann comes as a maiden, then the WerenArl is the goat-man Pan. As such he can be either the peaceful musician you met in the silhonell, or a wild-eyed being who wakes terror in the hearts of those who see him. And sometimes he is both.

The only folk who still give them reverence, at least by those names, are the weren. They are horned beings mostly, the Wild Folk. The muryan are numbered among them, for all that the lists in Wistlore place them among the erlkin. The weren were here long before the children of either the Tuathan or Daketh came to be. They take no sides in the struggle between Bright Gods and Dark. They are an amoral folk, lying outside the moral judgments that the Kindreds or the Daketh-born might apply to them. Sometimes they side with the Kindreds against the Dark, for they are the protectors of the worlds and will not allow them to be destroyed. But again, they cannot abide the endless order that the Kindreds would apply to each and every thing upon which they set their gaze.

Grimbold was quiet awhile and Minda tried to assimilate what she'd just been told. It was so much easier where she came from. There was just one god and he never had much to do with anybody, for all the preaching of his priests that it was otherwise.

"When Anann comes as a crone," she asked, "how does the . . . WerenArl appear?"

The Horned Lord's third aspect is that of a Grey Man. He is spoken of as a meddler, though other tales say he is a healer and a harper. He can take the shape of a raven or of other beasts and, together with Anann's crone-aspect, they create a balance between life and death.

"And so," Minda asked, trying to bring it all back to something tangible that applied to her, "the Pansign is what?"

It can be a ward sign, to keep ill thoughts at bay. When used offensively, it drives men and erls mad.

Minda stared down at her fingers. "I . . . I can do that?"

Grimbold shook his head. *That I do not know. And Camlin had no way of knowing if the power was in you or not when you shaped it, hence his fear.*

"But how *can* I know it? How come all of a sudden I can use mind-speech when I never could before?"

If it has to do with the Horned Lord, the Wysling said, *then I doubt any of us, from Taneh to the Lady, could explain. Little is known of the weren and less of the godlike figures that they revere. But if I were forced to hazard a guess, I would say it is the sword that works these changes in you. I spoke to you before of my fear. There is always a price, Talenyn. Using such a fey weapon could change you forever.*

"I don't know," Minda said. She touched her pendant through the material of her shirt. The changes had started in her before she ever found the sword. It started with the moor-man Jan Penalurick and his pendant. "I think I'd be changing even without the sword. It scares me, Grimbold. Sometimes I think I want the change, but at the same time it terrifies me." She shook her head. "I want to know who I am, Grimbold. *What* I am."

So do we all, the Wysling replied wearily. He glanced at the sun to judge the time. *The council will soon be in session.*

Minda nodded and collected her mug. Together they made their way back to the hall.

The council was held in a shaded glade, just north of Elenwood Hall. The oaks here wove their branches into a canopy above where dalin hung to light the dim glade. Aboveground roots formed chairs and supported the length of the table in the middle of the clearing. Minda knew everyone at the table from the night before. Seeing Taneh, whom she'd missed in the hall, she took an empty seat beside the Loremistress and plied her with whispered questions. How was she? And weren't these splendid clothes? And should she be up and about so soon? And wasn't Elenwood marvelous? And was she *sure* she felt well?

Taneh smiled. "I'm well enough now. But there was a moment in the void, before you keyed us through the gates. . . ."

"I couldn't have done it without your fixing an image of the henge in my mind."

"Perhaps," Taneh replied.

A chill rode up Minda's spine. "Don't say that," she said. "I'm still me."

The Loremistress laid a hand on her arm. "Of course you are. And yet something stirs in you, Minda Talenyn, else why are you here? Something fierce, yet fair."

Minda blinked at the solemn look in Taneh's eyes. She wanted to question her further, but Sian called the council to order and all too soon Minda was the center of attention. She studied the top of the table as she told them what had befallen her since first the dreams came, looking to Grimbold from time to time who obliged with clarifications where they were necessary. The erls were attentive and kept their questions to a minimum, but still the telling took them into the middle of the afternoon. When she was done, there was a long silence. Servitors from the hall brought tea and small cakes to see them through the long day. Not until they were gone did Sian break the silence.

"So," she said, directing her question at Grimbold, "you think Ildran is to blame for our sealed gates and Oseon's death?"

You think it impossible? the Wysling replied.

"Impossible? No. But somewhat unlikely. We are speaking of more than one henge, Ilan Grimbold. It isn't simply Cosrandra that is sealed. Allskeg, Peran, Southwell, Highfern—

all the gates of Gythelen are sealed. *All* of them. Our barden have a song or two of this Ildran and tell of his power—but such power? He is a muryan, not a god. Or has he become more?"

I fear he has become much more than ever he was. His hand is in this. What you have told us of Oseon's passing is too similar to what almost befell Talenyn and did befall Huorn's sister, Gwerynn. She was dream-slain and so was Oseon. So too might Talenyn have been if not for the intervention of this Penalurick. Have you tested the seal on Cosrandra?

"I have," Sian said slowly, "and it could have been spelled by Ildran, but the seal is strong—stronger than any muryan might spell it."

"And you feel that we must free the arluth Penalurick first?" Cothwas Holdmaster asked. "Why?"

I thought it plain. If our histories, scant as they are where they concern the weren, are correct, then Penalurick threw him down once. He knows Ildran. Perhaps only he, or so I fear, can defeat him again.

"Taryn Weldwen is at Goldinghall," Sian remarked. Her long slender finger rubbed at her temple reflectively.

How far?

"Two days riding," Dayan Harper offered.

Is there no swifter way?

Sian sighed. "A week past, we could have gated there swift as a thought. Now we must fare by slower ways. Still, I have steeds that can fare the distance in half the time. But that is the least of our worries. Ildran—if indeed it *is* him we're dealing with—will soon make his presence felt more strongly. I suspect that he, or his emissaries, will come to Gythelen. He slew Oseon for a purpose. Sealed our gates for a purpose. And if he seeks Talenyn, as you say, he will come. But why does he seek her?"

All gazes turned in Minda's direction and she felt uncomfortable under their scrutiny. She shifted in her root-chair, trying to think of something to say.

She wonders as much as any of us, Grimbold said.

"There is still the matter of the sword," Taneh added, speaking for the first time since the council had begun.

Minda glanced at her, worried. The Loremistress was still haggard and pale from her ordeal at Jasell Henge and in the void.

The sword and the Piper, Grimbold said.

Sian nodded slowly. "May I see the sword?"

At Grimbold's prompting, Minda had brought the sword along to the council. She drew it from its sheath now and laid it upon the tabletop, pushing it towards the Lady.

"'Ware its touch," Camlin said, remembering the erl who had tried to pick it up at Cosrandra Henge.

"It never hurt me," Markj'n remarked.

Sian regarded the blade with half-closed eyes, then made a pass over it with her hands. A crackle of blue flame rippled along the grey metal.

"This is a Tuathan blade," the Lady said, picking it up and turning it over in her hands with no ill effects. "It will never hurt a sure friend of its bearer. There are runes upon it, but I can't read them. They are in a tongue too old for my learning. The weapon is keyed to Talenyn's use, at least for the moment. I wonder who bore it in the elder days?"

She pushed it back to Minda. Taneh studied the runes, but shook her head as well.

"I have seen similar runes before," the Loremistress said. "In Wistlore we call them the god-tongue, yet we have none that can decipher them."

"A Tuathan blade," Cothwas murmured. The Holdmaster leaned forward, resting his chin on his hands as he studied the blade. "Then perhaps we are dealing with the Daketh, not Ildran."

Grimbold shook his head. *Not so. I know the taste of the Daketh's spells and it is not involved in this, at least not directly. The gods no longer walk Mid-wold. They have their own realms—and there is the Covenant.*

"It has been broken before," Merriwell Harper said, "if the sheaf upon sheaf of ballads and old tales that tell of its breaking are to be believed. Should a Dark God walk Mid-wold, then one of the Tuathan will rise against him. Always the Balance is held."

Aye, but remember, Grimbold replied, *that they are old tales. The gods need our reverence to exist. They will not break the Covenant and so risk the ending of the Many Worlds. For if Wayderness were to fall, who would there be to revere them?*

Sian shook her head. "Who knows what a god might want? But this we know: the weren *are* involved, for no matter where the muryan are placed in the lists of the Kindreds in Wistlore,

still they are the Horned Lord's children. And if we needed
further proof, we have this: Talenyn has met with the WerenArl
already."

"In a dream," Cothwas said.

"The silhonell," Merriwell corrected, "which is not quite
the same thing."

"Even so," Sian said, "do not belittle dreams. Dreams slew
my brother, and Ildran is the Dream-master."

Say, rather, a master of illusion, Grimbold said.

"It matters not what we call it," Sian said. "Oseon was slain
while he slept—supposedly safe in his own bed here in Elenwood. Still I concur with you, Grimbold, in that Taryn must
be summoned and the Penalurick must be freed. There was a
reason Ildran bound him in stone. It is my thought that Ildran
fears the moorlord. For that reason, if for no other, we must
free him."

"But the gates are sealed," Camlin protested. "How can we
free the moorman when we can't even reach him?"

Nods of agreement went round the table in response to the
Gatewarden's words. Minda was tired. The council had gone
on for hours and she was finding it hard to follow all the
arguments and counter-arguments. It all seemed very simple
to her: go to Taryn, have her show them the way to Weir,
rescue Jan, stop Ildran. What did it matter if muryan were
weren or not? Or if gods were involved or not?

"There's always these," she said, breaking the silence. "Jan
said they could take me to Weir." She drew the porthmeyn
pouch from the pocket of her jacket and spilled the stones out.
They fell with a clatter across the tabletop, drawing all eyes.

No! Grimbold said forcefully. *That would be folly indeed.
Not one of us here kens their use. With the gates sealed and
who knows what pressures bearing down upon Gythelen, we
dare not use them. The repercussions could prove disastrous.*

"Perhaps," Sian said. She touched a stone with her finger,
a measuring look in her eyes. "But Taryn would know their
use. So. Our talk has come full circle. Taryn must be summoned
before we can make any further plans. I will ride to Goldinghall,
with Talenyn to accompany me. With any luck, Taryn will
shed some light on these matters."

Rising, the Lady bowed to the council.

"I call an end to this council," she said, her voice suddenly
formal. "Is there any here who would gainsay me?"

Only Grimbold looked as though he wanted to disagree. But he sighed and nodded acquiescence.

"So be it," Sian said. "Tangle, would you have the steeds readied? Talenyn and I will ride within the hour."

A bustle and movement rose as the erls went about their business. Returning the porthmeyn to their pouch, Minda overheard Garowd and Markj'n as they left the glade.

"Thirsty work, all this listening," the giant was saying.

"My very thought," Markj'n replied.

Minda sheathed her sword and stood up. So it was beginning again, she thought, the rush and the tumbling and so little still really understood. But at least Taryn Weldwen was on *this* world. She looked up to find Sian standing close by her.

"I'm sorry to have brought all this trouble with me," Minda said to her. "It wasn't by choice."

"I know," Sian replied gently. "But don't take all the blame for it onto yourself. It began before you ever arrived. Our gates were already sealed and my brother already slain. This might seem to you to be a personal struggle, but it reveals itself, thread by tangled thread, to be so much more. It belongs to all of us now—whether we will it or not. All we can hope to do is put an end to it as quickly as we can and pray that there is no more damage."

She speaks the truth, Talenyn.

Minda looked to the badger and nodded glumly. "I suppose so," she said. Turning to Sian, she added: "Why didn't you just read me, like Camlin did at the henge?"

"Reading gives an essence; what we needed were details. We can take those from reading, but speech is easier and quicker. Mind to mind, the thoughts duck and play with each other, here one moment, there the next. Reading is best for an overview, and to judge the truth of a matter."

"Oh." Minda glanced at Grimbold and Taneh, then asked the Lady: "What about these weren? Nobody seems to like them very much."

Sian smiled, albeit sadly. "Most regard the weren with suspicion because they will not take sides in the struggle between the Bright Gods and the Dark. Is that not so, llan Grimbold?"

They are a chancy folk, the Wysling muttered.

"We know so little of them," Taneh added.

"What about Huorn?" Minda asked. "Is he something like the . . . Horned Lord?"

"Only in seeming," Sian replied. "But he *is* of the weren. The antlered folk such as he and the muryan are not always numbered amongst the weren because they often make a choice between Dark and Light. It's the *true* Wild Folk that make most of the Kindreds uneasy—unruly beings like hobogles or tabbykins."

Minda looked puzzled and Sian smiled.

"Sometimes you seem so hard and wise," the Lady said to her, "and then again sometimes you seem even younger than your seventeen years. I don't know what to make of you, Talenyn. Wisdom and innocence don't often abide in the same being."

The Lady's smile grew wider. In a moment a gaiety hung about her as though there were no cares in all the worlds, as though Ildran had never been. Minda grew glad of heart as she matched that smile, though she wasn't sure what there was to be happy about.

"Are you hungry?" Sian asked.

"A little."

"Well, we shall have a bite of food then, for we have a long ride before us and there'll be no time to break our fast upon the way. How are your hurts mending? Arenna told me you had a bad cut on your shoulder."

Minda hadn't even thought about her shoulder. She lifted a hand to touch it and there was no pain at all. When had she taken off the bandage? Last night before going to bed? Not this morning surely. And her cut knee, she realized, had long since healed without leaving a scar.

"I . . . I'm fine," she said slowly.

Grimbold and Taneh exchanged glances. Another mystery. But Sian paid neither them nor it any mind. Taking Minda by the arm, she led the way back to Elenwood Hall.

chapter four

Shadows grew long as they neared the hall, though once they were in the courtyard the swinging dalin dispelled them. Sian left the three of them with Markj'n and Garowd and went inside to fetch victuals. The companions made themselves comfortable on the grass, with the living walls of Colonog, the Lady's hall, at their back. The grass smelled sweet and they sat without speaking, sharing the moment of peace. Minda looked at their familiar faces...Grimbold, Taneh, Markj'n. Their presence gave her strength. Her gaze then met Garowd's serious countenance.

"I'd've liked to have come," the giant said. "There could be danger along that road, for all that you ride in the Lady's company."

Taneh nodded. "I've been in this almost since the beginning and would've liked to have seen it through to its end."

But that end will not come in Goldinghall, Grimbold remarked, *though by all that's holy, I wish it would. No, it is still not such a simple thing. Taryn is but one more step along this lengthy journey.* He shook his muzzle, plainly worried. *I, too, fear it for an ill thing that but the two of you ride south. Ildran no longer tries to hide his hand in this. He could well strike anytime, anywhere.*

"But could he fare swifter than these two might?"

They turned at Sian's voice to see Tangle Hallwife leading forth a pair of prancing steeds. The light of the dalin set highlights glinting on their golden hides. Brilliant white manes and tails streamed in the wind. They stepped lightly across the courtyard as Tangle led them, their hooves silent on the packed earth.

"Saenor and Mythagoran," the Lady named them. "Could even the wind outrun them? A star outshine them?"

"Broom and heather!" Markj'n said. "Those aren't horses— they're shape-changed erls, sure as I'm a tinker."

Minda stood up as the mounts were led closer, her mouth shaping an "O." "They're beautiful," she said. She touched the neck of the nearest one and stroked it shyly. The short hair was feather-soft to her touch. "Are you Saenor?" she asked.

The golden horse nudged her shoulder with his nose as though agreeing.

"Even so," the Lady said. "What now, llan Grimbold? Will they not bear us swift and sure?"

Swift indeed, was the badger's reply, *and as safe as they can. But still I fear. The Dream-master has been most noticeable of late by his absence. We met his work in a sealed gate, but have seen no other sign of him since Jasell Henge. I can taste his approach in the air, feel it in my bones. He is coming.*

"Then we must be away," Sian replied simply. "But first we will eat."

She gestured to a pair of erls that had followed her from the hall. They stepped forward to lay their food-laden platters on the grass before the company, then scampered away. Minda watched them go. They were both shorter than she but silver-haired. Were they young high erls? Then Sian seated herself gracefully and bade them eat their fill and Minda joined the company.

She cast admiring glances at the two horses while she ate. Saenor regarded her with reproach and she smiled. She reached for a piece of cheese to offer to him, then gasped as her pendant flared against her skin. At the same moment, the two horses reared, stamping their hooves when they landed and whinnying with displeasure. Sian bounded to her feet. With her head cast back as though listening, she stood. Her face darkened with anger.

"The gates!" she cried. "Ildran strikes!"

A few quick paces brought her to the side of Mythagoran. Smooth as a cat's spring, she was on the horse's back, heels touching its sides.

"Fly, friend! Run like the wind!"

And like the wind, they were off in a flurry of pounding hooves.

Minda ran to Saenor and, grabbing a handful of his mane, pulled herself onto his back. The horse reared as she unsheathed her sword. Blue fires erupted along its edges. From the direction of the henge, a slug-horn blew, answered by two, then three in the courtyard. Hastily armed erls issued from the hall and sped for the henge.

"Follow the Lady!" Minda cried to Saenor. The horse leapt forward at her command, hooves biting at the sod.

Minda had ridden before, but she wasn't a horsemistress. But the being that rode Saenor was not truly Minda anymore. Or if it was Minda, then it was also the spirit of the sword that burned blue in her fist.

Saenor pounded through the woods, skillfully avoiding the flood of erls that raced all about them. Far ahead the meadow could be seen, the henge looming grey in the growing twilight. A mounted figure neared the longstones, long golden hair streaming behind her like a banner.

Lights flickered and played between the standing stones. As Minda rode into the meadow, the sound of battle came to her ears. Dark shapes were in the henge, closing in on the erls that stood firm against them. But the attackers outnumbered the erls at least three to one and were driving them back. Then Sian was in amongst them—they were yargs, Minda saw— and magefire blossomed from the Lady's raised fists to char any that might dare lay a hand on her.

"Faster!" Minda cried. Saenor streaked for the henge with a renewed speed that took the last of her breath away.

Then she too was under the shadow of the longstones. Saenor sidestepped to avoid the first press of yargs that came at them. An axe rose out of the teeming mass and Minda batted

it away with the side of her sword with such force that it
shattered in the yarg's hand. She hardly felt the blow herself,
for the sword ruled her body once more.

She clung to Saenor's mane with one hand, her legs clamped
tightly about his girth, and cut away at the leering and howling
monstrosities that ringed her in. Her sword hummed as it cut
down first one yarg, then another.

She could feel the Dream-master in her mind now, and his
stench was in her nostrils, his mocking laughter in her ears.
Ildran grew stronger than the sword and she weakened under
his mental onslaught. His presence swelled in her, plucking at
her soul with tendrils of dark thought. She swayed in the saddle,
bones turned to water.

She rebelled, broke from his contact, with a strength born
of desperation. The sword moaned in her hand, its power filling
her. She let it take her completely, body and soul, and Ildran's
presence was gone. In his place, the sword sang its lust for
battle and the blood drummed through her veins.

The erls from the hall arrived, led by a roaring Garowd, his
father's axe whirring above his head. Markj'n was there, and
Grimbold as well. Saenor crashed through a press of the foe
before Minda and for a moment she was free of attack. She
turned to look at the kingstone, half blinded by the glare that
sprang from it. Something was forming above the kingstone.
The air crackled with power as a shadowy figure took solid
shape.

A Waster!

She heard the cry in her head but couldn't tell who had
voiced it. She stared numbly at the creature straddling the
kingstone. It stood a head taller than Garowd, but the pulsing
lights about it and the twisting mists that roiled through the
henge made it seem more immense still. Its skin was greyish
in hue, and its eyes were a burning ochre. Above its head it
held a staff that gave off darkness as a torch gives off light.

For the second time the sword's spirit was driven from her.
She saw the darkness gathered above the Waster's head. The
creature roared a deafening cry that stilled the wild din of the
battle. The darkness leapt from the staff to kill a half-dozen
erls and crack the kingstone under the monster. Arrows and
spears bounced from its hide, unable to penetrate. Again shadows erupted from the staff. Blades that were hacking at the

Waster exploded, their users charred in the sudden blackness that burned like a dark fire.

Then Sian was before the Waster. She raised her arms high and a golden storm of magefire awoke between her hands. Dwarfing her, the Waster eyed the fire and a huge grin split its heavy lips, revealing double rows of sharpened yellow teeth.

Join me!

Grimbold's voice blasted into Minda's mind with its intensity. But it was all she could do to stay on her horse as it stamped nervously under her, awaiting her guidance. The sword burned and crackled, fending off yargs, but its presence in her was gone. She saw only the Waster—its hollow gaze piercing hers, its power burning into her.

Talenyn! Grimbold cried. *Minda! The Lady has not the strength to face such a thing alone. Channel your power with mine—but control it!*

Power? Tearing her gaze from the Waster's, Minda clutched at Saenor's mane. A yarg's axe came whistling at her. She had no power. The sword almost tore her arm off as it lifted to meet the yarg's attack. Minda tried to open herself to the sword's power, to channel it as Grimbold had demanded it, but when it rose another power came at her call—a wild, uncontrollable surge of raw strength that sent her mind skittering in retreat before it.

Sian's magefire was like a star between her hands. The Waster was a darkness darker than the void between the worlds. Tears streamed down Minda's cheeks as she fought to keep the wild power inside her under control. Her pendant burned. There was a roaring in her ears. The raw wildness of what rose in her, surging and frothing like the sea, strained to break free. If she channelled this into Sian it would destroy the Lady as surely as the Waster's blast. And the horror was that it didn't come from the sword. It came from inside herself.

The moment was at hand. She could sense the sudden tension, the crackle in the air as Wysling spell matched high erl spell. The Waster's laughter thundered in the henge. Neither Wysling nor erl, alone or together, could match the darkness that gathered in the air above the Waster's head and the monster knew it. The shadow leapt from the staff to meet Sian's star of magefire and the world seemed to end.

Minda could see nothing, hear nothing. It was like being

in the void again, rushing helplessly into that black abyss from which there was no return. She knew Sian's pain, and the Waster's lust as it drove its power against the Lady. Meanwhile the power that could destroy friend as well as foe peaked and fought to break loose of her grip.

Talenyn! Grimbold pleaded desperately. *Help us!*

I can't! she wanted to cry, but the words choked in her throat. Precious seconds slipped away as she fought the wildness inside her. Darkness washed over Sian, leapt for her. The sense of the void thickened about her. The cold drove into her. Sian . . .

As she sensed the erl being swallowed by the dark, she loosed the power, channelling it like a darting bolt of lightning, not through Grimbold or Sian, but directly at the Waster.

It buckled under the onslaught, a howl of anguish tearing itself from the monster's lips, and its gnashing teeth bit into its own flesh. It buckled, swayed atop the cracked kingstone, but didn't fall. It was not enough. Power that would have destroyed either Sian or Grimbold merely staggered the Waster. It straightened, staff held on high once more, the darkness building. The power threatened to burn Minda herself now, but she dared not stop. Grimbold and Sian bent their wills to hers. Their strength filled her, staggering the Waster for a second time. Again it rose. The full weight of its merciless gaze fell on her. The darkness coiled towards her and not even her power could fend it off. The cold stabbed her so that she could not breathe.

She fell against Saenor's neck. She couldn't feel either the Wysling or the erl anymore. The sword's power was just a faint flicker before the Waster's might. And the wildness that come from deep inside her was failing.

A presence formed in the back of her mind. It seemed familiar, more so when it mouthed four simple words:

Strike with the sword!

Then it was gone, leaving an aftertaste of familiarity that there was no time to identify.

She kicked Saenor's flanks, edging him forward. As she approached, the Waster drew itself up to its full towering height. A great taloned paw swept the staff down to smash her. She fell from her mount's back, and as the creature bent down, she plunged the sword into its chest.

The staff never struck her. Ripple upon ripple of blue flames cut across the Waster's body, arcing to form a spinning circle the center of which was the blade held firm in her hand. The darkness fell back and warmth returned to her limbs.

She shuddered as she fought to drive more power through the blade. The others added their strength to hers. The pendant flared painfully against her skin and the sword burned in her fist. She fell against the cracked kingstone.

The Waster was gone.

Kneeling on hands and knees, still holding the sword, she shook her head slowly back and forth. Something sagged inside her—the wildness fading, the power withdrawing. The sword was dormant in her hand. She tried to understand what had happened. Twice the sword's spirit had been pushed from her. Where had the final power that burned the Waster come from?

Inside. From within herself.

Saenor nuzzled her side. She looked up, past the horse, to where the last of the yargs were being harried. Grimbold stood with his head bowed and Sian lay slumped against Mythagoran's neck, but her gaze met Minda's and she smiled weakly.

It is done, her voice whispered in Minda's mind. *But at such a cost.*

With the Waster defeated, the few yargs that remained died swiftly. The henge was littered with their corpses and with those of slain erls. So many dead . . .

Minda raised herself slowly and leaned against Saenor's side, staring with horror-stricken eyes at the carnage. Her gaze touched the kingstone.

Did we kill it? she asked.

Sian shook her head wearily. *Only a weapon such as the Waster itself bore could have slain it. Caryaln it is called, the shadow-death.*

Minda nodded, only half understanding still. Grimbold or Taneh had told her about it once.

But we have hurt it sorely, Sian said, *and it will not return soon. . . .* Her voice trailed off and she seemed to see her slain kin for the first time. Her eyes went hard and she pushed herself upright on her mount's back, a fist raised high.

"Ildran!" she cried aloud. "I curse you, Ildran! I curse you and will fight to see your dooming though the Daketh themselves ride at your side. I, Sian Gwynhart, swear this—on the grave of my brother Oseon and the dead of my people. Beware my wrath, Ildran!"

Minda stared at the transformed Lady of Elenwood Hall. Her lips were drawn back to bare her teeth and her face was dark with a cold anger. Garowd's words returned to her. "They crowd so much living into each moment." Sian looked as though all the hate that filled all the worlds ran through her veins at this moment.

A touch on Minda's arm startled her. She turned to find the giant himself standing at her side. The cloth of his tunic was hanging in tatters from him. Great welts and cuts marred his flesh.

"You did well, Minda Talenyn," he said gruffly, "and I thank you for your succor. Many more would've fallen had you not struck as you did."

A violent trembling shook Minda's frame as the last vestiges of the sword's influence left her. "Oh, Garowd," she cried. "So many have died."

The giant knelt by the stone and held her head against his big shoulder, gently smoothing her hair. "I know, lass, I know. But we live and we will see that Ildran is paid three times over for what he's done to us today. When Taryn comes we'll find a way to—"

He broke off in midsentence and they stared at each other. Minda could see the same thought take shape behind his eyes as formed in her own mind. There was a henge near Goldinghall. If Cosrandra had been attacked, what was to say that the other had not been attacked as well?

"Taryn," Minda said softly.

Sian was at their side; she had overheard their words, and shared their sudden fear. "I pray to Avenal that you are wrong, but we can delay not an instant. Weary as we are, we must ride now for Goldinghall."

Garowd lifted Minda to Saenor's back.

Grimbold? she called.

Sian has the right of it, the badger replied wearily. *There is not a moment to be wasted now.*

Minda searched the survivors for Markj'n, found the tinker helping a wounded erl to rise. Their gazes locked a moment— each comforted in knowing that the other had survived.

Sian touched her heels against Mythagoran's sides.

"Let us ride!" she cried. "Ride as never before!"

• • •

Saenor and Mythagoran bore their riders through the long night. League after league disappeared under their pounding hooves and except for the wind that whistled by their ears, that was the only sound they heard for the whole of their journey.

South and south they rode, through long rambling woods, across grass fields that stretched like seas, fording rivers to fare through still more forests, Minda clung shivering to Saenor's mane, trying to shake the aftereffects of the battle from her. For all their speed, the golden horses galloped with a gait so smooth that she found herself nodding off from time to time. She'd awaken with a start to clutch the mane all the harder, afraid she was going to fall off, only to doze again.

Two hours before the dawn, Sian drew up before a line of hills.

"The Stonecrop lies behind those hills," she said, "and beyond it Goldinghall and Peran Henge."

She seemed calmer now, though there was a hardness in her eyes. Sidling Mythagoran closer so that the two of them were knee to knee, the Lady touched Minda's arm. "There is still much about you that remains a mystery to me," she said, her eyes softening, "but know this. For your aid at the henge, you may always count on a welcome in Elenwood. I name you freycara ha kwessen—spirit-kin and friend. Now come, Talenyn. The last leg of our journey lies before us. Let us ride."

As one, they touched heels to their mounts and rode up the slope of the first hill.

chapter five

They forded the River Stonecrop where the Mylnwood meets the river in a cluster of oak, beech and hazel,
riding through the forest for another hour before drawing up
under the eaves of its outermost trees. Sian clutched mutely at
Mythagoran's mane as she stared down the long slope. Edging
Saenor closer, Minda looked for herself and stifled a small cry.

Below lay a wide valley, beyond it an endless roll of hills
that washed up against distant mountains. Closest to them was
Peran Henge, its stones broken and blackened as though scarred
by fire. There was only one power that Minda knew of that
could crack and burn henge stones like that. A Waster had
been here as well, leaving destruction in its wake. Beyond the
henge the remains of a great wooden hall were smoldering.
Smoke still hung low over its charred embers.

"Peran Henge and the Harperhall," Sian murmured in a
broken voice.

"That . . . that was Goldinghall?" Minda asked. She hadn't realized it was a Harperhall.

The Lady of Elenwood nodded. "Goldinghall was the Harperhall of all Gythelen, as Wistlore is in Langlin. It . . . oh, shall all of Gythelen fail?" For a moment the erl's sorrow was too much for her. Tears streaked her face and Minda gazed helplessly at her. Then Sian wiped the tears from her eyes with a rough motion of her sleeve. Her eyes hardened once more and cold anger cut across her sorrow.

"Shouldn't we—" Minda began.

"We should," the Lady said, not waiting for her companion to finish. "We must see if any survive, slim though the chance be. What defense had they against a Waster? They were mostly journeymen with rarely more than two or three Harpers in residence. Caught all unprepared by such a horror. But we must fare with caution. See? The enemy is still below."

Squinting, Minda could make out the small figures moving in amongst the fallen longstones and scrabbling through the ruins of the Harperhall. She hadn't needed her eyes, though, to know of the danger, for her pendant was hot against her skin, warning her. Sian made a quick motion with her hand and they withdrew into the wood.

"What do we do now?"

Sian shrugged, swinging down from Mythagoran's back. "We must wait until they are gone," she said wearily.

"But someone could still be alive down there. Taryn—or others."

"And shall we two storm an army? Shall we throw away *our* lives that we can use better for vengeance?"

Minda dismounted as well, stiff from the long ride. She stroked Saenor's brow thoughtfully before answering.

"We've got to do something," she said at last. "Down there is our only chance to free Jan and strike back at Ildran."

"Below lies death."

"But—"

She paused as she saw a sudden motion among the trees. A wolf appeared between two large oaks, loping soundlessly towards them. Sian stood back from Mythagoran, arms upraised to gather her magefire. The horses whickered nervously. But before Sian could attack, Minda stepped between the erl and wolf.

"No, Sian! It's Cabber, the wolf from Darkruin."

"That is no wolf," Sian replied.

The wolf paused a dozen paces away and inclined his head in greeting. *And yet I am what I am,* he said, his voice gruff and resonating in their minds.

"You!" Minda cried, recognizing the voice. "It was you!"

Now she knew who had called caution at Jasell Henge and later told her to strike the Waster with her sword in Cosrandra.

"You're like Grimbold," she added. "A mys-hudol."

Not so—though the difference means little at this point in time. The wolf sat on his haunches, lips pulled tight in a grin. *Cabber. I have wondered where you came by* that *name.*

Minda shrugged. "I had to call you something. Cabber just came to me and seemed to fit."

Fit it does, the wolf chuckled. *Better than you could know. I thank you for it.*

"There is nothing we know about you," Sian said. Her voice rang cold and sharp as a honed dagger. "Who are you and what do you want with us?"

You have named Talenyn your freycara; does your courtesy not extend to her friends?

"*Are* you her friend?"

The wolf met the Lady's gaze steadily. *Are you? No; bridle your temper, erl, and save it for those who are truly your foes. I came for a twofold reason: to see how the Little Wren wears her new strength after her ordeal with the Waster, and to bring you word. There are a few survivors that escaped and you will find them on the ridge beyond the wood that backs the ruin of the Harperhall. But you will need to go quickly if you would rescue them. Already a troop of yargs fares in that very direction.*

"Why are you helping us?" Sian asked, her distrust more than obvious.

"Sian," Minda began, tugging at the Lady's arm, but Cabber made it plain that he could answer for himself.

Why? He seemed to grow in stature before them, his voice matching the coldness in the erl's. *You must ask? Is my anger not plain?*

Minda staggered under the sudden onslaught of emotion that poured from the wolf. Her hand scrabbled for the hilt of her sword, but something, either the fact that her pendant made no warning, or a look in Cabber's eyes, stayed her hand. The sense of rage dwindled, then was gone. Minda stood still.

Taking a deep breath, she let her hand fall loosely at her side. She stole a glance at Sian, but the erl was still studying Cabber with a measuring look.

I must away, the wolf said as though nothing unusual had just taken place. He turned to go.

"Wait!" Minda cried.

Cabber paused, regarding her expectantly.

"A moment ago," she said, struggling to find the words, "you said something about coming to see how I wore my new strength. What did you mean by that? What do you know about me that I don't? Help me," she pleaded. "Please."

I am helping you. I, too, would see the green leaves grow on the High Tor once more, and know that the rowan bears its crown. But until you answer the riddle as to what you are, I can do no more.

"But I don't even know where to begin. What High Tor? What rowan? If you know, why can't you tell me?"

Cabber nodded his head sympathetically. *I know it is hard, Talenyn, but still you must try. Prevail as the Penalurick's name would have you do. Thus far you have done very well. Trust to yourself, look to yourself. Remain true to yourself and you will prevail.*

For a long moment the silence held between them. Almost Minda understood. The words High Tor and rowan nagged at her with a familiarity she couldn't connect to any memory.

Ildran is strong, the wolf added suddenly, *and grows stronger all the time. Fell and dark are his allies and he draws them from every realm. And strangest of all—dreams themselves hold our enemy. Ildran slays with dreams and harnesses those so slain to serve his cause. How can this be? It is a thing unheard of—yet it is. And it is because he can make illusion real, because he grows so strong, that the Shadowed flock to his banner.*

If you would do more, Talenyn, then do this: loose a call from your heart and gather the weren. It is your right.

At that Cabber turned and disappeared into the forest, as silently as he'd come. Minda stared at the place where he'd been sitting, her brow furrowed in thought.

"The weren..." she said softly.

"They are the Wild Folk," Sian told her, "the horned ones, the untamed."

Minda nodded, remembering.

"That one," Sian asked. "The wolf. He came with you from Dewethtyr?"

"Yes."

"Oh, I fear," Sian said. "I fear for all of us. 'Dreams themselves hold our enemy.'" The Lady thought of Oseon, her brother, and a shiver passed through her to think of him bound to serve the Dream-master's will. "This Cabber," she added. "What is his part in all of this? If he meant to aid us, why did he not speak plain?"

"You didn't understand either?" Minda asked.

The lady's shoulders slumped. "Almost I understand—but then my very ties to the Tuathan hold me back. This is a thing of the Middle Kingdom, of the Grey Ones, and they are not my people's gods. I find it hard to trust anything that has the touch of the weren about it."

Minda gave her a puzzled look. "After the council, when we were talking with Grimbold and Taneh, you made it sound like they were wrong to mistrust the weren. I almost thought that you were rebuking them. But now . . ."

"Sometimes," Sian said, "it is easier to speak than to do. You see they *are* a chancy folk." She sighed, put a hand on Minda's shoulder and stared into the distance. "The weren," she murmured. "And you must call them. It is your right, the wolf said. Where do you fit into this puzzle, Talenyn? Where in all of this does Cabber see you? And if he meant to tell us anything, why veil it in riddles?"

"He did tell us where we could find some survivors," Minda said.

She too was trying to unravel the riddles, but for her it was no new thing. It seemed all she ever did was worry at them without any luck. She didn't expect an answer now.

"Can we trust him?" Sian asked. "But then, what choice do we have? This much is plain: we will learn nothing biding here." So speaking, she mounted Mythagoran. "Again we must speed. Are you willing, Talenyn? Knowing that some few might live—shall we risk our lives to aid them? My doubt flees with a goal set before me, even by one of the wild folk. What of you?"

Minda took hold of Saenor's mane and pulled herself onto his back. "We ride," she said.

They touched heels to their mounts and the golden horses sped off once more, as tireless as though they hadn't galloped the whole of the night through.

They rode like a ghost wind, circling back through the Mylnwood, then across the low-backed hills that girded the fields around Goldinghall. As they rode, Minda wound her fingers in Saenor's mane and heard Cabber's words stinging in her mind. Over and over they went through her, like a battle march.

Gather the weren.

Images flooded her. She saw Jan's face, the small horns poking through his curls . . . Huorn and his mighty antlers . . . creatures more bull than man that walked on two limbs . . . others with the body of a stag and the upper torso of a man . . . skittering wee things with wiry limbs and ragged hair . . . tall gangly creatures all eyes and limbs . . . and all were horned.

See the green leaves grow.

A high crag lifted from moored hills . . . its heights wreathed in clouds while scrub, bush and tree burst into bloom at its foot . . . a hundred colors of green . . . bright against the grey stone of the tor . . . and atop . . . still figures . . . or were they henge stones?

The rowan bears its crown.

They *were* longstones . . . tall and straight . . . frozen in their long dance . . . forming a henge . . . by the kingstone a stunted rowan stood . . . its limbs drooping, branches lying broken by its roots . . . buds swelled along its branches and burst into leaf . . . the tree grew hale and wore a crown of red berries. . . .

Gather the weren.

The branches that lay on the ground took root . . . new shoots sprang forth, tined like a stag's antlers . . . weren and tor . . . henge and rowan . . . did she see her own face in amongst the branches?

Dreams themselves hold the enemy.

Darkness clouded the images . . . as black as the void between the worlds . . . as black as Ildran's presence in her . . . she rose and fell in the unknown darkness as though to the tide of an ocean of shadows . . . sinking . . . losing herself. . . .

Gather the weren.

The phrase drew her back out of the shadows, and the

moment was gone. She blinked to find that they had crested a hill. Sian spoke to her and the darkness fled completely.

Minda shook her head and looked to where the erl was pointing. Below them, a half-dozen men held a pack of yargs at bay. They guarded three slumped figures that lay between them and the face of a tall cliff behind them. In front of them lay a number of their own dead as well as the bodies of their slain foes. As Minda and Sian watched, the yargs massed for another attack.

The acorn pendant burned against Minda's skin. She laid her hand to her sword's hilt and drew the blue-edged blade, swung it above her head. Sian called forth her golden magefire until it crackled between her upraised hands. Voicing a wordless cry that rang between the hills, Minda kicked her heels against her horse's flanks. Saenor leapt forward and down, Mythagoran beside him.

Below, heads lifted at the cry and the sudden sound of hooves pounding on the hillside. The yargs turned from their intended prey to meet the oncoming pair with readied blades. Minda clung to Saenor's mane with one hand, willing the spirit of the sword to rise up and control her.

They were almost upon the enemy. Her sword burned blue, but the familiar sensation of its spirit ruling her body had yet to come. The yargs howled and danced, waving their weapons over their heads in anticipation. Minda bent all her will to freeing the sword's spirit.

The two golden mounts bore their riders in amongst the yargs and suddenly the sword possessed Minda with a force that still stunned her; but this time something twisted and broke deep inside her. She watched the sword rise humming in her fist to cut down the huge creatures all around her. It rang against axe and sword, cut through thick muscled bodies, her arms never tiring. Saenor turned and leapt under the sure pressure of her knees, bringing her to one foe after another. The sword bit into the faces of the howling yargs, spraying blood and shards of bone. The creatures broke and fled and she ran them down, slaying those that were spared from the bone-crushing hooves of her mount.

And then it was over. In less time than it took to count the yargs, the lot of them were slain.

"Is this Ildran's mettle?" Minda roared. The sword was lifted high in her hands and her voice sounded deep and strange to her ears. Sian turned, startled. "Is this his best?" Minda demanded. "This fodder?"

"Talenyn!" A stranger looked at Sian through Minda's eyes. *Sheath it!* the Lady cried.

I can't.

Her body was no longer hers to control. The other, the sword, the death-dealer owned it.

Sheath the blade! Sian commanded, her own voice deepening into spell-speech.

"Sheath it?" the being astride Saenor asked her. "And be weak once more—nothing but a maid?"

They faced each other across the bodies of the dead yargs, their mounts prancing with the stink of death in their nostrils, the resuced men staring at them.

Release her, Sian said. *By oak and moon and the staff of the father!*

The being roared, shaking the sword at her. Sian backed Mythagoran a step. She could see Minda still, her soul trapped behind the burning gaze of this other being. The blue flames licked and spat along the length of the blade.

"And be nothing?" the being demanded.

"Whatever you were," the Lady said, "you were not Minda Talenyn. The body you wear is hers. Release it."

"No! Too long have I been locked in cold metal."

Cold. The part that was still Minda shivered in some deep recess of herself. Ice knifed through her, numbing her. Strange thoughts, devoid of emotion, filled with sensations of great heights and vast distances, tumbled through her. She tried to sheath the sword, or simply fling it away from her, but her hand was not hers to control and the fingers were clenched on the hilt. She listened to Sian plead and argue with the being that possessed her, but it came as though from a great distance. She was so cold. And falling... growing smaller... dissolving.

Talenyn.

This voice, too, was distant—soft like the memory of a sigh. It seemed that she saw the face of a grave, ageless man with penetrating eyes boring into her own. She recognized the eyes.

Cabber? she asked in a small voice.

You are stronger than he, Talenyn. Sheath the blade. Send him back into its metal.

I can't. I've tried, and I just can't.

You can. You must. You will.

The words were quiet, but there was a power in them that could not be denied. She was no longer falling. The cold drew back. She rose up from the vastness that had swallowed her to wrestle with the sword for control. The hand that held the weapon trembled. The sword burned blue. Then slowly, one by one, the fingers opened and the weapon dropped from her hand.

Minda gasped, her heart pounding as bodily sensation poured back into her. She swayed on Saenor's back and would have fallen except that strong hands lifted her from the horse. She was drained. A violent trembling shook her slight form. There was a cool hand on her brow and dimly she could see Sian bent over her, a damp cloth in her hand that she was using to wipe Minda's forehead.

You *must control the blade, Talenyn,* she heard Cabber say, his voice faint. *Use it at your peril—for you will still need its strength more than once, I fear. But control it.*

Her vision swam and the voice was gone.

"Talenyn," she heard the Lady say.

There were faces behind Sian's shoulders—curious faces filled with wonder and concern, but mingled with that was a trace of fear. She closed her eyes to stop the spinning until she heard a plaintive voice calling.

"Jan? Is it Jan?"

Again she opened her eyes. A small girl knelt at Sian's side, her eyes oddly blank. The blind stare was fixed on Minda. The girl groped towards her, reaching out a trembling hand. The pendant woke on Minda's breast—only not in warning. It filled her with a bittersweet aching warmth.

"Jan . . . ?"

The girl had a cut above her sightless eyes and her face was filthy with dried blood and dirt, her hair matted and hanging to either side of her face in still tangles. Amidst the strands poked two small horns. The groping hand made contact with Minda's cheek. Something like a static spark licked between them before Sian could gently pull the hand back.

"Not Jan . . ." the muryan mumbled.

"No, Taryn," the Lady said. "She is another, but—"

"Not Jan!"

Taryn drew back, tears springing to her sightless eyes. A

man put his arm around the muryan's shoulder, murmuring comfort in her ear.

Minda's head started to spin again and she closed her eyes. Her pendant continued to pulse a warm pattern through her and she knew why Taryn had been mistaken. The pendant had been Jan's, it had called out to the muryan.

"Rest a moment," Sian said to Minda. "We'll move you in a bit. For now, be easy until I can see how sorely you were hurt."

The sword? she mind-spoke.

It's safe enough, Sian replied in kind. *I've sheathed it for you—and carefully enough, I'll tell you.*

It . . .

Hush, Talenyn.

Folds of darkness, comforting and cool, rose up in her mind to take her away. There was no terror in this darkness, only peace. For a moment she resisted, then she let herself slide into it and knew no more.

chapter six

Something tugged Minda away from the darkness that lay across her mind. For all that she struggled against it, seeking the peace of sleep, she felt it, heard it over and over again. It hovered at the edges of her mind like the eerie voices of the night winds in Darkruin, constant and demanding, until she could no longer deny it.

Opening her eyes, she looked into the dark skies of Gythelen, bespeckled with stars and with a waxing moon riding high. There was something she was trying to forget . . . or was it to remember?

Once she had had a sword with a soul of its own. When she used it to fight an enemy it possessed her and would return to its cold metal when the battle was done. . . . But surely that was a very long time ago? The memory seemed too old to be her own.

"Talenyn?"

She turned at the sound of her name. Her head was pillowed

with soft heather and grasses, freshly cut and sweet-smelling.
Sian sat beside her and Minda realized it was her voice that
had called her back. Beside the Lady was a thin man with a
bandage about his brow and his arm in a sling. His face was
deeply lined with age, his hair and beard grey.

"How are you?" Sian asked.

"A bit headachy. Have I been sleeping long?"

"The whole of the day."

Minda started to sit up and Sian gave her a hand. The rich
aroma of a herb and root stew reached her and she looked about
for its source. Sheltered under a stone overhang was a small
fire with a handful of men sitting around it.

"Where are we?"

"A league or so west of the Harperhall," Sian replied. "In
the Winding Hills. Are you hungry? Perhaps you should start
with some broth."

She took a bowl from the old man's hands and offered it
to her. Minda nodded. The broth was strong and full of flavor.
As she sipped at it, it seemed to warm a cold spot in her
stomach, a place where vivid recollections manifested themselves physically. The hands holding the bowl began to tremble.

"There . . . was a battle?" she asked.

Sian nodded. "Don't you remember?"

"Some. It seems like it happened a very long time ago. The
sword . . ."

Sian's eyes grew troubled. "Yes. The sword."

"It wouldn't let me go, would it?"

"No. But in the end, you let it fall."

"I remember." Minda shook her head. "But it doesn't seem
quite real. Did I hurt anyone?"

"Only yargs," Sian replied with a grim smile. Minda shivered and the Lady sighed. "Perhaps it's better that you don't
remember it too well. But beware of that sword, Talenyn. I
fear it now as much as ever Grimbold did. This is Gedwin
Masterharper," she added, introducing the man beside her.
"Dayan's father."

"Hello," Minda said.

She could see the Masterharper's resemblance to his son
and remembered his face as part of that half-dream, half-real
recollection of the battle. Gedwin gave her a smile.

"A-meir, Minda Talenyn," he said. "Well met. Your coming

was timely. My men and I owe you our lives."

Embarrassed, Minda looked down into her broth. In the bottom of the bowl she thought she saw an image, a blue-edged sword flashing. She shook her head and looked up.

"Why are we here?" she asked. "Are the yargs all gone? Why don't we return to Elenwood?"

"We are too weak to fare on by foot," Sian replied, "and Saenor and Mythagoran could scarcely bear the lot of us on their two backs. I sent them north to bring back folk with mounts for us all. As for the yargs, those we didn't kill are still milling about in the ruins of Goldinghall and the henge. A troop passed our hidey-hole an hour or so past, but it's been quiet since. We're safe enough for now, or at least as safe as we can be. I've dared a small fire for we all needed something hot in us. The horses will rouse Elenwood and help will come soon. But I fear it'll be another day or so before it does."

Minda said hesitantly, "The blind muryan—was she Taryn?" She remembered the muryan and her blind eyes, the touch on her cheek, but was the memory real?

Sian hesitated before she replied. "She was Taryn."

"Where is she?"

Sian motioned eastward with a sigh. "She is dead, Talenyn. Her wounds were great. We raised a cairn over her and the five journeymen of the Harperhall that fell."

"Dead?" Minda clutched the Lady's arm. "Tell me it's not true!"

"It is true."

Minda dropped her hand. Her face went ashen. "Then we're finished. Jan'll never be freed and Ildran's won."

"Not so!" Sian said fiercely. "Not while there is breath in us!"

"But—"

"We will fight the Dream-master and cast him down as surely as the Penalurick did before us—alone if we must. We defeated the Waster that he sent. So too will we defeat whatever else he sends against us. I will gather the wise from across Gythelen to our banner—erl Loremasters, warriors and Craftmasters. The cawran, Garowd's kin, will help us and Gedwin here has his harp-spells. We have power still! With Grimbold's and Taneh's wisdom and your power—"

"Sian," Minda said, "I don't even know what this power

is. It comes and goes at its own whim. And the sword I don't dare use again." She shuddered. "Grimbold was right. If Cabber hadn't helped me when he did . . ." Her voice trailed off as she remembered the wolf's words.

Use it at your peril—for you will need its strength more than once, I fear. But control it.

"*How* can I control it?" she asked aloud.

Remembering the being she'd confronted, Sian shook her head.

"Is it a Tuathan blade?" Gedwin asked.

"That's what Sian says."

"Whose? Do you know? Which of the Old Ones forged it? Who bore it ere it came into your hands?"

"I don't know," Minda said.

"With that knowledge I could help you," Gedwin told her. "The old legends tell of many enchanted weapons and the dangers that arise from their use. More importantly though, they tell how those dangers can be avoided."

"I found it in a museum on Dewethtyr. There were all sorts of weapons there. The sword drew me to it and it's helped me many times." She paused. "But I *can't* use it again. It takes over my body, pushing me back into a little corner where all I can do is watch. And this last time it wouldn't let me go."

"Yet in the end you defeated it," Sian said.

"Only with help."

"What did the wolf do?" Sian asked, remembering her own struggle with the sword's spirit.

Minda shook her head uncertainly. "He just told me that I was stronger than it."

"So it was *you* that defeated the spirit, not the wolf."

"I suppose. But if he hadn't come when he did I'm not sure I would have. Don't you see the danger, Sian?"

"Yes. But what will you do when Ildran comes? Will you use the sword against him, chancing the danger, or will you let him win?"

Minda set her empty bowl aside and met the Lady's gaze. "I don't know," she said softly. "I just don't know."

Sian smiled then, trying to reassure her. "Forgive me. I shouldn't press you. It's too soon to know the answers to questions only half realized. Would you like something stronger than that broth? There's still some stew left."

"No. Not yet. I've got to think a bit."

She looked down at her legs. Her trousers were tattered, shredded by the claws of the yargs, but the skin underneath was smooth and marked only by thin scars. It seemed a long time ago, that battle, but had only been a day ago, no more. How could the wounds have healed so quickly?

"Self-regenerating," Gedwin said, reading her thought. "Sian was washing your wounds and called me over. It was strange, indeed, to watch the cuts heal by themselves." He lifted the arm that was in a sling. "Do you have healing powers?"

"No. That is . . . I never . . ."

But she hardly heard him. The thin scars filled her with a dull fascination. What was she turning into?

She had a sudden urge to tear the pendant from around her neck. She lifted her hand, then stayed the impulse, staring instead at the hand itself. It was thinner than she remembered, harder looking, the knuckles sharp where before they'd just been little bumps. If she had a mirror, would she recognize the face looking back at her?

"I've got to think," she repeated, standing up.

Sian and the Masterharper rose with her. "Whatever happens," Sian said, "you are not evil. Remember that. Shadows have touched you, but you are not a part of them. There is a deeper mystery hidden within you that strives to waken. I can almost touch it. But whatever it is, it reads fair and unshadowed."

"There are many tales of possession," Gedwin added, "in the old ballads. Through them all, one thing stands out: remain true to yourself and you will prevail."

That was what Cabber had said, Minda thought. And Jan. Prevail like the wren . . . Talenyn.

"I will always help you, freycara," Sian said. "You have only to ask."

Freycara. Spirit-kin. Minda remembered the place where she'd first met Jan and where she'd seen the Piper. She wished she could reach it now, to gain herself a respite.

She glanced at the fire and saw that Gedwin's journeymen had doused its small flame—carefully, that it would not smoke—and were sleeping now. One man remained on guard. The camp was in a hollow, dug into the crest of a hill; the Winding Hills, Sian had named them. The sky was dark, the stars close and clear, the moon warm and friendly. A tall pointed crag fingered the sky to the north of the camp, towering over the hollow.

She turned back to Sian but couldn't find the words she wanted to say to the erl Lady. Sian nodded and touched Minda's cheek with a long slender hand, then, taking Gedwin by the arm, returned to the cold fire. Minda watched them go. She turned when they reached the sleeping journeymen and made her way to the base of the crag, settling down in the shadows there, out of sight of the camp. Looking out over the hills, she tried to call up the henge where she'd first met Jan. The sil-honell.

Could she only reach it when she slept? She pulled the pendant out from under her shirt, no longer wanting to throw it away. Its warmth comforted her. It hadn't been Jan's fault that Ildran had begun tormenting her. And this pendant was all that kept the Dream-master out of her mind.

How did her moorman feel, still locked in his stone prison, waiting for her? It was taking her so long to reach him and now, with Taryn dead, she might never succeed. Had he given up on her? Would he understand? She was bound to the muryan, though how or why she couldn't say. There was a bond between them.

Her pendant pulsed warmly and suddenly she was no longer sitting, watching the hills, but journeying across them. The coarse moor grass hardly bent under her feet. A sound came to her, like breathy reed-pipes, though it might only have been the wind. A sense of peace filled her, quieting her inner turmoil, and she knew that somewhere between one breath and another her spirit had slipped into the silhonell.

She paused to look back the way she'd come, to see only the endless sea of heathered hills. The sky above was still dark, but different constellations wheeled in its heights. It was hard to be afraid here. Hard even to remember the terrors of Ildran and yargs and Wasters and the sword.

Instead she called up Jan's features in her mind's eye . . . caught a glimpse of Janey sleeping in her bed above the bak-ery . . . Rabbert poring over a book in his kitchen, long legs stretched out on an ottoman made from a pile of fat art books . . . Huorn striding across a barren landscape like a de-sert. . . .

A raucous caw brought her back to her surroundings. She

turned to find a large raven perched on the twisty branches of a small thorn bush. The wind ruffled its feathers and again she caught a trace of a reed-pipe in the air. The raven fixed her with an unblinking stare.

The peace that fills you in this place lies within you as well.

She recognized the bird for what he was as his rough voice touched her mind.

Cabber?

Aye, Talenyn. The same.

What do you mean it's inside me as well?

The raven stretched a wing, ruffling the feathers, and cocked his eye to her. *That power in you, that fierce and wild power, was never meant for war. This is its true measure—and surely it is worth the struggle? Remember what you feel now, the next time the wildness rises in you, and perhaps you won't be so afraid of it.*

But it burns, Minda said.

And it heals as well.

Minda took a step towards him. *No more riddles,* she pleaded. *You know who I am. Tell me.*

Time you were returning, Talenyn. There is a need for you in the world where your body lies sleeping.

Before she could question him, the silhonell dissolved and she found herself in her own body, eyes blinking. The raven was perched on a rock beside her. When he saw she was awake, he lifted from the rock, his wings beating almost soundlessly in the still night air.

"Cabber?" she called softly.

Then she looked down and saw the long line of yargs marching below. Her hand flashed for the hilt of her sword before she remembered what had happened the last time she'd used it. Her hand closed on air. The sword still lay beside her bed in the camp. Just as well. Maybe she'd still have to use it again, but now was not the time. She could almost hear its sigh of regret from where it lay.

Slipping back towards the camp, she mind-spoke a warning to Sian so that by the time she arrived the Lady was already on guard. Together they watched the uneven line of yargs straggle by their hill and continue on into the moors.

You seem more at peace, Sian remarked as she turned from the view.

Minda nodded. *I went into the silhonell. It's peaceful there.*

I don't feel any less confused but the urgency is gone.

The endless riddling, the Lady said, *is perhaps more tiring than the perils themselves.*

They returned to the cold fire to ease the worries of Gedwin and his journeymen. Some of the stew was still warm and Minda helped herself to a bowl of it.

"I can't decide," Sian said while Minda was eating, "whether it would be safer to stay here tomorrow or if we should fare further west. We would have to travel slowly—both for you, Gedwin, and young Raeth Journeyman. The rest of us are not so sorely hurt."

Minda glanced at the sleeping men. There were only seven of them, all young, slender men, beardless, with hair no longer than the tops of their collars. Raeth was a dark-haired, serious boy no more than a year Minda's elder. He'd received a bad leg injury and could only hobble. She picked him out by the white bandaging on his leg. She didn't know the names of any of the others.

"Not west," Gedwin said emphatically.

Minda turned to regard the Masterharper.

"Why not?" Sian asked.

"Because there the weren hold sway and to fall into their hands would be almost as bad as being captured by Ildran's yargs."

Minda's ears pricked up but before she could say anything, Sian replied, "The weren mean no harm."

"Perhaps not to the erlkin, Lady, but they have no love for mankind. South of the Stonecrop it's a different matter from the north. In the south the Middle Kingdom still holds sway in the wild places. Mankind tore their holdings from the hills of the Wild Folk. They do not forget. They number few these days, true enough, but they do not forget."

"There *are* weren to the west?" Minda asked.

"There are," Sian replied thoughtfully.

"Then—"

Now is not the time to speak of it, the Lady mind-spoke.

Their gazes met and Minda knew that she too was remembering Cabber's words. They spoke of it no more, and Gedwin retired with the decision still to be made. Minda knew she wouldn't be able to sleep. Tired as she'd been, her day-long sleep and visit to the silhonell had filled her with a restless energy so she offered to stand watch. Finishing her stew, she climbed back to her vantage point by the crag, but stayed in sight of the camp.

From where she was, she could see Sian sitting straight-backed by the remains of the fire. She couldn't tell if the Lady was sleeping or not. *Did* erls sleep? She decided the Lady was meditating.

She turned to look over the hills and the porthmeyn pouch in her pocket dug into her side. Pulling them out, she looked at the small stones in the starlight. Without Taryn they were useless. Nothing more than a handful of grey rounded stones. A muryan gate, but without a muryan to show them how they were supposed to be used, they might as well be cabbages.

She put the stones, one by one, back into their pouch and slipped the pouch into her pocket. Again she turned to the hills, gleaming in the starlight. Were the weren that lived in them tall and barbaric like Huorn or more her own size, like the muryan?

The longer she looked westward, the more the hills drew her. Subtly, insistently, the pendant urged her to go to them. Hands clenched tightly into fists at her side, she held her breath, feeling the magic of those hills flow into her.

Almost she yielded. Then she turned on her heel and walked to the far side of the hollow, determined not to think about what lay west anymore. She was supposed to be on guard. The yarg patrols were east and south, with one band faring north to the Stonecrop. They were in for a rude surprise if they were still there when Dorren Fieldmistress rode south at the head of a troop of vengeful erls.

Kneeling in the rough grass, she pulled idly at a stem. Breaking it off, she chewed on one end, listening. It was quiet. She felt more alone here on this hilltop than she'd felt in Darkruin on her own. And it was hard to be doing nothing when there was so much to do. Here she stood guard over a half-dozen or so wounded harpers when she should have been away—to the west, perhaps, to try to gather these elusive weren, or north to Elenwood to make plans with Grimbold. There *had* to be another way to Weir.

Pulling the grass stem from her mouth, she stood up. As she was about to toss it away, a movement in the valley caught her eye. She leaned over the rocks and stared harder. Her pendant flared as she counted—one, two, a third there. Yargs. And something else that might have been men except they ran on all fours. Her heightened senses brought faint sounds to her ears, and her deepsight pierced the darkness.

Sian? she softly mind-spoke. *There's trouble.*

She turned long enough to see the Lady rise wordlessly to join her, then bent her attention to their enemies' stealthy approach. Sian brushed her arm as she kneeled beside her. Minda pointed out the shapes. The Lady looked and counted, then her gaze went past them and her finger stabbed the night air.

There! By those rowans. A Walker! Do you see him?

Minda's blood went chill. A Walker. The one from Darkruin, or another? It didn't matter. He'd be ready for her whichever he was.

There are too many of them and too few of us, Sian continued. *We must flee—and swiftly. Rouse the others while I keep watch.*

Minda hurried off to shake Gedwin and the journeymen awake. Finger to her lips, she woke them and told them to break camp. She went to her own bed, hesitated, then buckled on the sword before rejoining Sian.

They're warned and breaking camp, she said.

Good.

Where will we go? Minda asked. *Where can we go?*

Sian moved back from the hill's crest. Gedwin joined them and the Lady spoke aloud. "We go west."

"No," Gedwin said, shaking his head. "Not west. The weren..."

Sian faced him, anger flaring in her eyes.

Would you have us meet the enemy here? she demanded. *Or perhaps we should go to the ruin that was the Harperhall and give ourselves up to the main company?*

The Masterharper stepped back, stung by the force of her mind-speech.

There is a Walker below, Gedwin Masterharper, the Lady said, *with a score or more yargs and wode-woses. Will you stand and do battle with them or will you dare the hills? I am with you. What Wild One would dare lift a hand against the Lady of Elenwood Hall and those in her company?*

Gedwin's shoulders drooped and he nodded. "We will go west," he said, his misgivings still plain.

Sian looked from him to Minda. *Stealth and speed,* she said, *or at least as much speed as we can muster—those must be our defense. Do not draw your blade or raise your powers*

*while we flee and we may have a chance. The use of power
draws them, especially a Walker. You and I, because of what
we are, draw them as much as any power; but the pull will
not be as strong. And once in the hills, where our presences
can be confused with the weren, they could well lose us entirely.*

She glanced back at the camp and saw that the men had
packed what little they had in the way of possessions and stores
and had already left.

Shall we go too, Talenyn?

Minda nodded and fell into step beside the tall erl. She could
see the harpers ahead of them, moving through the heather.
Only two of them lagged: Gedwin who was both old and weakened from his wounds, and Raeth Journeyman who could fare
no quicker than a painful hobble. Reaching Raeth's side, Minda
slipped his arm over her shoulder and lent him her support. He
flashed her a grateful smile and they hurried on at the best pace
he could manage.

Glancing back, she saw Gedwin and Sian arguing about his
bringing along his harp. At length the Lady gave in and swung
the instrument onto her own shoulder, supporting the Masterharper with her free arm. The other harpers moved ahead,
deeper into the hills. Minda could tell by the set of their backs
that they were nervous, but obviously they preferred to dare
the possibility of meeting with the Wild Folk to the surety of
Gedwin's sharp words or the blades of the yargs that followed.
Or perhaps it was the fierce eyes of Lady Sian that kept them
moving on into the Winding Hills.

At any moment Minda expected to hear the cry raised up
behind them or to see a swift rush of leering yargs leap out of
the shadows on either side. It was hard to believe that they
might actually have lost them. Surely they'd attack in the next
few yards? But the next few yards passed safely enough and
then she was worrying about the next few and the long way
still to go. Raeth's weight began to drag on her and she wondered how long she could manage half carrying him as she
was. The journeyman's teeth were clamped tightly together to
bite back his pain.

This one can't go much further, she sent to Sian, *and I
don't think I can support him much longer.*

Gedwin fares poorly as well, came the Lady's returning
thoughts.

Should we make a stand?

She felt she had to ask. The very thought of drawing the sword again scared her more than the Walker and yargs combined. Already it seemed that she could hear it humming above her head, the hilt hard in her hand, the cold flames running the length of the blade.

Not yet, I think.

Minda concentrated on Sian's voice, using it to keep the potent lure of the sword at bay.

There's a menhir ahead on yonder hill, Sian continued. *Can you see it? We'll make for it and pray the Walker and his company pass us by. If they find us, the stone will lend us some strength. There is a feyness about such stones, a power that we may perhaps bind to our own purposes.*

Minda sent an affirmation back. The pull of the sword grew weaker. She glanced at her companion and tried to instill some confidence into him.

"That hill," she whispered softly, putting all the assurance she could muster into her voice. "When we reach the top of it, we'll rest."

Raeth nodded, his eyes narrowed with pain. But with a visible goal in sight, he was determined to reach it.

Minda thought she could hear their pursuit closing in on them. And when they reached the hill, what then? She didn't want to think about it, nor about the sword that slapped at her thigh as she tried to get Raeth to go a little more quickly. They reached the bottom of the hill and began the long struggle up its slope. The other journeymen had reached the crest and Gedwin and Sian soon topped it as well. Minda followed almost on their heels, dragging Raeth the last few steps. Reaching the top, she let the journeyman lie on the grass and dropped to her knees beside him, plainly spent.

Sian stood near Minda studying their trail. The journeymen huddled around the longstone, trembling with exhaustion and fear—though the fear was more for where they were than for what pursued them. Minda wondered at that.

"This was a mistake," Sian said aloud.

Minda rose wearily to her feet and stood beside the Lady. The dawn was streaking the sky and in its growing light they could see their pursuers closing in on them. The white robes of the Walker were plain to see now as they billowed in the wind. Minda swallowed hard, looking at him. Ranged before and behind him were at least two score yargs and the loping manlike beasts that Sian had called wode-woses. The horror of them was that they were so much like men, running on all fours with shortened hind legs and heavily muscled forelegs, manlike faces with wolf muzzles, deep-chested, with lean hind-quarters.

Minda turned and met Sian's gaze, reading defeat in the Lady's gold eyes. She started to say something, then the erl's defeated look was changed for one of anger. Sian flexed her fingers and tiny sparks of magefire flared between them.

"I was wrong," the Lady said bitterly. "I've exhausted us in this foolish run and now they have us. But it will cost them. Avenal hear me! It will cost them dearly!"

It can't end like this, Minda thought, then felt stupid for thinking it. Who said it couldn't?

The strident cries of the enemy rose in the thin morning air. Minda felt the touch of the Walker's mind like the slither of a wet tongue across her thoughts and shuddered. Her pendant was hot. Her hand reached to touch her sword's hilt and she felt her blood start to drum at the contact. A startled cry came from behind her.

She whirled to see the journeymen stumbling over each other in their haste to escape a hole that was opening in the earth under the longstone. Disbelief froze her. A figure appeared in the maw of a hole, amber light streaming from the space behind it.

The figure was a curious manlike being that seemed all legs and arms. Its torso was small and covered with a leather jerkin and trousers that hung just below its knees. Large owl-like eyes were prominent in its face, the cheeks hollowed, the ears pointed. Two small horns sprouted from its brow and dark stringy hair framed its thin-featured face. Minda took a step back, hand on the hilt of her sword. A word floated up in her mind. Weren.

"A hobogle," Sian breathed at her side.

The creature bent down on one knee before them. "A-meir, Lady," it said. "I, Jo'akim, heard your call and offer you sanctuary."

It—no, he—was speaking to her, not Sian. Minda regarded him blankly. "Ah . . ." she began, not knowing what to say.

"Into the hill," Sian said, nudging her. "The enemy is almost upon us."

The touch awoke Minda into action. The hobogle stood aside as they filed into the hill. For all that they feared the weren,

Gedwin and his journeymen were quick to move when the first yargs broke over the crest of the hill. Shafts of golden magefire burst from between Sian's hands and the enemy fell back in momentary dismay.

The rich smell of fresh-dug earth clung to Minda's nostrils as she made her way inside. Sian and the hobogle followed. The hobogle cried out a word in a strange language and the earth fell in on itself, sealing the hill with a rumble. They were safe inside, while the yargs pounded uselessly on the earth outside.

The hobogle grinned.

"They can pound for a thousand years," he said with a laugh, "ere this hill opens for the likes of them."

The huge owl-eyes turned to Minda.

"Why do you summon the Wild Folk, Lady?" he asked.

chapter seven

"Why did you call us?" the hobogle repeated.

She tried to collect her thoughts, but when she spoke it all came out in a jumble. "I didn't know I had, or that I could. The wolf—Cabber, that is—told me to, but I never really understood what he meant. I'm trying to help Jan, you see, because Ildran has him stone-bound, and Cabber told me to gather the weren—"

"Not so fast," Jo'akim broke in. "I can see this promises to be a long tale. Let us away to my hidey-hole so we don't have to shout over the pounding of yon yargs."

At that moment a violent trembling shook the hill. Something tugged at Minda's soul and she remembered the Walker in Darkruin pulling her out of her body. Dirt cascaded about the small company and Jo'akim looked up in alarm.

"Who is with the yargs?" he asked. "Who has the power to shake my hill?"

"A Walker," Sian replied simply.

215

A look passed between the erl and the hobogle that Minda couldn't read. She hoped that whatever differences lay between the two races wouldn't erupt into an argument. But Jo'akim nodded thoughtfully and looked away from the Lady.

"That is not good news," he said. "Such a creature could well break through. Come. We must hasten. Much as it pains me, I will have to close this hill as so many others have been closed."

Again a look passed between the hobogle and Sian. Minda remembered Gedwin saying something about having taken the hills from the weren. Had the erls been a part of that taking? She couldn't remember if that had come up.

"Do your ways lead north at all?" Sian asked.

"There's a north road," the hobogle said. "Why?"

"My Fieldmistress rides south to meet us. It would be better if we did not stray too far so that she may find us."

Jo'akim turned to Minda with a question in his eyes. She was uncomfortable when she realized he was waiting for her to—what? Give her permission? She nodded and the hobogle inclined his head to her, then motioned the others to precede him down the dimly lit tunnel. The light seemed to bleed out of the earth, a rich golden amber hue that lit the way without hurting the eyes.

The hobogle grinned approvingly when Minda stayed at his side. He waited until Sian had followed the last of the journeymen on down the tunnel before speaking again.

"It grieves me sore to close yet another hill—but what's to do? I am the last of my kin, Lady, south of the Stonecrop, you see. The men have harried us and kept us from all the old haunts as the erls did before them." He shook his head. "I should be bitter—Hoof and Horn, I *am* bitter—but I'm only one and lack the strength to carry out our ancient warring. Tell me this, though: are the erl and these men your friends? Do you travel with them willingly?"

"Sian is. She's the Lady of Elenwood Hall."

"The Lady of the erlkin herself, is she?"

Minda nodded. "The others are harpers, a Masterharper and his journeymen from Goldinghall. They're all that survived a yarg attack a few days ago."

"Harpers?" Jo'akim mused. "That's not so bad, then. They, at least, have remembered us in their ballads so that we don't fade entirely from Mid-wold."

Another violent shaking sent lumps of dirt falling about them. Minda could taste the Walker's rage at being balked by a mere hill. Her hand inched towards the hilt of her blade, stopping when she became aware of the movement. The hobogle noticed and shook his head as he eyed the sword.

"Now's not the time for such a weapon," he said. "But the hill must still be closed. Come, Lady. We should join the others."

"Why do you call me 'Lady'?"

Jo'akim regarded her with bewilderment. "But . . . you are to be revered. The power of the Grey Gods moves in you."

Now it was Minda's turn to be confused. "My name's Minda," she said. "Minda Talenyn. I'd rather you didn't call me 'Lady.'"

Jo'akim grinned wryly. "Little Wren? So be it. Come. We should go."

He led her into the tunnel. The hand grasping hers felt like old worn leather. The others were waiting at the far end, a distance of some two hundred yards. The journeymen eyed the hobogle fearfully and even Gedwin appeared nervous. Sian shrugged her shoulders helplessly.

"I've *tried* to tell them that you mean no harm," she said.

"How would you know, Lady of Elenwood, to whom I mean harm?"

Minda squeezed his hand in warning. "Please don't tease them."

"I don't tease men or erls," the hobogle said.

Minda joined the others at the far end of the tunnel. Jo'akim raised his arms above his head and spoke softly in the same strange language he'd used to seal the end of the tunnel earlier. It was as unlike Sennayeth as that elder tongue was unlike the common one Minda knew. Yet, when the hobogle spoke, there were words she almost thought she could understand.

In response to the weren's words came a rumbling from deep below. The ground of the tunnel shivered. In that earth sound it seemed there was language as well, words that echoed the hobogle's. He spoke again, as if replying to a question. Then a sudden thunder roared through the tunnel. A great wind whipped the tatters of Minda's trousers against her legs and spilled her hair into her face.

She heard Gedwin's men cry out fearfully, felt Sian stir uncomfortably at her side. Wide-eyed they watched the hill

collapse in front of Jo'akim. Dirt poured into the tunnel, coming
to a stop just before his feet.

"Mother, I thank you," they heard him murmur.

He turned to face the small company, his eyes dark and
strangely liquid.

"That will keep them from us," he said, "though the Walker
could still track us from overground. Shall we away?"

Minda nodded. Jo'akim smiled and approached her. Taking
her hand in his own again, he led her past the others.

Jo'akim's hidey-hole was deep underground. "In Underhill,
where the bones of the earth sleep," he told Minda. It was a
spacious chamber, shaped by rather than carved from the rock,
its walls veined with quartz and dark stone, the ceiling low
overhead. The same amber luminescence lit the room.

"Once the Stonecrop stored its heart-water here," the hobogle said, "creating the chamber and leaving it for my kin to
use when it was gone."

Sian looked up with interest and Minda thought of Colonog,
the heart-tree of Elenwood.

"But that was long and long ago," Jo'akim said. His owlish
gaze settled on Sian's face. "Once your hall belonged to my
kin, as well, and it was the Wild Folk that tended Elenwood
and the lands about it. Perhaps one day there will be erls living
here—or men."

He looked to where the harpers slept. Gedwin and his men
had managed to put their fears aside for long enough to appease
their grumbling stomachs with the hobogle's strange fare, a
mushroom stew served with a dark coarse bread that had a
nutty flavor to it. Afterwards they'd drifted off into sleep.

"The fey air wearies them," Jo'akim said with a sad smile.
"Ah, but I'll warrant their dreams'll provide ample fuel for a
ballad or two when all of this is done."

The three of them sat on flat stones with shaped backrests,
covered with dry moss. They sipped a drink that reminded
Minda of berry-flavored cider. She felt very much at home in
the hobogle's hidey-hole. Sian, though, sat stiff-backed, trying
for her companion's sake and for courtesy not to rise to the
hobogle's constant baiting.

At Jo'akim's insistence, Minda told her tale once again. He
listened attentively, head cocked to one side the while, refresh-
ing their mugs whenever they began to grow empty.

"Taryn dead?" he sighed when she was done. "I grieve to hear that. She was friendly to me, came to visit me Underhill once or twice. But then she was kin, of a sort, and didn't mind to spend a bit of time with a lonely hobogle."

"You're all alone?" Minda asked.

"Oh, yes. They've taken it all—the men and the erlkin."

Sian's eyes went hard, but the hobogle returned her gaze without flinching.

"Don't try to cow me, Lady of Elenwood. I've little love for you or any of your kind, and no fear. What more can you do to me? It's your folk that gave the manlings these hills so that they wouldn't settle north of the Stonecrop on land you'd already stolen from my people. These hills weren't yours to give. Had we been stronger—"

"Now isn't the time to renew old quarrels," Sian said. "All of Gythelen lies in peril now and with the gates sealed, we are helpless to send for aid."

"Perhaps," Jo'akim said. "And yet, does it not strike you as fitting in a way? Now you have perhaps an inkling of how we felt when, helplessly, we watched the manlings swell across our hills and us scarcely strong enough in numbers to do anything but hide."

"What would you have us do? It was land they wanted and they were many. Except for your kin, the hills were empty." She shook her head. "The old songs warned of their coming— told how we might stop them once, and once again, but never for all time. Their age has come to Gythelen while ours fades. Further south they swarm like ants across the land. And you could have come north. You were asked and would have been welcomed."

"What? Leave these hills to what charity you might spare us in a land *you* stole from us in the first place? Now where's the justice in—"

He broke off as Minda touched his arm. "Please. There's enough trouble without us adding to it."

Jo'akim sighed. "You can't know. But well enough. For your sake, we'll speak of it no more. I promised you my aid, and my aid you'll have. But it's only because it's you that's asked, Talenyn. You've the mark of the Grey Ones on you and I can't deny the calling you sent forth."

"Calling?"

"I felt you call me, here." Jo'akim touched his heart. "Long before you footed your way through my hills."

"What mark does she bear?" Sian asked.

"Penalurick's," Jo'akim replied. He stood to pace the chamber while he spoke. "Some say he's the oldest of the weren—some say he's a Grey One himself. I met him once and, though the years have rushed me by since that day, I'll not forget him."

He walked back to stand in front of Minda. A thin brown finger reached out to touch the acorn pendant lying on her shirt.

"There's his mark—not the shape of it, but the feèl of it. Old and hoary, sure as the bones of the earth. And he knew who it was he set his mark on. Doesn't matter what world you're from, Talenyn. The old blood's in you. And Penalurick . . ."

He moved away to pace again.

"If it's free the arluth you mean to do, then I'll go with you. Though all your talk of Ildran and enemies in dreams shivers me something fierce, still I'll come." He turned to lock gazes with Minda. "Ah, Minda Talenyn. We'll raise the weren—raise an army of them and cast Ildran down so far that his spirit'll never crawl back up into the light again."

The big owl eyes shone with fervor. His words sent a thrill running through Minda.

"But the gates," she said. "They're sealed. How can we reach Weir?"

"Weir? What need of that? We'll fare to Highwolding. That's where the arluth is—or so you've said. What need is there to fare to Weir?"

"But on Weir they know the way to Highwolding. No one I've talked to yet has ever *heard* of it before."

Except Cabber . . . and his talk of High Tor.

"Weir, Highwolding—they're both the same to us. One's as distant as the other. And we know about the same about both of them." Abruptly he stopped pacing again and sat down. Reaching out, he laid a brown hand on Minda's knee, his gaze searching hers seriously. "You'll find the way. You *know* the way, I'm certain of it. It's in there"—he tapped her head and grinned—"locked away. You've come this far with nothing but hope and luck to guide you and it was bravely done. Now we've but to finish the journey. The arluth knew what he was about when he named you Talenyn. Like the wren, you'll prevail. The very gods'll aid you."

Minda thought of Koevah. She remembered the image of

him in the church in Fernwillow—pot-bellied and round-cheeked, eyes wise but cold. Not a loving god. Not a helpful one.

She closed her eyes and images swam in her mind. She saw the Piper's face and the god of her homeworld faded before the bright fey wonder of him. His eyes were wise, too, but smiling and warm as a summer's day. He'd helped her once—opened her mind, her heart. Would he help her again? Behind him an antlered head took shape and then she saw yet another face, one she almost thought she knew. An old man with grey eyes. She shook her head and the images faded.

"We'll see," Jo'akim said when she opened her eyes to look at him. "We can only wait and see. Their hands have already touched you—see the sword and remember the silhonell. Even the wolf-raven Cabber could be their guide for you."

"He doesn't tell me *anything*," Minda said, "except for more riddles."

"And the sword was a coincidence," Sian said. "How could anyone know that Minda would come first to Dewethtyr, then find a sword that had lain there a thousand years or more? It's a Tuathan blade—and there is the Covenant. Neither Tuathan nor Daketh may walk Mid-wold."

Jo'akim grinned mockingly. "A Covenant they break whenever it suits them. But, high-born lady of the Tuathan's children, what of the Grey Ones—what of the gods of *my* people? Can you lay the rightful claim to them? What of the WerenArl and the Moon-mother? What Covenant binds them? They *are* Mid-wold. And if Ildran means harm to Mid-wold, do you truly think that they would stand idly by and do *nothing?*"

"No," Sian said after a long silence. "They would not. To see a Waster, yargs and wode-woses, a Walker stalking Gythelen. . . ." She shook her head. "They are evil, but they are not the Dark Gods themselves any more than my kin are the Tuathan." She met Jo'akim's gaze. "The Grey Ones would indeed make their presence felt."

Minda yawned just then and the grave look left Sian's face. "We've talked overlong for some," she said. "Rest is needed for the work that lies ahead of us still. We can begin to look for Dorren—my Fieldmistress, Jo'akim—sometime after tomorrow even. Can we go underground as far as the Stonecrop?"

The Hobogle nodded. "The north way leads a good way under the hills still, and there is a door near Mylnwood on the south bank of the river. We'll go there tomorrow afternoon."

"For this, I give thanks," Sian said formally.

Jo'akim inclined his head to her.

"I have heard," he replied in the same tone.

Long after Minda and the survivors of Goldinghall had fallen asleep, Sian and the hobogle sat quietly in the dim amber light, their old enmity lying between them like a physical barrier. The Lady thought of how she'd defended the weren to Grimbold and Taneh while the distrust lay thick in her own heart; and wondered if the Tuathan watched with approval or were angered as the lies passed her lips.

She sighed and Jo'akim glanced at her, his round eyes dark and unreadable.

"You accepted her very readily," Sian said.

"And you did not?"

"She came with those I trust."

Jo'akim shrugged. "If the Tuathan Avenal came to you, would you know her?"

"Surely. But are you saying that Talenyn is one of your Grey Gods in mortal guise?"

"No. Only that the *knowing* is the same."

Sian sat very still, thinking of that. Then she asked: "What is it that you want from her?"

The hobogle remained silent for so long that Sian thought he wouldn't answer. When he spoke at last, his voice was soft and held in it an old sadness.

"I sense in her the hope of my people," he said. "We are so few on most worlds—bound to the land, to our stones, to the very earth. In the long march of the years, this threat of Ildran can be seen as no more dire than the losing of our land. What Talenyn brings us is a hope, that the weren will prosper once more. Our numbers will never be great, but if she prevails in this trial, I see a time coming when we will have roots once more and neither Tuathan nor Daketh will steal them away again."

"We never meant you ill," Sian protested. "When we came to you with words, you met us with war."

"We saw beyond the words, Lady of Elenwood. You asked us for land and we knew that what we did not give, you would take. Was it not so?"

"It seemed we could never trust you."

"And that was a long time ago. But still"—the hobogle's gaze lifted to meet hers—"is it so different now?"

Sian shook her head.

"And Minda Talenyn," he asked, "when she raises her banner and the weren flock to it, what will you do? Will you stand with or against her?"

"We all stand against Ildran."

"But if Ildran is defeated?"

"I would never harm her," the Lady said. "I swore an oath; she is my kin now. Freycara."

Jo'akim nodded. "Word-kin. To me she is blood-kin. See that you remember your oath should such a choice ever arise."

"I will remember." Sian hesitated a moment, then reached out a hand, palm foremost. "Let there be peace between us, Jo'akim."

The hobogle regarded her steadily and she met his gaze without flinching. What he read in her never showed in his own dark eyes, but he laid his palm against hers.

"For now," he said. "Let there be peace."

chapter eight

They spent two days in Underhill.

For Minda the time passed all too quickly. For her these two days were like her briefest stays in the silhonell—a time to gather in the quiet and let its peace fill and strengthen her for what lay ahead. She spent much of her time talking with Jo'akim and Raeth, listening to their tales while telling them about her own life back in Fernwillow. It made her sad to talk of Rabbert and Janey and the good things she'd left behind, but she was happy to have the chance to share those memories.

Raeth was the only one of the survivors of Goldinghall to lose his fear of the hobogle. He delighted in listening to the other side of the old ballads he knew, where mortal was pitted against weren, so much so that he almost forgot the stabbing ache of his wound. Jo'akim—surprising even himself—took a liking to the young journeyman as well.

Sometimes Sian sat with them, but more often she tried to comfort Gedwin. His wound had begun to fester and she bemoaned the lack of healing salves. More than once she prayed that Dorren had had the foresight to bring a plentiful supply with her. The other journeymen kept to themselves, eyeing the hobogle and Minda (and Raeth for consorting with them) with an undiminishing wariness.

"They'll never be true harpers, not that lot," Jo'akim remarked. "They've no heart—and where's the harper without heart?" In the language of the weren, he told them, the two words derived from the same root word: truth.

"What about Raeth?" Minda wanted to know.

They'd both heard the young journeyman play on the Masterharper's instrument, airs that made Gedwin frown but transfixed Jo'akim and Minda with their simple fey beauty. Even Sian, whose erl musicians played with a magic that it was said could not be matched, stopped to listen when the young journeyman played.

The hobogle regarded Raeth now with such a long and steady gaze that the youth began to fidget. "He'll be a grand harper, in the old sense," Jo'akim said at last. "But he'll follow his own road, I think. The feyness of Underhill has touched him too deeply for him to ever go back to a Harperhall and learn to play only half truths."

"See?" Minda said, poking Raeth in the arm. "You're going to be the best there is. Jo'akim says so, and he should know."

Glancing at her, Jo'akim had to wonder once more. Though there was power in her, she seemed now to be no more than a young maid on holiday—teasing both Raeth and himself, laughing merrily.

"That's as may be," Raeth replied to Minda. "But I'm not sure if it's a blessing or a curse. Where will I go to study?"

"Find yourself a true harper and 'prentice yourself to him," Jo'akim said. "If he'll have you. There's still the odd one about here and there if you look hard enough. But you won't find them in a lord's court or a Harperhall. You must follow the roads, look in the hedgerows and small villages. Look where people have a heart and there you'll find one."

"You're too hard on Gedwin," Raeth said. "He's a good man and—"

"A fine harper. I've heard him play. But there's no magic

in his strings, Raeth, and it's magic you have—more in one finger joint than he's got in his whole body. Wouldn't surprise me if you have some of the old blood running through your veins."

"And if you don't find a harper on Gythelen," Minda said, "you could always go to another world." But then she remembered. The gates were sealed. They might none of them leave this world again. Sobered, she lost the moment's sparkle, and when the conversation went on, she was no longer a part of it.

Later that day Jo'akim asked Minda to come with him. He wouldn't say where they were going, only led her down deep and deeper into the earth. The tunnels were dark when they approached them, the amber luminescence awaking as they entered a new one, dying down behind them once they'd passed on.

"Where does the light come from?" Minda asked.

"From spells. They're simple to maintain and once set, require no further thought."

"Can all weren and erls do magic?"

Jo'akim shook his head. "No. Only those so trained. But they all have the potential to do so. It runs in the old blood, whether Grey, Bright or Dark."

For half an hour he led her through a confusing network of tunnels until they came at last to a small stone door that blocked the way before them. The hobogle spoke a word and a rune took shape in the air, soft and green, traced with gold. It dissolved into the door, which swung silently open. Jo'akim ushered her inside and they stood in a cavernous chamber.

The vaulted ceiling rose hundreds of feet above their head. The floor underfoot was smooth and warm. As the amber light chased the shadows away, shapes leaned out of the darkness and Minda gasped. Before her lay a fossilized forest, stone trees that stretched from one end of the cavern to the other. A soft sound like a wind was in the chamber and the boughs seemed to sway like a living forest, fragile stone leaves sparkling in the amber light.

"What is this place?" Minda asked in a hushed voice.

"This is my charge," Jo'akim replied. "Because of this I never followed my kin when they withdrew from these hills.

You must never speak of this to anyone, Talenyn—unless it be with your friend the Penalurick, or another of the weren."

A sense of old wonder stole over Minda, settling in her heart and making the war with Ildran and the sealed gates seem like a small and distant thing.

"What it is," the hobogle said, "is a fragment of Avenveres. There are pockets of the First Land on other worlds—some larger still, others no bigger than the spread of your hands— and the weren are their wardens."

Minda nodded, remembering that the muryan were called the shepherds of the longstones, the standing stones that were gates between the worlds.

"What does it do?" she asked.

Jo'akim smiled. "It does nothing, Talenyn. It simply is; isn't that enough? Think of it as a remembrance of what once was and what became of it. Or as a storehouse of ancient wisdom turned to stone—for in Avenveres even the trees had voices and some say that they were the wisest of all beings. I come here and walk under the stone boughs. Sometimes I dream that they speak to me."

"I've never seen anything like it. It's so beautiful."

"That it is."

Again she thought of the muryan and their stonework charges. "But," she asked, "couldn't this be used as a gate, too?"

The eagerness in her voice was plain but the hobogle shook his head. "No," he said. "It has no working purpose beyond its beauty."

He sounded terribly sad at that moment and Minda realized that she'd said the wrong thing. "I didn't mean to sound so . . . callous," she tried to explain. "It's just that I know that the gates are remnants of Avenveres and I thought . . . oh, please don't be angry with me."

"I'm not angry. Just . . . a little sad that the world has touched us in such a way that we can't look on such a thing and appreciate its wonder and its beauty without seeking some practical use for it."

Minda was crestfallen. She knew when he said "we," he meant her.

"I've disappointed you," she said.

"No. The turning of the world has."

When he turned to look at her she saw that his eyes were

glistening. "From time to time," he said softly, "I see in you a trace of how you were before Ildran laid his touch on you. I thought perhaps this place would ease that shadow somewhat. We were none of us born to be so grim, Talenyn, and you are so young to bear the burden that you do."

"Someone has to, I suppose."

Jo'akim nodded. "So it goes."

He turned to go, but Minda caught at his arm. "Please, couldn't we stay a little longer? Couldn't we walk under those trees for a bit and . . . and maybe dream?"

The owl eyes regarded her solemnly and a small smile touched the hobogle's lips. "We could."

He took her hand. They went forward and when, hours later, they returned to Underhill, there was such a serenity about them both that Sian regarded them curiously for the rest of the evening. But not a word of explanation was given by either of them.

On the following afternoon, Jo'akim took them along the north way, setting his pace to Gedwin's. As before, Sian supported the ailing Masterharper, while Minda lent her shoulder to Raeth; the other journeymen were not so sorely hurt and could manage on their own.

"If I could be guaranteed that you'd always be my staff," the young journeyman told her, "I'd not be so quick about seeing myself healed."

Minda blushed.

The sun was low in the afternoon sky when they stepped out of the hill. The Stonecrop glistened red in the sun's dying light and the Mylnwood was already in shadow. As the grassy door swung shut behind them, the clangor of battle rose over their conversation, and they looked at each other uneasily.

The sound came from downstream, its source hidden by a fold of the woods that marched almost to the river's brink. They made their way through the thickets cautiously. When they could finally see the source of the sound, a low cry escaped Minda's lips.

Dorren's troop had met a large patrol of yargs on the riverbank. Half her erls were still in the water of the ford, trying desperately to join their companions. The water frothed about them. On the shore, the remainder of the troop fought with the yargs. Though they were outnumbered two to one, the yargs stood their ground, fighting with a savageness that left more than one erl steed with an empty saddle.

Towering over both friend and foe, Garowd could be seen wielding his great axe. Grimbold was there as well, magefire blossoming from between his paws. Markj'n fought at his side.

Minda's fingers tightened on the hilt of her sword. The power of the sword's spirit strained to be let loose.

"No!" Jo'akim cried, forcing her hand from the hilt. "Now is not the time. We seem to have lost the Walker for now. Use that blade and you will surely draw him to us."

Minda nodded. With an effort she stuck her hands in the pockets of her jacket, fingers clenched into tight fists. She could still hear the hum of the sword, imagine its blue fire if she drew it forth.

But while she could do nothing, Sian was still free to act. She caught up a sword from the hand of one of the journeymen. With a terrible cry she stepped from the sheltering trees, the weapon raised high. The erls gave a great shout of triumph when they saw their Lady and returned to the struggle with a new will. The remainder of Dorren's troop rode up from the river and the battle came to an abrupt end as the last of the yargs died on the riverbank.

Minda and her companions hurried down the hill to join the victors. When they reached the bottom of the slope, Minda gave Raeth up to the care of an erl and rushed ahead of the others.

"Markj'n! Grimbold! Oh, it's good to see you!"

As she ran up, Markj'n thrust his paired tinker blades into the earth and swept her up in his arms, swinging her around.

"We'd near given you up," he said gruffly.

He set her gently down and she turned to greet the others.

"Ho, Minda!" Garowd boomed. He unslung a wineskin from his belt and offered it to her. "Is it late enough in the day for you?"

Grinning, she took the skin and had a sip before returning it to him. "I think so," she said. "Hello, Grimbold. Where's Taneh?"

She remains in Elenwood.

"Scribbling away for all she's worth an' then some," Markj'n offered. "I swear she's written out two books of notes since you left."

She sends her love, Grimbold said. *Ah, Talenyn. It does my heart good to see you safe and sound.*

Just then Jo'akim came up and Minda introduced him around. Grimbold nodded gravely to the weren, but his eyes were on Gedwin and his journeymen who were clustered together at the bottom of the slope.

These are all that survived the ruin of Goldinghall? the badger asked.

The grim reminder sent Minda's pleasure running from her. In all the excitement of seeing her friends again, she'd forgotten what had brought them south in the first place. Suddenly, she was acutely aware of the dead that lay strewn about them, erl and yarg, and a sour taste arose in her throat.

"Grimbold?"

They turned at Sian's call to see her beckoning to them. Subdued, Minda followed the others to where the Lady knelt by the corpse of a large yarg. The creature's reek assailed them but they all drew nearer as Sian pointed to the curious crystal that hung about its neck.

"What do you make of this?" the Lady asked.

Deep in the heart of the crystal, a red flame pulsed irregularly. The look of it set Minda's teeth on edge though she was hard put to explain why. The crimson flicker drew her gaze and she bent closer to look at it, her hands clenched as she leaned forward. The crystal filled her gaze and drew her into its bloody depths. A compulsion to wear it in place of Jan's pendant filled her. She knew she shouldn't, but the compulsion intensified the more she fought it.

"I sense an evil from it," Sian was saying.

The erl's voice was very distant.

Like a foul wind, Grimbold agreed. *It reminds me of something, though what—*

The need to touch the crystal exploded in Minda like a shock that stung her soul. She bent over the dead creature, fingers scrabbling at the jewel's fastenings. The others froze, watching her, but unable to move. Then Garowd's big hand was on her shoulder. He tugged her away and his axe was in motion.

As the big blade struck the crystal, a wailing cry knifed through Minda's mind. She bent her face to the ground, moaning in pain. Again Garowd struck. And again. Each blow shook Minda as though it struck her own body. She writhed in the grip of the crystal, her eyes rolling, her hands tearing at the ground. Then the crystal's grip faltered, loosened and was gone.

Minda opened her eyes to find her friends gathered about her, worry plain in their faces.

"Ballan!" Markj'n muttered.

Sian lifted her up from the ground. "Talenyn," she said. "Are you . . . ?"

"I couldn't stop myself," Minda said in a husky whisper. "It called out to me and . . . all of a sudden it was inside me."

"I heard it too," Garowd said. "But it will call no more."

Minda looked at the shattered remains of the crystal and shuddered.

"What was it?" Markj'n asked.

There was a long pause as each of them tried to understand just what it was that had happened.

"It was the enemy," Jo'akim said at last.

Yes, Grimbold said, nodding his head thoughtfully. *And now I know what it was—a holding-crystal. I remember reading of it in Wistlore. A spirit is encased within and it controls the bearer's body. I ought to have realized its purpose before it entrapped you, Talenyn.*

Understanding dawned on them.

"You mean it would've just taken me over?" Minda asked. Like the sword . . . like Ildran . . .

Grimbold nodded. *Its bearer was dead and it needed a new body. You are more . . . susceptible to such dangers than most. Without training, your spirit is too open and without the defenses it needs to combat such an attack.*

"Who controls the spirit?" Minda asked.

"Ildran?" Markj'n offered.

No, Grimbold said. *I would have recognized his touch.*

"*I* have never heard of such a thing," Sian said.

Grimbold turned to her. *They were created by the wizard Calthag, during the wars on Pelling, if I remember it rightly. He had a council of sorcerers who were slain in the third of the great wars that shook that world and their spirits he housed in holding-crystals. Through devious means he managed to overcome half the holdings on Pelling. Rather than slaying their rightful lords, he set these crystals—each holding the spirit of one of his slain council—about their necks so that their people would fight for him, thinking all the while that they obeyed their true lords.*

"Is Ildran leagued with this Calthag, do you think?" Markj'n asked.

No. Those wars were many longyears ago—before even my grandfather's father was born, Markj'n. In the end of that third war, a lord in south Pelling overthrew Calthag and so destroyed the crystals. And with Calthag's death, so too died the knowledge of how to construct them, or so it was always thought.

"But if it's not Ildran . . . ?" Minda began.

I cannot be sure. I do not feel Ildran's touch in this, yet who else could it be? Somehow he must have learned their secret. Yet what council of wizards does he command to fill these crystals, if it is indeed he?

Garowd was awkwardly brushing the dirt from Minda. She clutched at his big arm, trying to forget the feeling of the crystal being inside her. Then she remembered something else.

"Dreams themselves hold our enemy," she said softly.

Grimbold turned to her. *What did you say?*

Minda repeated her words, adding: "Cabber told us that, in the woods near Goldinghall."

Without further ado, she launched into a brief description of what had befallen Sian and herself since they'd arrived in the south. She glossed over the incident with the sword until Sian shot her a sharp look. Then, grudgingly, she told of it as well.

Bad tidings, the Wysling said when she was done. *I prayed with all my heart that I was wrong about the blade. But perhaps it is not so much evil, as merely too powerful. Where is Cabber now?*

Minda shrugged. "I don't know. He just comes and goes whenever he feels like it."

"You trust the wolf, Grimbold?" Sian asked.

I travelled with him. And though he hid his power well— and so too might hide an evil—still I trust him. His advice rings true, just as he himself rings true. But the oddity of that phrase: 'Dreams themselves hold our enemy' makes me wonder. We already know our enemy. Ildran. Master of illusion and called the Dream-master. Why would Cabber have felt the need to repeat what we already knew?

Minda looked from the broken crystal to Sian, then back. "Maybe he meant that those dream-slain or under his power are what's inside the crystals," she said.

She saw Sian's eyes grow bitter and knew the Lady was

thinking of her brother Oseon.

Grimbold sighed heavily. *Perhaps. But why would his victims help him?*

"Maybe they haven't got a choice," Minda said. "Maybe he's tricking them. Perhaps he has convinced them that we're their enemy."

Illusions. . . . The Wysling shook his head. *Events are moving too swiftly. We* must *break through the gates. If we could reach Wistlore, we might find an answer in its libraries. Jo'akim, do you know of a way?*

"Not I," the hobogle replied. "Ask Talenyn. The Grey Ones speak through her."

Grimbold regarded Jo'akim curiously, then turned to Minda. *Do you know a way?* he asked.

"No . . ." she began, then frowned. To her came a memory of Taneh bending over a map-laden table and the pendulum that moved in the Loremistress's hand. She'd asked if they could dowse a way to Weir and Taneh had replied that they couldn't without a map of all the worlds laid out before them.

What if they didn't need a map? All they needed to know was the shape of one henge on Highwolding. Couldn't she dowse the shape of the needed henge? Perhaps *that* was the secret of the porthmeyn—they were like a portable henge. With a pendulum and her mind attuned to Jan, couldn't she darynseek a henge-shape with the porthmeyn and use that henge to take them there?

"I think there is a way," she said slowly.

She spoke her thoughts aloud, her conviction firming as she laid her plan out before them.

No, Grimbold said flatly when she was done. *It is too dangerous. One miscalculation could spell disaster.*

"I agree," Sian said. "Here you at least have a chance. Ildran must come to you. Here you can confront the Dream-master without the danger of being lost in the void between the worlds."

"But it's Jan who's got to face Ildran," Minda said. "Not me. Without Jan we'll be slaughtered. Can't we at least *try?*"

But Talenyn, think of the danger.

Minda bit at her lip. She didn't *want* to think about it because then she'd be too frightened to try. She looked around the circle of faces—Sian frowning, Grimbold with his eyes dark and desperate, Markj'n still undecided. Only Garowd and Jo'akim nodded encouragingly, confident that she would choose wisely.

"Cabber said to follow my heart," she said at last, "and my heart says to try." She knelt on the ground, drawing the pouch of porthmeyn from her pocket.

"How far can you trust that wolf?" Sian asked.

Talenyn. Please reconsider.

She met Grimbold's gaze, then Sian's, and shook her head. "Markj'n," she said. "Do you have any thread?"

"Well, now . . ."

As the tinker dug about in his pocket, Minda searched out a suitable stone by the river. When she was satisfied with one, she returned and tied it to the thread that Markj'n had produced. Holding it above a patch of cleared ground, she closed her eyes, trying to clear her mind of all extraneous thoughts.

She focused on Jan, remembering the moorman's features and calling them up in her mind's eye, trying to find a sense of *place* about him. The pendant about her neck began to grow warmer and she smiled. It would help. Concentrating on that warmth, on Jan, she let the pendulum sway.

The others gathered close, watching as if spellbound. As the pendulum circled on one spot, Sian sighed and knelt beside Minda. She set a porthmeyn in the marked place. Minda lifted the pendulum for another try. With inheld breaths the company watched as stone after stone was set into place, some, when the pendulum refused to move on, capping two to form miniature triad dolmen to satisfy it. Then only the kingstone remained.

Minda gathered her inner strength and bent to the task. Her head ached with the effort. "Jan," she whispered, "help me."

She heard a faint breath of reed-pipe music, thought she saw for a moment against her closed lids the Piper, then the grey-haired man with Cabber's grin.

The pendulum settled into a spin in the midst of the tiny henge and Sian laid the last stone in place. Minda felt Garowd's hand on her shoulder and opened her eyes to see the stones laid out before her, each in its place.

"Well?" she asked Grimbold.

The badger studied the stones and shook his head. Each true gate had its own individual subtle difference. It was how the gates were keyed—by the shape of the henge, the star shapes in the sky above, the very feel of the air.

I am unfamiliar with this placement, he said at length. *Perhaps . . . ah, perhaps you are right. But if you are not, the danger—*

"Is all around us," Minda said firmly. Now that it was done, a rightness swelled inside her—pushing away doubt, easing the ache in her temples. When she spoke, her voice carried assurance. "It's going to work," she said.

"I've promised my aid," Jo'akim said then, "so I will come."

"And I," Garowd added immediately. "By my father's axe, I'll come and do what must be done. I'd not have you fare into danger without striving at your side myself."

Grimbold sighed. *I will see this through, though my heart misgives me.*

"An' you won't be rid of me either," Markj'n added. "Too much yarg-killing about here to suit me."

Sian looked at him sadly. "There will be even more killing where you fare now, Markj'n. I would come too, Minda, but I have my own kin to defend and care for. So many are slain."

"I understand," Minda said. "You have your own responsibilities, as I have mine. Will you say goodbye to Taneh for me?"

"That I will."

"Tell her I'll come back to see her, here or in Wistlore . . . if I can. And thank you, Sian."

I'll think of you often, she added in mind-speech.

Sian embraced her. *And I will think often of you, freycara. Go with strength—and return.*

Minda nodded as Sian stepped back. She took a deep breath and looked around. "Is everybody ready?" She met their steady gazes, glad of their company, but afraid. What if she was wrong?

She closed her eyes, keeping the shape of the miniature henge clear in her mind.

Jan . . . help us if you can.

The pendant pulsed softly. From far away a voice came to her mind. Cabber.

You do well, Talenyn, he said. *Hold me to you.*

As though his voice was the key that unlocked the hidden strengths inside her, she felt her power rise. Her thoughts reached out. They found Grimbold—uneasy but determined. The tinker—unconcerned and willing; Garowd and Jo'akim, boldly confident in her ability.

An amber glow sprang up about them. Minda felt Cabber's mind join hers—not to guide, but slipping into the web of thought that held the whole of the company together. The pendant filled her with the strength drawn up from deep inside her, from what Grimbold had named the taw, the inner well. Something like a door opened in her and her mind filled with knowledge of great importance, but she had to set it aside as she focused on . . . the henge . . . on Jan's presence that appeared to beckon to her like a distant star.

"Caeldh," she said softly.

The Secret Hill

chapter one

Darkness touched all Minda's senses as she keyed the gates. The opening word roared like thunder and the deep cold of the void stung her with such a force that the five beings under her care were almost torn from her grip. Quickly she bound them to her . . . badger and tinker . . . giant . . . wolf and hobogle . . . wove the net firm about them once more while she focused on the henge on Highwolding that, she prayed, was twin to the miniature henge she'd shaped with the porthmeyn on Gythelen.

In the silhonell a horned goat man lipped his reed-pipes; Minda heard the music and it healed her fears. Her own strength surprised and thrilled her. The power *could* be tapped, controlled. The memory of the Piper left her, but the faint music remained. The flare of gates flickered by but she passed them unheedingly, drawn by the power to one she needed. Would *it* be sealed?

Before the fear had time to take root, the gate was in front of her and she voiced the closing word, fiercely willing it to work.

"Tervyn."

Her voice sounded thin in the vastness of the void, but the gates drew them in on the echoes of the closing word. Spinning lights whirled about them, their dizzying motion almost breaking Minda's concentration. Then she felt solid earth underfoot and tumbled to the ground.

Just once, she thought, *I'd like to land in a slightly more dignified fashion.*

"Is everyone here—?" she began, opening her eyes. She froze in midsentence. The twilight lay heavy on Highwolding, as it had been drawing near on Gythelen, but its gloom did nothing to hide the vast array of figures that awaited them about the henge. There were yargs and wode-woses, strange squat beings that she'd never seen before that set her nerves on edge, men that were no longer men by the queer set of their features . . . and towering over them all, a Waster. It was the same one that they'd defeated in Cosrandra Henge—renewed, enraged. His gaze fixed unblinkingly on hers. His lips shaped a terrible grin, baring his teeth.

Her hand leapt for her sword and the sentient blade began to hum. She saw that many, many of the yargs had holding-crystals hanging from their thick necks. As her hand closed on the leather hilt of her sword, Jo'akim's fingers locked on her wrist, wrenching her from its hold.

"No!" he hissed as she fought him.

A flare of magefire erupted from Grimbold. Garowd's wordless battle cry could be heard as he lumbered to his feet, his great axe raised high. The hobogle's hand tightened its grip the more Minda struggled.

"Let me go!"

Jo'akim's free arm encircled her and he lifted her from her feet. She saw Markj'n struck down by a staff blow to sprawl across the kingstone. A full dozen yargs and those squat beings pulled Garowd to his knees. Jo'akim leapt into motion.

"Alive!" the Waster's voice roared above the din. "Take them alive!"

The hobogle made straight for the half circle of creatures that were bearing down on them from the left. For all her weight, he leapt effortlessly, straight over the heads of the howling creatures. Then he raced down the slope leading from the henge, making for the shelter of a far forest.

Minda beat at the hobogle with her free hand. She tried to find that power inside her, but the passage through the gates had weakened her. Behind she could see their foes and they numbered in the hundreds. Her friends were already down and a great wave of pursuers were hot on their trail. In their fore was the Waster, his long black staff raised high above his head.

Minda slumped in Jo'akim's arms, knowing that it was useless to struggle until her strength came back to her. The hobogle was simply too strong. She found herself hating him with a single-mindedness that surprised her. But she had reason to.

Because he'd stayed her hand, because he'd stolen her away, the others had fallen in the henge while they raced free into the night. She could have used the sword, used its power, but instead. . . . They were all dead.

The sword was awake, demanding. It slapped against her thigh, insistent, promising. *Free me,* it whispered, *and together we will slay them all—beginning with this creature that holds us captive.*

She strained again to draw it forth, but Jo'akim's grip didn't loosen for an instant and she was helpless.

The hobogle ran like the wind, his feet hardly touching the ground. The forest that had seemed so distant loomed suddenly before them, dark and shadowed with the settling of night in its heavy boughs. The sound of the pursuit grew steadily fainter, but gave Minda no cause for joy.

Free me, the sword said.

She could feel her strength returning to her, measure by tiny measure. Remembering how she'd tricked the Walker on Dew-ethtyr, she hoarded the power in secret. And still Jo'akim ran on; tireless.

Branches whipped against them, tree trunks rose up suddenly to be missed by a sidestep at the last possible instant. In utter silence the hobogle ran, not even breathing hard. The wood ended as suddenly as it had begun. Now they were racing uphill once more, thickets all about them until they too were gone and they crested a hill.

"There," Jo'akim muttered.

Minda's deepsight pierced the darkness to see a menhir on a distant hill. Behind she could hear the sound of their pursuit once more. Jo'akim had paused on the hilltop. Now he sped off again, racing for that tall lone standing stone just as the Waster broke out of the forest behind them.

"Ferral," Jo'akim named him, as though speaking to himself. "The Moor-render."

Minda gasped at their present speed. The hobogle fairly flew the remaining distance so that they neared that distant menhir quicker than any wind. In that last stretch, Minda gathered the last of the strength she needed.

We will teach him, the sword told her.

Grimbold... Markj'n... all dead...

He let our sword brothers fall while we fled, the sword whispered. *We could have saved them. The Waster fears us. We could have slain it.*

Garowd... even Cabber...?

Strike with your power, the sword commanded, *then draw me forth. Nothing will stand against our combined might.*

They had reached the hill and the menhir rose shadow-dark above them. Jo'akim, lulled by her passivity, set her down, then raised his arms to open the hill. Minda reached for the sword and its fire leapt through her mind, blue and cold. The movement caught Jo'akim's eye and he slapped her hand from the hilt, anger flashing in his eyes.

"Draw that blade and you doom us all," he said harshly.

Minda's hand twitched. The sentient sword fed her rage.

Kill him! it demanded.

Her fingers shaped the Pansign and a crackle of magefire leapt at the hobogle. His own fingers shaped a sign to twin hers and quicker than she could have believed was possible, the hand was raised to meet her attack. He staggered under the blow of her magefire, deflecting it from him, holding his defenses firm.

"Fool!" he cried. "Death is upon us, upon all the worlds, and you attack *me*? Ferral is your foe, Lady. And Ildran. But you have neither the wisdom nor the power yet to face them. The Penalurick must be freed. *His* is the strength."

He lies! the sword roared.

"You let them all die!" Minda cried.

"What use *our* dying or risking capture at the henge? Free, we've still the glimmer of a chance."

Free me! the sword commanded.

Minda shook her head and the magefire died. She couldn't

think, caught between the sword, Jo'akim and the pounding of
the Waster's tread that tolled like a death bell across the hills.

Free me and I will cut him down for you, the sword told
her. *Look at the creature. It could well be Ildran itself for all
you—*

Savagely, she pushed the voice from her head. She stared
at Jo'akim, pleading to understand, to be understood. Tears
streamed down her cheeks.

"They're all dead," she moaned. "I'm not strong enough to
go on by myself."

The ground shook as the Waster started up the hill.

"I can't..." Minda said. "Jo'akim..."

The hobogle roared out a word and the hill before them split
open. He pushed her inside, followed and spoke again. The
earthen opening closed behind them with a dull rumble. Unlike
Underhill on Gythelen, this tunnel was unlit, the air stale and
heavy with the smell of the earth. Minda's head spun in the
darkness. She was numb with sorrow. The sword muttered at
her side, pleading and cajoling now. From above them came
a pounding and the earth trembled. The Waster had come.

"There is a path before you," Jo'akim said, gripping her
arm and steering her towards it. A dull amber glow awoke,
pushing aside the shadows. "Follow it and it should take you
out into the moors once more." A sound exploded in her head.
"That is the word to open the hill. Find the arluth and free
him, Lady. I will hold this hill against Ferral for as long as I
can."

"No..."

She couldn't leave him behind as well. The anger still lay
between them—unexplained, unforgiven.

The hill shook with the Waster's fury. She was thrown
headlong to the ground, dirt cascading over her. She choked
on a mouthful as Jo'akim lifted her to her feet.

"You must go," he said. "There is no more time. Free the
arluth or everything will have been for nothing. Your own
trials, the deaths of so many, all will mean nothing if the worlds
fail. You are the hope of the weren, Lady. You *must* prevail."

Their gazes met in the dim amber glow. In his eyes, Minda
read understanding, hope, urgency.

"I'll go," she said, strengthened through the moment's sharing.

She fled down the dark tunnel. The ground shook again and

she stumbled, catching herself before she fell to flee on. The amber glow was soon left behind and darkness swallowed her. She could hear the Waster's roar of anger, though all the hill separated the monster from her, heard as well Jo'akim's answering jeer. And distant, distant, she thought she heard the winding of a horn, reminding her of Huorn, but it was gone so quickly that she couldn't be sure whether or not she'd heard anything.

On she ran, stumbling and brushing the walls of the tunnel with bruising force in her haste. Eventually she had to slow down to a walk when her breathing became too labored and a running pain stitched her side. The sword bouncing against her leg was silent now. All she had was the darkness and her sorrow for company. The tunnel wound on and on, endless. The darkness was thick and close and the press of the earth that surrounded her was a heavy weight.

At last she could go no further. She sank to the floor, leaning her head against the tunnel's dirt walls. Her deepsight was of no use in this utter black. The darkness oppressed her. Her strength fled in a wash of weariness and she wept. It was harder to face the emptiness inside than the dark that surrounded her.

Grimbold's striped features swam in her mind's eye. She saw Markj'n, smiling and chatty—he reminded her of Rabbert, she realized, which was probably why she'd liked him so much right off. And Garowd . . . less well known than the others, but they were still all so dear to her. And Jo'akim. . . . The ties that bound her to them were as strong as though she'd known them all her life.

She remembered a voice at the henge crying out to take them alive, but she knew her friends would have fought until they were slain. Grimbold or Sian had said that the Waster could only be killed with a special kind of weapon, but she couldn't remember what it was called. Something to do with shadows . . . like the darkness closing in all around her. None of them had a weapon like that, Jo'akim least of all. So she was alone again with a whole world to search looking for one stone-bound muryan.

And Cabber. What had happened to him? She knew he'd come to Highwolding with the rest of them, but she couldn't remember him being at the henge. Cabber with his shifting shapes and cryptic riddles. Wolf? Raven? Man? Where was *he* now?

Her tears had dried and she pushed herself away from the wall to stand up. Her sorrow seemed to have stepped beyond tears. With a queer sense of fatality riding in the forefront of her thoughts, she trudged wearily on down the tunnel. She touched her sword but it did not respond to the contact. Her pendant was warm, but more from her own body heat than through any magic it held.

Gather the weren, Cabber had told her. Well, she'd gathered one and by now he was dead. She certainly wasn't going to gather any more—even if they still existed on this world of yargs and Wasters. It had all come to an end, she realized. She couldn't understand why Ildran had even bothered with her. What threat could she possibly be? If it hadn't been for the help of her friends she'd have botched everything a long time ago.

The helplessness swelled in her until she couldn't stand it anymore. She stopped and looked up, calling the word Jo'akim had given her up to the roof of the tunnel. With a dull earthy rumbling, the hill opened and she scrambled up and out into the light of early dawn.

Blinking in the pale light like a mole, she surveyed her surroundings, her eyes needing time to adjust to the comparative brightness. She had no idea where she was or how to go about looking for Jan. Far behind her she could make out a great mountain range and remembered a brief glimpse of it when she'd first arrived at the henge. The sun was rising on her right, a bloody ball of flame against the dull grey smudge of the hills.

She sat down where she stood, half hidden in the tall gorse and heather, and tried to think. As the sun rose higher, the bleak grey of the surrounding vegetation was accentuated by its light, deepening her depression. The dullness of the sight weighed heavily on her. Even the blooms of the heather had lost their color. The land was a wash of grey for as far as she could see. Here and there a darker outcrop of stone or the odd greyish-brown thorn thicket stood out to relieve the monotony, but they were so grim in their own right that they did nothing to lighten her mood. She plucked a heather stem, staring at it idly.

Pausing, she looked at it with a sudden intentness, then stood and stared about herself again.

Seek my kin on Weir, she remembered the moorman saying,

as clearly as if he stood beside her. *Tell them I am in the Grey Hills . . . on Highwolding. . . .*

Hope blossomed in her. The Grey Hills. These had to be them. His stone prison was somewhere on these bleak moors, in these leagues upon leagues of grey hills.

She pulled the pendant from under her shirt, held it, savoring its warmth. It was all it had ever been. Only her own depression had cut her off from its influence. She turned in a slow full circle, concentrating as she had when she'd dowsed the henge with the porthmeyn. Northward . . . was the pull stronger? She repeated the circle. Yes.

Resolutely, she set out in that direction. Her weariness fled as excitement grew in her. Her stomach rumbled, but she pushed the thought of food away, concentrating instead on the pendant and what she could learn from it. She walked slowly, constantly checking for variance. Twice in that morning she had to correct her route, changing direction slightly, always following the pendant's faint tug. Near noon she came upon a small stream, trickling from a cluster of rocks. There she quenched her thirst and rested awhile before pressing on.

Thoughts rose unbidden as she walked, but she kept them at bay by allowing herself to think of nothing but the pendant. The constant watchfulness made her head ache. Towards evening, she was stumbling along at a snail's pace, numbly setting one foot in front of the other. Her gaze remained locked on the ground directly before her. The dull grey of her surroundings became nothing more than a blur. As the twilight darkened about her, her path took her up the side of a hill. Doggedly, she clambered up its slope. Though it was a gentle slope, to her befuddled senses and aching body it felt more like a cliff. As she topped it, the pendant flared in her hand and she raised her eyes slowly. A tall menhir stood brooding and ominous before her, rising darkly into the night. She stumbled towards it, not needing the pendant to tell her that this was Jan's prison. She felt no joy at reaching her goal, only weariness. Above, the night's first stars twinkled. She leaned her cheek against the rough stone and slid down to sit at its base.

"Jan," she murmured. "I've come."

Everything she'd held at bay through the long wearying walk went tumbling through her mind. Her friends dead; the Waster sure to find her soon; she did not know how to free

Jan. . . . Her eyes closed and she fought to stay awake. There was no time to sleep. But her exhaustion betrayed her and she slumped against the stone, lost in sleep's embrace.

chapter two

Minda was dreaming and her dreams led her through many strange realms until she slipped into the silhonell to find her spirit awake and aware, her mind alert, while still her body slept on. She was on a hilltop like the one in Highwolding, beside a menhir like the one that Jan was imprisoned in, but her thoughts were far from the arluth and his predicament.

Instead she watched the hills undulating with a crisp clarity into the far distances. She felt she could see beyond the mountains, could see into forever. Her sorrow and her weariness were wrapped into a tiny bundle and hidden away deep inside her, not by her own doing, but by some property of the spirit realm itself. The calm of the silhonell washed over her, and its peace stilled the warring inside.

The sound of reed-pipes came to her ears—low and breathy, soft like the whisper of wind through rushes. Floating above, within, beneath that sound were the ringing notes of a harp.

She turned slowly to search the shadows by the longstone from where the harp sounds came and saw the harper.

He knelt in the darkness, a grey shape in the grey hills. His fingers moved like water across his instrument's silvery strings, now plucking single notes, now chords, now rich harmonies, complementing the air of the reed-pipes that swelled and shivered until Minda felt she could bear their beauty no more.

She took a hesitant step towards him. The harper lifted his head and the moon, coming out from behind a cloud, lit his face with its silvery glow. A wolf's features flickered across his, a raven's dark eyes burned under bushy brows, then he was a man again—grey-cloaked like the longstone. Two small white horns pushed out from his forehead.

"Cabber," she said softly, standing perfectly still.

"So you have named me."

The music of the reed-pipes faded, became only the wind once more. The wolf-now-a-man took his hands from his harp and a stillness fell over the hilltop. Minda regarded him steadily, wonder touching her. Her deepsight made the most of the pale illumination thrown down by moon and stars.

He was slender and well shaped in his grey trousers and shirt, the darker shadow of his grey cloak spilling back over his shoulders in a waterfall of folds. His features were more striking than handsome, his eyes grey and clear, his hair a thick tangle of dusky locks. A wide-brimmed hat lay on the grass by his knee.

"The time has come for riddles to be unravelled," he said, "for questions to be answered. Ask, Talenyn, and I will answer."

Minda stood uncertainly in front of him, then slowly sank to her knees in the coarse moor grass. "Who are you?"

"My name is Cablin. I have been named Meanan by those who thought I was the Tuathan's Twilight Brother. I have been named Healer and Mender-of-Souls and the Grey Harper. The WerenArl's son I am, for I sprang from the loins of hill and moon. A hundred names I ken and my newest is Cabber. But Cablin my mother named me and, in the end when all names are done, when all shapes return to this I wear now, Cablin I remain."

"You're the Horned Lord's third aspect."

"No. He was my father and Arn was my mother."

Minda sighed. "What do you want with me?"

Silence lay between them as the harper weighed her words. "Peace," he murmured at last. "Peace and a return to the old ways."

"But what—"

"—has that to do with you? I will tell you now; but I must begin at the beginning."

Again he was quiet. He touched his harp and a fey note whispered forth, drifted across the hilltop, was gone.

"Imagine," he said, "the muryan Ildran—having tasted power in Weir, having ruled as its lord—imagine him being cast down by the true arluth of the moorlings, Jan Penalurick. Imagine him fleeing the arluth's rage, from one world to another, fleeing blindly and without hope, without a thought except to save himself.

"Who can tell where he fled, what he delved into in that flight, what better forgotten roads he wandered? But having tasted power once, power he must have again. And the holding-crystals gave that to him.

"You know of the Tuathan and the Daketh, how they may not walk Mid-wold because of the ancient Covenant. Yet their influences are still felt . . . light and dark, fair and foul, order and chaos. If one were to call to them long enough, that call would be answered. Ildran called—darkly, for what else did he know by then?—and one of the Daketh answered, lending him the knowledge he needed, showed him the way to shape the holding-crystals and so bind those dream-slain to his will, gave him command over the dark armies that feed on despair.

"You have seen them: the dalkwer, the Waster, the yargs. There was no breaking of the Covenant here, for no Daketh trod Mid-wold. Yet what need was there when they had one to feed chaos for them? That one is Ildran Dream-master, whose weapons are illusion and fear.

"To Highwolding Ildran came with his allies—the children of the Daketh and the spirits of those dream-slain that were bound to serve his will. Those dead innocents he housed in holding-crystals to heighten the powers and strengths of those who wear them. They came to Taplin Hill, this host, to where the High Tor reaches its henge moon-high, where dwelt the Wessener, the Gatekeepers."

"But Jan said . . ." Minda began.

An eyebrow lifted above a grey eye. "What did the arluth tell you?"

"He said that the muryan were the shepherds of the stones, that the gates were *their* charge."

"Did *he* tell you that, or did you hear it from Loremistress Taneh, or the Wysling Grimbold?"

When it was put like that, Minda was no longer so sure.

"They are not weren, those two," Cablin said, "and so they approach the Mysteries from a differing perspective than the wild folk hold. But they are partly right.

"The Wessener are the high born of the muryan. They are the blessed of Wayderness, the wonder of all the worlds. They keep whole the fragile Balance that binds Wayderness, one world to another. From the time when Avenveres still stood, they kept the gates awake, hallowed the longstones, the moors, the hills, the twilight and the moon."

"There were other worlds before Avenveres was destroyed?" Minda asked.

"There were," Cablin said. "But Avenveres was the first."

His hooded gaze looked beyond her, remembering. Again he touched his harp, and again the strings rang softly, echoed, faded.

"Ildran stole the knowledge of the secret entrances to Taplin Hill from the sleeping minds of the Wessener—for he is an illusionist, and a master of dreams. He brought his dark host and stole in upon the Wessener who numbered few in those days—less than three hundred all told. Against the physical strength of Ildran's army, and with surprise on the Dream-master's side, the Wessener were butchered before they could raise their defenses."

"But if the Wessener were so powerful . . . ?" Minda asked.

"He had the power of those dream-slain at his command," Cablin said, "Against that added strength—that *innocent* strength—the Wessener could not prevail. They were slain— they were *all* slain—save one and she was the youngest of the House of Taplin.

"Heavy with child, she fled in secret, using all the cunning wisdom of her kind, and escaped. In the confusion, in that terrible blood-letting and destruction, she was not missed, for it was all that Ildran could do to hold High Tor; and her fleeing left only the faintest of ripplings, a rippling that Ildran did not discover until years had passed.

"But then he pursued her."

Cablin sighed. His eyes were heavy with sorrow and he stared out across the moors once more as though watching the tale he told unfold across the grey hills.

"As Ildran had fled through the worlds to escape the Penalurick's wrath before, so did the last of the Wessener flee. But with the power of dreams at his command, with the power of those dream-slain to strengthen him, Ildran followed the cold trail.

"His quarry hid the traces of her passage well, making herself known to few on any world, and then to none. In time she came to a world where there was no magic and there she hid. She wrapped herself in a mortal's flesh and married the crudest of men, knowing that Ildran would never look for her in such company. By now she had given birth to her child and all that grew in her was a terrible need, a need to right the wrong; but she died before ever she could bring it to life.

"Years later, not knowing that she was dead, Ildran followed. He dream-slew those who had aided her along the way, adding their strengths to his growing store. And when at last he learned the truth, that the one he hunted was dead but had left behind a child ignorant of its heritage, his mirth knew no bounds. He vowed to make the child pay, but not all at once. It must be done slowly and savored. And so he sent out dreams to bind and mock the last of the Wessener and returned to his old game of dream-slaying the most innocent of the wise and harnessing their spirits to strengthen his armies.

"And he hid his deeds well, Talenyn, for he still knew fear. If all the wise on all the worlds were to rise they could cast him down. But this must never happen. The worlds must not rise for that is the way of Chaos, of the Daketh. And in that warring the gods would join, seeing their children set one against the other on such a scale. The Covenant would be broken and Wayderness, the Many Worlds, would go the way of Avenveres and be no more.

"No. Ildran must be broken on this world, by those now gathered to do him battle. And in the end a Wessener must sit once more on the rowan throne atop Taplin Hill. Not erl, nor Wysling, nor mortal. No. It must be a Wessener, and there is only one left in all the worlds."

His gaze weighed heavily on Minda and, following his tale, she could see what was coming, who it was that he spoke of.

No. Fear blossomed in her heart. Despair misted her eyes.

"You're wrong," she said. But she knew the words for a lie as she spoke them.

"No, Talenyn. That Wessener who fled—her name was Morwenna and her daughter she named—"

"No!" Minda cried. "It's not true!"

"It is true," Cablin replied, his voice ringing. "Is it such an evil thing to be the hope of the weren? To be a Wessener, hallowed even as the Grey Ones are?"

"You don't understand. It can't be me. Ildran's got nothing to fear from me."

"He should know such fear," Cablin said, "that the earth should tremble under his feet and the stars quake in the sky! He is cunning, Talenyn, but he lacks wisdom. Twice he has erred. He should have slain the both of you, the Penalurick and yourself, immediately.

"For see. Few on the Many Worlds know of Highwolding and the Gatekeepers, but the muryan of Weir are among that number. The Penalurick sensed a wrongness in the gates and came to Highwolding to investigate, to learn why they were profaned. He came alone, for was he not the arluth of the muryan? But no sooner did he set foot on Highwolding than Ildran trapped him, binding him in stone. So swiftly did the Dream-master strike that the arluth never knew what struck him.

"It was then that he let his thoughts range far and wide, seeking his kin for aid, seeking for anyone who might help him. He found you.

"I do not think he recognized you for what you were—your mortalness lay too heavily upon you. But still he saw beyond the trappings of a maid once-born and understood that you were more than what you seemed to be. He needed aid and, seeing that you required the same, he struck his bargain with you. His protection forestalled Ildran from taking you, but more, the pendant began to wake the dormant power that lay hidden inside you. When you set out to find the Penalurick, Ildran sent his minions after you. But you were growing in power and won through, time and again, against impossible odds.

"Ildran fears you, Talenyn, and well he should. You will be his downfall."

Her heart drumming, Minda shook her head. Her fingers plucked at the heather, shredding it nervously. She could hear

Ildran's mocking voice coming at her in the void as she spun towards the abyss.

You were the last of them. With you the line dies.

Panic thundered through her. She had to get up, get away from this madman with horned brow and his lies.

Cablin woke music from his instrument and the harp notes stilled the rush of her blood through her veins, the thunder of her heart, the wild panic. The music brought calm seeping through her spirit like a healing balm. She stared at the Grey Harper, the wonder returning as the calmness spread. Now she knew why he was called the Healer and the Mender of Souls.

And she knew that everything he'd told her was the truth. The realization spread through her on the echoes of the fey harping, lay still and silent inside her as the music faded, and could not be denied.

"But... alone..." she began.

Cablin shook his head. "Not alone. As you called Jo'akim to you, so have you called the weren forth. The power spoke from its hidden reaches within you, for all that your lips were still. An army of Wild Ones from many worlds has risen against Ildran's forces. Even now they do battle on the plains below Taplin Hill."

"Why did you never tell me? Why did so many have to suffer? So many died! Grimbold, Markj'n, Garowd, Jo'akim, and all those dream-slain. *Why*, Cablin?"

The Grey Harper sighed. His voice was sympathetic when he replied. "Not all are dead. Jo'akim drew the Waster away from you and has since joined the weren army. Some of your friends are Ildran's captives. But many have died, it is true."

"You could have come to me in Fernwillow," Minda said.

Cablin shook his head. "I did not know you until you keyed the gates and dared the void."

"But then?"

"How could I have told you sooner?" he asked. "All your life you've dwelt amongst the mernan—the once-born. Think how the sudden rising of your power would have destroyed you. As it is there have been times when it nearly killed you."

"It's no different now."

"Not so. Now you have had time to learn of it, to adjust to it a little. Now you are ready to face Ildran with a clear mind and the full might of your power at your command."

"But I'm *not* clear of mind! I feel like I'm... I'm crazy or something. Ever since the dreams first came..." Her gaze lifted to his, her eyes wild. "I can't do it. Why don't you fight Ildran? You know all the answers. You have power."

"I am a Healer," Cablin said, "not a Destroyer."

"Well, I'm not a Destroyer either."

But what of the Walker, and the battles with the yargs? an inner voice asked.

That was the sword, not me, she told that voice.

"When you were a wolf," she said aloud, "you fought at our side."

"As a wolf, I have a wolf's fierceness, a wolf's strength."

"Then be a wolf again."

Cablin shook his head. "A wolf could never stand up to the Dream-master and hope to prevail. In this, my true shape, I have power—but it is the power to make things whole; to heal, not slay."

"But you stand against Ildran," Minda said.

"I stand against Ildran because, should he triumph, Chaos will reign. War will walk across Wayderness and many will die. He would fall in that warring, but the cost would be too dear. Let the wise on all the worlds learn of his threat and they will rise to slay him. Then will the gods walk Mid-wold again and nothing will survive."

"But—"

"And I tell you this as well—should one of the Tuathan's children arise to set some bright order upon the worlds, I would stand against that one as well.

"But it is you, Talenyn, who are the last of the Wessener— the heir to the rowan throne on High Tor, and it is you who must cast Ildran down and set right the Balance once more. No other. Or the dark times will come to all of Wayderness as once they came to Avenveres. The arluth gave you a name, and you accepted it. Now you must earn it."

She could not deny the truth of what he said—it was the ability to follow through that she lacked. Power she might have, but it was not a simple matter like Taneh's setting a pen to paper.

"Your heart," Cablin said softly, touching his strings once more. "Your heart will show you the way. As it brought you here, so will it see you through your last trial."

"You don't understand, Cablin. I can't control it."

"I understand too well." The harp strings rang bittersweet.

"All too well. Do you think that I take joy in sending you into battle? Do you see me as some gamesplayer, carelessly moving the playing pieces across the board?"

Something Grimbold had said returned to her.

A Grey Man . . . spoken of as a meddler . . .

But meeting his gaze, she saw no joy in his dark grey eyes. Only pain. His harping ached with it.

"Return to your sleeping body," he said softly. "We will wake the arluth, you and I, together."

The silhonell blurred as he spoke, its sharp edges losing their clarity, the inner lights greying. Then she was awake in her own body, Highwolding's night skies dark above her, the Twilight's Brother standing over her, smiling a sad smile. The music was gone; there was no sign of his harp. His broad-brimmed hat was on his head now. Reaching down a hand, he drew her to her feet.

"What you said. . . ." she began in a small voice.

Already the words spoken in the silhonell seemed to be no more than words spoken in a dream—vaguely remembered, but left behind with sleep.

"Yes," he replied, nodding his head solemnly. "It was all true, Talenyn."

Minda lifted a hand to her forehead, feeling along her hairline.

"Not all weren have horns," Cablin said. "Just as some powers lie hidden."

Taking her hand once more, he faced the menhir and spoke a soft word into the night air—a word that shimmered amber and pale as it hung before them. Knowledge passed from the Grey Man to Minda. She spoke and her own word formed beside his. Hers was green and gold. The two runes merged with a crackle of power, then glided forward to flow into the tall longstone. The menhir flared at the touch of their spelling and a slender form tumbled from the stone to lie breathless before them on the heather.

"So slow his thoughts," Cablin said. "Like stone."

He knelt down beside the still form. Cupping the horned head in his hands, he breathed on Jan's face—a face that was as still and grey as the stone that had been his prison. The harper's breath left his mouth like a gold cloud, bathing the muryan's features with its radiance.

Minda knelt to take one of the muryan's hands between her

own. She could feel the stone thoughts plodding through him, felt them grow misty and begin to dissipate under the Grey Harper's healing. The deep gold eyes she remembered from her first meeting opened suddenly, startling her with their intensity. They saw straight through to her heart, reading all that had befallen her, all that she had become. A darkening sadness discolored the gold.

"You . . . ?" he whispered in a weak voice.

He tried to rise, but fell back. Cablin helped him to sit up, propping him against the menhir, his legs splayed before him like a marionette's.

"This much I can do," the harper said.

Again he laid his hands on either side of Jan's head. Watching, Minda could sense, almost *see,* the vitality stir in the muryan. He shook off the effects of stone and stone thoughts in a moment where he should have taken weeks to regain his strength. Cablin had been named a Healer, and rightly so, Minda thought. She caught Cablin's sudden smile. The hopelessness that lay so heavily on her melted away and she shared the Grey Harper's smile with a fey courage. A part of her wondered if perhaps the harper was working his healing spell on her as well. She couldn't find an answer in his gaze, and realized that it didn't really matter anyway.

chapter three

Night still held the Grey Hills in its spell when Minda and the arluth took their leave of Cablin. An unspoken bond linked the three of them at that moment, a close familiarity that had no root in logic, yet lay close in each heart just the same. United with the moorman at last, Minda realized the strangeness of her quest's ending. She'd chased across three worlds to free him so that he could defeat Ildran, only to find that she was expected to face the Dream-master herself. A queer twist of fate, indeed.

No. Not queer. But cruel. Capricious. She'd been named for luck, but could either name or heritage be enough against the Dream-master? She doubted her ability even to survive the encounter; it was not possible that she would prevail.

"You must," Cablin said in a soft voice. A trickle of harp music followed the sound of his voice, though his instrument was not at hand.

"You should leave that blade behind," the harper added. "It

will do only harm now if you keep it with you. This is a matter for the weren, not the Tuathan."

Minda touched the hilt and the hum of the sword's sentience went through her. "No," she said. "It's brought me this far and I won't leave it behind now. I don't know what it is, what or *who*'s trapped in its metal, but I won't leave it behind." Nonetheless, she took her hand from the leather hilt and shivered, remembering its power burning beyond control. The arluth and Cablin regarded her without speaking. "You said to follow my heart," she told the harper. "Well, my heart tells me to keep it."

"Your heart, or the voice of the sword?"

"My heart," she replied firmly.

But she wasn't nearly that sure. She only knew that she needed something more—that for all the magics and strengths hidden in her, when she thought of Ildran, of his power, his touch, she knew she needed a proven weapon in her hand.

She met the harper's troubled gaze and he shook his head. "I must go to the battlefield now," he said, "where the weren have met Ildran's armies. There is a great need for a Healer with so many wounded. I have played out my part in aiding you, Talenyn. The final outcome rests on your shoulders. Be strong and prevail."

As he spoke those final words, his form shivered, reshaped. The harper was gone, the music with him, and a raven lifted into the night air on long black wings, sped towards the far mountains.

Dursona, came the fading sound of his voice to their minds. *Camm serr lamm bren.*

They watched him go, their deepsight piercing the night's dark. When the raven was a speck, and then the speck was gone, Minda sighed heavily.

"I wish he was coming with us," she said.

The muryan at her side nodded. "We have need of a god's strength now. Keeping a gate sealed is not such a great matter, but the laying of such a spell requires a weirdling strength indeed—a strength that is Ildran's now."

"A god?" Minda asked.

Jan shot her a surprised look. "And what else would you call such a one? He is the Grey Man, Talenyn. The WerenArl's own son."

He'd said as much in the silhonell, Minda realized, but she'd never quite thought it all through. When he was near, she felt so strong. Now her eyes widened and a tremor of panic skittered through her.

She'd been talking with a god, calm as ever you please....

Jan did not notice the change in her. With Cablin gone, the closeness that held them together had loosened its bond. He knew a moment's awkwardness and looked away, to where the distant mountains made a jagged horizon between the dark sky and the darker moors.

"The way lies before us," he said, "long and wearying. Shall we go?"

Minda took a couple of deep breaths to steady herself. She followed the arluth's gaze with her own, and nodded. That way lay High Tor and Taplin Hill where Ildran held her friends still living captive. It was time to go.

The rolling hills between Jan's prison and Taplin Hill stretched for many leagues. They unwound swiftly beneath their feet. The stars wheeled steadily to the horizon and the moor winds licked at their skin. The silhonell and Cablin's healing powers had driven all weariness, hunger and thirst from them. The clear air of the hills filled their lungs, providing all the nourishment they needed and they went as quickly as though they'd borrowed the speed of the Lady Sian's two steeds, Saenor and Mythagoran.

But when the dawn brought its morning twilight to the hills and they drew nearer to their goal, the air grew bitter and they faltered. They tasted its leaden quality on their tongues and an oppressive weight settled across their shoulders. Minda felt Ildran's eyes on her. He knew they were coming and waited for them. And he had no fear.

They reached the hill where Minda had left Jo'akim and she stopped, staring aghast at its ruin. The longstone was toppled and broken in three. The rich soil of the hill lay gouged and thrown up in great fresh mounds, gleaming red and earthy dark in the light of the rising sun.

Moor-render, she thought, remembering what Jo'akim had called the Waster. Ferral Moor-render. *How* could the hobogle have escaped...?

Jan touched her lightly on the arm. "It grows too light. We

must hurry to the wood and work our way through its thickets
to High Tor."

She managed to force her tired legs into a run. As they
made it under the first overhanging boughs of the forest, a large
yarg stepped out of the wood's shadows. Her pendant flared
with its familiar warning and Minda dodged the grasping arms,
retching at the sudden reek of the creature. Before she could
regain her footing and draw her sword, Jan leapt into the air,
his legs scissoring, one heel lashing out to catch the creature
in the side of its head. She heard a dull crack as its neck
snapped, then Jan had her by the arm and was pulling her in
the direction of the hill.

I sense more than just that one, he mind-spoke. *Scattered
through the wood. Tread cautiously but be swift.*

She fell in behind him again, trying to copy his soundless
tread. But she knew no more of woodslore than she had in the
forest outside of Darkruin and was sure that she was raising
such a racket that every yarg from here to the hill could hear
her coming. And if they didn't hear the sound of her feet then
surely the pounding of her heart would warn them.

Jan dispatched two more yargs before they were through
the wood. He dealt death with a speed that defied reason.
Unarmed, he proved to be more dangerous than any weaponed
yarg, without even the need to use the magics she was sure he
had.

She glanced at the third one he'd slain. They seemed to die
so easily, for all their legendary prowess. But then the legends
told of battles between mortal and yarg, not of a muryan or
wizard facing them.

She hurried after Jan, frightened once more, and bumped
into him where he crouched behind a low bush.

There, he said, pointing ahead.

Minda knelt beside him, following his finger with her gaze.
The land rose from the edge of the wood and, from where they
were, she could see the tall crag that was High Tor. The sound
of the distant battle reached their ears faintly—weapons clash-
ing, horns winding, the roars of weren and yarg.

We should be there, a voice inside her said, and she knew
it was the sword speaking, awake once more.

She shook her head and the sword's mirthless laughter rang
in her mind.

How can your precious weren withstand Wasters and the

other horrors that Ildran throws against them? it asked. *You called them, you gathered them—but only to die. Free me and we could still rescue them.*

An image exploded in her mind. She saw herself leading an army of weren, the blue sword raised high. Jan was on one side of her, Grimbold on the other. Markj'n and Garowd guarded her rear. She was a wild-eyed warrior maiden, destroying her people's foe, slaking her need for revenge in the red blood and glory of war.

The sword strained, restless as a fettered beast. Her hand opened and closed at her side, but before she could draw the blade, Jan laid a hand on her shoulder. The interruption, small though it was, was enough to help her ignore the sword's voice. She turned to what must be done, ignoring the blade, and looked ahead to the final confrontation.

The muryan pointed out an opening in the rocky hillside, a cleft that led to the lower halls of Taplin Hall. The whole of the hill was hollowed, Jan explained, High Tor itself being where they'd find Ildran. But before they could confront the Dream-master, they must first win past the lower halls, over--coming whatever guardians Ildran had set there.

Are you ready? Jan asked.

When she nodded, he smiled reassuringly.

Then we will go! he cried.

They ran from the shelter of the woods, making for the cleft. The way was clear and they reached the first ridged back of the hillside without being discovered. Her pendant grew warmer, then hot, as they clambered for footing along the loose dirt of the slope. Rocks reared on all sides as they dropped from that first rise and scrambled down into the cleft below. The cleft was grassed with a look of disuse about it. There they paused, listening. All they heard was the sound of the battling on the further side of the hill.

The entrance to the lower halls lies beyond its second turn, the moorman said. Once, long ago, he'd walked those halls. But that was in a time of peace, before the Wessener were destroyed, before even Ildran had risen on Weir.

They padded along the cleft in silence, hugging one wall so that a chance observer from above wouldn't see them. Minda's pendant was like fire against her skin as they came to the hill itself. As they made their way around the first turn, Minda gripped Jan's arm.

Stop, she said. *There's danger ahead.*

I sense it too, the arluth replied. *But we must go on; we have no other choice. Ahead lies the only way open to us. Stay near to me and be prepared for anything.*

Cautiously, they edged forward. What was it that waited for them, guarding the lower halls? As they rounded the second turn, Minda stopped in her tracks. Be prepared for anything, Jan had warned. But for this?

The way ran straight before them, going a couple of hundred yards before vanishing into the hill. Granite cliffs reared on either side. And before the entranceway stood the guards: a giant, a badger and a tinker.

For one foolish moment, Minda's heart leapt to see them— then hope died. By their stance, by the blank hatred in their eyes, she knew Ildran had changed them. Markj'n had his blades drawn and ready in his hands. Garowd bore his great axe, holding it lightly, as though it weighed no more than a small hatchet. Grimbold stood on his hind legs, golden shimmers of magefire glinting between the long claws of his forepaws.

So, Minda Talenyn, the badger's voice rumbled in her mind, *we meet once again.*

The voice was familiar, but its tone was cold as hoarfrost.

She stared at them, unable to accept that they meant her harm. Jan tensed beside her. Minda reached out to the three with her mind, but hatred swept down the cleft, choking her. The sword muttered at her side.

"Grimbold," she pleaded. "Markj'n. What are you doing? Garowd. We were—we *are* friends!"

There was no reply, only the hatred in their eyes, and her voice faltered. It was then that she saw what she'd overlooked before. Around each of her friends' necks hung a pulsing crystal. These might be the bodies of her friends, but they weren't her friends anymore. Alien intelligences controlled the three now. Did their own souls now hang about the necks of yargs, strengthening them as they killed weren?

Hatred for Ildran rose in her—blind, white, sudden. And fear was swept away.

"If these were once your friends," Jan murmured, echoing her own thoughts, "then they are so no more. The holding-crystals have them in thrall."

Minda didn't answer. She wasn't even listening. The white

anger burned in her and she stepped forward. Jan pulled at her arm, but she shook him off. Was there a flicker of the Grimbold of old, hidden behind the cold stare in the badger's eyes? Did Markj'n still dwell in his body, sharing its use with another while he was helpless to control his actions? Was that Garowd's kindness still lurking behind the death that dwelt in his eyes?

The three guardians awaited her coming. Jan hurried to her side, tried to step past her, but she caught him by the arm and wouldn't let him by. There was strength in her now—a strength first woken by the muryan lord on that night he drew her into the silhonell and charged her with the task of freeing him. The ensuing weeks had tempered that strength, forged the new power in her. And she had the sword.

Her hand closed on the leather-wrapped hilt and she drew forth the strange blade that hung at her side. A brilliant blue flaring roared into life along its edges and its power burned in her mind.

The sword exulted in its freedom, its light blinding, the blue whitening. Minda fought to keep it under her control but it was like trying to stem a storm-frothed river with a pail. The blue fire thrilled through her veins. A wordless cry formed in her throat and burst forth from her lips like a peal of thunder. She shook the sword above her head and it exploded with brilliance. But it was not she who cried or shook the blade. The sword was too strong. She had thought she could control it, that what had happened on Gythelen was an accident, no more. She was wrong.

The three guardians, wearing the flesh of her friends, separated to meet the attack. Grimbold took the central position, with the giant and tinker ranged on either side. The sword drove Minda forward. She understood as she fought for control what the danger of the sword was. It wasn't made by the Tuathan so much as made *for* them. Flesh of Mid-wold, mortal or Wessener, must shrivel before a power meant only for the Bright Gods to wield. The blood in her veins flowed molten. Her body burned.

"Sheath it!" she heard Jan cry.

She knew she must, but the decision was no longer hers to make. Freed again, awake, the sword held control and would not let go. It would destroy her if she couldn't sheath it, and she wasn't strong enough.

Jan grabbed her arm. The sword turned in her hand. She

fought it so that when it struck, it was only the hilt that connected with the muryan's brow, knocking him to a senseless heap on the ground. A bolt of magefire erupted from Grimbold. The blade lifted to meet it, swept it aside. Its own power arced between them to strike the possessed Wysling, piercing his defenses.

Garowd and Markj'n came at her from either side. She could feel the sword's grin on her lips.

Child's play, it mocked. The words froze her with their amoral calmness.

She reached again for that hidden power that was her Wessener heritage, but the sword's spirit beat her back. Her arm lifted to meet Garowd's attack. The giant's axe shattered against the sword and she didn't even feel the force of the blow. Markj'n's tinkerblades were turned aside with deft ease. The sword licked through the tinker's defenses, leapt for his heart.

No! Minda cried.

Whatever madness had tricked her into keeping the sword, into loosing its sentience when she *knew* the danger, was not complete enough for her to allow the sword to kill her friends. Time seemed to slow as she bent her will against the sword's. Her body swayed as they struggled. Pain lanced through her— burning pain that rushed through her veins like waves of blue fire. The sword trembled in her hand, straining for the tinker's heart. Gathering her pain, Minda channelled her will through it. She let the sword complete its thrust, forced her hand to turn a fraction before it plunged into Markj'n's chest. The blade struck the pulsing crystal that hung around the tinker's neck, shattering it. A wail like a hundred souls dying tore through the cleft and Markj'n toppled to the ground. He lay like one dead.

Minda wept as he fell. She tried to bend down beside him, but the sword had turned its attention to Garowd.

Again she fought it, letting it strike at the crystal that hung around the giant's neck, rather than his heart. Another crystal shattered and Garowd crumpled to the ground like an empty sack. The sword vibrated in her hand.

Were Garowd and Markj'n dead? Or had they died before the crystals were hung about their necks? No time to think. There was still the Wysling.

Grimbold was rising on weak forepaws, his fur singed and smoking. He shook his striped head, still stunned from the force of the previous attack. Feeble gold magefire trembled weakly about him. He swayed before her, eyes unfocused. The sword leapt forward, dragging her arm with it. A third and final time she forced it to stab a jewel, not flesh, and the last of Minda's friends lay sprawled at her feet.

The sword stole that moment of confusion to break through her frail control. She could feel the heat building up inside her. Her arm glowed pale blue, growing deeper, dark and strong, flecked with streaks of white fire, like the sword itself.

It was feeding on her.

Panic rose gibbering in her mind—a huge backswell that overwhelmed her incomplete attempts to reduce the sentient blade in her hand to what it should be: a sword and nothing more. Fear coursed through her. The sword hummed, seeking a new foe. The sound of the battle beyond the hill came to her ears.

There! it roared. *We are needed!*

It hammered away at her ineffectual attempts to control it. Her body glowed like the heart of a fire. She staggered under its onslaught, barely managed to keep it from consuming her. The reality of here and now stretched thin as they struggled. Other dimensions shimmered in her heat-blistered gaze. She saw something take shape in the sky—a face, huge, craggy and grim, wreathed with flame-colored hair and an unruly beard. Was it in the sky . . . or in her mind? The sword—the force in her hand—was a Tuathan blade. Was it summoning its maker?

Opposite the first visage a death's head appeared—a bare skull with slender sinews of flesh holding its jaws in place. In sockets that should have been empty, baleful red eyes glared.

Greymin! the sword cried in welcome.

At the naming, Minda knew. The red-haired being was Greymin, the Skylord of the Tuathan. The sword had summoned its master. And with that god's coming one of the Daketh was taking shape as well.

If the gods should walk Mid-wold, if the Covenant be broken, all of Wayderness will fail. . . .

The knowledge pierced her like a knife thrust. The worlds would fail by her doing. The fault lay with her, on her shoulders. She was worse than—

Ildran.

The sword grew mad with joy as the Tuathan's visage grew more solid. It lashed about in her hand, beckoning to the Skylord. The flame that was her body, the unnatural flame that belonged to another dimension, was bright beyond imagining. The two faces, grim god's and Daketh's, waxed clearer still. Bodies took shape beneath them. The Skylord's lips were moving, but as yet she could hear no sound. Only the roar of the flames, and the sword.

Something snapped in Minda. Whether it was that her mind could simply bear no more, or that it was true that when death was upon you your past flashed before your eyes, she found herself falling back into times that had been, back and back to simpler days—before the dreams had come, before she'd left her homeworld to walk the roads of other worlds. She thought she was with her Uncle Tomalin.

They were standing one quiet night with the stars of her homeworld bright overhead, the woodlands running out before them, the fields of his farm on their right. The fields were all silvery in the magical light. She saw white splotches that were the beehives near the orchard. The wind was rustling the leaves of the apple tree, the grass about them. A nightingale sang in the distance.

That was the night she'd told him about Hadon, how he treated her. Tomalin had smiled sadly.

"Be like the reeds," he'd said. "When the wind blows 'em, they bend with 't, an' when 't's gone, why they're standing straight an' tall again, reaching for the sun. An' the grass underfoot. We'll be stepping 't down an' when we're gone, don't 't stand up again? An' where's the mark o' our passing?

"Do the same for a' the troubles o' this world. Bend with 'em an' let 'em blow o'er you. But when you're making your stand, be like the hills an' never give an inch. Give a listen to your heart, an' you'll ken which to do when. Give 't a try with Hadon an' see if 't don't work. There'll come a time when you'll be gone from him an' he'll mean nothing an'—looking back—you'll wonder why you ever let him bother you."

"Just give in?" she asked.

"No an' no! Never give in. Just give a little—like the reeds. Let him think you're doing what he wants an' then you'll live to stand up an' follow your own ways."

She'd tried to follow his advice when she returned to Fernwillow and found that it worked better than she would have thought. Many times, when she was sure that one of Hadon's towering rages would be the end of her, she'd learned to sidestep them. Bending, without giving in.

Remembering Tomalin and his gentle ways, something eased inside her. That hidden place that was filled with knowledge and power, and the skill to use both, opened under a gentle touch where all her pounding at it did nothing at all.

Bend, but don't give in. Like she'd done with the Walker in Darkruin. Like she'd done with the sword—allowing it to strike, but to strike what *she* wanted. Listen to your heart . . . Cablin had said as much.

She stared skyward, tears of pain and white fire blurring her sight. The two gods had not yet completely manifested. The sword pounded and hammered at her. She fought it for a second longer, then let it flow through her and fought no more.

The spirit of the sword hesitated briefly, then leapt through her with an exultant cry. It began to consume her. She held that pain to herself, used it as a focus. She fled before the sword's power, hiding her hoarded strengths under a mask of fear. Talenyn . . . the little wren that the Winter Lads chase, but never catch.

Her arm went up and high, the sword blazing in her fist. The sword allowed her the movement, though it saw no target. She brought the blade swooping down with terrible speed, down to where the still bodies of Grimbold and the tinker lay, where the giant's huge form was stretched out just beyond.

The dead are dead, the sword sang inside her, puzzled.

They are dead, she agreed.

She plunged the blade into the solid rock that was like an immense flagstone in front of the entranceway to the lower halls. It sank deep into the rock, cutting through the stone as though it were only earth. In the instant that it took the sword to realize her intent, Minda let the raw wildness inside her swell, storm through her, speed into the stiff fingers of her right hand, loosen her grip.

The sword fought her, understanding. But that moment's respite had been all Minda needed. Her fingers opened numbly and fell from the hilt. The fires died. She fell full length beside the sword, her body screaming its torment. With an effort that cost her as much as loosening her grip on the sword had, she raised herself to her knees and looked skyward.

There was nothing there. No grim Tuathan, no death's head. Only the clear blue skies of Highwolding. Silence fell upon the cleft as the dull roaring in Minda's ears faded. She hung her head, basking in the cool stillness, then heard from beyond the hill the sound of the distant battle once more.

She'd won no more than a skirmish, not even against their true foe. The war was not yet done. Ildran awaited her.

Her body grew cool, the sharp torment dying to a dull throbbing ache. She stared at her hands, her arms, marvelling that the flesh was unblistered, without a scar. Had there really been flames . . . consuming fires . . . ? Or were the scars all inside? Her gaze fell on the sword, standing upright in the stone, a short slightly curved length of dull metal. She closed and opened her hand, staring, thankful that the desire even to touch the blade was gone.

Grimbold lay beside her. She crawled to the badger's side, searching for some sign of life. He lay so still. She probed with her mind, found nothing. Weeping, she made her way to Markj'n and then Garowd, to find them the same. Only Jan lived. There was dried blood on his scalp and temple, a grim reminder of the sword's passion. At least his chest still rose and fell with a slow breathing, but the others, her friends, were gone.

She turned away from the muryan, collapsing on the ground as her grief overwhelmed her. They'd taken both her and all the danger that followed hard on her heels in stride—offered their help, their knowledge, their friendship, asking for nothing in return. Now they lay dead on a distant world with nothing to show for their sacrifice. She *should* have left the sword behind long ago. Should never have used it in the first place.

But if she hadn't, they might have all died without even leaving Darkruin.

More confused than ever, she wept. She was no brave hero in a jongleur's tale, no wizard nor swordswoman. . . . Then the tears left her, though she knew the grief would never end. If there'd been a hidden place of power in her, it now rang hollow with her sorrow.

She staggered to her feet, every part of her body protesting the movement. Drained, hardly able to set one foot before the other, she moved slowly forward, dazed like a sleepwalker. The darkness of the entranceway closed around her. She felt a tugging. As Ildran had known where she was, so now something inside her pointed the way to where he laired. She let the tugging guide her. She knew only that Ildran would pay for what he had done.

chapter four

The Dream-master's presence seemed close and thick in the darkness of the lower halls. Not so much a physical presence, as a foul taint that Minda remembered from her dreams. The cold touch in her mind. The mocking laughter.

She shuddered, moving slowly forward. Far ahead she could see a pale glimmering where the halls were lit. She forced herself to keep moving in that direction. With each step she took the air grew heavier with danger. As she could sense him, she knew that he was aware of her presence. He was waiting for her, expectant. Her coming was the final move in the game he played, though for her it was no game. Being here, moving through the lower halls of Taplin Hill, perhaps the same hall her mother had fled down all those years ago, was all too real. And yet there was a surreal quality to it, as though she read of it in a book or was watching mimers perform it. A dreamlike quality . . . a nightmare.

She reached the end of the darkness and stood just outside the spill of light, looking in from the shadows. A dalin hung high in a large central hall while more dalin hung at regular intervals about the chamber. The hall had a smooth-stoned floor and its woodpanelled walls had marvelous scenes carved on them—whole stories told, as panel followed panel. Once they'd been bright with lively colors, but that vibrancy had dulled, like autumn paling into winter. She stepped into the hall and touched one of the panels. A fleck of paint came away on her finger.

All things pass, change, grow, she remembered Rabbert telling her once.

It was funny how her thoughts kept turning to Fernwillow—to Rabbert and Tomalin and Janey, to the inn and Hadon's frown and Kate's brisk busyness. She remembered them all, but the memories belonged to a stranger. Rabbert, she thought, be thankful you didn't come.

There was nothing here but endings now. The faded panels, the empty halls, the Wessener. And over all, Ildran's presence hung like a shroud, dimming the dalin, his eyes on her, his black humor slithering across her thoughts. She shook her head wearily and stepped away from the wall.

The tugging in her head led her across the hall to another opening that led into a new tunnel. This issued into a larger hall and to stairs cut from white stone, bearing the marks of nailed boots and strange claws. The silence grew oppressive, the feel of Ildran's eyes upon her an unbearable weight. Where were his guards? No need for them now, she supposed, as she started up the stairs. This was between them now. Perhaps it had always been between just them—the Dream-master and the last survivor of these broken halls.

She reached the top of the stairs and paused once more. A wide hall ran in either direction, dalin-lit, doorless and curving out of sight each way. High above, one immense dalin hung. This dwarf-globe was like a constellation—intricately shaped, beautiful, and the only undamaged thing in sight. Here the wall panels bore the marks of sword and axe—senseless destruction by the hands of creatures who hadn't the wit to understand what it was they destroyed. The furnishings were so much kindling—broken chairs and the ruin of tables lay strewn about—and in places, the charred remains of fires blackened the stone floor.

The tugging pulled her to the right and she followed in that direction, coming to another stairway as she turned the corner. She paused again, hearing a scuffling sound. The noise came from the stairs that led up from the lower levels. Jan . . . ? But no. Her pendant cried danger and a cold chill rushed up her spine. If only she wasn't so tired. If only she were stronger.

She roused herself, and began to climb the new set of stairs, determined to confront Ildran under her own power, rather than being dragged before him as a captive. Perhaps he didn't know that she'd answered the riddle, that the power was no longer hidden inside her. Depleted, yes, but surely she could still make a stand?

She topped the stairs, silent as an indrawn breath. To the right two large doors stood ajar. Through them she could see a glimpse of the battle that raged below the hill, but it was too distant to realize fully. Of more pressing concern was the presence of the guards that lounged by those open doors. Some were yargs. The others were small, pale-skinned beings, all head and torso, that put her in mind of Jo'akim—though these reeked of evil. She shrank back a step or two. The guards hadn't noticed her. But from below, the sound of her stealthy pursuer rose as a whisper.

She could hear the guards shuffling as they eased stiff legs. For the moment they seemed more interested in the battle outside than in the hall they were supposed to be guarding. She peered from the stairwell again. The yargs jeered with one another in a rough language that was almost familiar. Across the hall lay another set of stairs. With luck . . .

She shook her head ruefully. The only luck she could hope for was to make her way safely to where Ildran would kill her.

She thrust the morbid thought from her. A deep breath helped to steady her jangled nerves. She expelled it slowly, then slipped silently across the hall. Her hand reached for the hilt of a sword she no longer carried; then she was across the dangerous expanse, hugging the wall. She made her way to the bottom of the stairwell and mounted it quickly.

She was in High Tor itself now. How she knew it, she couldn't say. The tugging drew her up and up to where Ildran waited. High Tor lifted like a gaunt talon into the sky, the tower of Taplin Hill. The very stones underfoot spoke to her familiarly. They eased her weariness. Her earlier exhaustion gave way to the amazing recuperative powers that was her inheritance from her Wessener parents. The closeness of the henge atop High Tor fueled it. Her taw, her inner strength, was still at low ebb, but her body moved more smoothly. She stepped up her pace and it answered the demand she put on it.

The stairs narrowed and rose in steady spirals. Doors led off from the landings she came to, but she passed them by. A sound arose from below. Her pursuer had been discovered. Was it friend or foe . . . ? The answer came swiftly. The guards laughed, calling out greetings to one of their own.

She peered along the banister and saw a swirl of white below. Pushing back, she hugged the wall, her heart thumping wildly in her breast. The Walker. She was almost more frightened of him than of Ildran.

She took another deep breath. Adrenaline banished her remaining weakness. She raced up the spiralling stairs now, taking them two at a time. Dark thoughts lapped at her—from Ildran? Or from the Walker? Her breath came raggedly, echoing strangely in the close confines of the stairwell. Her tension mounted. A scream was building up in her throat but she bit at her lip, choking it down. The utter futility of her coming here settled like an awful weight upon her. It didn't matter that she was the last of the Wessener. It didn't matter that she had their hidden powers. She was almost drained; the bitter struggle with the sword had seen to that. Why go on then?

To end it. She owed those who had died that much. To try to end it.

The stairs ended at a door. She stared at its grained surface, the dull shine of the brass latch, and wished she was anywhere but here. She could feel the Walker approaching, hear his tread on the stairs. Trying to find the resolve to open the door, she merely stood shivering in front of it. Going through would prove nothing. It was better to run, to try to make her way past the Walker, past the guards, while she was still alive. Run now—to return and fight when she was stronger. . . .

Shoulders heaving with suppressed sobs, she lifted the latch and stepped inside, closing the door softly behind her. She looked for something to bar the door with, but there was nothing. She leaned back against it, fingers still pressed against its ancient wood, and stared down a new hallway.

It was no more than a hundred feet long, with a door halfway down either wall and one at the further end. The tugging pulled at her. The end door. That was Ildran's.

Where was his touch now? Didn't he feel her . . . so near?

She could taste his thoughts in the air, roiling and curling about her. One nervous step she took, then another. When she came to the first door on the right, she opened it slowly to peer inside. It was a bedchamber with pannelled walls, tapestries and a comfortable-looking bed set in one corner. Bookshelves lined one wall. There was a hearth in another corner. She stepped inside, taken aback at the neatness of the room after the destruction she'd found below. Was this where the Dream-master slept?

Turning slowly, she studied the room, looking for something she could use as a weapon. Now was when she needed the Tuathan sword. The loss of that treacherous blade struck her like a blow, although when she'd fought with it outside the hill it was all she could do to be rid of the thing. There was nothing here that she could use.

She turned, stepped through the door, intent on what waited for her at the far end of the hall. Her rage was returning. The first faint touch of that hidden power stirred in her again. The henge stood directly above her, on the top of High Tor. It was that strength she felt filling her.

A sound came to her—a shuffle behind her that seemed to come from far off. She whirled, hands raised ineffectually in front of her, to face the Walker. His bald pate was shiny in the dalin light. Before she could move, he was upon her. A powerful hand gripped her shoulder, the long nails biting into her skin. She struggled and he slapped her so hard that her head rang.

Indeed, we have you now, his cold voice hissed in her mind. *Come along, wretched child. Ildran awaits you.*

He dragged her down the hall towards the final door. She drew on those faint trickles of power that stirred inside her, but the Walker's fingers only gripped her tighter and he laughed, unaffected.

Now it ends, she thought bitterly. Rather than confronting Ildran as Cablin had shown her she could, free with the hidden power of the Wessener at her command, she was being dragged before him, his helpless captive once again. Not dream-caught now . . . oh, no. Caught body and soul.

chapter five

It was dark inside, after the dalin-bright hall. Here only three candles threw a pallid light from the walls. The Walker thrust Minda through the door in front of him and she looked up from the floor to see Ildran at last. She stared at him.

He sat in a plain wooden chair—heavy snow-white brows hiding his eyes, a long grey beard hanging down to his chest, its end tucked into a broad white belt. His hair was the same grey, while his face, or what she could see of it, seemed like a kindly old scholar's—thoughtful and wise. His shirt and trousers were white and two small horns thrust from his brow— like they did from Jan's.

This was the Dream-master?

He looked more like one of the old men that frequented Rabbert's shop back in Fernwillow—scholars and book-dealers with fluttery hands and spectacles perched on the ends of their noses.

The room itself was unfurnished except for the chair he sat on and a large globe that was perched on a tripod in front of him. The globe reminded her of the holding-crystals, for it was the same deep red hue and pulsed with a similar rhythm.

The kindly face looked up and she shrank back. Seeing his eyes, she knew that the gentle appearance was a sham. The eyes were blood-red and without pupils, and the burning light in them spoke far more plainly of the twisted soul that lay inside him than any monstrous shape might have. He smiled. She wanted to look away, but she couldn't tear her gaze from him.

"So," he said in a soft voice. "What was it the moorman called you? Ah, yes... Talenyn. And you've come at last."

Minda shook her head, trying to keep the spell of his voice from lulling her. Its timbre was like Grimbold's, his abstracted manner like Rappert's. It was a trick. He had shape-changed. only the eyes were real; the rest was a lie.

Ildran's smile widened. "This is my true form," he said. "Am I so hideous?"

"You're evil."

"What do you know of evil?" he asked. "I have seen it, tasted it, lived it. Have you? I have walked Dalker—the realm of the Dark Gods. *I* have seen evil. Compared to them, I am no more than a babe, toying with my small games. But I have learned from them and will raise myself to their heights in time. Indeed, I will be evil then—to you, at least, or those who think as you do. But to my own mind? To those who follow me? I suppose it merely depends on one's point of view."

He chuckled softly. The camaraderie of his humor sent another thrill of fear through her. The room blurred in her sight, the candles becoming one, then a hundred, the white-haired man shimmering. Her eyes were filling with tears, she realized. No spell.

"I feel a certain warmth towards you," Ildran continued, "for no other has denied me as long as you have. Even before the moorman gave you your little trinket you were strong. But then, you were never a once-born, were you, Minda Talenyn? These halls, this hill, are your heritage, are they not? The Wessener. Proud they were, proud and mighty. But not so great that I couldn't slay them all. All save your mother Morwenna. But in the end I slew her too—though my hand was not there for the final blow."

He stroked the globe and its red pulse changed for a moment, deepened.

"The Wessener were such a doughty folk," he said. "And here you are, the last of their line. What shall I do with you, *Little* Wren? Perhaps you would join me?"

Mutely she shook her head. She concentrated on the henge that stood above this room, the grey stones reaching out to Highwolding's stars that fed her hidden strength, her taw, but all that stirred inside her was a vague flicker.

Ildran laughed at her reply—warmly, as though they were old friends. "Did you truly think that I would have you at my side?" he asked. "Scheming and plotting, driving me mad with that damnable innocence of yours?"

The rich laughter filled the room. She tried to withdraw inside herself, to hide from him, but there was nowhere to go. Everywhere her mind turned, Ildran's darkness was there, waiting for her.

"*I* was innocent once," he said at last, holding back his laughter. "But I lost it quickly enough. The Daketh whispered to me in *my* dreams and I learned of power and . . . other things."

He stroked the globe, and again its color deepened, the pulse slowed.

"Come to me," he said.

He spoke coldly, firmly, all humor gone. Enthralled, she could only obey. She moved across the floor until all that separated them was the globe. Ildran lifted his hand to touch her cheek, then grasped the leather cord that held her pendant, tearing it from her throat.

"A pretty bauble," he said, "but of little use to you now."

He dropped the pendant to the floor. With anguished eyes, Minda watched him grind it under his heel.

"Come, Talenyn," Ildran whispered, his voice kind once more. "Come let us dream, you and I. . . ."

Her gaze was drawn to the globe between them. Inside it she could see the battle that raged outside as clearly as if she were there. The miniature hillside in the globe was littered with the bodies of weren and dalkwer. The living weren were very few now. Amidst the flashing blades and mottled magefire, she could see the odd yarg wearing a pulsing crystal about its neck, wreaking havoc as three, four weren tried to pull it down. One of the Wild Ones—a man that seemed more like a bull standing upright than a man—reached the yarg with his weapon.

The yarg twisted aside, but not quickly enough to elude the thrust of the long axe. It struck true, shattering the holding crystal.

She felt Ildran shudder at that moment. His grip on her mind loosened slightly and then firmed again, as strong as before. A question rose in her mind that there was no time to answer. The globe disappeared and suddenly she was in her nightmare again—alone now . . . without even Jan's charm . . . ending as it had begun . . .

Roiling gases boiled over bloody landscapes. She plunged towards the ground in a stomach-churning descent, only to be tugged back up when she was bare inches from the molten rocks. Strange poisons filled her lungs, stung her skin. The air itself fondled her obscenely. Darkness leered on all sides, tearing at her with a life of its own.

She screamed and the sound issued forth as worms. They spilled out of her mouth, crawled down her neck, into her hair, over her skin. She screamed again and her throat thickened with more of the segmented creatures.

Fool, fool, fool! To come, when she should have fled. To face the Dream-master in his lair like some vainglorious hero of ballads, when all her power had been spent in her struggle with the sword.

Ildran's laughter echoed all around her, buffeting her with a physical strength. She was powerless before him.

Deep in her mind a tiny thought stirred, misty and unclear. She reached for it, but it slipped away, overcome by her terror, skittering back to whatever lost place it had left.

The dark pulled back and again she plunged for the ground, her leg brushing the lava. Fire ran up the limb. She screamed again. Worms covering her now, from head to foot. She choked on them, breathed them. The wriggling mass filled her throat, her lungs.

Kill me! she pleaded.

What? And spoil the sport?

His reply came as though from a great distance, yet echoed inside her.

Sport . . . sport . . . sport . . .

To him it was nothing but a game—despair for the sake of despair. He revelled in his control of her, playing her like a marionette, while she was as helpless as though she'd never undergone all those trials to reach him. All she had accomplished, learned, meant nothing. The deaths of so many had been for nothing. She had been defeated long before she left the inn in Fernwillow. And with death denied her, her mind frothed with madness. She reached for the echo of his mocking words, for it was the only reality that was left to her.

Sport . . . sport . . . sport . . .

On and on the word echoed and she followed it to its source.

Sport . . . sport . . . sport . . .

There was no coherence in what she did. She clutched at that one word, not even aware of why it was important to catch it. On it led her and Ildran laughed to watch her. He let the word slip and slide, twist this way and that, weaving a terrible maze that she could not follow, but follow she did. There was nothing else she could do. It was real where nothing else was.

What if she should reach him, following the word? Ildran thought—but the thought came too late. She was there, inside him, as he was in her.

As he knew her, so now she knew him. Everything he was was laid out before her in that one flashing instant. There was no magic involved in that knowing—no power required, no strength. She encompassed him and understood as clarity took the place of the madness in her mind.

Grimbold had guessed—but had not taken his speculations far enough. Ildran was the Dream-master, yes, but more he was a master of illusion. He had tricked them all—Jan, Cablin, the dalkwer, Grimbold, the Wessener. He had strength, but only because he had a pretense of power—the power of those dream-slain. His followers believed he would soon be all powerful in Mid-wold and they flocked to his banner.

But the power of those dream-slain didn't exist. The holding-crystals were a sham. The danger was real enough—his army of yargs, Wasters and dalkwer. But the holding-crystals were drawn from the memory of an old tale; the power of those dream-slain were an invention of his own mind. The crystals held some small power, but it was simply his own power, strengthened through the years not by those dream-slain but by his own painstaking researches. He hoarded it in the globe, focusing his will onto those who wore the crystals through that sphere. Only his illusions made his power seem more potent than it was.

It took only an instant for Minda to understand, for Ildran to realize that the game was up. The nightmare illusions fal-

tered. She was in the room in High Tor—and her hand struck
the globe and it fell to the stones, shattering, exploding with
a shower of magefire that seared them both.

Ildran lunged from his chair, trying to reweave his illusions.
But as the power of the globe exploded about them, she called
it to her use as quickly as he did to his. She felt the hidden
places inside her stretch with new strength and tore down Ildran's illusions as soon as he raised them.

They faced each other. Minda saw his face grow haggard,
drained of assurance, while her own confidence grew with each
passing moment.

She wove her own illusions between them using knowledge
stolen from Ildran's own mind. The room spun and churned.
The Walker stood forgotten. The power of the globe—Ildran's
long-hoarded power that had taken him untold years to garner—
replenished Minda's own, filling her taw until it swelled to
bursting. When she sent it back to him, its twistedness straightened out as it flowed through her, it became an anathema for
Ildran to touch. He withered under the onslaught.

Then Minda became aware of something else escaping the
destruction of the globe. The souls of those dream-slain *had*
been locked inside—kept there for Ildran's amusement. The
souls of those who wore the holding-crystals were there as
well. They fled into the ether in a wild rush, some exulting in
their new freedom, others weeping with despair when they
found their bodies long slain. Some rushed to fill still forms
that lay on the battlefield, and yargs that had collapsed when
the globe shattered arose to battle again. And three more fared
to bodies that lay just outside the entrance to the lower levels.

Minda's thoughts followed them, watched the spirits slip
into their familiar bodies, realized that the blood had never
stopped flowing through their veins, their lungs had never ceased
to draw in air. But the air was filled with the keening of those
who had no body to return to, those who were dead in truth.

Minda turned on the Dream-master. As her power had been
drained in the struggle with the sword, so was he emptied now.
She grew in stature as she faced him, all her need and sorrow
and pain focused into one final blow. Her power roared like a
storm in the chamber, a blinding power that struck the Dream-
master and rebounded to knock her to the floor, drained and
spent herself.

The power grew and grew, feeding on itself until it flared with a terrible intensity—and died. Darkness filled the room. The candles had been snuffed out in that final maelstrom.

Ildran was dead.

She raised herself on trembling arms. The Walker was still present. She could hear his stealthy movement in the darkness, feel his tension as he poised to strike. It didn't matter to him that Ildran was dead, though it had been the Dream-master who had tricked him and his kin into what was now a useless struggle. She knew he remembered that she'd bested him once. He'd held back until her battle with Ildran was done. But now she was fair game.

She lifted an arm across her face, warding herself from the blow she knew must come. Slowly she got to her feet, backing cautiously away from where she'd fallen. She sent a testing thought, down into the hidden reaches where her taw was, but only vague flickers stirred; slaying Ildran had drained her once more. Minda stood helplessly in the dark. Her power would return in time, but time she didn't have.

Magefire flared in the Walker's hands. Minda dropped to the floor, feeling its power burn the air above her, its passage singeing her hair. Spots danced before her eyes, then the darkness returned. She moved quickly to her left where she'd seen the door in that one instant of brightness. But before she could reach it, the door burst open and dalin light spilled into the room.

The sound of a horn thundered in the confines of the room. Minda and the Walker turned to face the door. Huorn stood outlined in its frame, his horn lifted to his lips, his antlers brushing the top of the doorframe. In his free hand he held a staff that Minda had last seen in the hands of the Waster. He let the horn fall to his chest and lifted the black staff.

"Ferral is slain, Walker."

His words rang loud and hard in the room. The tableau held for a long breathless moment. Fear flickered in the Walker's eyes and he leapt for the door—not to attack, but to flee. He knew the weapon that Huorn bore. It was the shadow-death, caryaln—created to slay his kind.

The staff moved as though it had a life of its own. The Walker lunged for safety, magefire crackling about him, but the staff went up and Huorn drove it into the creature's chest.

The Walker's wailing death cry was the last thing Minda heard as unconsciousness washed over her in a wave.

For a long moment, Huorn stood in the ensuing silence, his antlered head bent. Then tenderly he picked Minda up and carried her from the broken halls.

EPILOGUE

So Green Leaves Grow...

Minda awoke to find herself in the henge that straddled the top of High Tor. The long day was over and Highwolding's twilight stars shaped constellations in the grey skies above. Around her, in the henge, an amber glow came from the old giant stones and she met with the survivors.

Grimbold was there, weak and gaunt, half his fur missing while the remainder was charred. Markj'n and Garowd, scarcely able to stand, leaned against a menhir. The tinker flashed her a quick smile, then grimaced at the pain that the small movement brought him. There were others she didn't know, weren that seemed more alien than ever in this moment between unconsciousness and waking, and again some she did.

Jan was there, his gold eyes dark with concern. Jo'akim lay propped up against a menhir, heavily bandaged. Huorn stood over her with a question in his eyes. The question fled as she raised her hands to him. He helped her stand.

"I should have known," she began, "in Darkruin . . ."

He silenced her. "How could you have known?"

There was a stranger there that seemed familiar to Minda—a small wizened man in a grey cloak, a long wisp of beard falling against his chest, a tall staff in his hand. Then she knew him for Cablin, in yet another guise. He nodded a greeting to her.

Few could have done as well as you, Talenyn, last of the Wessener.

Minda bowed her head. She still felt weak, but something lay inside her now that would never leave, something older and wiser than had lain in the heart of the girl she'd been, fleeing Fernwillow for her life. Understanding of her heritage had not answered the riddle of who she was—who she *really* was beyond the words of Wessener and Gatekeeper and last of a line—but that was as it should be. She knew herself as well as anyone could, and that would have to be enough.

She looked around at the faces of her friends and allies, then her gaze fell on a small stunted tree that grew near the kingstone. As she watched, buds sprouted, uncurled into leaves that were bright and green. She smiled to see it grow, never questioning the wonder of it. She saw that tree as it was, bravely shaking the gloom of Ildran from its heart, and as it would be, crowned with red berries.

"The rowan blooms," Cablin said. "Give thanks, for this is a sight allowed to few."

"This is my home now," Minda said softly to those gathered. These empty halls . . . they wouldn't stay empty, not if she could help it.

"And you are welcome in it—forever and always."

She thought of Rabbert, far way in Fernwillow, and longed to see him again. Would he come and stay in Taplin Hill with her? There were erls and even more magical folk for him to meet and he could move all his books here and never have to sell one of them again. There was room enough here for him to let them multiply to his heart's content.

Another's features came to mind, that of the journeyman Raeth, and she felt a curious sensation stir in her. She smiled, knowing in that moment what Janey saw in Wooly Lengershin, and wondered if Raeth could be convinced to learn his harping here. . . .

She sighed. There was time enough for that sort of thing

later. For now her eyes were shiny with tears. She wept for
relief that Ildran was truly gone, that her friends were safe,
and that here, amongst those friends, she had found a home.
She looked from face to face again and saw in each gaze the
promise that they would stay and help to rebuild the wonder
that had been Taplin Hill. It would be their home as well. One
face she missed, and she looked again, but Cablin was gone.
All that remained of the Grey Man was the faint echo of his
harp's strings, then they too faded until only the memory of
them remained.

*A barrow was dug for those who had died. Above it, a tall
menhir was raised with the names of all those slain inscribed
upon it in Sennayeth runes. Ildran and the dalkwer were burned
in a pyre that lifted its flames for three days and two nights.
In the twilight of that last day, a wind came up from the Grey
Hills and scattered the ashes far and wide until only a circle
of blackened ground remained.*

*And as the barrow and menhir stood there as a monument
to those who had fallen, so nothing ever grew in that barren
circle, as a bitter reminder so that the dark times might never
return.*

GLOSSARY

of Sennayeth Words &
Unfamiliar Terms

[Note: (S) indicates Sennayeth words.]

a-meir (S)—*well-met*

Anann—*the earthmother, moongoddess; also called Arn; has three aspects, that of maiden, mother and crone; also called simply Mother or Moon*

Arn—*see Anann*

arluth (S)—*lord (arluth gan menhir means "The lord of the longstones" and arluth gan hal means "The lord of the moors")*

Avenal—*Tuathan Lady of Earth and Moon*

Avenveres (S)—*the First Land*

Balance, the—*see Covenant*

Ballan—*Tuathan Lord of the Travelling Folk*

barden (S)—*itinerant musicians and singers*

Cablin—*the son of the WerenArl and Anann; called variously the Grey Harper, the Grey Man, Healer, Meanan, Meddler, Mender-of-Souls and the Twilight's Brother*

caeldh (S)—*open*

Carn ha Corn (S)—*Hoof and Horn (refers to the WerenArl); an exclamation*

caryaln (S)—*literally "shadow-death"; refers to weaponry that can destroy Wasters and dalkwer*

cawran (S)—*giants*

Cernunnos—*the Horned Lord, Anann's consort; also called WerenArl or Wild Lord and Pan the Piper*

Chaos Time—*when the gods warred on First Land and Avenveres was destroyed*

colonfrey (S)—*heart-water; a gift from the trees of Elenwood on Gythelen that speeds growth and recovery of spiritual sores*

Colonog (S)—*heart-tree; the name of the Lady's hall on Gythelen*

Covenant, the—*an ancient agreement between the Tuathan and Daketh (that some say was forced upon them by the Grey Gods) that states, in part, that they may no longer walk in Mid-wold. If one of either does come to the middle realm that lies between their own, a member of the opposite gods of the same rank is permitted to come as well, to maintain the Balance that was broken in the Chaos Time resulting in the destruction of Avenveres.*

Craftmasters—*the wise of the erlkin*

Daketh, the—*the Dark Gods*

dalin (S)—*globe-shaped lights made by dwarves*

Dalker (S)—*the realm of the Dark Gods*

dalkwer (S)—*low born of the Daketh; includes Walkers and yarg chieftains*

Dark Gods, the—*see the Daketh*

daryn-seeking—*dowsing*

dralan (S)—*one who can seek with the power of his mind*

drokan (S)—*base-born yargs, trolls, etc.*

dursona (S)—*godspeed*

erlkin (S)—*an elfish folk, divided into high erlkin, who are the First Born of the Tuathan's children, and the low erlkin, who are the Second. High erls are a tall, golden folk, not bound to any one place. Low erls are much like their*

cousins the weren, or wild folk, and are usually bound
to their forests, if they are wooderls; their hills, if they
are hillerls, etc.

freycara (S)—*spirit-kin; a term of kinship amongst the erlkin
that can be equated with the once-born's term "blood
brother"*

god-tongue—*Loremaster/Loremistress term for the runes of the
Tuathan*

Grey Gods, the—*the gods of the Middle Kingdom who ruled
before the coming of the Tuathan and the Daketh; namely
Cernunnos and Anann, and their son Cablin.*

Great Mysteries, the—*Loremaster/Loremistress term for any
of the great unsolved riddles, such as who created mankind.*

Grey Harper, the—*see Cablin*

Grey Man, the—*see Cablin*

Greymin—*Skylord of the Tuathan*

Gwynhart (S)—*fair-of-spirit; surname of the Lords and Ladies
of Elenwood on Gythelen*

Hafelys (S)—*summer-court; name of Grimbold's homeworld*

hobogle (S)—*hill-dwelling weren*

holding-crystals—*possessed jewel that controls the wearer*

Horned Lord, the—*see Cernunnos*

kemys-folk (S)—*beings that are half-human and half-beast*

keying—*term used for opening and closing the gates between
the worlds*

Kindreds, the—*see the Seven Kindreds*

kwessen (S)—*friend*

llan (S)—*variously holy one, wise one, elder, depending on
the context*

Loremaster, Loremistress—*historian*

Meanan (S)—*the Twilight's Brother; see Cablin*

mernan (S)—*mortal; once-born, as opposed to the Kindreds
who live more than one life*

Middle Kingdom, the—*is often used incorrectly to describe
the realms of the erlkin and other of the Kindreds; it is
in fact the realm of the weren, but as the years go by
the usage has blurred to refer to either*

Mid-wold—*term used to refer to the realms that lie between
the realms of the Tuathan and the Daketh*

muryan (S)—*weren moorfolk*

mys-hudol (S)—*talking beasts*

Old Ones, the—*usually refers to the Tuathan; sometimes, when used by a weren, refers to the Grey Gods*

Once-born—*see mernan*

Pan—*see Cernunnos*

Pansign—*weren spell*

Penalurick, the—*Jan Penalurick, the arluth of the muryan*

porth (S)—*the gates; plural is porthow*

porthmeyn (S)—*gate-stones*

Seven Kindreds, the—*the children of the Tuathan in order: the high erls, the low erls, the mys-hudol, the cawran, the dwarves, the kemys-folk and mankind, though the Tuathan make no claim to the last and they are cited as one of the Great Mysteries*

Sennayeth (S)—*the high or ancient tongue first spoken by the weren on Avenveres and later adapted by the Seven Kindreds as their own*

Shadowed, the—*refers to the children of the Daketh or anyone who has dealings with them*

silhonell (S)—*literally "the inner realm where spirits walk"; the spirit realm*

skeller (S)—*mutated bats found on Dewethtyr*

ster-arghans (S)—*star-silver; a precious metal*

stone-bound—*an enchantment that literally binds the body into a stone—usually a menhir*

tabbykin (S)—*weren; small stone spirits*

Talenyn (S)—*Little Wren; Minda Sealy*

taw (S)—*inner strength; usually that which is used for spell-working*

tervyn (S)—*close*

tosher root—*a bitter root; normally used in ale-brewing to give body*

Tuathan, the—*the Bright Gods, the Gods of Light*

Tyrr—*Sky Father of the Tuathan*

Walker, the—*dalkwer; named by its curious gait; specializes in far-seeking like the dralan of the Kindreds*

Waster, the—*First Born of the Daketh*

Wayderness (S)—*the Many Worlds*

wenyeth (S)—*mind-speaking*

weren (S)—*the Wild Folk*

WerenArl (S)—*literally "Wild Lord," see Cernunnos*

Wessener, the (S)—*high born of the muryan; the Gatekeepers*

Wistlore—*renowned halls of learning and Harperhall on Lan-
    glin*
wode-woses (S)—*manlike creatures that run on all fours*
wooderl—*low erlkin, usually bound to a particular forest or
    tree*
Wysling—*wizard*
yaln (S)—*death*
yarg (S)—*troll-like creatures with bodies like men, triangular
    heads, large wide noses and large ears*

Fantasy from Ace
fanciful and fantastic!